PREDATORY GAME

This Large Print Book carries the
Seal of Approval of N.A.V.H.

PREDATORY GAME

CHRISTINE FEEHAN

THORNDIKE PRESS

A part of Gale, Cengage Learning

GALE
CENGAGE Learning™

Detroit • New York • San Francisco • New Haven, Conn • Waterville, Maine • London

GALE
CENGAGE Learning™

LIBRARY OF CONGRESS CATALOGING-IN-PUBLICATION DATA

Feehan, Christine.
  Predatory game / by Christine Feehan.
    p. cm. — (Thorndike Press large print romance)
  ISBN-13: 978-1-4104-0920-1 (hardcover : alk. paper)
  ISBN-10: 1-4104-0920-1 (hardcover : alk. paper)
  1. Parapsychologists — Fiction. 2. Female assassins — Fiction.
  3. Telepathy — Fiction. 4. Psychokinesis — Fiction. 5. Large
  type books. I. Title.
  PS3606.E36P74 2008
  813'.6—dc22   2008017610

Published in 2008 by arrangement with The Berkley Publishing Group, a member of Penguin Group (USA) Inc.

Printed in the United States of America
1 2 3 4 5 6 7 12 11 10 09 08

For Adam Schuette, with love

FOR MY READERS

Be sure to write to Christine at christine@christinefeehan.com to get a FREE exclusive screen saver and join the PRIVATE e-mail list to receive an announcement when Christine's books are released.

ACKNOWLEDGMENTS

I want to thank Domini Stottsberry for her help with the tremendous amount of research necessary to make this book possible. Brian Feehan and Morey Sparks deserve much gratitude for talking rescues and action and answering endless questions! As always, Cheryl, you are incredible! Thanks to Dr. Chris Tong for his patience in trying to teach me about everything from physics to biology, and to Tyler Grinberg and Cecilia Feehan for their help in working with impossible theories. And of course, I would never get anywhere without Manda!

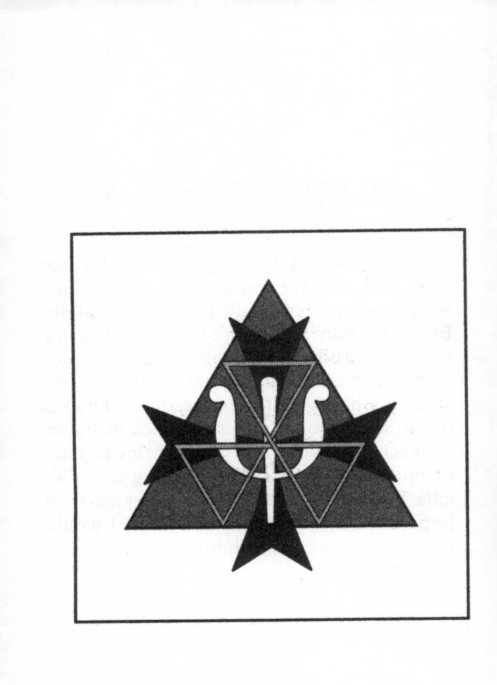

The GhostWalker Symbol Details

SIGNIFIES
shadow

SIGNIFIES
protection against
evil forces

SIGNIFIES
the Greek letter *psi*, which
is used by parapsychology
researchers to signify ESP or
other psychic abilities

SIGNIFIES
qualities of a knight—
loyalty, generosity,
courage, and honor

SIGNIFIES
shadow knights who protect
against evil forces using
psychic powers, courage,
and honor

nox noctis est nostri

THE GHOSTWALKER CREED

We are the GhostWalkers, we live in the
   shadows
The sea, the earth, and the air are our
   domain
No fallen comrade will be left behind
We are loyalty and honor bound
We are invisible to our enemies
and we destroy them where we find them
We believe in justice and we protect our
   country
and those unable to protect themselves
What goes unseen, unheard, and unknown
are GhostWalkers
There is honor in the shadows and it is us
We move in complete silence whether
in jungle or desert
We walk among our enemy unseen and
   unheard
Striking without sound and scatter to the
   winds
before they have knowledge of our

existence

We gather information and wait with
endless patience

for that perfect moment to deliver swift
justice

We are both merciful and merciless

We are relentless and implacable in our
resolve

We are the GhostWalkers and the night is
ours

PROLOGUE

The lights from oncoming cars hurt his eyes and seemed to pierce right through his skull, stabbing at his brain until he wanted to scream. He quickly tuned the radio station until the soft, sexy voice of the Night Siren flooded the car. It was taped, but it helped. His vision tunneled, so that everything took on a dream-like quality. Buildings flashed by, cars appeared as streaks of light rather than solid matter.

"Where are we going?"

He jumped. For a moment he had forgotten he wasn't alone. Throwing an impatient glance at the whore seated beside him, he felt the terrible pounding in his head, which had just begun to ease, return. In the dark she looked a little like the woman he needed. If she kept her mouth shut, he could pretend. Tempted to tell her she was going to hell very soon, he forced a slight smile instead. "You're getting paid, aren't you? What difference does it make if we drive around for a little bit?"

She leaned forward and fiddled with the radio.

He slapped at her hand. "Don't touch anything." He had the station tuned right where he wanted it — needed it. The Night Siren's voice was drifting out over the airwaves, making his body hard and his head clear. The woman wasn't going to make it through the hour if she touched that dial again.

He kept his eye on the car he was following. He knew what he had to do. He had a job and he was damned good at it. The whore was such a good cover, and gave him such an anticipation of the pleasure to come later. He hadn't been caught yet. Damn Whitney for his interference. The doctor had threatened to send someone else again. Stupid man didn't like his reports. Well, fuck him. The doctor thought he was so superior, so intelligent, and was worried — *worried* — about the situation deteriorating. What a crock of bullshit. There was no situation, nothing was deteriorating. He could handle surveillance on a GhostWalker any day of the week.

Whitney thought his precious GhostWalkers were supersoldiers to be revered. Well, screw that. GhostWalkers were genetic mutations, aberrations, abominations, not the fucking miracles Whitney purported them to be. The entire lot of them should be wiped from the face of the earth, and he was the man to do it. They were government experiments that should have been scrapped long before they were ever let loose on the world.

He saw himself as the guardian, the lone man standing between the mutants and the humans. *He* should be revered. Whitney should bow down to him, kiss his feet, thank him for his reports and his attention to detail . . .

"You never told me your name. What do I call you?"

The voice jerked him out of his reverie. He wanted to slap the little whore. To pound his fists into her face until there was nothing there but bloody pulp. To take her head between his hands and hear a satisfying crack just to shut her up, but that was for later. If she kept her mouth shut he could fantasize that she was the Night Siren.

The Night Siren belonged to him and he'd have her soon enough. He just had to get rid of the GhostWalkers once and for all. And then she'd do everything he told her.

"You can call me Daddy."

17

The whore had the audacity to roll her eyes at him, but he resisted the urge to punish her. He had other plans for her.

"I am a naughty girl," she said and leaned over to rub his crotch. "And you obviously like me that way."

"Don't talk," he snapped, and sighed when she opened his jeans. Let her just go to work on him while he took care of business. It would keep her mouth and hands occupied. He could look at her skin and hair and everything would be all right. It was going to be a long night tonight, and at least he could look forward to later.

Up ahead the car he'd been following pulled to the curb. It was a strange thing to do, but he couldn't get caught — and he couldn't lose them. He pulled over as well and waited while the whore worked on him, the rush beginning to flood his veins like a drug.

CHAPTER 1

Saber Wynter leaned back against the plush seat in the low-slung sports car and stared incredulously at her date. "Am I hearing you right?" She tapped a long, perfectly polished fingernail against the armrest. "You're saying you've taken me out on three dates, and you're claiming you've spent a hundred dollars . . ."

"A hundred and fifty," Larry Edwards corrected.

One dark eyebrow shot up in disbelief. "I see. One hundred and fifty dollars, not that I have any idea what you spent it on. Your favorite restaurant is a truck stop."

"The San Sebastian is no truck stop," he denied hotly, staring into her violet-blue eyes. Unusual eyes, beautiful and haunting. He had noticed her voice immediately on the radio — the Night Siren, everyone called her. It seemed a husky whisper of pure sensual promise. Night after night he'd

19

listened to her and fantasized. And then when he met her . . . she had great skin and a mouth that screamed sex. And those eyes. He'd never seen eyes like that. She looked so innocent, and the combination of sexy and innocent was just too hard to resist.

But she was proving to be difficult, and damn it all, what did she really have to brag about? She was skinny, looking like a lost waif, nothing to be all haughty and uptight about. In fact, she should be grateful for his attention. As far as he was concerned, she was nothing but a tease.

She shrugged in a curiously feminine gesture. "So you think because you spent this money on three dates it entitles you to sleep with me?"

"It damn well does, honey," he snapped. "You owe me." He hated that distant, clinical look she gave him. She needed a real man to put her in her place — and he was just the man to do it.

Saber forced a smile. "And if I don't — how did you so delicately put this? — if I don't 'put out,' you intend to dump me off right here in the middle of the street at two o'clock in the morning?"

She hoped he would make a move or force the issue, because he was going to get a lesson in manners he was never going to

20

forget. She had nothing to lose. Well, almost nothing. She had stayed too long this time, made too much of a life for herself, and if she wiped up the floor with good old Larry the Louse before she disappeared, she'd be doing the women of Sheridan a favor.

"That's right, darling." He smirked at her complacently. "I think you'll agree you need to be a little reasonable about this, don't you?" He slid his hand along the back of her seat, fingers not quite touching her. He wanted to. Usually by now he was doing a lot of touching, loving watching the woman squirm. Loving the power he had over them. He didn't understand why he wasn't forcing her mouth to his, yanking open her blouse and taking what he wanted, but as much as he longed to do that, there was something inside of him warning him to go slower, to be a little more cautious with Saber. He was sure that very soon she would sit quietly and he'd be able to do whatever he wanted with her. He expected her to cry and plead for him not to leave her there, but instead, perfect little white teeth gleamed at him like bright pearls, making his stomach clench.

He looked so smug Saber wanted to slap his boyish good looks right off his face. "I've got some bad news for you, Larry. The sad truth is, I'd rather pull out my fingernails one by one than sleep with you." She slipped out of the low-slung car. "Your breath stinks, Lar, and let's just face it — you're a creep." She slammed the door with such force he winced visibly.

Fury swept through him. "This is a bad section of town, Saber. Drunken cowboys, drug dealers, deadbeats. Not a good idea to stay here."

"Better company, I'm sure," she taunted.

"Last chance, Saber." His eye twitched angrily. "I'm doing you a favor here. Sex with a scrawny thing like you is no Fourth of July. Basically you're a pity fuck."

"So tempting, Lar, so very tempting. Did that get results from some scared teenager? Cuz it's really not working with me."

"You're going to be sorry," he snapped, furious that nothing he said seemed to get the reaction he wanted. She talked down to him like a princess to a peasant and made him feel like slime under her shoe.

"Don't think it's over, hotshot," she warned, still hanging on to her smile. "This will make a great little story on my radio show. I'll build an entire program around the theme: worst jerk you ever dated."

"You wouldn't dare."

"You're not dealing with a sixteen-year-old, Larry," she informed him coldly, too angry to laugh at the situation. He had no idea who — or what — he was dealing with. The idiot. He thought he could force her into sleeping with him by threatening to dump her in a bad part of town? She wondered if his plan had actually worked for him before. The idea made her fingers itch to get at him. She held on to her cool and stared him down.

Swearing furiously, Larry revved the motor and, laying a trail of rubber, screeched away, leaving her standing in the middle of an empty street.

Saber stamped her foot as she glared at the disappearing tail lights. "Darn it, Saber," she muttered, kicking at the curb in frustration. "If you insist on going out with jerks, what do you expect?" She was tired of trying to be normal. Weary to death of pretending. She was never going to fit in, not in a million years.

Raking a hand through the mass of thick, blue-black curls spilling in unruly confusion around her face, she took a long, slow look around. Larry hadn't been kidding — it was an appalling part of town.

Drawing a deep breath, she muttered, "Just wonderful. There are probably rats down here. Starving rats. This is not good,

Saber, not good at all. You should have kicked the hell out of him and stolen his car."

Sighing heavily, she headed down the cracked, dirty sidewalk toward the only streetlight, which illuminated a telephone booth. "It will be my luck the stupid thing is broken. If it is, Larry," she vowed aloud, "you will definitely pay for your sins."

Because, of course, she couldn't have a cell phone like everyone else. She didn't leave paper trails for anyone to follow. Next time, if there ever was a next time that she was stupid enough to go on a date, she would take her own car and she would do the dumping.

A forty-five-minute wait for a cab. Bravado would only carry so far. She was not going to wait forty-five minutes in the dark surrounded by rats. No way. How incompetent of the taxi service not to have planned their resources better.

In a fit of temper she slammed the phone in its cradle, giving only a fleeting thought to the dispatcher's ear. Saber kicked the side of the booth and nearly broke her toes. Howling, jumping around like an idiot, she vowed eternal revenge on Larry.

She should have stayed in the car and faced him down instead of letting him drive off. He was a worm crawling his way across the earth, but he was no monster. She knew monsters intimately. They dogged her every step, and soon — far too soon if she didn't leave — they would find her again. A slime-bag like Larry was a prince in comparison. Larry certainly hadn't recognized the monster in her. If he had touched her . . . She pushed the thought away and made herself think *normal.* She should have decked him though, just once, for all the other women who would be put in the same situation because he liked power. She was fairly certain most women would have had the desire to at least punch the bastard.

Saber sighed softly and shook her head. She was putting off the inevitable. She wasn't walking home and she couldn't very well stay where she was. She was going to pay royally for this, but what was one more lecture out of several hundred? Fighting for a deep controlling breath, she punched in the numbers, her fingertip unconsciously using a rather vicious stabbing motion on the blameless telephone.

Jess Calhoun lay sprawled out full length on the wide, leather, specially built futon, staring up at the ceiling in the darkness. Suffocating silence surrounded him, wrapped him up and pressed heavily down on him. The sound of the clock ticking was only in his mind. Endless seconds, minutes. An eternity. Where was she? What the hell was she doing out at two thirty in the morning? This was her night off. She wasn't at the radio station working later than usual, he'd already checked. Surely she hadn't been in an accident. Someone would have notified him. He'd called every hospital in the area, at least he could console himself with the knowledge that she wasn't in any of them.

His fingers curled slowly into a fist, beat impotently once, twice, on the leather. She hadn't told him she was going out. She hadn't even called to say she would be late. One of these days he would be pushed too far by mysterious, elusive Saber Wynter, and he would just strangle her.

The first memory of her washed over him unbidden, reminding him it was his own folly that had landed him in such an uncomfortable position. He had opened the door ten months earlier to find on his doorstep the most beautiful child he had ever seen, worn suitcase in hand. No more than five foot two, she had raven-colored hair, so black that little blue lights gleamed through the riot of curls. Her face was small, fragile, with classic delicate bones and a faintly haughty nose. Soft flawless skin, full mouth, and enormous violet-blue eyes. She had an innocence about her that made him want — no, *need* — to protect her. She was shivering unbearably in the cold air.

She'd wordlessly handed him a piece of paper with his ad on it. She wanted the job at the radio station, vacated when his night crew had been killed in a car accident. The accident had left everyone shaken, and Jess had taken a long time before he thought about filling the position, but he'd recently advertised for someone.

It had been her eyes and mouth that had given her away. This was no child wrapped in a thin denim jacket several sizes too large, but a young, exhausted, exotic, disturbingly beautiful woman. Those eyes had seen things they shouldn't have had to, and he wouldn't — *couldn't* — turn the young woman with those eyes away.

It had taken a moment to close his mouth and move back into the foyer, inviting her in. His hand had completely enveloped hers, yet he could feel the strength of her grip. Beneath the deceptive peaches-and-cream skin were muscles of steel. She moved with flowing grace, her carriage so regal he pegged her for a ballet dancer or gymnast. When she had finally offered a tentative smile, she had taken his breath away.

Jess raked a hand through his hair, cursing himself for inviting her in. From that moment, he had been lost; he knew with a certainty he always would be. Over the past ten months she had cast a spell and he didn't even want out. He had never had a reaction to a woman the way he had to her. He couldn't let her go, no matter how illogical that had been, so instead he'd opened his home, offering her the job as well as light housekeeping in exchange for a place to live.

Of course he'd investigated her; he wasn't entirely out of his mind. He owed it to his fellow GhostWalkers, members of his elite military team, to know who was sharing his house, but there was no Saber Wynter in existence. It wasn't exactly shocking, he suspected she was hiding from someone, but it was very unusual that he couldn't find out every last thing about her, especially when he had her fingerprints.

The shrill ringing of the telephone sent his heart slamming hard against the wall of his chest. His hand flew out, the swift striking of a coiled snake, and snatched up the receiver. "Saber?" It was a prayer, damn her, a blatant prayer. He inhaled deep, wishing he could draw her into his lungs and hold her there.

"Hi, Jesse," she greeted him breezily, as if it were noon and he hadn't been climbing the walls for hours. "I sort of have this teeny little problem."

He ignored the relief racing through his body, the tightening of his muscles at the sensual sound of her voice, and the instant hard-on that never quite went away when he thought about her — which was all the time. "Damn it, Saber, don't you dare tell me you landed yourself in jail again." He really was going to strangle her. A man could only take so much.

Her sigh was exaggerated. "Honestly, Jesse, do you have to bring that silly incident up every time something goes wrong? It's not like I tried to get arrested."

"Saber," he said in exasperation, "holding out your hands with your wrists together is asking to be arrested."

"It was for a good cause," she protested.

"Chaining yourself to an old folks' home to call attention to conditions is not exactly the right way to go about changing things. Where the hell are you?"

"You sound like an old grumpy bear with a sore tooth." Saber tapped out a rhythm with a long fingernail on the booth wall, one of the nervous habits she'd never overcome. "I'm stuck out here near the old warehouses, sort of, um, like by myself — without a car."

"Damn it, Saber!"

"You already said that," she pointed out judiciously.

"You stay put." Cold steel was in the deep timbre of his voice. "Don't leave that phone booth. You hear me, Saber? I'd better not find you throwing dice with a bunch of deadbeats down there."

"Very funny, Jesse."

She laughed, actually laughed, the little brat. Jess slammed down the phone, itching to shake her. The thought of her, so fragile and unprotected, down near the warehouses, one of the worst parts of town, scared him to death.

Saber hung up and leaned weakly against the wall of the phone booth, momentarily closing her eyes. She was trembling so hard she could barely stand. It took an effort to pry her fingers, one by one, from the receiver. She hated the dark, the demons lurking in the shadows, the way the black night could turn people into savage animals. Her job at the radio station, the job she owed to Jess, couldn't have been better suited to her, because she could stay up all night.

And tonight, her first night off in ages,

had to be spent with Larry the Louse. He just had to dump her butt in the worst section of town he could find — not that she couldn't take care of herself, and that was the problem. It would always be the problem. She wasn't normal. She should be afraid of what lurked in the night, not afraid of harming someone.

She sighed. She had no idea why she had gone out with Larry at all. She didn't even like him or his rotten breath. The truth was, she didn't like any of the men she dated, but she wanted to like them, wanted to be attracted to them.

She sank down in the small booth, drawing her knees up to her chest. Jesse would come for her, she knew it. It was as certain as Jess's silly story about needing someone to rent the upstairs apartment, or how it was so cheap because he needed someone to do light housekeeping for him.

The place was a palace as far as Saber was concerned. Wide open spaces kept immaculately clean. The upstairs was no apartment, had never been an apartment. The second upstairs bathroom had been added after she had moved in. The huge, well-equipped weight room and full-size swimming pool were an added enticement that he'd said she could use anytime.

For the first time in her life, Saber had swallowed her pride and had taken a handout. The truth was, as much as she hated to admit it, she had never had cause to be sorry, not once since she'd moved in — except that she'd known she couldn't stay too long. Jess was the real reason she stayed — not his house, the swimming pool, or her job. Just Jesse.

She closed her eyes briefly and rubbed her chin on her knees. She was getting far too attached to the man. Six months ago it wouldn't have occurred to her to call for help, now it didn't occur to her not to. The revelation made her uneasy. It was time to leave, past time to leave, she was getting too comfortable. Saber Wynter had to go out in flames and a new identity had to rise from the ashes, because if she stayed any longer, she was in terrible danger, and this time, it wasn't going to be anyone's fault but her own.

The van rumbled up to the curb in record time. Jesse thrust his handsome face out the window. His eyes were dark with shadows as he looked her over rather anxiously. The drift of those gorgeous eyes had her stomach flipping when she didn't want to feel anything but relief.

Saber stood up slowly, a little shakily, and

dusted off the seat of her jeans, allowing herself time to recover.

"Saber," he growled, cold steel very much in evidence.

She hopped in, leaning over to give him a quick kiss on his shadowed jaw. "Thanks, Jesse, what would I do without you?"

The van didn't move, so she made a slight face at him and, under his watchful gaze, she snapped her safety belt around her.

"Let's not find out." Velvet over steel. He said the words in exasperation, his glittering eyes sweeping her small, slender figure possessively, assuring himself she wasn't hurt. "What happened this time, baby? Someone convince you these little warehouses are death traps and you decided to commit a little arson?"

"Of course not," she denied, but she studied the buildings with a prejudiced eye as they drove by. "Although now that you mention it, someone should probably look into the problem."

Jess groaned his annoyance. "So what happened, angel face?"

She shrugged with casual disdain. "My date dumped me off after a little tiff."

"I can imagine," Jess said, but something dark and dangerous began to smolder in the depths of his eyes. "What did you do?

Suggest stealing someone's chairs from their porch? A raid on the YMCA? What was it this time?"

"Has it occurred to you that it just might be Larry's fault?" she demanded indignantly.

"Sure, for all of two seconds, although I intend to find this friend of yours and beat him to a bloody pulp."

"Can I watch?" Saber grinned at him, inviting him to laugh at the entire incident with her. That was the thing about Jesse she loved so much; he was so protective and dangerous. He gave the illusion of being a teddy bear, but underneath . . . underneath all that muscle was something deadly that drew her like a magnet.

"It's not funny, you little brat, you could have been mugged, or worse. Now what happened?"

"I'm quite capable of taking care of myself," Saber informed him haughtily. "You know I can too."

"I know you think you can. That isn't quite the same thing." He turned probing, hawk-like eyes on her. "Now stop avoiding the question and tell me what happened."

Saber stared sightlessly out the window. It almost made her resentful that she was going to tell him. She didn't want to, but for some reason she seemed to tell him anything he asked. Worse, she never felt uncomfortable with him afterward. She was definitely getting too close — and that meant she had to leave him.

Leave *him?* Where had that come from? Her stomach dropped out from under her and her heart did a strange little flip that was very alarming.

"Stop sticking your obstinate little chin out, Saber; it always means you're about to become stubborn. I don't know why you bother, since you always tell me what I want to know in the end."

"Maybe I don't think it's any of your business." She said it decisively, pretending she felt no guilt.

"It's my business if you have to call me out at two thirty in the morning when one of your lowlife boyfriends dumps you out on the street."

Instantly Saber's temper flared to life. "Hey, I'm sorry I bothered you," she said belligerently, because the way he made her feel was scaring the hell out of her. "If you want me to, I'll get out of your precious van right now."

He sent her a long, mocking, ice-cold stare. "You can try, sweetheart, but I can guarantee you won't make it." His voice gentled, became a velvet caress, smoothing over her skin and sending a current of electricity snaking through her bloodstream. "Stop being your usual contrary self and tell me why he dumped you."

"I wouldn't sleep with him," she muttered in a low voice.

"Run it by me again, baby, this time looking at me," he suggested silkily.

Saber heaved a sigh. "I wouldn't go to bed with him," she repeated.

There was a long silence while he opened the security gate by punching a code into the remote control opener and maneuvered the van down the long winding drive and into the large garage.

Jess, using his heavily muscled arms, hoisted himself into his waiting chair. His electric one, Saber noticed. "Come on, honey," his voice was so unexpectedly gentle she found herself blinking back burning tears. "You can ride on my lap."

Saber managed a small smile, although her gaze skittered away from his all-seeing eyes as she curled up, snuggling against his chest, drawing comfort from his presence. He was as hard as a rock. Her bottom slid over the large bulge in his lap, sending a thousand wings beating against the walls of her stomach. She sat on him all the time, and he was always hard. Always erect. There were times when she desperately wanted to do something about that — like now — but she didn't dare change their arrangement. And it wasn't as if it were all for her. She wished it was, but he never once made a move on her. Not one.

Jess could feel the trembling of her slender body. His hand brushed the pulse beating so frantically at the base of her throat. For a moment his arms closed protectively around her, his chin resting on the top of her silky head. She had to feel the monster of a hard-on, but she never said a word, simply slid her bottom over him and settled down as if she fit there perfectly. If she could ignore the damned thing, so could he.

"Are you sure you're all right, Saber?" he asked quietly.

She nodded, making a little sound of affirmation, muffled against the broad expanse of his chest.

The wheelchair was locked in place, the lift lowering them to the ground. Normally, Jess preferred his lightweight racing chair. He propelled it manually, maneuvering it with ease, liking the exercise, the control, the freedom to play. But at the moment, he was grateful for his larger, heavier electric chair. It left his arms free to cradle Saber against him. She seemed a little lost tonight, very vulnerable, and she rarely showed him that side of her. Saber preferred humor to anything else and used it often as a barrier between herself and the rest of the world.

Once in the house, he took them straight through to the darkened living room. His hand tangled in her hair, fingers massaging her scalp, easing the tension out of her.

"So facing me was preferable to sleeping with this bum, hmm?" he teased gently.

She turned her face up to his. "I would never sleep with someone I wasn't in love with." And she wouldn't either. She was going to live her life to the best of her ability. She was going to make friends, have causes, know what fun was. And damn it all, just once, just one time, she was going to know real love. When that time came she'd give that man her body, because she wouldn't have anything else to give him.

"You never told me that. You mean all these idiots you date . . ."

She sat up abruptly, would have jumped from his lap, but his arms came up to circle her slender form, effectively holding her prisoner. She glared at him, furious. "Is that what you've been thinking of me all this time?" she demanded. "You think I just go to bed with anyone at all?"

Actual tears sparkled in her eyes, tugging at his heart. "Of course not, angel face."

"You're such a liar, Jess." She shoved at the solid wall of his chest again. "Let go of me. I mean it. Right now."

"Not like this, Saber. We've never had a fight before and I don't want to start now."

For a moment she stayed stiff, holding herself away from him, but she couldn't stay angry with Jess. With a small sigh, Saber lay back against him, the tension draining out of her. His arms were the only place she ever felt safe. The darkness was everywhere, waiting, watching. She could almost hear it breathing, waiting for her to climb the stairs and go to her lonely room.

She couldn't remember clearly the first time Jess had pulled her onto his lap, probably after one of his outrageous races, but it had always been the same. The moment his arms closed around her, she felt as if she never wanted to leave. Maybe that was why she'd allowed their relationship to go so far. It was why she'd stayed too long and taken too many chances. She couldn't bear the thought of walking away from him, and that made her just plain stupid.

"So, are you going to hide from me or are you going to accept my apology?" His chin rubbed the top of her hair.

39

"If that's the way you apologize," she sniffed indignantly, "I'm not sure I will ever forgive you. I don't like what you think of me."

"I think the world of you, and you know it." He tugged at a particularly intriguing curl. "Is, 'I'm sorry,' good enough?"

"I hope we never get into a really serious fight." Saber slapped at his hand, but she was more irritated at herself than him. She could stay right where she was forever, just inhaling him, feeling the muscles of his body and the warmth of him spreading through her with a luxurious heat she'd never known before.

He laughed softly, the sound feathering down her spine like the cool touch of fingers.

Instantly Saber lifted her head, horrified at the disturbing sensations in her body. "I'd better go upstairs, Jesse, and let you get some sleep." Because if she didn't get away from him, she might make a fool of herself and give in to the urge to feather kisses up and down his throat and over his jaw and find his oh-so-disturbing mouth . . . She jumped up, her heart pounding.

Reluctantly he allowed her to escape. "I know you better than that, baby; you'll go upstairs and keep me up all night with your ridiculous pacing. Go get your bathing suit on, we can go swimming."

Her face lit up. "You mean it?"

"Go," he ordered.

She walked across the hardwood floor to the bottom of the stairs and paused to look back at him. In the dim light he could see her perfect profile, breasts thrusting invitingly against the thin material of her pale blouse. His body tightened even more, hardened into a painful, familiar ache that wasn't going to go away anytime soon. Jess cursed beneath his breath, knowing he would spend another endless night, like so many others, craving the feel of her soft skin and haunting blue eyes. He'd never had a reaction to a woman the way he did to Saber. He couldn't keep her out of his mind, and if she was anywhere near, his body hit overdrive in seconds.

Hell, she didn't even have to be near to him. The sound of her voice over the radio, her scent lingering in the air, her laughter, and God help him, just the thought of her turned his body into one painful ache.

"Thanks, Jesse, I knew you wouldn't let me down. I don't know what I'd do without you."

He watched her walk up the stairs, thinking about her words. It was the second time

41

she had made that statement to him tonight. And there had been a new note in her voice. Wondering? Was she finally noticing he was more than a man in a wheelchair? That wasn't fair; half the time she didn't seem to notice the wheelchair, but she didn't seem to notice the man either.

He ached for her, fantasized about her, dreamed about her. Sooner or later he was going to have to claim her. Ten months was long enough to know she was wrapped inextricably around his heart. He might be in a wheelchair, his legs useless below the knees, but everything above was in top working order, demanding satisfaction, demanding Saber Wynter.

He sighed aloud. She had no idea she had knocked at the devil's door and he'd invited her in. He had no intention of giving her up.

Saber turned on every lamp on her way through her sitting room to her bedroom. She stood at the window, staring up at the stars. What was happening to her? Jess had taken her in — against his better judgment, she was certain. They had become best friends almost immediately. They liked the same movies, the same music, they talked for hours about everything, anything. She laughed with Jess. She could be the real Saber Winter with Jess. Outrageous, sad, happy, it never seemed to matter to him what she said or did — he simply accepted her.

Lately she had been so restless, lying in bed thinking of him, of his smile, the sound of his laughter, the width of his shoulders. He was a handsome, athletic man, wheelchair or not. And living in such close proximity to him often made her forget the wheelchair completely. He was totally self-sufficient, cooking for himself, dressing himself, driving himself all over town. He bowled, played Ping-Pong, and every day without fail, he lifted weights and went swimming. She had seen his body. It was that of a top athlete. His arm muscles were so developed he could barely touch his fingertips to his shoulders; his biceps kept bumping. Jess had told her the nerves below his knees had been damaged severely, and were irreparable.

He disappeared for hours into his office, the one room she never went into, and he kept it locked up tight. She'd caught glimpses of high-end computer equipment, and she knew he liked gadgets, that he had been in the Navy — a SEAL team — and still received countless calls from his friends, but he kept that part of his life away from her and it was just as well.

Did he think of women? They certainly thought of him. She had seen dozens of women flirting with him. And why not? Good looking, wealthy, talented, the sweetest man in Wyoming, Jess was a great catch for anyone. He owned the local radio station where she worked, and he did other things as well, things he wasn't so forthcoming about, but it mattered little to her. She just wanted to be close to him.

Her fist closed over her lacy curtain, bunching material in her fist. Why was she thinking these stupid thoughts about a man she could never have? She didn't deserve to be with a man like Jess Calhoun. He never complained, never talked down to her. He was arrogant, used to being obeyed, no question about it, but he always made her feel special. He was exceptional, extraordinary, and she was . . . she was going to have to leave soon.

Idly, she let her gaze stray to the road. For a moment her heart stopped. A car was parked in the trees just beyond the security gates. A tiny red circle glowed brightly as the occupant inhaled on a cigarette. Everything in her froze, became utterly still, her breath catching in her throat. Her heart began to race and her fingers twisted the material of the curtains until her knuckles turned white.

Then she could see the couple necking, the man struggling to hang on to his girl and the lit cigarette. Most of the tension slipped from her body. Of course. This was a perfect parking place, a dead-end road.

Ten months ago, Saber had turned down that same road thinking she would avoid people. She had actually camped on Jess's property for a few days before it got so cold she was certain she would freeze to death. That was before he had installed the security gates and the high, fancy fence.

Had he done that for her, because she was almost always nervous those first two months, before Jess had made her feel as if he could keep her safe from the entire world? Or was there some reason he felt the need for security?

Saber sighed as she dropped the curtain back in place. Did Jess see far more than he should? Was he aware that for all her crazy antics and bravado, she was really afraid all the time?

Thoughtfully, she peeled off her black denim jeans and pale lime blouse, perfect attire for one of Larry's favorite dining holes. "A hundred and fifty dollars," she sniffed indignantly, aloud. "He's such a liar. The meal didn't cost more than a can of dog food. Who does he think he's kidding?"

She pulled on her one-piece charcoal gray and salmon bathing suit. It hugged her breasts, emphasizing her narrow rib cage and small waist, rode high in a French cut over her small hips. Saber raked a hand through the thick mass of raven curls, yet carefully avoided the sight in the mirror. Hastily she donned a T-shirt, caught up a towel, and hurried down the stairs to join Jess.

Subject Wynter. Put in a situation where dispatching the problem would solve it, subject chose to call for aid. In the few short months she has been with Subject Calhoun, she has lost her edge. She spotted me, yet was fooled because she wanted to be fooled. She grows weaker as time passes, her training forgotten as she is lulled into a false sense of security. A few more weeks and we should be able to reacquire her without much trouble or risk. I was able to introduce the virus into her system and it should begin to work almost immediately. At that time I may gain entry to Subject Calhoun's premises. He is much more difficult, alert all the time.

"What are you muttering about?" The

46

woman sitting beside him had been applying her lipstick in the rearview mirror as he dictated.

He glanced once more up at the empty window before turning to look at her with a cold smile. "You aren't finished yet." He unzipped his pants and dragged them down, catching her by the nape of her neck. "Let's see if you can earn all that money you're charging me."

He turned up the music and leaned back against the seat, closing his eyes as she went to work on him. He blew a circle of smoke and crushed out his cigarette, allowing the rush to overcome him. It was an amazingly powerful feeling to sit back and enjoy her, knowing it would be the last thing she ever did. Knowing she worked and worked to please him, thinking she would be getting such a lovely tip, and instead . . .

He moaned and forced himself deeper, holding her head even when she tried to struggle, forcing her to accept all of him, forcing her to clean him up before he took her head into his hands and, smiling, broke her neck.

CHAPTER 2

The indoor pool was warm and inviting, lights dim, casting intriguing shadows on the tiled walls. A mosaic of trees with shimmering silver leaves crept up to the ceiling, woven into the pattern of the cool mint tiles. From the doorway, Saber waved to Jess and watched him slide silently into the water, the muscles in his arms bulging with strength. His skin gleamed a deep bronze, dark hair tangling over the heavy muscles of his chest and angling down his ridged abdomen to disappear into blue swimming trunks.

He definitely had a body on him. She stared at him often, although she tried not to, and she knew every defined muscle. When he moved, it was with total grace. He was always alert and ready, yet still when he was at rest, unlike her. She fidgeted, always moving, always wary of standing in one spot.

Her breath caught in her throat as she

watched him glide through the water. He reminded her of a sleek, powerful predator, silent, deadly, moving with deceptive laziness as he cut through the water.

Saber couldn't take her eyes from him, watching the power in him. He'd never told her what had happened to his legs, but the scars were still red and raw and the doctors visited him often. She knew he'd had numerous operations, but it wasn't something he ever discussed. He worked out and he went to a physical therapist daily. He excelled at swimming. Once, he'd stayed under so long, she'd dived in, terrified he'd drowned, only to have him scare her by grabbing her around the waist and tossing her to the surface. No wonder he'd been a Navy SEAL; he was more at home in the water than out of it.

When Jess halted, using powerful arms to tread water, Saber dropped her towel on the deck and dove in, not wanting him to catch her staring at him.

Jess dove right after her and met her beneath the water. His hands spanned her waist and shot her to the surface. She erupted from the water laughing, came down, eluding his outstretched hands, and dove beneath him. They played an energetic game of tag and football. Saber was the football. They raced, tried a strange form of water ballet, and finally ended up clinging to the bars that ran the full length of the pool.

Breathless, her eyes dancing, Saber wiped droplets of water from her face. "This was a great idea, Jess."

He hooked one arm around the metal bar and lay lazily floating, buoyed by the water. "I always have great ideas. You should know that by now." He sounded impossibly arrogant.

She sent a jet of water at his smug, grinning face, squealed, and dove to the center of the pool when he retaliated. By the time she had surfaced he was sitting at the water's edge striving for innocence.

Her heart jumped just looking at him. His smile. His laughter. The way his eyes lit up. How could she have ever gotten so lucky as to find him? She sent another column of water shooting toward him, then turned and swam away. She spent several minutes doing hard, fast laps, driving herself, trying to push her body into fatigue.

Jess settled into the hot tub and turned on the jets, allowing the water to massage his damaged legs. He sat in silence and watched her small body cut efficiently through the water. Strangely, when she swam, his body always went on alert, every sense flaring into self-preservation mode. She was a beautiful swimmer. She moved with the rhythm of a ballerina, silently and gracefully. He knew she had fast reflexes. He'd even tested them a time or two, simply because of this — the way she swam.

When she allowed herself to forget he was near, she swam fast like a racer, but when he'd asked if she'd ever competed, she'd flicked him a glance of such utter disdain that when one second later she'd laughed and said of course, he knew she was lying to him.

He should have used that — added it to the things he knew about her and continued to search for her true identity. She had a valid driver's license, but her prints didn't match the prints in the system. Not even close. He wiped his face with the towel and continued to watch her perfect form. It was mesmerizing to see the way she shot beneath the water as she made the turn, gliding half the distance to the other side before surfacing to stroke. Not a single sound gave her presence away, even as she surfaced, and that was more than fascinating to him. He practically lived in water, and just how could she be so completely silent?

Saber. He played with her name in his

mind. A sword — for justice? She'd taken the name, obviously. And where did Wynter fit in? Things just didn't add up with his roommate, yet he couldn't bring himself to put his team on it. He sighed as he watched her surface again, looking first at the shimmering leaves on the tiles and then up at the ceiling.

She looked so exotic, yet innocent. She was thin, but there was muscle beneath that smooth skin. She turned her head and found him — and smiled. God. It hit him like a punch in the gut. His body immediately heated, blood rushing, centering in his groin, until he thought he might burst with need. The wariness was ingrained in her — those violet-blue eyes, so unusual, so haunted, were always restless, searching for an enemy.

He knew part of the reason she relaxed with him was because he was in a wheelchair and she didn't perceive him as a threat. It wasn't that she didn't see — or recognize — the predator in him; she simply didn't believe the threat existed any longer.

"Are you going to swim all night?"

"I'm thinking about it," she conceded. "It's this or the hot tub."

"I feel compelled to point out the hot tub is much warmer and that you're turning blue. The color looks good on you though, it goes with your eyes."

She laughed, the way he knew she would. He loved that he could make her laugh — *really* laugh. Genuine and happy. It had taken months of patience, but she had finally let him in, just a little bit. She trusted him. But maybe she shouldn't. She had a false impression of who and what he was, but he wasn't about to scare her off by showing her the real Jess Calhoun. She could believe this life, the radio station, the songwriting. The man who treated her gently.

Saber climbed the ladder, shivered, and hurried to the hot tub, taking a seat opposite him. "I didn't realize I was so cold."

That was another thing he'd noticed about Saber — she ignored her comfort level, even pain, as if she could block sensation for long periods of time.

"Where'd you meet Larry?" Because he was going to have a few words with the man. "What's his last name and where does he work?"

She made a face. "He's a bartender, and believe me, Jesse, he's not worth the trouble, so back it on down and forget the whole thing. It was my own fault anyway." She leaned her head back and closed her eyes.

"I don't know why I do half the things I do. Going out with Larry was a bad idea and entirely my fault."

"Why did you go out with him?"

She looked relaxed, something Saber rarely did. She was in constant motion, like a hummingbird. Her hands were always restless. She skipped or danced across a room rather than walked. Sometimes she'd leap over the furniture — she'd even cleared the couch one day, and it was longer and wider than most. She was a puzzle he couldn't quite figure out.

Saber opened her eyes to look at him through the rising steam.

Because of you. She went out with utterly rotten cads because she didn't dare fall in love with Jesse. That was so lame — so stupid. She couldn't have someone decent, so she went out with men knowing she couldn't hurt them — ever. She would never hurt an innocent.

She didn't have time to censor her thoughts. Not even to herself had she ever admitted that she couldn't look at him anymore without wanting him. She wanted to trace every line in his face, memorize the shape and texture of his mouth, slide her fingers through that wealth of beautiful hair that fell haphazardly in all directions. She couldn't close her eyes and not have him in her mind. She smelled him in every room. When she inhaled, he was there, drawn so deeply into her lungs that she felt possessed by him.

Afraid he might read too much on her face, she looked away from him, studying the tiled mural. "Who knows why I do anything I do, Jesse."

He didn't have the ability to read minds. *She had spoken telepathically to him.* Every cell in his body went on alert. Her words were clear, absolutely clear in his mind. *Because of you.* She was capable of projecting her thoughts into his head. Not only had she been clear, she had done it easily, with no energy spills at all, no surge of power to give her away. Never once in ten months of living with him had she slipped up. Not one time. And that spoke of specialized training — not merely specialized; it took rigid discipline to be good enough to go undercover and never make a mistake. He wasn't going to buy it that she just happened to find his home, find him, and be trained in telepathic communication. God. Jesus. He couldn't bear it if she was undercover playing him for a fool.

He sat in silence, stunned at the revelation, furious with himself for not seeing it

55

coming. Maybe all along he'd suspected, but he hadn't wanted to know. She was so beautiful. So right for him. Who sent her? Who put those shadows in her eyes? The wariness on her face? *Because of you.* What exactly did that mean?

He kept his features expressionless while he studied the situation from every angle. If she'd been sent there to kill him, she would have done it already. If she was spying, she would have tried to get into his office and he would have known. He didn't believe in coincidence, so just how much danger was he in? And how much should he tell the others? He'd kept everyone away from Saber, purely for selfish reasons, although maybe he'd known the truth all along.

"What? No comment? You've gone awfully quiet, Jesse, and you always have some little lecture to pull out of your long list of them. I guess the truth is, I wanted to feel something for someone. He seemed like fun in the bar. Good looking. Somewhat intelligent."

He'd been a creep. She'd purposely gone out with a sleaze, just as she always did, because she didn't want to hurt a really nice man. Wherever she was currently calling home, she knew she could never stay. She wanted to do all the normal things a woman would do when she pretended she was living life like everyone else, but she never wanted anyone hurt on her account. She'd already caused enough hurt for a lifetime.

She sighed and punched her fist into the bubbles. "It was stupid. I won't be doing it again."

"It was stupid," he agreed. "And no, you won't be doing it again."

She glanced up at his face. It looked as if it were chiseled from stone. That was Jesse on the outside. Jesse on the inside was . . . mush. A slow grin spread over her face and amusement slowly lit her eyes. "You're so bossy. How does anyone stand you?"

"Not very well, which is why I've lived alone until you came along. Even my parents avoid me." He flashed her an answering grin and, using the bars, pulled himself from the hot tub to the platform he used for drying off.

For a moment all she could do was stare in awe at the power in his arms as he lifted his body. Realizing she was ogling him again, she hastily jumped out, turning away from him to shut everything down.

"So what's with the T-shirt, angel face?" Jess idly toweled his hair.

"I always wear a T-shirt swimming." Saber shivered as the cold air hit her wet body.

She strove for the ideal tone. Nonchalant. Breezy. She could do breezy — she'd honed that to perfection. "You know I do, it isn't anything new."

"I know, but you can't exactly get sunburned indoors," he pointed out, and reached for his thick, terry cloth robe. "I've explained that before, but you didn't take much notice." He paused in the act of putting on his robe. "Where are your sweats?"

"I forgot them." Saber was drying herself off as fast as possible.

"Come here," Jess ordered softly in exasperation.

"I'm all right," she assured him, looking anxious.

"It's a hell of a lot easier for you to come over here than it is for me to go over there, but if you insist." Jess shifted his weight, reached behind him for his racing chair.

"All right already," Saber was beside him in an instant. "Do you always have to have everything your way?"

He grinned mockingly, and without preamble caught the bottom of her T-shirt and pulled it right over her head. Saber froze in place, her heart thundering in her ears, but Jess was already enfolding her in his warm robe.

"You already know the answer to that one,

baby." With the ease of long practice and the help of strategically placed bars, Jess lifted himself into his chair.

Saber pulled the robe close, tightened the belt around her small waist. "Someone spoiled you, Jess. Patsy?" She named his older sister.

"Patsy!" He groaned the name. "Patsy was far too busy ensuring my soul was saved. You ought to know that. How many times have you heard her lectures on the two of us living in sin?" He spun the chair around, balanced on the two back wheels for a long moment before streaking through the wide-open halls to the living room.

"Will you stop doing that?" Saber jogged after him. "One of these days you'll be showing off and you'll go over backward." She scooped up the thick comforter lying in a heap on the sofa and tossed it to him. "And it's all your fault we get lectures. You started the whole thing."

"I did?" Jess tucked the blanket around him, one eyebrow shooting up. "I was not the one who came strolling out of my bedroom wearing one of my shirts and nothing else when she came to visit."

His smile did something to her heart. "It wasn't like that and you know it. You didn't even mention having a sister, dragon king.

How was I to know who she was? And you know very well why I was in your bedroom, wearing your shirt."

"Another one of your unfortunate accidents — a mud puddle, wasn't it?"

"Laugh about it." Saber swept a hand through her wet hair, glaring at him. "You dropped me in the mud puddle on purpose. I know you did. I wasn't about to go dripping up the stairs and into *my* bedroom. And I wasn't going to stand around in filthy clothes."

"You decided all by yourself to pay me back by dirtying up my bedroom," he pointed out. "And it wasn't my idea for you to come out of my bedroom looking as sexy as hell when my nosy sister showed up. You did that all by yourself."

Saber stamped one bare foot in feigned outrage. "Hey now. I did not know she was here. You could have warned me." Only Jesse had ever made her feel this way — joy, laughter, a sense of belonging. Fun. He created fun. "I was not about to stay dirty. You knew very well I had taken a shower and put on your shirt. I was being silly — it was a joke. I did *not* look sexy. I'm totally incapable of looking sexy."

Amusement softened the hard edge of his mouth. "Yeah? Who says? Believe me, honey, you looked sexy. I didn't blame Patsy for jumping to the wrong conclusion."

"And you didn't deny it when she did," Saber accused, snuggling deeper into his robe, wishing it were his arms, wishing she dared press her mouth to his.

"Neither did you. As I recall, you wound your arms around my neck and looked provocative." Deliberately he provoked her, wanting the shadows gone from her eyes, wanting to see her laugh, the real thing, the one that she reserved for him alone.

"Provocative?" Violet sparks were fairly shooting through her blue eyes.

She looked young, tousled and very tempting, so small in his huge, thick terry cloth robe. If he reached out, he could catch the lapels of the robe and tug her close, bring his mouth to hers and just go up in flames.

"Provocative," he said decisively.

"Now that is untrue and you know it, Jesse." She wrinkled her nose in disgust. "Provocative. What rot. And you pulled me onto your lap prior to my winding my arms around your neck. Which, incidentally, was a major mistake; it should have been my hands around your throat. I had no idea Patsy was your sister. I thought she was some ex-girlfriend you wanted to get rid of. I was merely obliging you."

"Ha!" he snorted inelegantly. "More like you thought she was a new one *you* wanted to get rid of."

Saber's bare feet beat a little tattoo on the floor in total frustration. She looked around for something to throw at his head, and settled for her damp towel. "You wish, caveman. Don't flatter yourself. You are so arrogant, Jesse, it drives me crazy."

He reached out, captured her hand, and brought her fingers to the disturbing warmth of his mouth. "You love it, baby." His thumb feathered over her knuckles, sending little darts of fire racing along her nerve endings. "You love arguing."

She jerked her hand away as if she'd been burned. Maybe she did, but she wasn't admitting it. "One of these days someone is going to take you down a peg or two."

He shrugged his powerful shoulders, his smile mocking. "It won't be you, angel face."

"Don't count on it, dragon king. As it happens, my week to cook is coming up fast. I know at least seven recipes for tofu. Shape up or eat soybean."

Jess burst out laughing, the sound so infectious she found herself joining in. "Vengeful little brat, aren't you?"

"You know it." Saber didn't bother to deny the accusation. "I'm going upstairs."

"Is that an invitation?"

"Stop leering, although I can tell you're very experienced at it," she retorted. "Good night."

He let her get to the bottom of the stairs. "Don't keep me up all night with that mournful twanging garbage you refer to as music."

"Mournful twanging garbage?" Saber echoed, outraged. She raced up the stairs, his soft, goading laughter following on her bare heels.

He didn't like her usual country music, did he? She rummaged through her collection of CDs. "Just the thing," she murmured happily and cranked up the loudest, most obnoxious rap song in her collection. Jess would appreciate good country music after listening to an hour of really loud rap. She took her time in the shower, shampooing her hair, allowing warm water to cascade over her cold, shivering body. She even sang, very loudly, feeling righteous and pleased with herself.

By the time Saber had finished toweling herself off and blow-drying her hair into complete disorder, Jess was throwing things at the ceiling.

Her grin wicked, she stopped the rap music. "Did you want something, Jesse?"

she called using her sweetest voice.

"I surrender. White flag," his muffled voice replied.

"I thought you might," Saber said smugly.

Jess shook his head as the music stopped. She had a mean streak in her. She knew he often wrote songs and that the sound of whatever she was blaring would hurt after a couple of minutes. It made him laugh, though, as he pushed the wheelchair down the hall to his private office. He keyed in his code and waited for the doors to part.

Once inside with the doors closed and locked and the security system switched on, the smile faded from his face. He was going to have to dig a little deeper and find out just who Saber Wynter really was. He couldn't let his feelings for her get in the way of business. And God help them both if she was there to do damage, because he wasn't altogether certain he could kill her. With a sigh, he pushed the thought from his head and went to work.

The computers and phone lines inside were all clean. He hit speed dial. "We're clear. Send the information and let's do this. When you come in, don't make any noise at all. She won't be asleep."

"I know the drill by now."

The abrupt click told Jess he was in for

trouble. Logan Maxwell wasn't happy with him. He hadn't been when Jess told him about inviting Saber Wynter to live in his home. He hadn't bought the story for one moment that Jess needed a housekeeper, any more than Saber had. Neither had pushed it. That was the power of the wheel-chair. Logan would have reamed him if he hadn't been staring down at him, facing the chair. But if Logan knew Saber was tele-pathic, he'd put a gun to her head, Jess's objections be damned.

Jess rolled the wheels back and forth, rock-ing himself while he thought about that. Everything had some advantages, and a GhostWalker learned to take whatever he had and use it. Jess was sure as hell count-ing on Logan to continue to notice the chair and not the man, because Logan was like a brother, but Saber — well, Saber was wrapped around his heart. There would be nothing left if Saber was gone.

The moment Logan slipped inside the secure room, he kicked the wheel of the chair and glared at Jess. "What the hell are you doing these days? Do you have any idea what time it is? And that — that woman never goes to sleep. You're damned lucky this room is soundproof, because she's pac-ing again. What's up with that?" He reached

65

around Jess and poured himself a cup of coffee.

"Hello to you too." Jess glanced up at his fellow GhostWalker. Logan was wearing a frown, his blue eyes flat and cold. "I can see you're in a great mood."

"We're supposed to be catching a killer, Jess, not catering to your girlfriend."

"Go to hell, Max," Jess snapped. "I'm getting the job done. And if you don't want to work with me, the door's right there. Don't let it hit you in the ass when you leave."

"Whoa. What a grump." Logan rolled his broad shoulders and flashed a small grin. "You're not sleeping with her yet, are you? The great Jess Calhoun, studmaster of the SEAL team, shot down by his housekeeper."

Jess responded with a rude gesture and shoved a chair at him. "You get the grunt work tonight for that crack."

Logan dropped into the chair and they went to work, moving with the ease of much practice, sifting through the files and reports, searching for a name. A single specific name. They both hoped they'd recognize it if they came across it.

After an hour Logan pushed back and shook his head. "This looks bad for the admiral."

"No way. It's not him. The traitor's hidden deep," Jess said with a small sigh. "I will not let myself believe Admiral Henderson is in any way involved. He can't be that good of an actor, and he sure as hell isn't stupid. Right now he's our only suspect, and would that be the case if he were guilty?"

"We've been at this for weeks, Jess," Logan said. "Have you run across one single name that has the pull and clearance needed to orchestrate this kind of double cross, a person who has been involved with every mission?"

"He's head of the NCIS. He's one of the most decorated rear admirals our nation has. He's been the sole commanding officer for our GhostWalker team since we were formed, and he's looked out for us," Jess protested. "It isn't him."

"Who then? Give me someone else." Logan threw his hands into the air. "Anyone else. Because as far as I can see, he's the only one who has known every time we've been sent out. He gave the order to send Jack to the Congo. When Jack couldn't go, he sent Ken in his place. The Norton twins were tortured beyond human endurance. Have you seen Ken? They're lucky they got out."

Jess pushed his hand through his hair and

slapped the desk hard with the flat of his hand in frustration. "I know. I visited him in the hospital when he first came back."

Few people know about the GhostWalkers, even in Washington. The Special Forces teams from every branch in the military had been tested for psychic abilities, and anyone who scored high had been given the opportunity to continue forward into the GhostWalker program. The soldiers were given specialized training before, during, and after the experiments, and the results had been incredible. Of course no one had known genetic experimentation had also taken place. Knowledge of the GhostWalkers was on a need-to-know basis, beyond security clearance. They were top-secret weapons sent out only when the circumstances were dire. But someone very high in the chain of command wanted them dead.

"Someone knew. Someone knew we volunteered to be psychically enhanced, and they have to know Peter Whitney carried the experiment even further. He has God knows how many women out there he experimented on as well." Jess shook his head. "Someone knows, Max, and it isn't the admiral."

"Maybe Louise Charter, the admiral's secretary. She's been with him twenty years, and when we investigated her before, she came out clean, but let's go there again and see if we missed anything." Logan knew he sounded as reluctant as he felt. They'd looked at Louise thoroughly. Nothing had been missed and they both knew it.

"My gut says it isn't the admiral," Jess persisted.

Logan let out his breath. "All right. Then what are we doing here? We're looking through every single report that ever had anything to do with the GhostWalkers, except that not a single mission was ever in a report. This paperwork is all bullshit. So tell me what we're looking for, Jess."

"Every GhostWalker volunteered to be psychically enhanced. At least the men. While it's true we didn't know about the genetic enhancement, my guess is, if we had, we'd all have gone for it. Someone wants us all dead, and what we're doing is trying to find out who."

"True," Logan nodded his head, knowing Jess was thinking out loud. The man was brilliant, right up there with Kadan Montague, another GhostWalker and one considered a genius. If anyone could figure the mess out, it was Jess or Kadan.

As if reading his thoughts, Jess glanced at him. "Kadan is running point for Ryland's team. He's looking at their commander, General Rainer. He's finding the same thing we are. The buck stops with his general, and he doesn't believe it any more than I believe Admiral Henderson is betraying us. So what do we know for certain, Max? We have to go back to the beginning on this one if we're going to unravel the mess and find our traitor."

Logan shot him a faint grin. "We know for absolute certain that we were all as dumb as jackasses to agree, and that we're all royally screwed. Well, with the sad exception of you, who can't get your housekeeper to cooperate and give you one or two extras. That might change if you weren't such a cheap son of a bitch."

"I might throw you out in another minute." Jess's voice was mild.

"Actually she's kind of cute," Logan persisted. "And when she talks on the radio, man she sounds like sin. Maybe I'll give it a try and see if she likes my type."

"I'd have to shoot you," Jess said. The walls expanded and contracted. Beneath his chair the floor shifted ever so slightly, and on the desk several objects moved. He took a deep breath and let it out.

Logan was joking. Teasing. The kind of bantering they always did back and forth, but for some reason, the mere thought of Logan hitting on Saber sent his gut twisting into hard knots.

Logan glanced around, leaned back in his chair, and laced his fingers behind his head. "You know you picked a bad time, Jess."

Jess sighed, not bothering to pretend he didn't know what Logan was talking about. Hell yeah, he'd picked the wrong time and the wrong woman. "Yeah, I'm very aware of that. Don't worry, I have my priorities straight."

"Do you? Because this could get ugly. If the wrong person gets wind of this investigation, they'll come after you, my friend. They'll kill you and her. And most likely they'll do to both of you the kinds of things that were done to Ken, just to see what you know and who you told."

Jess knew Logan was right. Worse, he knew he had put himself and maybe even his team members in jeopardy by not revealing that Saber was telepathic. Dr. Peter Whitney had experimented on young girls years earlier, and there was no doubt in his mind that Saber was one of these women. She could have other, much more dangerous, psychic gifts. Most of the GhostWalkers did. But he couldn't give her up. It made no sense, but he couldn't do it — not yet.

"You've got to tell me what's going on, Jess," Logan said, shifting in his chair, leaning forward. "We've been friends too long for you to shut me out."

Jess nodded. "Give me a few days to sort through all this. We're not even close to finding the traitor yet, so there's no way we could have spooked anyone. Just let me figure things out."

"Don't wait too long," Logan cautioned. "In our business, things go to hell very fast." Idly, he picked up a folder sitting beneath a lamp on the desk and turned it over and over in his hands. Jess leaned forward to take it and immediately Logan flipped it open. "What is this?"

Jess held out his hand. "Nothing important."

Logan inhaled sharply. "Don't bullshit me. This is your medical file. Bionics?" He was silent a moment flipping through the thick pages. "Lily sent you this, didn't she? For God's sake, Jess, she's Whitney's daughter. We've already got some bastard trying to kill us all, we've had our brains opened wide and our DNA altered, isn't that enough for you? Tell me you didn't agree to do this."

Jess remained silent.

"Bionics." Logan murmured the word

aloud. "Another experiment?"

Jess shrugged, trying to look casual. "The latest technology. Eric Lambert told me about it first when he was here checking on me. He said Lily Whitney has already advanced it."

"And convinced you to be her guinea pig? You don't think that what her father did to us was enough?" Logan took a breath. "Do you really trust her, Jess? I know she's married to Ryland and he's one of ours, but . . ."

"She lives in that house, knowing every minute of every day that Whitney has to be able to see and hear what she's doing so she can keep track of him. She lives in hell, Logan. Yeah, I trust her. She's helped every single GhostWalker in some way, from the exercises she teaches us to help shield our brains from outside disturbances, to making each of us financially independent. Without her, we wouldn't have half the data on Whitney that we have. She uses the computers to spy on him."

"How do you know she's not a double agent?"

Jess shook his head. "We're all getting so paranoid. Look at what we're doing to the admiral. We've known the old man for years, but we're looking into every aspect of his life. Now you don't think we can trust Lily?

If there's one person here who has suffered the most, who has given up everything, it's her. She knows he can find her, maybe even get to her, but she sticks herself out there so we can keep track of him. Without those computers we're dead in the water. He'll go under and we'll never find him."

"You're betting your life on her," Logan growled. "She's very much like her father."

"That isn't fair. She's brilliant like her father, otherwise she's nothing like him." He pushed aside the little voice in his head reminding him of the iguana and lizard DNA as well as the adult stem cell regeneration drug he'd been administered. It would sound far too close to Lily's father's experiments.

It was Peter Whitney, a billionaire with an extraordinary mind, who had managed to talk them all into his psychic experiments, not telling them — or anyone else — that it wasn't the first time he'd tried it on human beings. He had first experimented on orphans, infants, small children he'd had complete power over — including Lily, the child he'd adopted. As time went on they discovered he had also genetically altered them all. And he had continued his experiments, so no one knew how many women or men had been affected. Lily was trying to find out.

"I worked with her a lot while I was in the hospital recouping," Jess admitted. "She's committed to helping the GhostWalkers, *all* of them. She wants to find the other women and track down any other teams he may have worked on, so they can eventually live semi-normal lives."

"None of us are ever going to be able to do that," Logan said. "You know it as well as I do. And letting her experiment on you with bionics . . ."

"What do I have to lose?"

"Your life."

"You just said none of us were ever going to have one," Jess pointed out. "In any case, it's too late. I've committed to the program."

There was a long silence. Logan leapt out of his chair and paced across the room, swearing under his breath.

"It's that woman upstairs, isn't it, Jess? She's making you crazy, man." Logan turned to face Jess. "I'm not going to let this happen. I mean it. We've been friends too long. If she doesn't want you because you're in a chair . . ."

"That's not it and you know it. I wanted to try this. Once Eric mentioned the bionics program, I studied it, and when I took it to Lily, she asked me to let her see if she could improve things a little. With my enhancements, she wanted to add a few things that might work better for me." Things that would regenerate cells so his legs would actually work, things like iguana DNA and cells from his bone marrow. Who really knew what was in that bone marrow, since Peter Whitney had already added to the strange DNA that was now his?

"It's still an experiment."

"I didn't walk into it blind. You know me better than that. I won't stop until I find out who the mole is, and I'm going to walk again."

Logan shook his head. "You're not giving me much choice here, Jess."

"I'm aware of that. Let's get back to work. We've got a couple of hours to go through the rest of these reports. Maybe something will jump out at us."

Logan took another look at the file on bionics and then tossed it on the desk with another shake of his head. "Stubborn son of a bitch."

"You don't know the half of it." Jess flashed a small grin and went back to work.

Subject Jess Calhoun. Called in another GhostWalker tonight, Logan Maxwell. Calhoun is definitely still working with the SEAL Ghost-Walker team. At this time I have no further data on what he might be up to. Could not get the opportunity to plant the devices, as the virus has not reacted as we'd hoped. Wynter's system is quite resistant. Will try again and up the dose. Need your input and help with finding the security flaws. So far, cannot penetrate without detection. Please advise. Both subjects appear to have the same vulnerability. If their adversary is not enhanced, neither appears to have any alarm or radar going off. Your observations were correct, and I believe you should take steps to correct that in any future models.

The man clicked off his small recorder and leaned back against the plush leather seat as he switched on the radio. Immediately the car was flooded with the voice of the Night Siren. Sensuous. Like silk sheets. He felt it penetrate right through him, stroking his skin and hardening his groin. He adjusted his legs and closed his eyes, listening, knowing she was talking to him. He could feel her fingers, her tongue and mouth. So erotic. So much promise.

He shouldn't have dispatched the whore so soon. She wasn't anything like that voice, but she had a good mouth on her. He unzipped his trousers and began to

77

stroke himself to the sound of Saber Wynter's sexy voice.

CHAPTER 3

"For all my night owls out there, this is a special love song from the Night Siren to you." Saber sent her soft, whispery voice out over the airwaves, punched in the music, and stared up at the clock for the hundredth time.

Her head was shrieking at her, she had a sore throat, and she had wiped beads of sweat from her forehead more than once. She couldn't even come up with decent dialogue for tonight's program. The sexy Night Siren of the airwaves was as sick as she could possibly be. She had been at work exactly two hours and she was ready to surrender.

Saber rubbed her temples, trying to soothe the awful pounding. She had fallen asleep at six in the morning and, unusual for her, had slept all day. The sore throat and headache had been with her from the moment she'd opened her eyes.

"Jesse spent the day doing incantations," she muttered resentfully. He had looked the epitome of health as she went off to work, but he had been distant. Well, that wasn't exactly true. Jesse was never distant, but she felt he was closed off to her, and he was never that. She sighed and laid her head down on the desk, using her arms for a pillow. She was too sick to figure anything out.

Brian Hutton, her soundman, waved to her from the other side of the glass, indicating the telephone. When he mouthed Larry's name, Saber wrinkled her nose in distaste and shook her head. Just the idea of the louse increased the awful pounding in her temples. She was going to have to go home, crawl in bed, and hope she could fall asleep with the lights on.

She flicked a switch. "Brian, I'm not going to make it tonight," she said with genuine regret. She had never missed a day of work, had never even been late. It meant something to her to be able to go to work, however brief her stay always was. She liked having a clean record, knew they would think well of her after she left.

"You look like hell," Brian informed her.

"Oh, thanks. I needed to hear that. Would you cover for me so I could go home and get some sleep?"

"Sure, Saber," he agreed sympathetically. "It's just as well, the crazies are calling in tonight."

Her fingers wrapped around the microphone, and everything inside of her stilled. "What crazies, Brian?" She had waited too long. She should have left weeks earlier.

"Don't worry about it," he reassured. "We get them all the time, that's why I'm here, to weed them out. I always make sure I clue you in on the death threats. The nut tonight was very persistent, but he wasn't out to gun you down or save your soul. He was just another weirdo, probably looking for a date with the owner of that sexy voice."

Saber forced a laugh, forced her tense muscles to relax. "If they could only see me now." But she would have to be more careful than usual. She'd grown too comfortable here. Too comfortable with Jess.

Brian pulled one of her tapes and found the entrance he wanted. They did a silent countdown and her voice feathered out into the studio.

Saber breathed a soft sigh of relief, dropping her head into her hands. All she wanted was to crawl into a hole and hide.

Brian entered the sound booth and wrapped a comforting arm around her shoulders. "You're burning up. You okay to drive? Or do you want me to call you a cab?"

She patted his hand, shifting out from under him on the pretense of gathering her things together. "I'll be fine, Brian, thanks. Rest, orange juice, chicken soup, I'll be here tomorrow night with bells on." She held up her car keys. "I didn't lose them this time."

He grinned at her. "That's a shock. Wait for the security guard. You know how Jess is about you wandering around in the parking lot alone this time of night. He'd have my job first, then my head, if I let you."

"Poor Jesse." Saber smiled at the thought of him in spite of the fact that even her teeth hurt. "He really thinks I'm a pack of trouble, doesn't he?"

Brian grinned at her. "He's right too. Come on, I'll walk you down."

"Thanks, I'm fine, really, but next time you want to take a day off, do it on someone else's shift. The day sound guy, whatever his name is . . ."

"Les."

She rolled her eyes. "He's a grump and a bore. Last night was no fun at all working with him."

He grinned at her. "I'll be sure to plan all my future days off around your schedule."

She thumped his shoulder, knowing sarcasm when she heard it. "The phones are lighting up all over the place."

He shrugged, uncaring. "Probably that nut. He's called six times already tonight. I don't want to talk to him."

"Might be," Saber agreed. "But on the other hand it could be our mighty boss. Ever think of that?"

Brian's smile faded instantly. He was halfway down the hall by the time Saber lifted a heavy hand to wave before matching her short strides to the security guard's longer ones.

The ride home seemed longer than usual. Saber was so sick she could barely keep her head up. She never got sick. She was so used to her body's natural immunity to illness, it was rather alarming to find she had a high fever. If she wasn't so afraid of calling attention to herself — and Jess — she might have considered seeing a doctor.

Saber parked her small Volkswagen bug beside Jess's large, custom-made van. Her car looked incongruous next to the huge bulk of the van. She glared at the pair of cars, thinking of how many times Jess had teased her about how small she was. She kicked the tire in a spurt of resentment. So like the two of them. Mutt and Jeff. She didn't belong here. She could never belong here and she had to get the backbone to leave — and soon.

The large house seemed unusually dark and spooky as she entered it. Saber resisted the urge to flood the room with light, not wanting to disturb Jess. She did enough of that on the nights she didn't work, keeping him awake with her phobias.

There was no sound to warn her, yet suddenly Saber couldn't breathe, adrenaline pumping into her body, freezing her halfway through the foyer. There was no scent, no breath, no stirring of the air, but she knew, an eternity too late, she wasn't alone.

Something snagged her ankles and she sprawled facedown on the hardwood floor, the breath knocked from her body. Before she could roll or retaliate, she felt the cold, deadly kiss of a gun barrel pressed against the nape of her neck.

It all happened in seconds, yet time slowed down so that everything was crystal clear for Saber. The faint lemon in the polish on the wood floor, the beating of her heart, the pain in her lungs, the deadly feel of metal against her skin. Everything stilled as if she'd been waiting.

They were here. They had hunted her, stalked her, and now they were here. Jesse. Oh God, she thought wildly. Jess was alone, asleep, vulnerable — what if they had hurt

Jesse? Her vision tunneled, everything inside her coiling, ready to strike. She would have to kill the intruder in order to protect Jesse. Even if her assailant killed her, she would have to take him with her.

The moment she put her hands palms down to push up off the floor, he shoved harder with the gun. "Don't do it."

She had to get her hands on him, make him think she was a woman terrified out of her mind. She just needed that one moment where she could wrap her hand around his wrist, feel his pulse, his heartbeat . . . Saber went crazy, thrashing, trying to turn, arms flailing out at the gun to knock it aside. "Go ahead, shoot! Do it! Get it over with. I'm not running from you anymore." She caught at the gleaming barrel as she sat up, pulled it against her head. "Do it!" She judged the distance to his wrist. A moment, just one heartbeat and she had him.

To her surprise, her assailant suddenly swore and yanked the gun back.

"Saber!" Jess's voice was hoarse with a mixture of fear and anger. "Are you out of your mind sneaking in here like that? I could have shot you."

Fury and relief met fear head on, mingled, and melted together in a violent swirl of emotion she couldn't contain. "You pulled a gun on me?" She flung herself at him, swinging at him with a clenched fist. She could have killed him — had come within a hairsbreadth of killing Jesse. Oh God, she could never — *never* — have lived with that.

He caught both of her wrists, tipped her off balance, and brought her up hard against his legs. "Stop it, Saber." He gave her a little shake when she continued to struggle. "I had no idea you were coming home. It's hours early. You hate the dark and yet you didn't turn on a single light." He made the words an accusation.

She was trembling uncontrollably, so close to tears it terrified her. "I was being considerate," she hissed. "Which is more than I can say for you. Let go of me, you're hurting me." She could have killed him. She *would* have killed him. Why hadn't she known it was him? She always recognized his scent, his warmth. She hadn't even recognized his voice. Maybe she had on some level afterward, but not at first, not when he'd come at her in the dark. Why? What had been different? Her mind raced with questions, but anger and hurt and terror overtook reason.

"Are you calm?"

"Don't patronize me. You put a gun to my head. God! I live here, Jesse, I can come and go as I please. And what are you doing sitting up at one o'clock in the morning, lights out, with a gun?" she demanded.

Suddenly she knew. She felt another's presence, a witness to her hysterical outburst. Stiffening, she turned slowly. Saber caught a glimpse of a shadowy figure hastily backing out of sight. Tall, abundant curves. Saber's heart plunged right down to her toes. A woman. Jesse was with a woman in the middle of the night. A stranger. With the lights off. Worse, Jess was so willing to protect that stranger that he had actually lain in wait with a gun. Betrayal was a bitter taste in Saber's mouth. *And why hadn't she scented the woman?*

A small flame began to smolder. Had he held the woman in his strong arms? Run his hands through her hair? Kissed her the way Saber had so longed for him to kiss her? Oh God, they'd probably been making love, right there in the living room. The fire spread. And the woman had witnessed Saber's lack of control. Her gaze was riveted to Jess's hard features. It was a silent accusation of betrayal and she didn't give a damn if he knew how she felt. She'd spent way too long here, risked too much. *Damn you to hell for this.*

Saber evaded his instinctive move toward

her, pressing the back of her hand to her mouth. She felt betrayed, utterly betrayed. If it was possible to hate Jess, right at that moment, she did.

"Saber." There was an ache in his voice.

She whirled around and ran up the stairs, for the first time in years not caring or even noticing that the lights were out. She went straight through to her bedroom, her chest burning, fighting for air, her head pounding. She flung her shoes one after the other at the wall and threw herself facedown on the bed. If this was normal, it sucked. She didn't want normal anymore. She wanted to disappear, let Saber Wynter die and someone else, someone who didn't — *couldn't* — feel like this take her place.

Jess doubled his fist wanting, needing, to smash something. In ten months Saber had never once come home early from work. The security guard should have called him, damn it. Brian should have called him. Why was she home? And what the hell was wrong with her? She hadn't known it was Jess holding the gun, he had been shielding the scents and sounds in the room, yet she had fought like a wildcat, even going so far as to scream at him to shoot her.

Instantly he felt the jarring note. Not him.

She believed him to be someone else. He winced as he heard her shoes crash against the wall. Who? Who had she expected? He moved toward the darkened living room.

A soft muted sound stopped him cold. Saber was weeping, a muffled, heartbroken sound that tore his heart right out of his chest. Damn the GhostWalkers and the all-too-necessary security precautions. Damn the security guard and Brian for withholding a warning.

"I'll go." His guest moved out of the shadows.

"I'm sorry for the inconvenience," Jess forced himself to say. He couldn't very well tell her to go to hell. Louise Charter, the admiral's secretary, had risked her life to hand deliver a small digital recorder to him, yet at that moment, all he could hear, could concentrate on, all he cared about, were the soft sounds of distress emanating from the bedroom upstairs.

Saber never cried in front of him. Not even if she was injured. Tears might sparkle for a moment, but in ten long months, Saber Wynter had never cried.

Jess knew he was bordering on rudeness when he ushered Louise from his home with unseemly haste. The moment the door was closed he waited impatiently for the lift. It seemed to take an endless amount of time. He had a mad desire to try jumping his wheelchair up the flight of stairs, balancing on two wheels.

Why had she come home? He remembered the feel of her satin skin burning his. Of course. She was ill. There could be no other reason conscientious little Saber would leave her job. He didn't let himself remember the cool steel in her eyes when she'd first turned, the ease of her body rolling, and her hands coming up in a classic defense. Only the hurt, the betrayal in her eyes — *in her voice* — mattered. Her voice had slid into his mind with such ease, such clarity, such pain.

The lift carried him to the second floor and his racing chair glided silently through the sitting room to her bedroom. He paused in the wide doorway, his dark, stricken gaze on Saber's slender form. She was on her stomach, her tear-stained face buried in the crook of her arm.

His heart turned over. One thrust of his powerful arms and he was at her side, his hand tangling in the riot of curls. "Baby." He groaned it softly in a kind of anguish. "Don't, don't do this."

"Go away." Her voice was muffled.

"You know I'm not going to do that," he

replied, keeping his voice low. "You're sick, Saber, I'm not just leaving you up here to fend for yourself." His hand stroked her hair. "Come on, love, you've got to stop crying. You'll get a headache."

"I already have a headache," she sniffed. "Go away, Jesse, I don't want you to see me like this."

"Who can see? It's dark in here," he teased, hands sliding to her shoulders in a calming rhythm.

"Where'd your little friend go?" Saber couldn't stop the words from tumbling out, could have bitten her tongue off for doing so. As if she cared. He could have fifty women, a whole harem over every night while she worked at the station.

Jess found himself smiling in spite of everything, and had to hastily control his voice. "You're running a fever, little one, let me get you a cold cloth. Have you taken any aspirin?"

"So perceptive of you to notice." Saber sat up, rubbing her eyes with her fist, furious with herself for crying. She swept a hand through the mass of raven-colored curls in a vain effort to smooth the disheveled mess. "And I can take an aspirin all by myself."

He was already halfway to her bathroom. "True, but would you?" he queried as he pushed open the door.

Jess had designed the remodel of his house, making certain that every door was comfortably wide, everything was low enough for him. Now, he was particularly grateful that he'd made certain he had ease of movement upstairs as well as down. Ignoring the lacy scraps of female underwear hanging to dry on the towel rack, Jess scooped up a washcloth.

Saber made an effort to pull herself together. So she wasn't feeling good. Big deal. So her best friend in the entire world had scared the hell out of her. Big deal. Jess was sneaking around with some woman he didn't want her to know about. Rotten, stinking, no-good bum. Saber smoldered with resentment, frustration, and something that was far too close to jealousy.

Just what was he doing with all the lights out? How often did Jezebel visit while she was gone? It wasn't like Saber didn't tell him about every single disgusting date she went on. They had endless discussions about them. She didn't sneak behind his back.

Jess stifled a small grin. It took tremendous effort for him to keep his expression blank. Her violet-blue eyes spit fire at him. Jealousy meant she cared, whether she wanted to care or not. Something stirred in him deep down, something gentle and tender and long forgotten.

"Baby," he said gently, "if you continue to look at me like that I'm bound to fall dead on the floor." The cool washcloth moved over her burning face, stroked down her neck.

"Good idea, great idea, in fact," Saber snapped, but she didn't pull away from his ministrations.

"Shall I call Eric?" He pushed back her hair.

Eric Lambert was the surgeon who had saved Jesse's life, Saber knew, a really big deal, apparently famous among doctors, and he still made house calls — at least to Jess. Sometimes he came with another doctor, a woman, although Saber had never met her. But she knew Jess had been violently ill after the last time they'd both come; she didn't want any part of that.

"I've got the flu, Jesse," she reassured him in spite of the fact that he deserved the death penalty. "No big deal, I don't need a doctor."

"You need to get out of these clothes." His voice dropped a husky octave.

"Don't hold your breath." Having an affair without saying a single word when he wanted to know every detail of her dates? How dare he?

"Who did you think I was?" He slipped the question in with all the precision of a skilled surgeon wielding a knife.

Beneath his hands she went still, blue eyes skittering away from his. One finger nervously twisted a lock of hair around it. "I have no idea what you're talking about."

Jess lifted the washcloth, caught her chin in a firm grip, and forced her to meet his steady, probing gaze. "You're getting to be a terrible liar."

Saber jerked her chin free. "I thought you were safe in bed, caveman. Why do you think I was stumbling around in the dark? I was being considerate. How was I supposed to know you were carrying on a clandestine meeting with the local harlot?" Furious, Saber sat up and switched on the dim lamp on her nightstand. "I can't believe you actually tripped me and held a gun on me."

"I can't believe you behaved so stupidly. If I had been an intruder, you'd be dead right now," he bit back, dark eyes glittering.

"Well, maybe I knew it was you all along. Did that ever occur to you?" Saber jumped up, putting distance between them.

"Like hell you did."

"Don't you dare get mad at me. I wasn't

the one pointing a gun at *your* head. I didn't even know you had a gun in the house. I hate guns," she declared. But she knew how to use them. She could break one down and put it back together in seconds, less than that when needed. She was fast, efficient, deadly.

"So I noticed." He smiled in spite of himself.

She paced the length of the room with the familiar flowing grace of a ballet dancer. "Well, just who did you think I was, some private investigator hired by that woman's husband?"

Jess didn't even blink. "I don't know what you imagined you saw," he began.

"I saw a woman. She ducked into the shadows," Saber was adamant.

"It happened so fast, honey, and you were frightened."

"Hit the big slide, Jesse," Saber said rudely.

"I'm not exactly certain what that means."

"Don't you laugh. Don't you *dare* laugh. It means go to hell, and for your information, I wasn't that scared. I *know* I saw a woman." She crossed her arms over her chest and tilted her head to scowl at him. "Not that I blame you for wanting to deny her existence. Her dog probably wants to deny her existence. But I know what I saw."

"Okay, okay," he said soothingly. "You saw a woman hiding in our living room, I believe you. Now get out of those clothes and into your night things."

Saber glared at him. "You're patronizing me, pretending to pretend to believe me."

His eyebrow shot up. "This is far too complicated to sort out with you so ill. I can't even follow the logic of that. If it makes you feel better I'll close my eyes."

She considered throwing things at him, but her head was pounding and she was unbearably hot. "So keep them closed," she ordered and stalked into the bathroom.

Saber was observant; he had to hand it to her, although it shouldn't surprise him. She was running a high fever, was terrified of the dark, and must have been even more so by his unexpected assault. Yet she had noticed that whisper of movement in the darkest corner of the room. And her movements had been calm enough, calculated, and might have worked on someone with less training.

She emerged, clad in a long T-shirt reaching halfway to her knees, looking more beautiful than ever. "Are you still here?" she demanded as she flounced across the floor to fling herself on the bed.

"Did you take aspirin?"

"Yes." She made a face at him to show him he wasn't forgiven. "Are you happy?"

Jess sighed softly. "You're still angry with me."

Saber curled up in a little ball, facing away from him, actually hunching a shoulder. "You think?"

It took one powerful motion of his incredibly strong arms and Jess had shifted himself from his chair to her bed. Saber's slender body stiffened as he stretched out beside her, but she didn't protest.

He pulled her close, fitting her into his shoulder, amazed at how soft her skin was, how fragile and small she appeared next to him. He reached out a lazy hand to snap off the lamp.

"Don't."

"It's time for you to sleep, baby," he prompted, plunging the room into darkness with a quick flick of his fingers.

Instantly he felt the shudder run through her body. "I sleep with the light on."

"Not tonight. Tonight you sleep in my arms, knowing I'll keep you safe." He stroked her hair tenderly.

"I have nightmares if the lights are off," Saber admitted, too sick to care.

His chin rubbed her silky curls. "Not

when I'm here, Saber, I'll keep them away."

"Arrogant dragon king," she murmured drowsily, reaching to lace her fingers with his. "Demons wouldn't dare cross you, would they?"

"Who did you think I was, Saber? Who are you running from?"

There was such a long silence Jess was certain she wouldn't answer. Finally she sighed. "You're imagining things. I'm not running from anyone. You scared me is all." There was the tiniest note of amusement in her sensual, silky voice.

Lying next to her should have produced the familiar relentless ache, but instead he felt a deep peace, something he had never experienced, stealing into him. She felt intensely hot despite the fact that the air in the bedroom was quite cool and he had only pulled a sheet over them.

"Maybe I should call you a doctor," he murmured. "Eric could be here in a couple of hours."

Saber sighed. "Stop fussing, Jesse," she pleaded. Her fingers tightened around his. "I'll be fine."

He held her, feeling her body relax in the shelter of his, her breathing slow and rhythmic. Jess buried his chin in the mass of silky raven corkscrews, enjoying the feeling of just lying next to her, of being close to her.

Sometime later he must have drifted off, his dreams mildly erotic, not the usual flaming fantasies Saber aroused in him. The first sign of her distress awakened him, a soft little whimper, her body jerking convulsively.

She rolled suddenly, her hand coming up and toward him, a knife slicing fast toward his jugular with deadly accuracy. The movement was smooth and practiced. He caught her arm, slammed it down to the mattress, twisting almost to the point of breaking her wrist, his thumb finding a pressure point to force release. She never made a sound. Didn't cry out in pain, even when he dug his fingers in hard enough to bruise.

Jess was enormously strong, genetically enhanced, and worked out daily in order to lift his own body weight all the time, yet it was difficult to subdue her. "Wake up, Saber," he hissed, giving her a little shake.

The knife dropped from her hand and slid off the bed, but she rolled, ramming her elbow toward his jaw. He took the blow on his shoulder and caught her by the throat, slamming her down to the mattress.

Saber fought back, her eyes wild, haunted, his name on her lips. "Jesse!" She called for him again, the sound so filled with pain, so raw with terror, he felt actual tears stinging his eyes.

"For God's sake, Saber, wake up. I'm here. I'm here." He pinned her wrists, holding her down so she couldn't continue the attack. "You're having a nightmare. That's all it is, just a bad dream."

He knew the exact moment she became aware. Her body stilled, stiffened. Her gaze jumped to his face, examined every inch of his features, searching his expression for reassurance. He slowly released her and lay back beside her, turning so his body curled protectively around hers.

"Someone's in the house, Jesse, I heard a noise." She shuddered and leaned her burning forehead against the coolness of his.

"It was a nightmare, baby, nothing more."

"No, someone's in the house. Downstairs." She clutched at his shoulders. "Lock my door. Is my door locked?"

He smoothed back her hair with gentle fingers. "No one can get in, you're safe with me."

"Turn on the light, we have to turn it on. No one will come in if the light's on," Saber insisted desperately.

"Shh." He pulled her into his arms, burying her small, delicate face against his chest. She was trembling, burning hot against his skin. Tenderly he rocked her back and forth.

"Nothing is wrong, Saber. I would never let anything happen to you."

Her heart slammed hard against his chest, her pulse racing so frantically, Jess tightened his hold.

"It wasn't a dream. I know I heard a noise, I know I did." One hand curled into a fist, beating a tattoo against his shoulder. The other stroked the bulging line of his biceps in agitation.

There was something intensely intimate about the feel of her fingers tracing his muscles, despite the circumstances. His body stirred in response, painfully tight, urgently demanding. He ignored it, imposing the strict discipline that had kept him alive for years. He simply held her, rocking her gently, stroking her hair soothingly, not answering her wild imaginings.

It was some time before her body ceased trembling and she lay quietly in his arms.

Jess brushed a feather light kiss over her silky curls. "Feeling better?"

"I think I'm making a fool of myself," she replied in a small voice.

"Never that, honey," he murmured with gentle amusement. "You had a bad dream. Probably that rotten music you listen to."

She nuzzled his chest, liking the steady beat of his heart beneath her ear. "Country

101

music is good music."

"After the other night I decided I could get to like it. What in the world were you playing, anyway?"

"You don't like rap?" Her laughter was muffled. "How did I know you wouldn't like that particular group?"

He tugged a curl a little bit too hard in punishment, then rubbed the spot soothingly when she squealed. "Because I write number one hits all the time and not one of them has ever been rap."

"Egotistical maniac," she accused. "Not everyone has to listen to your music."

"That's true, baby, I don't care if the entire world stops listening." His lips brushed her hair again. "Except for you. Not only are you required to listen, but you're required to like it." He gave the order gruffly.

She laughed softly, relaxing against him. "So sing to me."

There was a long silence. Jess cleared his throat. "Say, what?"

"Sing. You know. *Ooh baby, baby, dum de dum.* Sing."

"I don't sing, I write. Music and lyrics. Write, Saber. And I sell them to other artists. I work for the navy. I don't have a band."

"Why is that, Jess? You're obviously independently wealthy, you have a reputation as a songwriter, yet you're still in the military. You're in a wheelchair."

"I hadn't noticed."

"You know what I mean. Why are you still in?"

"Who said I was?"

"I've lived here ten months. I know you're doing some kind of job for them. Or am I not supposed to know?"

"You're not supposed to know."

She settled deeper into his chest, looking up at him with humor in her eyes. "Fine then. I'll be ignorant. Sing to me, Jesse. If I can't have the light on, and we can't discuss how utterly stupid it is for you to stay in the military, then you can at least sing."

"Is this what I have to look forward to the rest of my life?" he asked, bunching her hair in his hands.

"A fate worse than death," Saber agreed drowsily.

At least she hadn't demanded to know what he meant. Jess mentally shook his head. He couldn't afford any more mistakes like that. Saber didn't stay in one place very long and lately she had become restless, looking over her shoulder. Was she getting ready to leave? She had said she wasn't running anymore. He couldn't take the chance of making her more nervous, because he damned well wasn't going to let her go, and he was finding out every single one of her secrets whether she liked it or not.

"Jesse." Saber sounded petulant.

He eased back against the pillows, Saber's head on his chest. "A song, huh?" Jess sighed heavily. "You're so high maintenance."

"Quit stalling," she murmured.

Jess closed his eyes and allowed the feel of her satin skin, the clean feminine scent of her to seep into him. He swallowed the lump in his throat and sang Saber her song. The one he wrote for her, the one that beat in his heart, his head, every time he looked at her or thought of her. A slow, dreamy ballad.

She moves like an artist, graceful and free
Like the paint on a canvas that flows
   easily
Oh, but those haunting eyes
They make me realize
The depths of my emotions stirring inside
She's the woman I dream of
A child at play
Crusading for others, in her own special
   way

When I think that it's over, it's only begun
When I look in her eyes . . .
Oh, but those haunting eyes
They make me realize
The depths of my emotions stirring inside
Like the flight of the butterfly in gentle
    breeze
Her delicate features are so clear to see
She's a woman, a warrior who never
    gives up
Oh, but my elusive butterfly
She makes me realize
The depths of my emotions stirring inside

Jess felt her tears on his chest as his voice faded. His hands tightened possessively, one in her hair, one around her waist. He didn't need words, her tears were enough. Did she feel the deep emotions stirring in him? Did she realize he was baring his soul to her? He allowed her to hide, not wanting to push her when she was so vulnerable.

Saber drifted off into a fitful sleep. He waited until her breathing was slow and even before he reached over the side of the bed and found the knife. Very carefully he slid it by the tip into the small pouch on his chair. He could examine it in the morning, lift any prints, find out if anyone other than Saber had handled that military issue knife.

He held her most of the night, sometimes sleeping, more often than not simply lying awake, enjoying the feel of her in his arms. Her fever abated somewhere close to dawn, and regretfully, Jess eased himself from her side, knowing she wouldn't be happy if she woke to find him in her bed, reminding her of her tears and their shared emotional night. She wouldn't know how to handle it, and with her so close to running, he wasn't about to take any chances.

Subject Wynter arrived early. I doubled the dose we first agreed on in order to infect her. Her system is much more resistant than believed. Will find a way to get more blood from her to work with. She continues to move away from her training with each day. I believe you are correct in insisting on isolation and daily training. The longer she goes without exercising her skills, the more rapid her decline. Subject Calhoun has had visitors frequently. Lily Whitney and Eric Lambert visit him on a regular basis but almost never when Wynter is at the house. Lily is under heavy guard during the time that she's with Calhoun, so snatching her would be next to impossible. We will see how Wynter fights off the infection and whether Calhoun calls for medical care.

He snapped off the recorder, wishing he

could linger, but he didn't dare tonight. He was taking too many risks, and he couldn't chance being caught. Death came swiftly to those who failed. He wanted the prize they dangled in front of him. Enhancement, both psychic and genetic. He could take what he wanted then. Yeah, and he was having fun along the way. The next time maybe he'd bring entertainment again. He loved the look in the whore's eyes as she realized just what he intended to do. His seed had been smeared all over her face and on her protesting lips at the very moment she'd understood he would have her life too.

"No, honey, you didn't please me nearly as much as you thought you did," he whispered aloud and glanced up at the window, smiling with a cold, dark promise.

CHAPTER 4

Saber opened her eyes slowly, reluctantly. Beside her, the bed was empty. She felt achy and sore, but the fever was gone. What in the world had happened to make her so sick? She was never sick — never — and it had been a shock. She hadn't handled it very well either.

She rolled over and caught the sides of the pillow to inhale deeply Jess's distinctive male scent. It flooded her lungs and made her stomach do a strange little flip. He had lain beside her, holding her in his arms, singing her to sleep. Her mouth curved at the thought. He said he couldn't sing, but she loved his voice. The thought of it, of his song to her, had a warmth spreading quickly through her entire body.

She took another quick sniff of the pillow, wondering whether she should wash the pillowcase immediately before she became obsessive over it, or leave it forever, slip it into her emergency pack so if she had to run fast she would always have it. No one was around to see her, so she rolled like a cat over the spot where he'd slept.

Jess. He smelled so good all the time. He smelled safe and clean and so very male. With a little sigh she forced herself to get up. She had awoken earlier than usual. She tended to stay up all night and sleep in the mornings and early afternoon. Having no idea what she was going to do with herself, she forced her body into motion, taking her time in the shower, savoring the feeling of the hot water on her skin.

She couldn't get Jess out of her mind. The feel of his hard muscles, his enormous strength, the tenderness in his voice. For a moment she closed her eyes, allowing hot water to cascade over her head and just dreaming. Letting herself believe, just for a moment, that she could have a life. A home. A man. She wanted to belong to Jess Calhoun. Her eyes flew open in shock. Oh God. She was in trouble. She had to get out before it was too late. How had she let this happen?

She pulled on her clothes as she tried to calm her wildly beating heart. Her mouth went dry. Jess Calhoun was not for her, no matter how much she wanted him. When had it happened? When had she allowed herself to believe her own fantasy? She stared at herself in the mirror while she blew her hair dry, trying to make her mind focus on what to do next. A sane woman would leave. Self-preservation would dictate that.

As she turned off the dryer she heard the soft murmur of Jess's voice. Something — some note in it — caught at her, raising every alarm. He sounded stressed. Not a lot, but she knew him now, she paid attention to every detail, and Jess was upset.

Her heart slammed hard in her chest as she carefully set the blow-dryer aside and reached beneath her mattress for her knife. It wasn't there. She swore under her breath and crossed to her pack, placing her feet with care so that she made no noise. Her mouth firmed and her hands were steady as she put on her belt, gun sliding into the holster smoothly and throwing knives slipping into each loop. If Jess was in trouble, she was going to be prepared.

She had promised herself she was through with killing, but . . . She couldn't let herself think about that. It would only mess her up. Moving without sound, Saber kept her back to the wall, making the target small as she eased through the bedroom door to the upstairs balcony. There were two places where the boards squeaked. She avoided both, although the stairs would be more difficult. She should have fixed them, but she thought it was a good warning system if anyone tried to sneak up them while she slept.

"It's so good to see you, darling," a woman's voice purred, followed by a telling silence. Saber stiffened in the doorway of her small sitting room, picturing Jess being soundly kissed. Her fingers curled around the gun.

"Chaleen. I have to admit you shocked me. You were the last person in the world I expected to hear from when I picked up the phone." There was that note of stress again. Whoever Chaleen was, Jess wasn't happy to see her.

Tinkling laughter pealed out. The sound grated on Saber.

"I knew you'd be pleased."

"What in the world are you doing in Sheridan?"

Jess didn't sound pleased at all. Chaleen had to be an idiot if she thought he was. Saber eased out into the hall. The alert was still pounding in her body, a warning that all was not right.

"Why, I came to see you, darling." Chaleen's heels clicked on the hardwood floor.

"I've been on planes for simply days."

Saber padded silently on bare feet to the balcony overlooking the living room. The woman was tall and slim, with breasts that were too good to be true. Her hair was sleek and sophisticated, her clothes elegant. Saber despised her on sight.

"So how did you find out where I was?" Jess asked. "I thought I'd covered my tracks."

Saber leaned on the banister, unashamedly listening. Chaleen? Who was named Chaleen? She wrinkled her nose in disgust. And did Chaleen darling have to purr at Jess? Why couldn't the witch talk like a normal woman? Even her perfume was drifting up the stairs. Saber sniffed in distaste and curled up out of sight but where, if they stayed in the living room, she could hear every disgusting, purring word. Or, if the woman wasn't out for sheer sex like she sounded to be, then Saber could put a bullet in her head before she made a wrong move against Jess.

"I ran into your parents in Paris." Chaleen settled herself on the plush sofa, crossing her silk-covered legs to show them to their best advantage. "I still can't believe it, such a tragedy. Poor Jess had his wings clipped in such a brutal way." A long red-

112

tipped nail traced delicately through the fur of her coat.

"Cut the crap, Chaleen, you left the moment you found out."

"I loved you too much to see your pain, Jess."

Saber rolled her eyes. What rot. Jesse. Jess and Chaleen. How juvenile. It grated on her nerves the way darling Chaleen said it. Jess. Chaleen purred it. Tasted it. Saber's fingers tightened around the gun until her knuckles turned white. Fuming, she missed Jess's response, but not Chaleen's tinkling laughter. The sound made her want to throw up — or shoot somebody. Little did Chaleen darling know she was seconds away from death.

"Oh, darling! You're so funny! And so brave, to bear this horrendous burden so heroically. But why bury yourself in this backwater town? You'll never be happy here. You need excitement, the hunt. You'll wither here." Chaleen fluttered her lashes, ran a restless hand along her silken leg.

"I've managed not to wither so far." Jess sounded bored.

"Jess, I'm just so devastated to think that such a virile, sexy man could have been struck down so cruelly."

Saber winced at that, and nearly bit a hole

in her lower lip. How did the carcass wearer know that? Sexy. Virile. Good old Chaleen had better keep her red-tipped fingers to herself.

"You've always needed a real woman, one who could satisfy your appetites, and now . . . Oh, Jess. Can you . . . I mean . . . is it possible for you to . . ." Chaleen trailed off, a hand to her throat.

Furious, Saber jumped up and rushed to her bedroom. That — that disgusting hussy. She was throwing herself at Jess. And she was doing her best to make him squirm, make him feel less than a man. The viper. She was trying to strip him of his pride. Well, Saber would be damned if she'd stand by and let that happen.

She tossed clothes in all directions, searching for something sexy. She didn't own anything sexy. And how was she going to compete with a five foot ten blonde with more cleavage than good manners?

She caught a glimpse of herself in the mirror over her dresser. A slow, saucy smile curved her soft mouth. There was no competition. She drew on Jess's shirt, the one she always wore to bed, the one that made her feel so close to him every time she put it on. The one that had his scent all over it.

Saber tossed her gun aside, the knives following, and kicked her jeans into the corner of the room, wishing she could be in two places at the same time. She wanted to hear every word that painted witch said to Jess.

On bare feet Saber padded down the stairs, clad only in lacy underwear and Jess's shirt.

The vamp was wound around Jess, running her poisonous, bright red fingernails through his hair, bending low to murmur in his ear, clearly in danger of falling out of her dress.

"Jesse." Saber wasn't above using the Night Siren's whispery voice. It worked on the airwaves, why not at home? "You didn't tell me we were expecting company." She smiled, syrupy sweet. "I take it this is the *old* friend you told me about." Saber maliciously emphasized the word "old" and just for fun giggled as though Jess had given her an amusing tale.

Jess held out his hand to Saber, grinning in conspiracy. "Chaleen Jarvos, Saber Wynter. Chaleen happened to be traveling through Sheridan and was kind enough to look in on us, angel face."

Chaleen straightened abruptly, glaring daggers at Saber, cold hazel eyes sweeping her up and down. "Who is this little urchin, Jess?" she demanded.

115

Jess brought Saber's hand to the warmth of his mouth. "Is that what you are, love? My little urchin?"

Saber laughed and rubbed her cheek along his knuckles. "I'll run in and grab your robe." She glanced up at Chaleen guilelessly. "Would you care for coffee?"

Saber made herself look as innocent as possible, but deep inside she was as cold as ice. This woman might be Jess's ex-girlfriend, but she was definitely far more than that — and she was a threat to Jess. Those eyes were flat and cold and filled with venom. Chaleen Jarvos was someone other than who she pretended to be.

"I doubt Chaleen will be staying that long," Jess said.

"Jess!" Chaleen purred the name. "I've traveled all this way to see you, talk to you." She made a gesture encompassing the house. "This isn't you, you're no family man. You were born for wild excitement, not this cutesy little home scene. You're wasted here."

Saber's arms circled his neck. She pressed against the back of his chair. Jess could feel the heat of her body, the warmth of her breath. She smelled fresh and clean in contrast to the heavy, cloying perfume Chaleen had poured over herself. A part of him wanted to send Saber far away, where Chaleen couldn't sink her claws into her, and another part of him desperately wanted her there.

Saber gave a husky, intimate laugh. "Don't worry, umm, Carlene, is it? Jess is definitely not wasted here. And we provide each other with more than enough — how did you put it? — wild excitement." She exchanged an intimate, bedroom smile with Jess, bending her head slightly to brush the side of his shadowed jaw with her soft, satin lips. "Let me just run and get the robe."

"It's Chaleen." The blonde glared furiously, tapping her high heel on the hardwood floor. Miffed that Saber sailed right out of the room without so much as acknowledging the correction, she paced back and forth. "I cannot believe that a man of your caliber, of your education, Jess, would team up with a little . . ."

"Urchin," Jess mocked.

"Exactly!" Chaleen pounced on that. "We have a past, we know each other. We've shared danger, excitement." She placed her hand on Jess's thigh. "We've shared each other."

"That was a lifetime ago, Chaleen. Another world."

"A world you belong in. Losing your legs

117

can't change that." Chaleen loomed over the wheelchair. "You need to come back, be part of it all again. Maybe you are already. I can't imagine that you'd give up your work for that silly little kid. She has to be just out of high school. You need a woman, not a child." She flashed a smile. "You are working for the navy, aren't you, Jess?"

Saber cinched the belt of the terry cloth robe tighter around her small waist, wishing for one moment the tie was around Chaleen's scrawny neck.

Jess leaned forward, circling Chaleen's wrist with his hand. Saber's heart dropped right down to her toes. What if she had guessed wrong? What if this vampish viper was the mystery woman from the other night? What if she was making a fool of herself, leaping to Jess's defense when he really didn't need or want it? She held her breath as Jess lifted Chaleen's hand.

Everything in her stilled. The world narrowed, tunneled. She was suddenly focused and in complete control. Because if he kissed Chaleen's fingers, Saber knew with certainty that Chaleen Jarvos was a dead woman.

Jess dropped her hand as if it were distasteful. "I'm exactly where I want to be, Chaleen."

Saber slumped against the wall with relief, closing her eyes briefly, distaste of her first, most primal reaction to an enemy beating at her. *That* wasn't a normal reaction. Had she waited too long to leave? Had she already become the very thing she'd always feared she was? She pressed the heel of her hand to her forehead even as she strained to listen to the conversation.

"This is my world. Sheridan, Wyoming. And Saber is everything I need. Go back to your boss and tell him I put in my time and I want to be left alone."

"But there's so much more you can still do. All your people, they're still loyal, they still trust you. Your name could open doors."

"Who are you looking to contact?"

"I need some answers, Jess. You know who I work for. Whatever you're doing is pissing off some powerful people." Chaleen pinned him with a cold gaze. "They know you're involved in something big. No one is buying your legless charade. I'm trying to keep you out of trouble, and watching you pretend to be an idiot for your little teenybopper is making me want to throw up."

"Sorry, I don't do that kind of work. And my injuries are fully documented. Whatever you're looking for isn't here."

"Damn it, Jess, you don't want to mess

119

around with me." Shifting suddenly from purring, Chaleen sounded as hard as nails, bringing out a protective streak in Saber she didn't even know she had. "I'm trying to save your hide here. You've got some investigation going and it's raising flags all over the place. The FBI. The CIA. I'm hearing your name everywhere. For God's sake, something like that will get you killed."

Saber held very still. There was actual fear in Chaleen's voice. She might have come for information on whatever Jess was investigating, but she was genuinely concerned for his safety. Was Chaleen an assassin? Saber moved into a better position to get her away from Jess if she tried anything. Just what was Jess doing, anyway?

"I have no idea what you're talking about."

"Damn you, Jess. You were always so fucking closemouthed. This isn't a game. You always think you're playing chess instead of living real life. You're making enemies and they'll be coming after you."

Chaleen definitely sounded threatening. Saber forgot about trying to get information and moved into the room. She circled Jess's neck with her arms. "Sorry I took so long, love," she murmured.

Chaleen glanced at her diamond-studded watch. "Did you run?" she snapped.

Saber ran her fingers through Jess's thick, dark hair. "Pardon me?" she asked, her voice dripping with sweetness.

Chaleen gathered up her fur coat and Gucci purse. "You're making a big mistake, Jess." The purr was completely gone from her voice, leaving it cold and disdainful.

Jess's eyebrows shot up. "Don't threaten me, Chaleen. Take that back to your people: you don't want to threaten me."

For a moment the hazel eyes glowed yellow, the unblinking stare of a dangerous cat, and then Chaleen was smiling. "You misunderstand me, I wouldn't presume to threaten you. So nice to meet you." She didn't bother to look at Saber, some battle still being waged between hazel and dark brown eyes.

Saber, frightened for Jess for no reason she could think of, clutched convulsively at his biceps. Without taking his eyes from Chaleen, he reached up to cover Saber's hand in reassurance.

"Okay," Chaleen capitulated. "You're out of it."

"I hope so," Jess replied ominously. "Saber, make some fresh coffee for us, baby. And drink a glass of orange juice."

Reluctantly Saber allowed him to move away from her, across the room, escorting the blonde toward the front door. Jess never ordered Saber to do things like make coffee or drink orange juice. The juice, she was certain, was because of her fever. The coffee was a ploy to get her out of the way. She hesitated, worried about leaving him vulnerable to Chaleen, although he seemed to feel the issue was closed.

And she did feel lousy. Her head hurt, her body ached, and there was no doubt she needed aspirin. Muttering to herself, she ground fresh beans and obediently put on a pot of coffee.

Jess found her slumped in a chair, elbows on the table, head cradled in her hands. He glided up beside her on silent wheels. "Are you sure you should be out of bed, angel face?" he asked gently.

"Of course not," she retorted, without looking up. "The place is being overrun by your women. Someone had to do something."

His mouth twitched but he remained silent as he poured her a glass of orange juice and set it next to her elbow. "Drink."

She lifted her head. "Chaleen? Is someone really named Chaleen?" Her voice held a wealth of scorn.

He tactfully refrained from pointing out she had an unusual name too.

Saber drank half the glass in a gulp. "How many more should I expect?"

"Now, honey," he soothed, deliberately feeding the fire. "She's very nice."

"Some people probably thought Jack the Ripper was nice too. For heaven's sake, Jesse, she wears dead animals." She glared at him as if he'd slain and slaughtered the poor creatures with his own blood-soaked hands to make Chaleen darling's coat. "You were actually the lover of a woman who wears dead animals. That's so disgusting."

He tugged at one of her wild curls. "She's not that bad."

Blue eyes shot violet sparks. "Oh yes, she was — is. Who should I expect next? Attila the Hun's wife? You owe me for this, hot shot. I've probably saved you from a fate worse than death. That vamp had designs on your virtue." She had designs on more than that, but Saber was going to have to take a little time to figure out what.

He nudged the juice a little closer to her, silently urging her to drink more. "I don't know, Saber, it might have been fun."

"Don't give me that, Calhoun." Saber raked a hand through her hair in total exasperation. "You were terrified she was going to throw herself at you and you know it. I could see it in your eyes."

He grinned at her. "Hallucinations again. I'd better call the doc in after all."

She rolled her eyes. "The last time your doctor was here, he insisted I get a flu shot right along with you, and look what happened. I've never been sick until now and what do I have — the flu."

"Drink your juice." This time he shoved the glass into her hand.

She sent him a smoldering glare, but when he didn't wither, she took a sip. "Actually, I don't blame you a bit for wanting to change the subject. If I had such poor taste in my youth, I wouldn't want to dwell on it either," she sniffed.

"So did you? Have bad taste I mean? In your youth?"

Instantly a shutter slammed down, laughter fading from her dancing eyes and leaving them veiled, shadowed, even haunted. Saber shrugged the question away casually, too casually. "Good juice, Jesse. Is this fresh squeezed?"

"Of course. What else would I do with you ill?" He ran his knuckles along her cheek in a rough caress. "How are you feeling this morning? I was worried last night."

"Better. I'll go to work tonight," she assured him.

"Saber, don't be ridiculous. You're not

well." He laid a cool hand on her forehead. "You're still running a fever."

"I'm better," she insisted.

"Uh-huh, I can tell." He couldn't help smiling. Sitting curled up in the oak chair, clad in his robe, black hair tousled, long lashes sweeping the curve of her cheek, Saber was irresistible. Jess had to touch her, wanted to hold her. His finger traced the back of her hand, just to keep the contact. "I am your boss, baby, and I say you don't go to work tonight."

She tilted her chin. "Do I get it off with pay?"

"You drive a hard bargain."

"I'll get your coffee," Saber volunteered.

"Sit. I'll get the coffee. You finish that juice and get back to bed." Jess easily reached the coffeemaker sitting on the low counter.

"So, all right, I'll admit I'm hooked. Does Chaleen work for the CIA, or is she some agent for another government?"

Jess concentrated his entire attention on pouring himself a cup of coffee.

Saber ruffled his hair. "Never mind, dragon king. I don't want you to have to lie to me."

His hand reached up to cover hers, fingers sliding sensuously between hers. Before she could pull away, he captured her hand,

125

brought it to his chest. "I'm willing to trade, baby."

Saber could feel the steady beat of his heart. For some odd reason she had the urge to lay her head on his chest. She couldn't look into his probing eyes. "I don't have anything to trade."

His eyebrow shot up, but before he could respond, the shrill ringing of the telephone interrupted them. He grinned, white teeth flashing. "You have a guardian angel." Jess reached a lazy hand out for the receiver. "Yes?"

Saber rolled her eyes at his unconventional greeting. A faint scowl flitted across his features, and for a brief moment his dark gaze rested on her small face.

"She's ill, Les, she's not coming in to-night." Deliberately, he ignored Saber's frantic signals, holding the receiver away from her, fending her off with one hand.

"I can go in if they need me," she hissed. Her gaze slid over his rough good looks and narrowed speculatively. Was that a smear of bright red lipstick along the bluish shadow of his jaw? Her fist clenched. Had he allowed that witch to kiss him?

"What kind of calls? Threats? What the hell does 'not exactly' mean?" Jess sounded impatient. "If someone is harassing the station, or Saber in particular, call the police."

"No." Saber made another grab at the telephone, her face pale. "Jesse," she wailed when he whirled his chair around, keeping his back to her, preventing her from getting to the receiver.

"What exactly is he saying? Yes, that's right. Call the security company, have them double the guard around the station. Brady's security tonight? Have him give me a call. Sure, Les, thanks for calling." He dropped the receiver in its cradle and turned his chair to face her.

"That was my phone call, Jesse," Saber protested, her heart slamming in alarm, "you had no right to keep me from it."

As usual, he didn't seem to be the least bit intimidated or upset by her outburst. "Sit down before you fall down," he suggested calmly. "You're trembling."

"With anger," she exploded, but she did sit, afraid her shaking legs wouldn't support her.

"With fear. Tell me about it, Saber. Who are you expecting? Just how dangerous is he?"

Stubbornly her chin went up. "It is not my fault some crackpot is calling the station. It happens. It doesn't have a thing to do with me. Triple the guard at the station for all I care."

"Don't worry," Jess said, "I will. Les says the man has called nine times, last night and this morning. Brian recorded a couple of the calls on his shift as well. He hasn't threatened you, but he wants to meet you."

"Everyone wants to meet me. I'm cute."

"Your voice is sexy as hell and these creeps get all sorts of ideas."

"Will you please wipe that disgusting stuff off your face? I can barely stand to look at you," she snapped.

His eyebrow shot up. "What disgusting stuff?"

"You know very well. You just had to let her kiss you, and you've got her lipstick all over you."

His eyes burned black velvet. "You'll have to do it, honey. I can't see it."

Saber shook her head. "No way. You let her put it there, you can just get it off yourself."

Jess shrugged. "I guess it will just have to stay."

She glared at him. "You know where she kissed you."

"I don't remember." He had to work to keep the grin from his face.

Furious, Saber jumped up, wet a cloth, and bent over him, scrubbing at the offensive smear of lipstick along his jaw. "I could just smack you one, Jesse."

He pulled her onto his lap, exactly where he had planned to have her from the moment she had come downstairs. "Thank you, baby, I appreciate it. I wouldn't have liked going around all day with Chaleen's brand on me."

"But you would have." Saber wasn't ready to forgive him. "All day, just to make me crazy."

"Would it have?"

"Of course."

"Well, since we're talking." He pulled the military issue knife from his pack and held it up in front of her. "I thought I'd return this to you."

She went absolutely still. "Where did you find that?" She didn't touch it.

"You had a nightmare. Before you woke up, you tried to protect yourself."

Saber jumped off his lap, careful to avoid the knife, and stared at him, a look of horror stamped on her pale face. "I did what? I attacked you, Jesse?"

Tears swam in her eyes, and when he moved toward her, she backed away, putting one hand on his arm to keep him at a distance. "No. No. If I did that, it's not safe for you anymore. I have to leave. I can't believe I did that."

It wasn't the reaction he wanted or expected. If she was an actress, she was the best he'd ever seen. He could feel her distress, waves of it rolling off of her, distress and fear. Both emotions were broadcast so strong they swamped him. His body reacted with signs of stress, heart rate increasing so dramatically that he pressed his hand to his chest.

Her eyes widened even more and she snatched her hand away from him, rubbing her palm on her thigh, fear in her eyes. "What's wrong? Is it your heart? Jesse, answer me right now."

He felt instant relief, the heaviness in his chest easing, his heart slowing to normal. "I'm fine, baby, just sit down and stop getting upset over nothing."

"Pulling a knife on you is not 'nothing,' Jesse."

"I pulled a gun on you. We're a violent couple."

"That's not funny. None of this is funny. I keep the knife in my bedroom for protection, but I never thought I'd ever have a nightmare and try to use it on someone. I can't stay here."

Saber took a deep calming breath and forced air through her lungs, trying to remain calm. Oh God, had she almost killed him? First with her touch and then with a knife? She wanted to run fast and far away from herself.

The faint humor left his face, leaving his expression bleak and cold. "Don't be ridiculous, Saber. You can throw the knife away if you're afraid, but leaving doesn't solve anything."

If only it were so easy as throwing away a knife.

"Leaving keeps you safe."

"Does it? Does it really?"

She was so upset. She'd never been sick before — not once in her entire life. And she'd never made such a mistake before, yet was Jess in danger? Did Chaleen present a danger to him? And there was the uneasiness she couldn't shake, that feeling of being watched. She'd even gone out the night before around four in the morning and patrolled the parameters of the property, but she hadn't seen anyone. She intended to do the same tonight, because she was going to make absolutely certain she wasn't bringing her hell down on Jesse.

She hopped up, needing to put distance between them. "I don't want to talk to you anymore. I'm going upstairs."

A muscle twitched along his jaw. "Go on,

Saber, run like a little rabbit, stick your head under the covers."

Saber fled without a backward glance, racing for the sanctuary of her room. She'd pulled a knife on Jess and he'd been able to disarm her. It had to have been because she was still asleep. He couldn't use his legs. He was helpless, really. Burying her head in the pillow, she tried to make her mind blank, tried to block out the image of hurting the one person in the world she cared about.

But he *was* helpless. And he had enemies, maybe as many as she did. Someone had to take care of him. He didn't realize how vulnerable he really was in that chair. He needed her. Needed her to watch over him. She lay awake staring at the ceiling, trying to figure out the right thing to do without having to give him up.

Subject Wynter. Something happened tonight while I was away. Subject left the residence, which leads me to believe the virus had little effect on her. She nearly caught me. I was about to turn on the road when she pulled in before me. In order to keep from giving myself away I continued on away from the residence. I believe she is beginning to suspect she's under surveillance. I believe we're going to need another pair of eyes and ears to maintain adequate . . .

He stopped dictating abruptly.

He didn't want anyone else around to witness any fun he might have while gathering information — after all, that was his business. He erased the entire tape. It wasn't his night for surveillance. If she'd left the residence and hadn't been caught, that wasn't on him. No one would be the wiser that he'd wanted another glimpse of her window, that sometimes he just sat listening to her voice on tape and staring at her bedroom in the hopes he'd catch a glimpse of her. He found it exhilarating to sit just down the road from her, in plain sight, creating his plans for the sexy little siren — he had so many.

CHAPTER 5

"Wake up, Saber," Jess called from the bottom of the stairs. "I know you can hear me. Come on down here."

He had to see her. It was pathetic how much he needed her, how much joy she brought to his life.

"Go away." Her voice was muffled, confirming his suspicions that she had the covers over her head to block out the sunlight. "I just got to bed."

Saber wasn't certain she could face him. The idea that she had tried to kill him had haunted her all night. And what if she hadn't tried to use a knife? He would never have known, would never have been able to defend himself.

"It's your own fault you didn't go to bed last night. And you can forget any sympathy from me, not after the way you woke me up at five a.m. with that crap you call music."

She answered him with total silence. She was ashamed of her loss of control. She covered her face with her hands and could have wept in despair.

Downstairs, Jess heaved a sigh. "I'm serious, angel face, you don't get down here in five minutes, I'm coming up after you. And if you put me to all that trouble, you won't like the consequences," he threatened.

He heard her stirring, muttering. Something hit the wall and he grinned. Saber padded down the hallway on bare feet, rubbing her eyes drowsily with her fists. At the banister, she leaned her head over, her shining hair an intriguing mass of unruly curls. She was wearing what looked to be one of his old shirts, one he was certain he had tossed out recently. The thought made him smile.

"What exactly do you want, dragon king? Because this is totally uncivilized behavior," she accused. "Even for you."

She looked incredibly small and feminine, her huge eyes so drowsy they seemed to be an open invitation to temptation. She looked like sin and sex to him, all rolled up together, and his body responded in the now-familiar way, hard and aching with a demand he was afraid would never quite be sated.

"My willpower is dwindling away," he muttered.

"What?" Saber looked more confused than ever. "Jesse, you are making absolutely no sense. Not that I think you make much sense anyway, but it's only noon. Noon is the same to me as three in the morning is to someone else. I am in deep sleep mode. I don't care how cute you think you are, go away and stop bothering me."

"Stop complaining and get down here. Patsy's on her way." Cute? She found him cute? Like some teddy bear. That was worse than if she'd called him sweet. He was going to show her cute if she kept looking at him like that.

"Patsy?" Saber groaned and shook her head. "Oh, Jess, no. I cannot take your sister on no sleep. She thinks I'm ten and you're a pervert out to ruin my virtue."

"Well, don't feel bad. Usually she thinks the woman is a vamp and is after *my* virtue so really, you're the lucky one this time."

She sat at the top of the stairs, smoothing her shirt tail over her knees, her hair wild and her lashes drooping. "Poor Patsy. She's always trying to look out for someone. I like her, I really do, but she's . . ." She stopped, searching for the right word to describe his older sister.

He found himself smiling. She always managed to make him smile. "A stick of dynamite? Come on, baby, grab a shower and eat something. By the time she gets here, you'll be in great shape."

"I'm never in great shape around Patsy," she muttered. "Can't we pretend I'm not here? I could stay up here sleeping." Patsy was wonderful and so loving, but she wanted to take care of Saber. No one had ever tried to take care of her. She was a very solitary person and the people around her had always avoided touching her — with good reason. Patsy, however, had no idea of personal space. She hugged and kissed and generally tried to run Saber's life — in the nicest way possible of course, and maybe that was the biggest problem. Saber was growing too fond of her as well.

"And leave me to face her alone?" Jess scoffed. "No way. Not a chance in hell. Get dressed and get your very awesome ass down here." Jess rubbed his shadowed jaw thoughtfully. "I'd better shave."

"Jesse," she wailed, trying not to be pleased at his "awesome ass" comment. "Why drag me into this? She's your sister." He looked good. He brought such sunshine into her life. And he made her feel special, as if he couldn't deal with life without her.

She wanted him. *Wanted* him. Ached for him.

"You're my housekeeper. Helping out with guests is part of your job. Now stop being a little complainer and get down here."

Saber forced a glare when she wanted to laugh, just because he was incredibly beautiful and he wasn't holding a grudge over the way she'd tried to stab him. "You owe me big time for this, Jesse."

Jess regretfully turned his back on her, although the sight of her lingered in his mind. Saber couldn't have been more beautiful if she had spent all day locked in a beauty parlor with a team of makeup experts. The sight of her slender, bare legs and fresh, soft skin put far too many erotic thoughts in his head.

Saber was falling in love with him, she just didn't know it. He rubbed his jaw, hoping he was right. He was happy around her. He loved their strange conversations and her causes. He liked watching the expressions chase across her face. She *had* to be falling in love with him. She was running in every direction but the one she should be. She belonged with him, and whether it was the right time or not for either of them, he was going to make certain she stayed where she belonged.

Patsy Calhoun was tall with a woman's curvy figure, a generous mouth, and rich dark hair spilling around her face in a soft feminine sweep emphasizing her cheekbones. Normally she was smiling and looked sophisticated and in absolute control, but when Saber opened the door, she was leaning against the wall in tears.

Saber glanced back into the house, looking in desperation for Jess to appear, but he was in the kitchen brewing tea for his sister. "What's wrong?" She sounded more clipped than compassionate because it scared her to see Patsy in tears. She placed a comforting hand on the older woman's arm, feeling inadequate but wanting to help. The moment they came in contact, an instantaneous prickle of awareness ran down Saber's spine.

"I'm sorry." Patsy looked down at her, the tears spilling over. "I guess I'm more shaken than I thought."

Saber wrapped her arm around Jess's sister and urged her into the house. Patsy was trembling, and Saber's prickly awareness was now a full-blown radar attack. She kicked the door closed and took Patsy through to the kitchen.

Jess glanced up, the smile fading from his face. "What happened, Patsy?" His voice was calm, but his eyes were sharp and penetrating. He maneuvered around the chairs and took his sister's hands. "Tell me, honey."

Patsy sank into a chair. "I'm sorry, I'm being silly. It's just that . . ." She trailed off again and began to weep quietly.

Saber hastily got her a glass of water. As she leaned over Pasty's shoulder to pass her the water, she felt the tingle of a low-level vibration emanating from the woman. Keeping all expression from her face, she rested a hand on Patsy's shoulder and let everything in her shift to find the rhythm of Patsy's body. She was very suspicious that she knew what that vibration of energy was.

"Patsy?" Jess leaned toward his sister. "Just tell me, honey."

"I dropped by the radio station this morning." Patsy's hand trembled as she lifted the water glass to her lips and took a sip. "It's the first time I've been there since I lost David."

Jess glanced at Saber. "David was Patsy's fiancé."

Patsy nodded. "I own the station with Jess and I thought I should begin to take an interest again, so I went in and wandered

140

around. It was upsetting, but I really feel like it's time."

"That's good, honey," Jess encouraged.

Now Saber was picking up both rhythms, Jess's and Patsy's, because Jess was holding Patsy's hand. It was interesting that they were so different. Being siblings apparently didn't make their individual biorhythms similar. Jess gave off a very strong, steady beat, the blood moving through his body with an ebb and flow that suggested power. Patsy . . . Saber frowned, not liking the rhythm. Something was a little off. The blood didn't seem to move the way it should. She took a breath and tried to drown out Jess's beat as well as the strange little vibration so she could catch the flow of Patsy's blood, the echoes of the heart chambers.

"I talked to some of the men and then I left. I was driving down the winding road leading to the main highway, and just as I was approaching that hairpin turn . . ." Patsy's voiced hitched again.

Jess let go of her hand to get her a small towel from the sink. That allowed Saber to align her body rhythm with Patsy's. Yes, there was a definite swish that shouldn't be there as the blood flowed through a chamber of her heart, almost as if it wasn't going

141

through properly and was backing up. Along with that Saber could pick up that strange vibration, the energy low and tuned to . . .

She straightened, covering her gasp of alarm. Jess's exact tones. The receiver, somewhere on Patsy's body, was tuned to look for Jess's tone exactly. She inhaled and exhaled, pushing air through her lungs. Chaleen's warnings were well-founded. Someone wanted to know about Jess's secret investigation, enough to use his sister to slip a receiver into the house.

"Take your time, Patsy," Jess instructed. "Tell me what happened."

"I was approaching the turn. I took it very slow and I know I was already shaken, I always am, but this SUV came out of no-where, off a little dirt road directly across from the curve, and it hit my bumper. My car went spinning right for the cliff. I nearly went over, Jess. I came to a stop right beside the guardrail. The SUV kept going."

Jess's granite features went so still it looked as if he had been carved from stone. There was a sudden, telling silence. The walls of the room seemed to expand and contract, and Saber's heart leapt when the floor beneath her shifted slightly. She glanced at the coffee table and saw that items levitated, moved, and trembled. Power surged in the room. Energy. She glimpsed Jesse's right hand curling slowly into a huge fist.

Jess Calhoun was no SEAL. At least he was no *ordinary* SEAL. For a moment she couldn't breathe. Even her brain froze. He moved the walls, the floor, and the objects on the table. He had to be involved — very involved — in the GhostWalker project. And anyone in that project — anyone who knew about that project — was her mortal enemy. She had never had pain around him, never had to worry about headaches and the problems that came with psychic abilities. She thought it was the house, or the fact that they just fit, but he had to be an anchor, a GhostWalker who drew energy away from others.

He had to be trained. And very skilled. They'd lived in the same house for months and she'd never suspected. She *always* knew when a GhostWalker was close. They gave off a different energy field. Damn. Her gaze slid to the window, the door, calculating the distance. And what about her emergency pack with her money and her important things? Could she get to it? Did she dare take the time? Did she have time to pack everything that mattered?

If Patsy went down, Jess would concentrate his attention there and that would give her an opening to escape. Did he suspect she knew? She had to act natural. Had to appear as if she was only concerned for Patsy and her safety. And what had really happened? Saber shook her head, trying to clear her brain. Patsy had a bug in her pocket tuned to Jess, not Saber, so what did that mean? She had to think.

"I'll be right back." Saber flashed a small sign to Jess, hoping he would just let her walk out.

"Where are you going?" Patsy caught at her hand.

"I need to take a quick look at your car, honey," Saber said. "It'll just take a minute." Because if Patsy was telling the truth there would be evidence.

Jess gathered his sister close. "You're all right, Patsy."

"I know, it's just that it was so weird that it was right in that same spot where I lost David, almost as if it were meant to be."

Saber was on her way out of the room, but the floor rolled and she turned back to see the horror on Jess's face. He looked stricken. Pale. She couldn't bear it, even though she was terrified that he was her enemy.

"Patsy, don't say that," Jess snapped. "I

mean it. You're not meant to die because David did. That's bullshit and you know it."

He glanced up at Saber and motioned her to check the car. She realized his fear was no act. He was genuinely afraid Patsy had nearly driven off the cliff on purpose.

She hurried through the house to the front, where Patsy liked to park her car. The sleek fire engine red convertible suited Jess's sister. Saber walked around the car until she came to the rear bumper. Black paint, scrapes, and dents marred both the bumper and the rear end of the car on the left side. The car had definitely been hit, and fairly hard. It would have put the convertible into a spin. Patsy had been lucky.

On one hand Jess was a GhostWalker and the two of them being in the same place at the same time couldn't be a coincidence. On the other hand, Patsy's car had been hit and she had come in wearing a bug tuned specifically to look for Jess's tones. He was conducting some covert investigation that was riling people up everywhere, which meant he was probably in more trouble than she was. If she had any brains at all, she'd leave.

"You're stupid, Saber," she murmured aloud. "Stupid."

She'd stayed ahead of Whitney by being

smart, by being on the move and leaving no trace behind. She knew how to conceal herself right out in the open, and she was still free because she always — *always* — played it smart. So what was she doing considering walking back into that house?

She stood in the front yard, staring at Jess's house, her heart pounding, and realized the truth. She loved him. She had let herself fall in love with him. And he was her enemy. Did he know about her? How could he not? There was no such thing as coincidence, not in her world. How many men and women had Whitney actually experimented on, opening their minds and removing their filters, enhancing their psychic abilities and genetically altering them? Certainly the chances of accidentally running into one in Sheridan, Wyoming, were very small.

"Leave, Saber. Walk into the house, pack your things, grab your emergency pack, and leave while you can," she said aloud as firmly as possible. "He's a GhostWalker, and wheelchair or not, this is a setup. If he's in trouble, that's his problem. You can't go back to Whitney. You have to look out for yourself. You do. So go now."

Her heart ached — an actual pain that seemed like the point of a knife stabbing deep. She shook her head and made herself go in. She'd be casual. She'd walk in and tell him about the car, excuse herself, and get out.

She pressed her hand to her chest as she made her way through the living room. She loved the house. Loved everything about it. She loved the way Jess's scent lingered in every room. Masculine. Spicy. She inhaled to breathe him in as she stopped in the doorway and just looked at him. Even in his wheelchair he was an imposing figure. He looked up, his eyes meeting hers, and her heart nearly stopped at what she saw there.

Raw desire mixed with something else, something she'd never seen before. Could he love her? Was it possible? She pushed a hand through her hair, suddenly uncertain of what to do.

"Baby? What is it? You look as upset as Patsy."

The caress in his drawling voice warmed her when she hadn't even known she was cold. She shook her head. "There's black paint as well as scrapes and a large dent in her car, Jesse. Someone hit her." And there was a listening device somewhere on her person. Saber had to find it and destroy it. "Did you go anywhere else today besides the radio station?" She poured tea and added a little milk, setting the cup down in front of Patsy. She was very casual, moving around Jess's sister to stand at her side so she could once again rest her hand on Patsy's shoulder in comfort.

"Just the police station to report the accident."

Saber nodded. "Maybe you should have gone to the hospital and let them check you out. You didn't hit your head did you? Or hurt your neck?"

She had it now. The low-level energy was coming from Patsy's jacket pocket. Anyone could have dropped it in as she passed by them on a sidewalk.

She was fairly certain that it was no accident that someone had hit Patsy's car and then taken off. But why? Saber studied Jess's face. He looked cool until she looked at his eyes and felt the volcano simmering just below the surface. He was enraged, and that meant he'd come to the same conclusion Saber had: someone had tried to harm his sister. But if that was so, then who put the bug in her pocket? She looked at Jess again as he leaned forward, his sister's hand in his, murmuring comfort to her.

She had been with him nearly eleven months. When she was close to him, he stilled the demons that plagued her. Not because he was a GhostWalker and an anchor, but because everything inside her was at peace when he was near. He made her laugh. Not a fake, polite smile, but a genuine laugh. More than that, she liked him, liked being with him. He was intelligent and could talk about any subject she was interested in. Jess was her best friend.

She couldn't believe he was really betraying her. She couldn't bear it if he was involved in a conspiracy against her. She took a breath, let it out, and turned away to keep her composure. There was something so endearing in watching him comfort his sister, that look of love on his face, the gentleness in him.

But the fact remained that he was a GhostWalker and she was on the run and Whitney would do just about anything to get his hands on her. But could she leave Jess when he might need her the most? There was a listening device tuned to the exact frequency of his voice — she'd worked with rhythm and sound enough to know Jess's when she heard it. Still, her mouth was dry, her heart fighting for acceleration, which meant her body was in flight mode.

Jess chose that moment to look up at her and smile. The warmth in his eyes, the tenderness, swamped her.

Okay. She would try to gather more information and just keep her guard up every second. That meant watching him taste their food and drink in case he put a drug in it to sedate her. She shoved a hand through her hair and sighed. The complications were enormous and she was crazy to stay.

"Saber," he asked, his voice gentle, "is something wrong?"

"I'm upset that this could happen to Patsy," Saber said, and it wasn't altogether a lie. She hated that Patsy might be in danger as well.

Patsy immediately reached out and caught her hand. "I'm all right, just a little shaken. If it hadn't been that exact spot, I'd be all right. I go there often and put flowers just over the guardrail. I had no idea that dirt road was there or that anyone lived on it. It's a scary drive to come off of, onto that highway right in the middle of a hairpin turn."

Saber took the opportunity to move very close to Patsy, zeroing in on the listening device. One tiny burst and the bug was toast, but if she didn't direct it exactly, she could destroy everything electronic in the house. Worse, she was sincerely worried about Patsy's heart. Something was off, the rhythm not quite right. If she blew it, she

could kill Patsy, and that didn't bear thinking about.

"Tell us what was so important before all
this happened," Saber encouraged, knowing
she was opening a can of worms, but determined that Patsy would stop crying. "Let
me take your jacket for you, and you just
relax and have tea and tell us what's up."

Patsy straightened immediately. "Yes. I
had something very important to discuss
with you both."

Saber reached down to help Patsy out of
her jacket, not giving her a choice in the
matter. Jess raised his eyebrows at her, not
at all pleased that they were about to get a
lecture. Both of them knew what was coming, and Saber had deliberately invited it.

Patsy lifted her chin and glared at her
brother, which was difficult to do when he
had just been so loving to her. "I have come
to save Saber from your playboy tendencies,
Jess. You're a hound dog and you know it.
She's a sweet, innocent girl who needs my
protection and I intend to give it to her."

Saber hid a grin at Jesse's aggrieved look
and carried the jacket across the room to
the doorway leading to the living room. She
needed to get it as far from Patsy as possible.

Saber hung the coat in the closet and,

glancing back toward the kitchen to assure herself no one could observe her, placed her hand on the listening device and concentrated on keeping the electromagnetic pulse streamlined toward that one small object only. The brief surge of energy eliminated the faint vibration so she could breathe a sigh of relief. She'd check the computers and Jess's cell phone as soon as she could, but she was fairly certain she'd kept the pulse centered on Patsy's jacket pocket.

"Very funny, you two," Jess said as Saber reentered the room. "It's a good thing I'm not sensitive."

"I'm thinking you need to go to the hospital for a checkup, Patsy," Saber said, changing the subject abruptly, knowing Jess would follow her lead if only to get out of another lecture.

"Saber's right, Patsy. You could have internal injuries we don't know about," Jess agreed.

Patsy rolled her eyes. "You're both just saying that to distract me. Saber's much too young, Jess, to be living with you like this."

"Actually I just look young," Saber said. She might be small and waiflike, not tall and elegant with womanly curves, but she certainly was a fully grown woman. "I'm a lot older than you think." But she couldn't very well tell her age when she didn't know it herself. Whitney wasn't big on giving out that kind of information. She hadn't known people celebrated things like birthdays and Christmases and anniversaries until very recently. "And truly, when you came in that day and we were clowning around, it was only a joke. Jess is always a gentleman with me."

"Even when I don't want to be," Jess muttered under his breath.

Patsy leaned forward. "What did you say?"

"I said I'd never hurt Saber, not in a million years, Patsy," Jess assured.

"I'm sure you wouldn't hurt her deliberately," Patsy said. "But she isn't like your other bimbos."

Saber leaned her hip against the wall and grinned at Jess. "I see Patsy's met Chaleen. She was here recently, Patsy. She wanted to pick up where they left off."

"Jess!" Clearly aghast, Patsy reached out to her brother. "Are you all right?"

"Of course I am. Saber sent her away."

Patsy cast Saber a grateful look. "I detested that woman. She only pretended to enjoy all the things Jess liked. And she really didn't like the family."

"Families can be scary," Saber admitted.

"Not ours," Jess said, holding out his hand. He noticed she was staying far away from him and knew it was a bad sign. "Come here."

Saber crossed to his side, hiding her reluctance. The more she was with him, the more physical contact they had, the more she knew she would be trapped by her own feelings for him. But she put her hand in Jess's because she couldn't resist.

Jess tugged at her until she was close to him and he could catch the nape of her neck, dragging her head to his level to brush a kiss in her hair. "I'm sorry, ladies, but I have an appointment with my doctors, so I'll have to leave you two alone. Patsy, don't you dare persuade Saber to leave me. I wouldn't survive it."

"Just the opposite. I'm going to persuade her she needs to make an honest man out of you."

Jess flashed a quick smile at his sister. "I'll love you forever if you manage to convince her."

"You'll love me forever anyway," Patsy said.

He pushed himself out of the room, hearing Saber urging Patsy to go for a quick checkup, even if it was just to her own doctor, "just in case."

Jess entered his office, upset over Patsy's supposed accident. Coincidences were piling up and they were beginning to strain the bounds of credibility. And Saber, well, she was just acting weird.

He had a meeting with Lily and Eric about the bionics and he wasn't looking forward to it. By now the therapy, visualization, and drugs should have been working, but he still couldn't walk. He didn't need to be wasting his time with doctors who weren't doing him any good.

Something was wrong with Saber and he was terrified she was on the verge of pulling a vanishing act. If she took off, he'd never find her. And that scared the holy crap out of him.

Lily and Eric were both waiting, greeting him from their respective monitors. "How are you feeling?" Lily asked.

"Like I can't walk," Jess replied, an edge to his voice. "Hell, you used enough iguana and lizard DNA to turn me into a reptile. I thought it would regenerate the cells with or without the drugs you're pumping into me."

"You have to have patience, Jess," Eric said. "We told you, this course of treatment has never been tried on a human. The theory is sound and it worked on a few lab animals but we didn't have time to even perfect that."

"A few lab animals," Jess echoed. "That's great. Just great. If my tongue starts to grow and I suddenly develop a taste for flies, you'll tell the others why, won't you?"

Lily passed a hand over the mound of her stomach. She looked like she had swallowed a basketball. "I know you're upset, Jess. But this will work. We just have to give it a little time. Are you still having trouble with bleeding?"

He shrugged. "Sometimes."

"And you're not overdoing it? You only do your therapy when you have someone with you, right?" Eric said.

Rather than lie Jess scowled at them. "I'm beginning to think neither one of you really knew what you were doing when you talked me into this."

"I told you it was highly experimental," Eric pointed out. "When I said it had never been tried, I meant it had never been tried."

Lily leaned forward. "I'm working on it, Jess. You know I'll keep going until I get it right. Your body hasn't rejected the bionics, and that's the biggest hurdle. We just haven't yet managed to get them hooked into your brain. If worse comes to worst, we can go back to the power pack idea."

"Which gives me a few hours and then I'm back in the chair, still a liability if I'm on a mission."

"So you really want to go back into the field," Eric asked.

"Of course." But he was no longer so certain. He didn't want to leave Saber behind. "Look, there's nothing new you're telling me. I'm going to sign off now and get some other things done."

Lily nodded. "We'll figure this out, Jess."

He lifted a hand at both of them, inexplicably angry with them and with himself. He had agreed to the surgery. Neither had lied to him about the possibility that it wouldn't work, but he had been so certain. Iguanas and lizards regenerated tails, why not find a way to regenerate his damaged nerves so his bionics would be directed by his brain, just as if his legs were all his?

He needed Saber. He needed to hold her. To be with her. To just breathe clean fresh air and forget that he might not walk again after his hopes had been raised. He went looking for Saber because she was the one person who soothed him when he was ready to explode with frustration or anger. She was in the kitchen putting dishes away.

"Is Patsy gone?" Jess asked.

Saber nodded. "A little while ago. I tried

to get her to go to the hospital and get checked out, and I really think you should call her and try to persuade her. Sometimes things show up later. She shouldn't take any chances."

"Patsy's stubborn. Maybe if she wakes up tomorrow and hurts like hell, she'll go."

Saber pressed her lips together to keep from insisting. "Are you all right? You look upset. If you're worried about Patsy, I still think you should have a doctor check her out and then hire security — a bodyguard, someone to keep an eye on her."

Jess had already planned to do just that. In fact, he was going to make a few phone calls. He was feeling restless.

He dragged both hands through his hair. "I'm feeling cooped up. Let's get the hell out of here and go on a picnic."

Her eyebrow shot up. "A *picnic?*"

"Yeah, a picnic. You know, blanket on the ground —"

"Cold ground," she interrupted.

"Blanket on the *cold ground,*" he repeated. "Wicker basket loaded with goodies especially prepared for outdoor dining. You know — picnic."

"I know what a picnic is, Jesse, I just don't understand your sudden urge to go on one, especially now when nature is about to

158

dump a ton of snow on us."

"It's just a bit brisk. You'll love it."

"Yeah right. Me and the penguins." But he was starting to grin and the sparkle in his eyes was irresistible. Darn him. He knew she couldn't resist that teasing look. "Suppose I agree to this ridiculous picnic idea. As you've just pointed out, picnics involve food." She opened the refrigerator and pointed with a smirk. "Hate to burst your bubble, Calhoun, but that looks empty to me."

"Give me some help here, you little whiner. We'll stop at the store. I need some enthusiasm from you."

"All right already," Saber capitulated. "I'm enthused. I can't wait." And she couldn't. She'd never been on a picnic before. It was one of those things normal people did. Normal, just like she'd always wanted. "Where are we going?"

"You'll see. Dress warm and don't forget your gloves," he instructed.

Saber allowed herself to really study his face. It was difficult to read Jess; it always had been. She felt comfortable with him, alive and happy. And there were no headaches, no bleeding from her mouth, nose, or ears. When she was close to him, she could handle all the energy flooding her brain, all the emotions and the bombardment of sound assaulting her. She had never questioned that, but she should have. Only a GhostWalker who was an anchor could draw the energy away from her, and Jess Calhoun had to be an anchor. Was that why she felt so close to him? Because he was like her?

Had she really deceived herself all these months? He had to be very well trained to have concealed his part in the program from her. Ordinarily she could spot a Ghost-Walker a mile away, but because Jess was in a wheelchair, it hadn't even occurred to her that he could possibly be in that program.

"What is it?" he asked again, his voice soft.

It was tempting to just blurt out her fears, her questions. But she knew better. Jess had been a SEAL, and once a GhostWalker there was no going back. He still worked for the military. He was involved in some kind of top secret investigation. She was well aware of the secret visits, the men she never saw come and go. She should have suspected, but the wheelchair had thrown her into a false sense of security.

"Saber?" he prompted.

"Nothing." She forced a smile. She was taking this one day with him, for herself, because it was probably the only day she would ever have with the man she loved.

Subject Calhoun's sister arrived today. I managed to drop the listening device in her pocket earlier after I heard she was going to visit her brother. He must have jamming equipment in his house, because it did no good. I couldn't pick up on anything and it abruptly stopped working. The good news is, she is back in town, and if needed we can use her to control Calhoun. He has shown us that he is willing to sacrifice his life for anyone he loves. It is his greatest weakness and one we can capitalize on. Give me the go-ahead and I can take the sister.

He would love to get his hands on haughty Patsy, looking down her nose at him, brushing him aside as if he were nobody. He could teach her manners and enjoy every moment of it. He was frustrated that the listening device hadn't worked after he had gone to all the trouble of planting it, especially since it had taken so long to get the exact frequency worked out. Weeks of listening to Jess's voice for hours on end, over and over, recording the exact wavelength. Whitney had all these little experiments he wanted done. And the other — he was just as demanding. It was exciting to be a double agent, play both sides and collect fat paychecks, but if he didn't get the results both wanted soon, they would send someone else to do the job, and that was unacceptable. He had plans for the Night Siren. Big plans.

CHAPTER 6

Jess had been all over the world and he had chosen Sheridan, Wyoming, as his home, not only for its warm, friendly people, but because of its rich history and the year-round activities. It was a beautiful city close to the Big Horn Mountains. It was home to him, and after he had been put in a wheelchair he had planned to stay — until Lily and Eric had talked to him about the bionics program.

He still had nightmares about how he'd gotten into the wheelchair in the first place. He often woke up drenched in sweat, his heart pounding, pain twisting his gut into knots and his legs jumping with the memory of first the bullets slamming into his bones, and then the torture that followed. It had seemed endless, a sea of pain, the pattern of blood splattering the walls, memories of the brutal men slamming objects into the mess that had been his legs. He remembered it so vividly. Time hadn't dulled any of it. Nothing had helped until he opened his door and let Saber Wynter into his life. The nightmares hadn't stopped, but since Saber's arrival, they had eased.

Saber remained silent as they drove through the streets, but as always, he felt peace steal into him when he was with her. His response was strange, since Saber wasn't exactly a restful person. She had too much energy and too many causes, but every time he was with her, he felt happy. On their evening walks, she often jogged beside him as he wheeled his chair along Main Street, past the scenic buildings.

She was enhanced. Whether he admitted it to himself or not — or even whether she did — she was a GhostWalker just like him. She was good — too good — and that meant she'd been trained, or she would have slipped up long before now.

Being a GhostWalker explained her voice, so popular on the airwaves that his little radio station was becoming a huge hit. It explained her need for solitude. She wasn't an anchor and she couldn't be around other people without pain. It explained everything but why she was in his home. Because no matter how much in love with her crazy ways he was, he couldn't ignore the fact that she had to be a plant. That was the only explanation he could think of to explain why her fingerprints hadn't kicked a red flag back at him.

He drove the van west on Loucks Street, but was so busy watching Saber he nearly missed the turn onto Badger. Kendrick Park was dead ahead. This time of year, with the air cooling rapidly but the snow not yet here, few people used the park. Big Goose Creek bordered the park, with its wealth of evergreens and tall, elegant cottonwoods.

"Perfect picnic area. All the tourists say so," he commented, looking carefully, cautiously around. Suddenly his senses were prickling — nothing too big, but a definite hit. His hand slid over his pack to feel the weight of his gun.

Saber laughed. "This park is packed in the summer. I thought for sure you were taking me to Fort Phil Kearny. You've been promising for three months."

"True, I also said we'd go to . . ."

"Buffalo Bill Museum." She laughed. "There's so much to do. We couldn't miss the rodeo, that would have been a sacrilege." And she wanted to do it all before she left — she wanted to do it all with Jess, because nothing would ever feel the same again.

"Would you rather go to the Fort? We

165

could go exploring." He paused in the act of gathering up their supplies. He had room here if an enemy attacked, both room and cover. He'd rather stay.

"No, this is perfect. I'd like a little peace and quiet, maybe take a nap since I didn't get much sleep last night." She shivered a little in the cool air. "You did bring blankets I hope."

"I remembered everything with no help from you."

She flashed a sassy grin at him. She hadn't helped him pack for the picnic because she'd been trying to come to terms with the fact that Jess was more than a Navy SEAL; he was part of a GhostWalker team. It explained everything, especially why she could so easily be in his company. She had never been able to tolerate being around people for very long until she was with Jess. He was definitely an anchor and he drew energy away from her. She should have known. Well, on some level she had known; she just hadn't wanted to bring it out in the open and examine it.

They made their way to a secluded area near the stream, where water bubbled over rocks and where they had a good view of anyone approaching them. After spreading the ground sheet out at the bottom of a thick tree trunk, Jess slid from his chair and sat with his back propped against the tree, blankets — and gun — within easy reach.

Saber sat a foot away, facing him, the wind playing with her hair. "I could stay here forever," she said softly. And she wanted to stay with him.

"That could be arranged," he agreed.

Saber pushed silken strands from her face. "Sometimes I can't tell if you're serious or joking."

"I told you, honey, I take you very seriously."

His black gaze bored into her, causing her womb to clench. She looked away. "Can you imagine all this a hundred years ago? The battles fought in this country? The famous Indians and frontiersmen who walked this ground?"

"Red Cloud, Chief Dull Knife, Little Wolf," he recited.

"General Cooke, Captain Fetterman, Jim Bridger," Saber listed, not to be outdone. She knew her history. She could read a page and recite it verbatim.

Jess sighed. She was probably going to relate every historical event that had ever taken place in Sheridan County including the building of the Sheridan Inn and the stories of its resident ghost. He liked history but not right now. Saber was running from him just as surely as if her feet were burning up the pavement.

"Are we going to talk about the Fetterman Battle or about us?" he asked, his voice gentle.

"The Fetterman Battle." Saber sent him a quick, almost desperate smile.

"How did I know you'd say that?"

Saber shrugged. "We could talk about cooking or restaurants."

"I could shake you."

"Restrain yourself."

"Family, baby," he suggested. "Let's talk about family. Are your parents alive? You've never mentioned them."

Saber scratched at the ground sheet, avoiding his probing gaze. "I grew up in an orphanage," she said abruptly. "There's not much to say, is there?" It was almost a challenge, as if she were daring him to push the issue.

She was going to run if he pushed; he could see the wariness in her eyes. Jess allowed the subject to pass, leaning with deceptive laziness against the tree, staring up at the clouds in the sky and then allowing his gaze to search every square inch around him that he could see. The ground. Brush. Even the trees.

Saber yawned, quickly covering it with her hand. "It was a good idea to come here, dragon king. It's peaceful."

Jess's hand snaked out and tugged at Saber, unbalancing her. With a little squeak, she fell over against him, her head pillowed in his lap. His hand came up to caress her silky hair, lingering in the abundance of curls.

"Take a nap, angel face," he coaxed. "I'll watch over you."

She relaxed against him, smiling as he tucked a blanket around the two of them. "You know, Jess, I love your house. If I haven't told you that before, thank you for all the remodeling you did to make it perfect for me to live there. It was thoughtful of you and not at all necessary, but I'm so glad you did."

"I thought it was our house now," he replied mildly, intrigued by the blue high-lights the sun was putting in the black of her hair. "It feels like our house."

Her soft mouth curved. "It does, doesn't it? I've been happy these last months, happier than I've ever been. You're a good friend."

His fingertip traced the velvet outline of her lip. "Is that what I am, honey?" Amusement colored the deep timbre of his voice.

"A good friend? You're beginning to sound as if you're delivering a eulogy. 'It's been great, Jess, but I'm out of here.' "

Her teeth nipped his finger. "It's not at all like that and you know it."

"So tell me what it's like." He was careful to keep his voice quietly bland.

Her lashes swept down to lay like two thick crescents over her eyes. A jolt of electricity hit him hard in the stomach. For one moment his hand trembled badly as he forced his body under rigid control, then he was caressing her hair and earlobe with gentle fingers.

"I move around a lot, Jesse. You know that. I've been in New York, Florida, and several other states before here, not to mention different cities in each state."

"Why?"

"Why?" she echoed. The tip of her tongue touched her full lower lip.

"Why," he insisted, suppressing the groan threatening to rise in his chest.

There was a long silence, so long he was afraid she might not answer. "This is the most time I've ever spent in any one place. I'm getting far too attached to everyone. The people in this town are the nicest I've met anywhere. And if I stay much longer with you . . ." She trailed off with a sigh.

His hands moved over her face, tracing delicate bone structure as if committing it to memory. "It's already too late, baby," he said.

The long black lashes fluttered, lifted, and beautiful violet-blue eyes touched his burning gaze and then skittered away quickly. Her throat rippled. As she made a slight movement of withdrawal, Jess tightened his hold possessively and waited for the resistance to drain out of her.

"I thought you wanted to talk seriously." He ruffled her hair because he couldn't resist the corkscrew curls springing everywhere over her head.

"That was you."

"Little coward."

She caught his hand in both of hers, held it against her cheek, wild emotions racing chaotically. "I am, I'm sorry." She choked the words out, sudden tears burning far too close. It was going to tear her heart out to leave him.

His hand cupped her cheek, thumb sliding firmly along her jaw. He bent his dark head slowly to hers, blotting out the sky, the light, until finally there was only Jess.

His mouth hovered inches from hers. "I won't let you leave." He said the words so quietly she barely caught them.

Her breath caught in her throat, mind and body at war. Everything in her yearned for this, craved him, while the sane part of her shrieked for self-preservation, screamed for her to jump up, save herself. His hand spanned her throat, felt the pulse fluttering wildly against his palm like the wings of a captured bird. He murmured something in an aching voice, his breath warm against her skin.

His lips slanted over hers, feather light, velvet soft, yet firm. At the first touch of his mouth her heart slammed in alarm against her breast, and her blood took fire. His teeth nipped at her lower lip. It was her startled gasp that gave him access to the warm, silky, moist interior of her mouth.

Everything changed. *Everything.*

His arms tightened around her, dragging her closer, the hand around her throat forcing her head to remain still, giving him exactly what he wanted. Pure black magic. He was everything male, sweeping her token resistance away, drinking her sweetness, exploring every inch of her mouth.

Pure feeling. The ground seemed to shift beneath her, colors whirled and blended. Her body was no longer her own, familiar, under control. It flamed into life, craving, crawling with the need to be touched, caressed. If any man in her life had ever kissed her before, Jess wiped him from her mind for all eternity. His mouth was on hers, hot and hard, so that her brain melted into mindless compliance, branding her as irrevocably his.

Saber moaned softly in despair. She was losing herself, clutching desperately at his heavily muscled shoulders to anchor herself to some reality.

Jess lifted his head reluctantly. She was so beautiful, staring up at him with such sensuous confusion he nearly ignored her distress. Saber pushed at the wall of his chest with her small hands, her strength easily overcome, but he obediently straightened, leaning back against the solid tree trunk. She sat up hastily, scrambled what she thought was a safe distance away, and kneeling, faced him.

"Lord, Jesse." She breathed his name in awe. "We can never do that again. We don't dare. We nearly set the world on fire."

A slow smile curved his mouth. "Personally, I was thinking it would be a good idea to repeat the experience. Often."

She touched her full lower lip with a cautious fingertip. "You should be outlawed, a woman isn't safe around you."

He resisted the urge to caress her face

with his hand, not wanting to destroy her illusion of safety. "It wasn't just me, angel face."

She shook her head in adamant denial. Jess ignored the gesture, intrigued by the play of light in her shining hair. God, he wanted her. It was far more than a relentless physical craving. It was everything wrapped into one. He'd had beautiful women and flash affairs, but he'd never felt like this. Not where love and lust met, intertwined, and became so tightly woven together they were one and the same.

"This can't be," Saber said. "I have to go, Jess. Things are getting out of hand and I can't control them. I don't want to control them."

As she started her retreating move, Jess's hand snaked out with lightening speed and shackled her wrist. "Oh, no you don't, baby, you're not getting away from me." His grip was immensely strong, but he didn't hurt her — he never did.

Blue eyes flew, startled, to his dark ones. Dragon king, she always called him. He was wreaking havoc on all her senses. "Jesse," she made a breathless little protest, already feeling lost.

"It's too late, Saber. You're in love with me, you're just too damned stubborn to admit it to yourself."

"No, no, Jesse, I'm not." She sounded more frightened than convinced.

"Sure you are." Relentlessly, he drew her back to him until she was so close the heat between them threatened to erupt into flames. Beneath his hands he could feel her trembling. "Think about it, honey. Who makes you laugh? Who makes you happy? Who do you run to when you have a problem?" His fingers found the nape of her neck, sending little tongues of fire licking along her spine.

She took a deep steadying breath. "It doesn't matter. Even if you're right, which you're not, it wouldn't matter. I have to leave."

His fingers curled over her shoulders, gave her the gentlest of exasperated shakes. "Stop saying that. I don't want to hear it again. Don't you think I'm aware you have some deep, dark secret in your past? Somebody you're running from? That's what doesn't matter. You belong here, Saber. In Sheridan, Wyoming, with me, in my home, right by my side."

She went pale. "You don't know what you're saying. Jesse, I don't have any deep, dark secrets, I just like to travel. I can't help myself. I just get restless and pick up and go." He knew. He knew about her. How? Or maybe he didn't. Maybe she was panicking and he really thought she had a creep for an ex-husband and she was hiding from him. Let it be that. Please, please, let it be that.

He released her with a smile. "You can't lie worth a damn, Saber."

"Really?" She stuck her chin out at him. "Well neither can you. You have a few deep dark secrets of your own."

He nodded. "I'll admit it. I have a high security clearance and can't talk about my work much, but that shouldn't affect the two of us or our relationship."

He was admitting it. Her heart went into overdrive, pounding so hard she pressed a hand to her chest to alleviate the ache. He was a GhostWalker, highly trained in dealing death. And he was skilled in psychic abilities. Wheelchair or not, she wasn't safe with him. Pressing her lips together, she ducked her head. She didn't want to pursue the matter any further. Not now. Not today. Most of her life was pretense. This was her one chance at a day with Jess. The only one she might ever have.

Jess could sense the panic in her, the confusion and reluctance. He sighed and let it go. "We'll drop it for now. Just make me a promise; give me your word of honor you won't ever try to leave without discussing it first with me."

"You won't discuss it," she said in frustration. "You'll stop me."

"Promise me."

"That's not fair."

"Saber." He tapped her chin with his index finger.

"Oh, all right. I promise," she gave in with bad grace. "I'm hungry. I didn't have breakfast, lunch, or anything else in between. Are you going to feed me or what?"

Jess would take his small victory. Backing off, giving her space, seemed the lesser of two evils. Saber's mood swings were mercurial. He could easily read her rising panic. He needed to soothe her, alleviate her fears. She was desperately hiding the truth from him, but it didn't matter, because he already knew she had to be one of Peter Whitney's experiments.

Whitney had taken girls from orphanages around the world, kept them locked up, and performed psychic and genetic experiments on them long before he had done the same to grown servicemen. He'd given them the names of flowers and of seasons — *Winter.* She used the name Saber Wynter. Winter was more than likely what Whitney had called her.

He had entered the GhostWalker program of his own free will. And he'd known when he'd made the decision to enhance his psychic abilities that he would remain government property for the rest of his life. Wheelchair or not, he was still a powerful and dangerous weapon. No one was going to just forget about him and let him live his life out in peace. He had agreed to the bionics experiment partly for that reason.

Okay. He'd agreed to it because he missed the action of combat. Riding a desk just wasn't his thing and never would be. But then along came Saber and he suddenly wasn't thinking about saving the world anymore. Settling down seemed much more appealing, and she'd been with him long enough now that he couldn't imagine his life without her. But he'd made the choice as a grown man. Whitney had taken these girls, these *infants,* and instead of giving them a decent home, he'd made them into science projects.

He felt the hot surge of anger and deliberately forced it down. "You're closest to the picnic basket, angel face," he said very gently. "Pass me a sandwich."

Saber, grateful for the change of subject, dug into the wicker basket. "Cream cheese?"

"That's yours. I get ham," he said.

The color was slowly coming back into Saber's flawless skin, the tension easing out of her. She avoided touching him when she handed him his sandwich. He let her get away with it. "Drink, woman," he commanded. "Where's my drink?"

Saber handed him a mug of hot chocolate. "Tell me about Chaleen."

He nearly choked. "Why would you want to know about her?"

Because she was still hanging around and Saber didn't trust her for a moment. But she didn't mind playing the jealous woman if it got her what she wanted. "She's after you. I think that was made pretty plain. She gave me the look women reserve for competition. So tell me about her."

"If you want to know about Chaleen, I'll tell you, although there's really not all that much to tell." Because he had to be careful.

She could tell he was reluctant. "You don't have to." She tilted her head. "But I did overhear part of your conversation and it sounded as if she was warning you about an investigation you're conducting." She held up her hand when his piercing eyes went flat and cold. "I'm not fishing for details, but I think she's a lot more than she wants you to know. She's coming off as your friend warning you, but I could feel . . ."

She had a million secrets she couldn't tell him, so it seemed unfair that he would have to reveal something obviously private to her — but she did want to know. She *needed* to know, because Chaleen was a dangerous woman, and she had to figure out just how dangerous she was to Jess.

Jess shrugged. "I met her skiing in Germany. It seemed innocent enough and she was beautiful and intelligent and loved doing all the things I did. She seemed perfect. Of course she was too perfect and I should have seen that, but I was too wrapped up in the sex to be thinking I might have been set up."

Saber winced. Sex. She didn't want to think about him having sex with perfect Chaleen, but she'd asked for this. She bit her lip hard to keep from interrupting.

Jess leaned back, pressing his head against the wide base of the tree. "It was so stupid, really. I knew better. I wasn't some dumb kid. She began asking me questions about my work. Nothing big, nothing to raise alarms, but still, it should have. I just took it that she was interested, and believe it or not, I actually felt guilty that I couldn't tell her anything."

Saber drew up her knees and rested her chin on them. She could see clever Chaleen manipulating a man into feeling guilty.

"At least at first I felt guilty. Somewhere along the line I realized she really didn't like all the things she pretended interest in. She was only acting."

Chaleen had probably studied him, found out his every interest, and become the person he would be attracted to before she'd moved in on him. Chaleen — black widow spider. Saber twisted her fingers together, already afraid for him. If the woman had come back, she'd come for a reason.

"An assignment went bad. I was taken prisoner, and tortured. I'd been shot in both legs so they smashed what was left of my lower legs to try and break me. They wanted me to give up a colleague." He looked at her, wanting her to know what kind of man he was. "I didn't."

She rubbed her palm over his thigh in silent sympathy.

He still felt it sometimes, those blows landing on the raw gaping wounds, felt the bones shattering inside his skin. His stomach knotted and for one moment bile rose. He fought it down. "I stared at the ceiling for three straight weeks after they brought me to the hospital. Just stared at it, without seeing or speaking."

Instantly her eyes clouded and she caught his hand in both of hers. "Oh, Jesse, how terrible for you. I didn't mean for you to relive a horrible memory." She knelt close to him. "I'm sorry, so sorry I brought this up."

His hand shaped her face, caressed her soft skin, traced her delicate cheekbones. "Don't be sorry. I wanted to tell you or I wouldn't have."

"Were your parents with you?"

"I wouldn't see them, I couldn't. I had to decide on my own what to do with the rest of my life. I didn't want anyone to pressure me one way or the other. The decisions I made had to be mine, ones I could live with. But Chaleen came. And went. I wasn't of use to her anymore, or to her bosses. I couldn't give them anything, so there was no point in our engagement."

Her heart dropped. He'd been engaged to Chaleen. Had he loved her? Really loved her? Perfect Chaleen was probably perfect in bed. Saber was so far from perfect at everything there wasn't even any contest.

His thumb slid over her mouth. "I realized that I didn't love her, that I never really had. So I didn't retaliate. I just let her go and chalked it up to a lesson learned. I have a job that someone out there is interested in

— a lot of somebodies. And they want to know what I'm doing." His fingers slid to her curls and fisted there, holding her still while his gaze drifted over her upturned face, inspecting her expression.

His eyes went flat and cold. "I won't be so nice if I find out you're deceiving me, Saber. You, I care about. You got under my skin. So if you're working undercover, now's the time to tell me, because if you ever betrayed me, I would break your neck."

The tone of his voice and the look in his eyes sent a shiver down her spine. She didn't doubt that Jess would come after her if she deceived him in the way Chaleen had.

"I don't care about your secret life, Jess, not the way you mean it. I care about you."

His smile was slow in coming. He was probably the biggest fool in the world, but damn it all, he believed her. He believed those large, beautiful eyes, even with the shadows in them. Deliberately he glanced at his watch. "We'd better eat if we're going to. The temperature out here is dropping rapidly."

Instead of drinking the warm liquid, Saber put the mug down and stretched out, snuggling under the cover, close to him. "I think I could take you in a fight."

"Oh really?" Amusement crept into his

voice, and his arm curved around the top of her head, fingers tangling in the silken strands of her hair. "You could take me?"

Her fist thumped his hip. "Don't say it like that. Do you have to make everything sound sexual?"

"I'm feeling that way." His hand stroked her temple. "You drive me crazy."

He'd never just come right out and said it before. She wasn't stupid. She certainly knew he was physically attracted to her, although after seeing Chaleen and knowing she and Saber were complete opposites, she wasn't certain why.

She tapped her fingers on her knee and stared at the surrounding mountains. She had to give him something of herself. It wasn't fair otherwise. He'd told her things, hurtful things that mattered, that were real, and just once, she wanted to give him something of herself.

Saber was silent and Jess remained so because of the little giveaway nervous tattoo of her fingers.

"I was trapped in a sort of hole in the ground once. It was completely black." She watched his face carefully. She was giving him . . . too much. Enough to hang herself, yet there were abused children every single day. He would naturally think that of her, rather than something so bizarre and coincidental as that she was also a GhostWalker.

Jess went still inside. He could hear the catch in her voice as she revealed a traumatic event in her life. There was the faintest of tremors in her body. This was the real thing, not something made up to appease him. The suppressed emotion in her said it all and he felt rage — ice cold rage. He wasn't certain he was prepared to hear this.

"I couldn't see my own hand in front of my face. After a while I thought I was going crazy. I couldn't even breathe."

She didn't look at him, but kept her gaze on the mountains. "There were bugs. Oh God, so many bugs. They crawled on me." She brushed at her arms and face as if to remove them. He saw her throat convulse as she swallowed hard and knew she was unaware of the tears gathering in her eyes. "I didn't think I could stand it. I lost track of time. A minute, an hour, days. I could hear myself screaming, but not out loud, only in my mind. I didn't dare make a sound. I would have never gotten out."

The silence stretched between them. He was afraid of speaking, afraid his voice would break. He couldn't touch her, couldn't move his hand those scant inches separating them. He was shaking with anger unlike anything he'd ever experienced, and if he didn't stay in control, the results could be deadly.

Saber became aware of the ground undulating beneath her. The trees trembled and the water in the fountains shot up like geysers. A branch in a nearby tree cracked ominously. She leaned into him, laid her head against his shoulder, and put a calming hand on his thigh. Instantly his hand covered hers and he took a deep breath.

"It's all right," she soothed. "I'm all right." He was furious on her behalf, close to a loss of control — no good thing for any Ghost-Walker. It should have reminded her that Jess was dangerous, in or out of a wheelchair, but all it did was make her happy.

"How old were you?" His voice was very quiet. He brought her hand to his mouth and kissed her palm, trying to find a way to make it all better.

"I think I was about four the first time. We weren't allowed to show fear and I was afraid of closed in and dark places. That sort of weakness just wasn't allowed where I grew up."

He didn't have to ask who had done such a thing to her. Whitney, damn his soul to hell. Peter Whitney had taken this child and tortured her to make or break her.

"That's why you like every light in the house on."

Her hand clutched his shirt, fingers curling around the edge of the material, brushing his bare skin. She didn't seem to notice so he left it there, covering her hand once again with his own and pressing her palm into his chest.

"I guess they never managed to scare the fear out of me," Saber admitted. She touched his leg with the tip of her nails.

"Bastards." He was careful not to ask who "they" were.

She had no idea why his reaction sent a heat wave crashing through her entire system. She took a breath and let it out, catching at his wrist to distract them both. She looked at his watch. "I need to get ready for work."

"You have hours, take a nap."

"Out here?" Did she dare when they might be under surveillance?

"Sure, listen to the water, you were just saying it was peaceful. You tell me something from your past and immediately get nervous and want to run." He slid down, pillowing his head on a rolled-up blanket. "Come on, mystery lady, get over here where you belong."

Saber hesitated only a moment, then

snuggled close to his side. The feel of his body curved protectively around hers was fast becoming familiar, comfortable, as if this was where she belonged. She was tired and the fresh air and absolute beauty of their surroundings, along with Jess's presence, made her intensely happy. She cradled her head in the hollow of his shoulder, one slender arm flung across his broad chest, and closed her eyes. "If you hear or see anything suspicious, or anyone else comes near us, promise you'll wake me up."

So she felt it too, then, Jess noted. He let his gaze drift around them, quartering the area to make certain no one was near. "I will. Go to sleep."

Jess held her, caught somewhere between heaven and hell. Having already tasted the honeyed sweetness of her mouth, he craved more. His mind was at peace, holding her in his arms, but his body was crawling with need. Slow, he reminded himself, slow and gentle. Saber was worth every ache, every sleepless night. She needed protection whether she knew it or not, because if Whitney had put her in a hole in the ground and she had escaped, then he would be coming after her.

He didn't want to think of the other possibility — that Whitney had sent her to spy on him, to report how close to the truth he was in his investigations. God help them both if she was betraying Whitney, yet that didn't feel right to him. She was too close to bolting. A spy wouldn't be running, she'd be trying to get closer to him.

Saber didn't like snow, certainly not to drive in. First a series of bad storms, and the weather would be breaking sooner than usual. Once the snow fell Saber would be less inclined to take off and he would have all winter to tie her securely to him.

The words of his song echoed in his mind, a reality to him.

Oh, but those haunting eyes
They make me realize
The depths of my emotions stirring inside

Haunting eyes, haunting refrain, and all so true. Every time he looked into her violet-blue eyes his heart turned over. This was one woman he would never be over. Every day strengthened his feelings for her, his assurance of how completely he was committed to her.

Saber slept with the innocence of a child. Deeply, quietly, still in her sleep, where awake she was quicksilver. It was dark when she opened her eyes, and he knew the very instant by the way her body tensed, her swift intake of breath.

"You're all right, baby." He breathed it softly in her ear, firmly turning her in his arms. "I've got you. If you open your eyes you'll know you're perfectly safe."

His hands were possessive, his breath warm against her skin, his husky, sexy voice swirling a fierce heat in the center of her body. Saber moved against him restlessly, an unconscious enticement.

"Am I?" She whispered the words, craving the feel of his mouth feeding on hers, needing him there in the darkness.

There was no hesitation. Jess needed her every bit as much. He caught her head firmly in the crook of his arm, fist beneath her chin, and brought his head down to hers. There was nothing of the sweet gentle persuasion he had coaxed her with before. He was too hungry for her. He took possession of her mouth without his usual self-imposed control. Male domination pure and simple. Hot, heated, demanding, an assault on mind and body, his tongue an invasion, mating wildly. It was a turbulent storm sweeping her into a primitive world of pure feeling.

A rush of damp heat, her breasts swelling, aching, her skin ultrasensitive. Jess's hand moved under her shirt, rested on her narrow rib cage, fingertips brushing the underside of her breast, sending a wave of fire darting like tongues across her skin.

Saber wrenched herself away with a little despairing cry, rolling away from him, from his fully aroused male body and hard threatening muscles. "Jesse, we can't do this." It was a heartbreaking moan. Hopeless, forlorn, tinged with desperation.

Jess laid perfectly still, staring up at the thousands of stars blanketing the sky, afraid if he moved he would shatter into a million fragments. His body raged for release, his head pounding savagely. He wanted her with every cell, every fiber of his being. Inside, warning bells were shrieking at him. He could not lose her through clumsy handling.

What the hell was wrong with him? He knew she was afraid. The furthest thing from her mind was any sort of commitment.

He struggled for control, forced a note of amusement into his voice. "Sure we can, honey." He pulled himself into his chair with the ease of long practice. "It's the perfect night for it. You're a woman, I'm a man. Those little twinkling things overhead are stars. I believe it's referred to as romance."

Saber sat a few feet from him, arms across her chest. She was fighting just to breathe normally and there was Jesse, laughing at her inexperienced reaction. She had an uncharacteristic urge to slap his handsome face. Patsy was right. He was a cad. Her body was crying out for his, uncomfortably not her own, and he was calmly gathering everything up, ignoring her obvious distress. She sure as hell wasn't perfect Chaleen whom he had perfect sex with.

Jess watched Saber rake an unsteady hand through her hair and bite at her full lower lip. In the moonlight she looked wildly erotic, impossibly sexy. He had to look away, his jeans so tight they hurt, his body actually trembling.

"I think talking about Chaleen darling and her perfect sex put ideas in your head," Saber grumbled. "Either that or Patsy, with all her talk of bimbos."

"You hardly qualify," he said dryly.

Saber tested her legs, standing up to gather the picnic supplies into the basket. Her blue eyes flashed purple sparks at him. "Is that an insult, Jesse? Because if it is, you can take the big slide."

He laughed softly, the sound inviting. "You have such a way with words. Here, I'll carry that," he said as she took the basket from his lap. It looked nearly as large as she was.

"Don't start with the short jokes," she cautioned. "I'm not in the mood."

He followed her, keeping up easily with a single thrust of his powerful arms. "You mean like: Hey! I'm sitting down and I still have a couple of inches on you."

She stopped so abruptly he ran right into her, catching her waist, laughing at her squeal of outrage as he pulled her down onto his lap. "What's wrong, Saber, does it hit too close to home for comfort?"

Saber circled his neck with her arm. "Oh, shut up," she snapped, but he could hear the answering laughter in her voice.

She couldn't help but admire the easy way he maneuvered the chair over rough terrain with her added weight and the awkward load of blankets and picnic basket. They were both laughing when they reached the van. But by the time they were home, Jess was quiet, thoughtful, almost remote.

Saber tried desperately to push away the feel of his mouth, his hands, as she dressed for work. It was a good thing she wasn't trying to go to bed. There would be no such thing as sleep.

Elation, euphoria poured through his system

along with sheer adrenaline. He was so much cleverer than Whitney's precious enhanced soldiers. He could have walked right up to them and sliced their throats. He'd stalked them, *together,* and neither had been aware of his presence. He was so good. The best. So skilled and yet had none of the training the two of them had. All that time he had circled them, fantasizing about how he would end them both, laughing to himself, feeling so high. He almost couldn't come down from it. All that money spent, all that training, and here he was, a mere foot soldier without a single enhancement, just brains and skill, eluding both of them.

It didn't surprise him in the least. He'd always been superior to others, but this should prove it even to Whitney. Whitney, who put his intelligence above everyone else, who believed himself a god. How many mistakes had the man made? His pheromone receptor research had made fools of the soldiers and whores of the women. Look at Wynter kissing the cripple when she should have killed him. Calhoun was inferior now. Useless. He should have had a bullet in his head a year ago, but no, they wanted his DNA. He was going to have to take over her training, because Whitney certainly hadn't gotten it right. It was becoming harder and harder to wait, to play the game and play the role of a puppet. He wanted to up the stakes and shove it right under their noses now that he knew he could. Oh yes, this was going to be fun.

CHAPTER 7

Someone was stalking them. Saber slipped into the garage and looked carefully around. Nothing was out of place, yet someone had been there, and they were good, very good, because she had an eye for detail — a photographic memory that alerted her the moment something was even a hair off. It was time to step out of her dream world and confront reality head on.

Jess was a GhostWalker. She was a Ghost-Walker. He had been recruited and trained as an adult already in Special Forces. She had been taken from an orphanage and raised in a laboratory and then later a training compound. How in the world had they both ended up in Sheridan, Wyoming?

Saber carefully went over Jess's car and then her own, searching for an incendiary device. She needed her electronic equipment to be absolutely certain the cars were free of bugs, so that would have to wait. But as far as she could tell by listening and feeling, both vehicles were clean, and she had always been right. She slipped into her car and sat for a moment, contemplating what to do.

She tapped her fingernail against the dash of her car and stared at herself in the rearview mirror. There wasn't a single line in her baby soft skin. Her too-big eyes were fringed with long feathery lashes and held a look of absolute innocence. She could barely look at herself sometimes. Her innocence had been lost when she was sent out on her first mission at nine years old. She glanced down at her hands expecting to see blood — something — some evidence of the evil that lurked inside of her, but even her hands looked young and innocent.

She looked back into the mirror. She'd made a promise to herself that she would never go back to that life, but she wouldn't — couldn't — abandon Jess. She didn't believe in coincidence, but there was no way Jess could have planned for her to show up at his home. She had wandered down his road, hoping to find a place to camp before winter set in and she had to move on. She had gotten his name off an Internet site for radio station jobs when she'd looked for an opening in Sheridan.

Her voice was one of her best assets. Radio stations were the easiest places to find work, and if there was no opening, she could often use her voice to persuade them to hire her anyway. She knew Jess had suspected she was a battered woman on the run. He had hired her for work at the station and offered to let her rent the upstairs in return for light housekeeping. How could someone have manipulated their meeting? And if they had, what was the purpose?

She bit at her lower lip while she sat there turning it over in her mind. She couldn't leave, not when someone was hunting Jess. She was just going to have to be very alert and know that either of them, or both, could be in danger every step of the way.

Jess watched on the monitor as Saber drove her car through the gates and disappeared from sight. He touched a fingertip to the screen, right over the spot where the Volkswagen's taillights had been. He should have insisted on a guard for her. Someone was watching them. Someone who knew how to bypass the kind of security he had, knew exactly where the camera's blind spots were and had utilized them to invade Jess's territory. He had known the moment he'd gone outside. He doubted if the intruder had breached the house, but he'd followed them to the park. Jess knew they were being hunted.

There was no hesitation as he caught up the phone, punching in a number few people had access to. He knew when he needed help. He had to bring in part of the team and spread them out. No matter how much he loved Saber — or because he loved her — he had to notify those he trusted that someone was orchestrating something big.

He didn't like the idea that he couldn't keep Saber safe himself, but he couldn't allow his ego to get in the way. He was still recovering from the operation, and he'd taken too many chances using Zenith in an effort to heal faster. Lily and Eric had counteracted the drug twice and had had to give him blood when his cells went ballistic on him. He'd had the surgery before Saber had come into his life. Maybe he wouldn't have had she gotten there sooner, but his life had loomed ahead endlessly bleak as he'd listened to Eric outline the technology. It seemed possible, more than possible, to not only walk again, but to be of use.

He let out a sigh. Once again he'd agreed to be an experiment. The military was using bionics for soldiers, but they wore outerwear, nothing as advanced or as complicated as what he had inside of him. He did most of his intense therapy at night while Saber was at the radio station. It was safer for Lily Whitney-Miller to visit when no one was around. She always came with her husband, Ryland Miller, leader of the Special Forces GhostWalker team, and Eric Lambert, the surgeon who had saved Jess's life. Eric often was on standby during a mission, ready to fly anywhere in the world to assist a fallen GhostWalker, and he came often to treat Jess.

After talking to Logan and arranging for his team to come quickly, he went to the pool. Standing, he dove into the water and used the bionics, forcing his brain to develop neural pathways needed to command his new legs. Cell regeneration was happening, but at a much slower rate than anyone had anticipated. He had to be careful because one of the drugs they used was so danger-ous. It healed — and then it killed.

He swam, trying to direct his body to think through the mechanics of each kick. He stood in the shallow end near the net-work of bars and performed exercises. The water made him light, so if his legs failed — as they often did because his concentration was not exact — it didn't matter, although he knew Lily would be upset with him for working alone.

When they had operated, he had been so certain he would just stand up and walk. It wasn't anything like that. All of his training in the SEAL program, his GhostWalker training, none of it compared to this. His head ached constantly. His legs shook and were weak. Pain flashed up his thighs and into his hips. He fell constantly, and that was the worst. His legs just went out from under him, refusing to work if he wasn't thinking about the mechanics of how they worked every second. The smallest distraction could bring him down.

He cursed over and over as he forced his brain into the pattern of telling his legs how to work. He visualized each muscle, the pathways he needed, the ligaments and tendons, pulleys to force his legs to take small steps. Sweat ran down his body along with droplets of water when he pulled himself to the stairs and sat, his lungs burning and his head screaming.

He'd given himself another bloody nose, the only thing that made him quit. He didn't want another transfusion. He snagged a towel, furious that he'd ever agreed in the first place. His legs were too weak to hold him up. He exercised twice a day and did physical therapy, but here he was every day, exactly the same, his legs shaking and his head aching and nothing to show for it.

Noticing that the water in the pool bubbled in reaction to his anger, he took several deep breaths to calm himself. He was mostly angry that he couldn't tell Saber. That she wouldn't tell him about her life. They lived in the same house. He'd seen love in her eyes, tasted it on her lips, yet they couldn't talk about who they really were.

Cursing, he caught the bars and pulled himself to a standing position. It always amazed him how everything looked so different when he stood up. It amazed him how different he felt. He was a strong man with an amazing amount of upper body strength, his thighs were strong, but the weakness in his calves could send him crashing to the ground in a heartbeat.

He was going to walk to his chair. His fingers curled into two tight fists and determination molded his mouth. He would do it this time. It was only a couple of feet. It was a matter of visualizing the way a leg worked and giving the information to his brain to carry down his body to his calf and foot.

He took a step. Beads of sweat dripped into his eyes. He forced air through his lungs. Jackhammers drilled at his temples and pain shot up his leg. He held the picture in his mind, everything working in tandem, his muscles contracting and expanding. He took a second step. He was so close to his wheelchair, only a scant two feet. A part of him wanted to try to sprint and another part wanted to lunge, keeping his feet in place so he wouldn't have to use his brain anymore.

His legs shook and he went down hard, crashing to the cement before he could stop himself. He banged his head and one elbow against the ledge as he sprawled awkwardly on the ground. Hell, he couldn't even fall right anymore. The legs just went with no warning, not giving him enough time to roll or simply brace himself with his arms. He lay there, furious at himself, slapping the cement with his open palm, alternating between swearing and trying to breathe.

The telephone rang, but he was too far away to reach it. He swore again and dragged his body using his arms over the cement tiles. He left a streak of blood behind as the rougher spots took skin. Patsy's voice came on, ordering him to pick up. He caught at his chair and just lay against it, resting for a minute. Finally, using his upper body strength, he managed to crawl into his chair. By that time Patsy had given up and left him alone. He was grateful. He didn't want to talk to or see anyone. For just a few moments he had felt totally helpless.

He rolled into his office and slammed the door, locking it, although no one was there to interrupt him. He stared in the mirror at the blood running from the cut on his head and sighed. It was going to be a long night. Technically he should call Lily and report the injuries. With even a small amount of Zenith in his system, he was at risk for bleeding out from even a minor lesion, but he'd be damned if he'd tell her or anyone else he fell.

"Holy crap, Saber," Brian said. "You really know how to stir the boss up. He's cut you off for the rest of the evening. And he's angry. Really angry. I'm not certain you're going to want to go home tonight."

Saber leaned her chin on her palm and eyed him with suspicion. "You didn't by any chance call him and tell him to tune in to the broadcast, did you? Because I don't think he usually listens to it."

Brian put his hand over his heart dramatically. "You're killing me."

She fanned her lashes at him, struggling not to get up and kick him. "You should have a little loyalty, Brian. Someday you may need a favor."

The smile faded from the soundman's face. "He's my boss too. He'd fire me over that stunt you pulled — not you, *me*. Everyone at the station knows he's gone on you. And he's protective as hell. Sending out an invitation to a crazy man is over the top, Saber, even for you. You can't talk in that voice and not expect to get a million whacked-out or drunken callers. One time and look, the board's lit up like a Christmas tree."

"You didn't need to tattle on me. We're grown-ups for heaven's sake."

She pushed her hands through her hair in agitation. She'd used her enhanced voice to lure the man who had been calling the station into calling again. She had sent her soft, sexy voice with that buried compulsion out over the airwaves. "To that special someone out there so anxious to reach me, I'm waiting for that call. For my romantic listeners we have a little mood music."

Brian had thrown his arms into the air, furious with her. "Calhoun is going to murder you," he mouthed through the glass.

And the tattletale had called the boss. If Jess had heard that recording, he would have known instantly she was using an enhanced voice. Any GhostWalker would. It had definitely been a calculated risk, but she'd just lost if Jess had heard her. She could have strangled Brian for his interference.

She wanted to take the fight away from Jess's home. If Whitney had sent someone after her, let him come out into the open and try to take her. Hell yes, she'd meet a hundred nutcases if it meant she could keep Jess from harm. Let him be mad. He may have been the biggest badass in the navy at one time, maybe even in the GhostWalker program, but he was locked to a wheelchair now, and she wasn't going to let anyone hurt him.

"I have to agree with Calhoun on this one, Saber. Men like this, calling the station, they think they're going to go out with you. They're fixated on you. You can't agree to meet them. You can't take their calls and encourage them."

She bit back her argument and forced a smile. "You're probably right. I don't like to be afraid, and he's so persistent, I thought if I talked with him I wouldn't be nervous anymore."

Brian scratched his head, frowning. "You've always laughed about these nuts calling you. I didn't realize they bothered you."

"Not usually. It's just that he's so persistent, you know?" She was supposed to look and act scared, but she didn't have very much experience in that department. She tried a tentative smile and fluttered her eyelashes, feeling pretty silly. She couldn't very well admit she planned to beat the crap out of the guy if he touched her or kill him if he threatened Jesse.

"Calhoun put plenty of security guards on the place," Brian assured her. "No one can get in here. I'll make certain a couple of them escort you to your car every morning when you get off work."

"You and I both know security guards aren't always the best, Brian."

He shook his head. "You don't have to worry. Calhoun hired the real deal, not the rent-a-cop version. These men know what they're doing — at least that's what Calhoun said."

Saber made her smile even brighter. "Thanks, Brian. I really appreciate your reassuring me. I won't do anything stupid like that again. I feel much better now that I've talked with you about this." She was going to have to find another way to draw out the caller and assess the threat.

Brian grinned at her, obviously relieved now that she was cooperating with him. He turned away to take the phone calls and she slumped back in her chair and began her Night Siren show.

Jess paced the length of the living room and open foyer, back and forth, back and forth, thrusting powerfully at the wheels of his racing chair. Saber had been asleep eight hours now; if he didn't hear her stirring soon he was going to wake her up. And not so gently at that. What had she been thinking last night? Daring some nut to call her. Inviting him to do so. It was just like her.

What had Logan said this morning? Brian had followed her home from the station last night. Why? What was going on between them?

"What are you doing down there?" Saber demanded, leaning her mop of curls over the banister. "Practicing for some kind of race? Wearing holes in carpets?"

"We don't have a carpet," he pointed out. No one should look that sexy when they first woke up. Everything went out of his head, leaving a burning desire to pull her into his arms, take possession right there.

"Who needs a carpet, you're making train tracks," she laughed, sweeping a hand through her unruly hair, the action pulling her nightshirt taut across her breasts.

Jess let his breath out slowly. "Very funny. Little comedian, aren't you? Get down here."

She grinned at him, a saucy, teasing grin. "I don't think so, Jesse. You sound like a grumpy old bear again. Patsy call?"

"I'd like to get my hands on you." He meant it as a threat but a vivid picture of her writhing naked beneath him rose up to taunt him. He groaned aloud. Time was catching up with Saber Wynter fast.

"Yeah?" she challenged, tilting her chin, blue eyes dancing with mischief. "What'd I do this time? Leave my nylons hanging in your private bathroom? Did your midnight caller find them and get angry?"

"You're enjoying yourself, aren't you?" he asked.

Her foot slid over the bottom railing, calling attention to her bare legs. "If I'm getting to you, I'm having a great time." She laughed at his pained expression.

"Will you get down here?" he demanded, exasperated.

"I need a shower. And I have to dress. It wouldn't do to have Patsy catch me parading around in my night things."

"I could care less if Patsy walks in. Damn

it, Saber, I'm running out of patience."

"Oooh!" Dramatically she clutched at her heart. "I'm so scared!"

Jess couldn't help himself, he burst out laughing. "You're such a brat. I'm coming up."

"No!" Alarmed, Saber caught at the banister. "I'll be right down. Really, Jesse, I promise. Five minutes."

He wanted to kiss that look right off her face. She could wreak havoc with his body so easily. "All right." He conceded her the time grudgingly. How was he ever going to gain the upper hand with her, when all it took to wrap him around her little finger was a flashing look from her blue eyes?

He entered the kitchen to make her fresh coffee. Upstairs the water went on and he found himself smiling. She took more showers than anyone he knew. The smile faded as the image of the radio station's night soundman rose up.

Brian Hutton. Tall, muscular, good looking, he was twenty-seven years old, closer to Saber's age. At least he thought so. He didn't even know her age. How close were they? Funny, he had never thought to be threatened by Brian. Saber had worked with him every night for ten months, nearly eleven, and she talked about him often. Why would the man follow her home from work?

Everyone at the station knew Saber lived with Jess, at least half of his employees thought she was sleeping with him. He had never corrected the assumption.

Saber ran into the room, barefoot, hair still damp in little ringlets all over her head, eyes dancing at him. "Did I make it?" Abruptly the smile faded and she hurried to his side, sweeping back the hair that was falling across his forehead. "What have you done to yourself?"

His body stirred uncomfortably, jeans suddenly tight. "You're two minutes late." He tried to sound severe.

"Jesse, answer me. You cut your head. It looks bad. There's bruising and swelling. Maybe you should call the doc."

He caught her wrist and pulled her hand away, irritated that she could see the evidence of his fall. "It's nothing. Let it go."

Saber heard the bite to his voice, hesitated, and then poured herself a cup of coffee. "So what's up, caveman?" She brushed fingertips along the corner of his mouth, sending white heat coursing through his blood. "Stop frowning at me, Jesse. Your mouth is bound to freeze that way."

Strong white teeth snapped at and caught her index finger and drew it into the moist cavern of his mouth. His eyes burned black velvet as he used his tongue to caress her finger. She wasn't going to embarrass him, and he felt the tension in him drain away.

Faint color tinged her cheeks, blue eyes skittered away from his. She pulled her hand back as if he had burned it. "So what's this all about?"

He studied her small, slender form, the ribbed cotton scoop-neck T-shirt, the figure-hugging black denim. She looked ready to flee at the slightest provocation. He resisted the urge to capture her wrist. So close, yet so far away. He wanted her to make up her own mind, bind herself to him. At the same time, he wanted to just take possession finally, irrevocably, and never let her go, the hell with her choices.

"Are you going to sit down or are you going to be flittering all over the house like a little butterfly? I can just see us having a decent conversation with me following you all over."

She perched on the countertop, regarding him warily over the rim of her coffee mug. "Conversation? Uh-oh. What have I done?"

"What makes you think you've done anything?"

Her bare foot tapped the cupboard. "I know you so well, dragon king, you only get that particular look on your face when you're burning to give me one of your lectures."

"Do I give you lectures?" He frowned.

She grinned. "Oh, I don't mind. I think you're kind of cute when you do, and I don't really listen anyway."

"That makes me feel good, baby. Honestly, I really feel so much better now that you've shared that with me." The frown had vanished and there was a distinctly wicked gleam in his dark eyes. Jess eased his chair around the table until he was directly under her feet. The counter was low, built for him to use easily. "How well do you know Brian Hutton?"

It was the last thing she expected, and it wiped the sassy grin right off her face. "Brian?" she echoed. "I don't know. As well as I know anyone at work I guess. He's great at his job. What do you want to know?"

"What kind of relationship do you have with him?"

Saber looked completely confused. "We're friends, I like him, why? Has he been dipping into the till or something?"

"What's he like?"

"You know him better than I do, Jesse, he works for you." Saber rested her bare feet on his knees. "What's this all about?"

213

He shrugged. "Nothing important, I just wondered what you thought of him."

She studied his handsome face, and then finally shook her head. "Oh, no. This is really getting to be a bad situation here. We can't have Mr. Straight-as-an-arrow lying. You need to give yourself lecture four. The one on telling the truth."

His fingers curled around her bare ankle. "You are in a precarious position, Saber," he pointed out.

"Am I?" She put down her coffee cup, tilting her head to one side. "So let's hear the truth. Why the interest in Brian?"

Jess sighed heavily. "He followed you home last night."

"He did what?"

"Followed you home. With this weirdo calling the station asking about you, anything unusual worries me."

"How do you know he followed me?" she demanded suspiciously. "You were in bed when I got home."

"You thought I was."

Saber shrugged. "He objected strenuously to certain portions of my broadcast." Saber grinned at the memory. "He did a lot of jumping around and yelling."

"We'll discuss my opinion of your stupidity later," he promised. "Maybe Brian was

214

worried about you."

"More likely he was worried about his job if anything happened to me. I think you intimidate him."

"I doubt that. We lost three of our crew in that car accident. There'd been a big celebration at the station — Patsy and David had just announced their engagement. David handled the night program. He, his soundman, and the day soundman were driving down the hill when they lost control of their car and went over the cliff."

"Where Patsy was hit? The same place?"

He nodded. "I hired both Brian and Les about three weeks before you arrived."

Her heart jumped. A car accident? Three people from the radio station had died and that had created a job opening. She was in so much trouble. She forced a smile. "A good choice too. Brian's brilliant at his job. I couldn't have made it without him those first few weeks. He really taught me so much."

She wasn't giving her opinion of Les, the day man. She was just glad she didn't have to work with him very often. "If Brian was worried about me to the point he had to follow me home, I'll apologize to him."

"You won't say a word," he ordered. "Until I know a little more I don't want you

215

letting on to Brian that you know."

"Intrigue! How bizarre."

"Stop being flippant. Just what did you think you were doing last night?" There was an edge of anger to his voice.

"I wanted to talk to the man. Is that such a wild idea? Honestly, Jesse, you can look so intimidating when you want to."

"I can be intimidating when I need to be. You were asking for trouble last night and you know it. I can't blame Brian if he was worried, you scared the hell out of me. Have you ever listened to yourself? You sound sexy, Saber. Very erotic. You can't tease this guy."

"I'm not teasing him. I don't want to be afraid of him either. I figured I might as well find out what he wants. And in any case, if he ever caught up with me, he'd find out I'm not in the least bit sexy."

His palm slid up her leg from ankle to calf and back. "No? You obviously don't see yourself the way I do."

His touch sent little tongues of fire licking along her spine. Muscles bunched in her stomach and along her thigh. Her womb spasmed. Wild color spread, turning her complexion rose. She ducked her head, avoiding his hungry gaze.

"You're not to do it again, Saber. No more

216

invitations to this man. You don't know what he's like. You could be feeding some sick fantasy of his. I mean it, you're not taking any phone calls. I called Les this morning and Brian will be told this evening."

"You can't do that. Phone calls are a big part of my show — you know that."

"I can do anything, baby, I own the damn station."

"Don't you dare pull rank on me, Jesse. If this were Brian's show you would never have said such a stupid thing!"

"Brian isn't you."

"And that's supposed to justify it? You can't mess with my show."

"Well I just did. No calls," he ordered, implacable and stony-faced.

Her chin tilted at him. "And what if that makes it worse? It could, you know."

Jess's palm glided over her smooth skin in a mesmerizing caress. "You don't believe that."

Saber bit at her full lower lip. "Well, maybe not," she admitted reluctantly. "What if I just don't take his call? Brian can vet them all first, and if it's him, Brian just won't put him through." She could barely think with Jesse's fingers on her, brushing back and forth in that amazing way.

"I had Les send the tapes over to me. This

is a nutcase, honey, and he'll call again. And if Brian can say you can't take calls from anyone, this nut will have no reason to think he's being singled out."

"That's crazy. Wrap me in bubble wrap, why don't you?"

"Better yet, why don't you stay home from work for a few days? We can say you're ill." Jess's hands dropped lower to take her foot into the palm of his hand, massaging it gently. "We could go on a trip together, honey."

"What kind of trip?" In spite of herself Saber was interested. Going away with Jess would be heaven. Going anywhere with him.

"You name it. I don't care."

Saber sighed, reached out to brush a lock of hair from his temple with gentle fingers. "You can take me dancing and we'll call it good."

"You do love dancing, don't you?" His eyes met hers, black with hunger. Saber felt as if she were dissolving, melting into him. She actually leaned toward him, her breath catching in her throat, heart thudding painfully.

The shrill ringing of the telephone had both of them jumping. Jess swore under his breath. Saber pressed the back of her hand to her mouth.

"We don't have to answer the damn thing," Jess groused.

"It's the only safe thing to do," Saber said unsteadily, lifting the receiver. "Hello."

Jess winced at the sultry sound of her voice.

"Saber, I'm glad you're up already."

"Brian, what's up?" Saber reached down to ease the grip Jess had on her calf.

"I thought maybe we could grab a bite to eat before work tonight. It's silly for us to take two cars," Brian said.

Jess could hear that clear, carrying baritone. He wanted to rip the phone right out of her hand and tell the stud of the radio station where he could go. People were fired over lesser infractions. Saber's soft laughter grated on his nerves.

"Thanks for thinking of me, Brian, but I always take my own car. It's a new rule I made after an unfortunate date. I thought your apartment was clear out in the other direction." She glared at Jess's frowning face, flicked his chin with her index finger.

He caught her finger, carried it to his mouth, took wicked enjoyment in her swift intake of breath, the sudden cloudiness in her blue eyes.

"I've moved," Brian informed her. "So what about meeting me for dinner?"

Jess removed her finger from the warmth of his mouth. "I'm taking you dancing, remember, baby?"

Saber rolled her eyes. "Another time, Brian. Jess and I have plans tonight."

"And every other night," Jess said under his breath.

Saber caught it anyway, grinning at him as she nodded at whatever Brian was saying. "See you tonight, Brian, right, goodbye." She hung up. "Jesse, you're so outrageous. It will serve you right if I insist on you taking me out every single night. I thought you liked Brian. He's really very nice."

"He's a damned playboy."

Saber shifted sideways, jumped to the floor, dusting off her hands on the seat of her jeans. "So are you. Your own sister said so. And a cad."

"I'm a nice cad."

She flashed her sassy smile. "Well . . ." She tilted her head to one side pretending to consider. "I think you're right."

"I've got to put in a couple of more hours working," Jess said.

Saber nodded, knowing Jess could disappear into his office with his high-tech equipment and be there for hours.

"It's about time," she teased. "I was afraid

I'd end up supporting you."

"It might come to that." He glided over the smooth floor toward the hall. "What are you going to do?" If she was going out, he needed to notify Logan.

"Swim a few laps, lift weights, and eat."

"If I work too long, come in and yell at me."

"And risk you biting my head off?" She feigned shock. "Not even Patsy braves the dragon in his inner lair."

He paused in the doorway. "Am I really that bad?"

She laughed. "I'd like to lie and tell you no, but when you're in the middle of working, you definitely object to any interruptions."

He had to follow the lead the admiral's secretary, Louise Charter, had given him. He had a feeling time was running out on him and he needed to find the traitor in the chain of command as soon as possible, before someone else was set up to die.

"This time I'll make an exception, I promise, honey. If I get caught up, come and get me."

She nodded and watched him as he moved easily down the hall. There was something so fluid, so powerful in the way Jess moved, she loved to just watch him.

■ ■ ■ ■

Snarling with rage, he slammed his fist repeatedly into the wall, tearing holes into the Sheetrock. How dare Whitney send some enhanced bastard of a soldier to reprimand him. How dare the son of a bitch order him away from Calhoun's sister. It wasn't his place? He'd show them his place. *And how had Whitney known?* He kicked the chair, splintering it into pieces, stomping on it for good measure.

He had managed to penetrate Calhoun's security and make it inside the fence without being seen. *He* had done that, not one of Whitney's finest. Screw them. He could get in and out of the house at will. He could go right now, right this moment, to Calhoun's sister's house and spend all night cutting her into little pieces, maybe send them one by one to the cripple — no, send the pieces to Whitney — so fuck him. How would Whitney like that?

He'd placed a listening device right outside the kitchen window. Calhoun had a jammer, but he was so much smarter at electronics than that enhanced bastard — than all of them. Had any of Whitney's elite soldiers gotten that close to Calhoun?

And she would be gone this evening, dancing the night away with her lover. Well, he'd leave her a little surprise in her bed. In her panties. All over her entire damned room. Screw Whitney and his orders. And as for the cripple, well, tonight was going to be his last night. He was going to have him beaten to death right in front of the little whore. Whitney and his enhanced soldiers could choke on that.

CHAPTER 8

All this agonizing over Saber was inspiring.
Jess was beginning to believe songwriters
needed to suffer to produce good material
— because this song was *good*. Every single
note hauntingly beautiful, just like Saber.

He had started out working to unravel the
mystery of that small digital recorder Louise Charter had brought to him. The recorder had been sealed in a plastic bag and
locked in the office safe when she found it,
and she hadn't been the one to put it there.
The admiral had nothing whatsoever to do
with her office safe. According to Louise, he
didn't know the combination. If it was a
plant to incriminate the admiral, whoever
had placed the recorder there hadn't known
that only the secretary had access to the
safe.

The recording was in bad shape. He could
hear voices, but was unable to catch the
words, even with his advanced equipment.

In the end, he thought it best to turn the recorder over to the soundman of the team, Neil. The man could do almost anything when it came to sound. And once that was taken care of . . .

The need for Saber consumed him, so he poured his frustrations into composing and everything else just went to hell. For the first time in his adult life, he wanted to quit his job with the military, so that if Saber was in his home for any reason other than because she wanted to be, the secrets would no longer matter and they could be together.

"Jesse?" Her soft siren voice cut through his thoughts, a note of hesitation so endearing he was already smiling as he turned to open his office door. For a moment his heart seemed to stop beating.

Saber was dressed in a figure-hugging, royal blue, off-the-shoulder dress. The skirt flared from the hips down to a hem of ragged tails. She had touched her long thick lashes with mascara, colored her full lips a pearly pink. The wild riot of curls spilling around her face gleamed with highlights. She was so incredibly beautiful his stomach clenched and his heart did a crazy roll.

"Did you still want to go with me?"

"You're not going without me, not looking like that," he said, black gaze moving

225

hot and hungry over her.

She performed a little pirouette for him. "What do you think?"

"I think you can break hearts in that dress." Not to mention raise a man's temperature a few hundred degrees. Jess wiped at the little beads of perspiration forming on his skin. To hell with the dancing. He had other, far better ideas in mind.

"You like it then? I bought it on a whim a couple of months ago. You know me, I never wear dresses." She looked pleased at his response.

"I'd better get cleaned up to at least be presentable if I'm going to be seen with you. You look absolutely beautiful, Saber."

A faint blush stole into her cheeks. "Did you get quite a bit of work done?"

He nodded as he followed her into the hall, unable to take his eyes from her slender form. Just the way she walked suggested music to him. She was beautiful, and while he dressed, all he did was fantasize over her. He took care with his clothes, wanting to impress her, wanting her to feel the way about him that he felt about her.

Saber waited while Jess changed into his dark Italian suit, the charcoal gray one. The one that always made Saber melt inside when he put it on. She loved the tangy,

226

masculine scent of him, the way his hair was so neat except for that one persistent, very sexy lock of hair that always fell across the middle of his forehead.

In the van he sat for a minute, simply looking at her. His gaze was possessive, admiring, everything Saber could ever have wanted to see. It caused a rush of moist heat, the swirl of butterfly wings, and made her mouth go suddenly dry. She moistened her lips with the tip of her tongue, and then swallowed hard when his hungry gaze followed the movement.

"Jesse," she protested breathlessly.

"Kiss me." His voice went husky with raw need. He needed her kiss, the feel of her lips, her mouth, his body burning with desire, craving the honeyed taste of her.

Even as her brain protested, her body was already leaning toward his, wanting the heat that flared between them, wanting just one more taste of the forbidden.

The moment his mouth claimed hers, the trembling started. His teeth teased at her full lower lip, insisting she open to him. Hesitantly she obeyed, liquid fire rushing through her veins, arousing something fierce and primitive in her that matched the savage in him.

His tongue claimed her mouth the way

his body meant to claim hers, hard, thrusting, sweeping her up with him, a wild mating tango that went on forever. Her heart, soul, and body belonged to him in that moment, melting, merging, straining to be part of him.

Lack of adequate air tore them apart. Rather than let her go, Jess's hands framed her head, his lips wandering over every inch of her face and throat. Saber moaned softly, clinging to the hard muscles of his shoulders.

"Do you want to stay home, baby?" He whispered the enticement, a sorcerer bent on tempting her.

Her breath left her in a rush and she stared at him, shocked and pleased and closer to agreeing than she wanted to admit. "We don't dare, Jess."

She didn't dare. He, however, was altogether a different story. With Saber, he'd dare just about anything — give up anything — even his career if necessary. Very gently Jess put distance between them. It took a minute to control his breathing, to get his raging body under some semblance of control.

"Glory, Jesse, you have got to stop doing this." Saber fanned herself with her hand, blue eyes so dark they were violet.

"Personally, angel face, I'm becoming quite partial to 'doing this.' " He set the van in motion, a small, crooked smile softening the hard curve of his mouth.

An answering smile hovered on her lips. "Well, don't think it's going to be a habit. We're liable to set the neighborhood on fire, we're that combustible."

His eyebrow shot up. "I don't think you're being the least bit open-minded about this, Saber."

"It's a matter of survival," she informed him. Her long lashes concealed the expression in her eyes.

He flashed his predator's smile. "Exactly. Now you're getting the idea. It is a matter of survival." There was no laughter in his voice.

She frowned, bit back a response, deeming it more prudent to remain silent. She was definitely not getting the better of him. In fact, she had a sinking suspicion she was losing ground fast. She wanted him so bad. More than she'd ever wanted anything in her life, yet he would always be out of reach. Even if a miracle happened and he really fell in love with her, she'd never be able to stay.

"Amazing," he teased. "Saber Wynter without a word to say."

She stared out the window, refusing to be provoked.

Jess's laughter faded at her discomfort, and he reached a hand across the intervening space to brush her cheek with caressing fingertips. Saber jumped and turned her violet-blue gaze on him. Haunted eyes. It was Jess who swallowed hard and looked away.

The club was relatively small, suggesting intimacy. Most of the patrons knew each other and greeted Jess and Saber immediately. Saber stood at Jess's side, her hand in his as they moved through the crowd to their table. Jess ordered her usual 7UP and orange juice without a murmur, one of the many things she appreciated about him. Saber never touched alcoholic beverages and normally her dates acted almost offended by it, or treated her as if she were a child who needed coaxing. Jess simply took her preference in stride.

The band was good, playing a mixture of rock and roll and slow romantic tunes.

"Jess. How good to see you." The voice came from behind them, startling her. Saber hadn't been aware of anyone approaching, and that was disconcerting. Normally, she was aware of everything. Her heart jumped and then began a quick hammer in her chest. She turned to see a couple right behind her, so close she could have touched them. Too close to have slipped her notice. She hadn't scented them, felt their energy or rhythm, and her radar hadn't gone off. Her heart sank. Jess had to be shielding them.

"Ken. Mari." Jess held out his hand to the man.

Ken was covered completely in scars. It looked as though someone had sliced him into little pieces. He seemed as tough as steel, and his eyes were ice cold and watchful. Mari looked small beside him, but the way she moved was a dead giveaway.

These were GhostWalkers, not just friends of Jess. He had called in his team. She should have known he'd realize someone was watching them. She should have anticipated that he'd call on his friends. She was slipping, and now she was virtually surrounded by the enemy.

Jess caught her hand and tugged until she was beside him, so close she could feel his warmth. "Saber, these are good friends of mine. Ken and Mari Norton. They're newlyweds, so expect them to suddenly gaze into each other's eyes and forget we're here. Ken, Mari, this is my Saber."

Deliberately Saber forced a smile, studying the other woman, trying to place her, trying to figure out if they'd ever been in the same compound. Whitney had several training facilities and he liked to keep the girls in groups, but he separated the groups and introduced different training techniques in an effort to find what worked best. She'd never seen Mari before, but there was no doubt she was a soldier, a GhostWalker.

Saber stuck her hand out, her breath catching in her lungs — waiting. Would they take her hand? Did they know? If Whitney had sent them to retrieve her, they'd hesitate or find some excuse not to touch her. They'd fear even her touch.

Mari took her hand immediately, a welcoming smile on her face. "It's so good to meet you."

Ken not only took her hand, but covered it with his other one. If they knew about her, they were too good to show fear. "So you're the woman who has finally put Jess in his place."

For a moment she thought she hadn't heard right. "It's not like that . . . ," she began to protest, but Jess reached up and took her hand right out of Ken's and kissed the center of her palm, his gaze locked with hers. She lost her train of thought.

"She's the one," Jess admitted. "She'll

deny it, but that's because she's an outrageous little liar. We were just about to dance."

Ken leaned close to him. His voice was a pseudo-whisper. "It was Mari who dragged me here too. I sympathize greatly."

Mari smiled and shook her head. "I can't dance at all. Ken loves it."

Ken wrapped his arm around her waist and took her out onto the dance floor. She slipped easily into his arms. They didn't dance so much as hold one another and sway.

Jess's black gaze burned possessively over Saber. He glided easily onto the floor and held out his hand to her. Saber's smile was slow, unconsciously sexy, blue eyes clinging to his. She slid onto his lap, circling his neck with her slender arms, slowly relaxing against the wall of his chest, head on his shoulder. Jess's hand slid up her back, his other swaying the racing chair to the slow, sensuous rhythm of the music.

She was unbearably soft, her skin hot through the thin separation of their clothing. Their hearts beat together, his body stirring to a fierce arousal all too noticeable against the back of her bare thigh. She smelled fresh and sweet and Jess couldn't resist sliding his tongue along her neck, tasting soft, scented skin. His teeth nipped experimentally, the hand at her back drawing her even closer so that he could experience the reaction of her body. She laid her head on his shoulder, her hand tapping out a rhythm on the nape of his neck.

Saber was lost in the music, in the hard strength of his body. It was a melting heat, a merging of souls, a slow, erotic pulsing of blood and instruments, body and mind. It lasted an eternity, forever, it lasted a heartbeat, a moment.

As the soft strains of music faded away, the real world forced entrance to their private sanctuary. Bereft, Saber lifted her head, eyes starry, breath impossible to control. She looked as if he'd made love to her and for a moment Jess tightened his hold, almost forgetting where they were.

A swift upbeat number had couples breaking apart. Ken clapped Jess on the back. "Enough of that, you two," he reprimanded. "Let's see some moves."

Reluctantly, Jess allowed Saber to slide from his lap, closing his eyes against the savage ache as her firm, rounded buttocks slid enticingly over his lap.

"Is that some kind of challenge?" He winked at Saber, his voice a little bit husky, his breathing not quite under control.

Ken nodded. "You got it, Calhoun. You and Saber are supposed to be so hot, at least that's the word from Max." He winked at Mari. "Well, maybe you already are."

"Very funny." Saber moved back, hips swaying to the beat of the music, feet picking up the rhythm. She didn't know who Max was, but they'd all obviously discussed her in the context of her belonging with Jess, and she was absurdly pleased about that.

Jess smiled, a slow sensuous response to the rhythm of her body, easily tilted his chair, balancing on two wheels, moving with her, around her, Saber around him, close, apart, eyes locked on one another. Her body flowed with all the grace of a ballerina and the strength of a gymnast. She was a wild little thing of pure beauty, music mysteriously coming to life.

It was obvious they were in a world of their own, the only two people on the dance floor. It looked as though every moment had been choreographed to perfection, a swirl of man, woman, and machine. Jess's ability to spin, jump, and glide in his wheelchair was phenomenal. Their soft, muted laughter and wild, skillful dancing continued for several songs.

Ken and Mari, laughing together, joined

Saber and Jess at their table.

"So are we the champions?" Jess asked, grinning at his friend.

"I give up," Ken conceded. "You two can keep your crowns."

"I can't dance at all," Mari admitted. "Ken makes me look good, but I don't think I'll ever get the hang of it. Where'd you learn to dance like that, Jess?"

Jess sipped his drink, eyes on the perfection of Saber's face. "This lady right here. She loves to dance, and has music going all the time. She'd nag me all the time, until I had no choice."

He smiled at Saber tenderly.

You have it bad, Jess. Ken sent the thought telepathically. *She's definitely a GhostWalker, but Mari has never seen her before. Have you checked her out?*

Jess tried not to react to the faint hint of suspicion in Ken's voice. If the positions had been reversed, he would have been suspicious as well.

"Well, she taught you well," Mari said, shyness in her voice. "You're very good."

Saber had the impression Mari wasn't used to crowds. Ken slipped his arm around her waist, bending to brush her temple with a quick, tender kiss. They were obviously not pretending to be married for her benefit

236

and that made her feel safer. Maybe Jess hadn't called in his team. His friends would want to check up on him, visit him and make certain he was doing all right. She wanted to believe Ken and Mari were just at the club to have fun with Jess.

"He is good, isn't he?" Saber said with pride.

Mari nodded. "I've never seen anything quite like that."

It was kind of funny that they were all sitting at the same table pretending they were all just friends — normal people — instead of their reality. Saber had learned to handle the crush of energy others gave off, but it was difficult over long periods of time. She usually avoided crowds. Mari wasn't an anchor either and she would have the same problems being out in public. It gave Saber a kindred feeling toward Mari.

"I love to dance, and Jess was so good about dancing at home with me."

Home. Jess liked the way she said it. He'd never thought much about having a home. He'd taken it for granted, growing up in a loving family the way he had. He wondered what Saber's childhood had been like. He knew Mari's had been extremely difficult. Jess reached for Saber's hand, thumb feathering over her knuckles. "It was fun," he said decisively. "Although I think she's always afraid I might fall over backward."

"That's because you deliberately scare me." She laughed because she couldn't help it as he caught at the wheels to do a pop-up. "Stop, you know I hate that."

"Stop showing off for your woman," Ken ordered. *She's laughing but she's really worried about it.*

Jess shot his friend a shut-up look, but he stopped teasing her. "I do it all the time, honey, and I never fall."

"I know," Saber sipped at her drink and flashed him a reassuring smile.

That was the problem right there, Jess decided. That smile. Like she was taking care of him, watching over him. Afraid he'd hurt himself. He knew where all the exits and windows were. He knew who would be the most dangerous men in the room in a fight. He knew the make and model of every car in the parking lot and exactly how they were parked. He knew which of the customers were armed and which ones he could take — most likely all of them — without breaking a sweat and still sitting in his wheelchair. But she didn't see him as someone who could take care of her.

He wanted to shake things up. He was tired of pretending to be less capable than he truly was. But he couldn't tell her the truth because he was a top secret national security weapon. And most likely, she couldn't say anything to him for the same reason.

As if reading his mind, Ken gave a small shake of his head. *Mari thinks she's on the run.*

Was he really that transparent? He wanted to lean across the table and kiss her. She melted when he kissed her, forgetting all about the chair. Jess sighed and sought a safe topic of conversation. "How's Briony? Her baby must be due soon." He found Saber's hand again, tangling their fingers because he needed to touch her. "Briony, Mari's sister, is married to Ken's brother, Jack."

"Jack and I are twins," Ken explained. "And so are Mari and Briony. Briony is expecting twins."

"How did that happen?" Saber asked. "Because that's plain scary."

Ken laughed. "It's a curse in my family. We always have twins. The men in our family find women who produce identical twins. It's either a blessing or a curse, we're not certain which."

Mari shot him a look. "Not me. My poor sister is terrified of having children and with two of them coming, I can't blame her."

Saber was horrified. "Two? I've never even held a baby."

"Neither have I," Mari confessed. "Briony hasn't either, but I told her I'd help her. Jack is really good with her."

"Jack has these books he's always reading," Ken said with a little grin. "On pregnancy, having twins, labor, and now parenting."

"He makes us all read them," Mari added.

Saber felt tears burning behind her eyes. It was so unexpected she wasn't prepared for the emotion overwhelming her. Their voices, she decided, held so much love, so much warmth. They were a family. Jack and Briony. Ken and Mari. And now children. Somehow they'd made it out of the insanity that was the life of a GhostWalker.

She wanted to ask them so many questions, but at the same time she wanted to beat back hope. Because if you hoped and then it was taken from you, life was far worse than ever before. She had escaped, but Whitney kept coming after her. Sooner or later he would catch up with her, and she would be dead, because there was no way she'd ever go back to that hellish captivity. She'd die first. How had Mari gotten out? And was Briony a GhostWalker as well?

Why had Whitney let them leave? Why was he leaving them alone and not her?

Jess tugged at her until she came out of her chair and settled on his lap. "Dance with me again, baby," he said, keeping his voice soft and low. The look on her face was heartbreaking. If there was ever a moment in his life when he really considered breaking security clearance, it was right then.

Her arms circled his neck and she relaxed into him as he powered the chair onto the dance floor. He found a quiet corner where the shadows felt intimate. The music was soft and soothing. Saber relaxed into his arms, burying her face against his throat.

He spotted Logan Maxwell in the crowd, and Martin Howard at the bar. He felt better knowing they were close. Whoever was watching them would get more than they bargained for if they made a move against Saber or him. Logan wielded power with infinite skill. Ken was one of the toughest GhostWalkers in the business. Martin was lethal in any situation. Mari was an unknown to Jesse having recently married Ken, but if she was strong enough to stand with Ken, then she was welcome.

Jess wasn't losing Saber. Her running days were over, and if she was still working for Whitney, then he would see to it she knew exactly who and what Whitney really was.

"What's wrong?" Saber's whisper was in his ear, in his mind, sliding over his skin like a caress.

He made himself breathe. "Nothing, baby. I'm just enjoying holding you."

The chair swayed to the music. He knew the others could read him. They would know how deep his feelings for Saber really went, but at that moment the only thing that mattered to him was keeping her safe.

Outside, Neil Campbell would be lying up on a rooftop or in a tree somewhere with a night scope. Ordinarily Ken and Jack Norton took up sniper duty, but with Jack's wife so close to having her babies, and Ken having the only female partner available to their team, Neil pulled the task of providing cover.

The last notes of the music faded away and Jess maneuvered the chair through the crowd back toward the table. Saber stayed on his lap because she wanted a few more stolen minutes with him. The path opened up along the wall, and her legs brushed against a very good-looking man with ice-cold blue eyes, wide shoulders, and muscles in his arms to rival Jess's.

The moment she brushed against him, an

electric current sizzled through her body and she had to force herself to keep from looking up. *GhostWalker.* Damn it. Damn it, she'd waited too long. The man was an enhanced soldier, an anchor if she wasn't mistaken, and no one was safe now. She had to get Jess out of the bar as quickly as possible and maybe — oh God, she couldn't believe she was considering it — she had to find a way for Ken and Mari to escort them to the van. Unless . . .

For a moment she couldn't breathe, her breath hitching, but she was a professional, and if Jess was betraying her, delivering her back into Whitney's hands, then she'd better be prepared for anything. She was surrounded, and they couldn't know that she knew. But would Jess allow her to snuggle onto his lap if he'd been told about her? She had to think. Maybe excuse herself and go to the restroom. She could be gone in seconds. Saber was an expert at disappearing. They'd have a man, maybe two outside, but she could make it out. Eventually they'd find her gear. She sighed. If Jess was really in danger, then she was leaving him vulnerable.

Jess knew immediately that Saber had identified Logan as a GhostWalker. She didn't change expression or even stiffen,

243

but for one split second her breathing had caught.

You're made, Logan. Even with me shielding, she knew.

I felt it when she touched me. Logan did a mental shrug. *It doesn't surprise me in the least. I was shocked that the two of you had been in the same house for so long and neither knew about the other.*

Saber had her arms around Jess, her palm curled along the nape of his neck, skin to skin, and she felt the current of energy arc in the air, from Jess to the stranger. She automatically tuned her biorhythm to Jess's to get the feeling for the current. The brain activity gave telepathic communication away every time. She knew exactly what part of the brain did what and where the pulses came from. He was talking to the man with the ice-cold blue eyes.

She kept the rhythm of her heart exactly the same. Her pulse didn't leap, not even when it entered her mind that she could be in a trap, with Jess as the bait — all-too-aware bait. He knew them all. And he was talking to them. If she slipped into his rhythm, she might even pick up the exact pathway and eavesdrop.

She didn't dare think that Jess had betrayed her — not for real — because if he

244

had, she didn't know what she might do. Would she — could she — kill him?

"Saber, talk to me," Jess said. She was moving away from him. Not physically. If he didn't know her so well he wouldn't have sensed any difference in her, but he felt a jarring note, as if his energy had fit with hers and now it bounced back as if she had turned away. "What's wrong?"

She wanted to shake him. She detested playing games, but she had no choice. "Nothing." Now she sounded sulky and felt inadequate. The moment they returned to the table, she jumped off his lap. "Nothing at all." She even managed a quick, bright smile. Who smiled before they killed? She'd undergone tests most of her life, mental, psychological, physical, and emotional. She'd always been too emotional to please Whitney. He'd come close to terminating her several times, close to using her in one of the programs few survived, but by that time, she'd caught on. She knew she had to play his game and be better at it, because in her world, being the best at dealing death meant surviving.

Mari indicated the drinks on the table. "The owner sent us another round."

There was no more sipping at drinks or trusting her companions, not even to pretend. She watched Jess take his drink and lift it with a nod toward the bartender. Ken tipped Mari's glass and then Saber's. She was careful about actually putting her lips to the rim. A dusting of poison could kill in an instant. Appearing distracted by a dancer, she set the drink aside, still standing, tapping her foot to the beat.

"This is great music," she said to no one in particular, allowing her gaze to drift over the crowd. Men and women who could handle themselves had a distinct look. She touched a few potentials, men who looked good in a fight, men who carried themselves with confidence, who moved with easy, sure steps and flowing muscles. She couldn't discount the women as a threat either.

Mari was a soldier. There was no doubt in Saber's mind. She'd gone through the same extensive training Saber had, and it had been thorough. She probably knew more ways to kill a man than most individuals in the room. She'd gone through psychological and emotional testing. She was trained extensively in weapons and hand-to-hand, but more importantly, she had been put through test after test on her ability to think in a crisis. On how to remain cool and calm, how to be as cold as ice in any given situation.

For the first time in her life, Saber was grateful for the years of training, for all the times she'd been punished for showing emotion. Jess had betrayed her, sold her out to the other GhostWalkers. By all rights she should terminate him.

"Have you met Jess's sister, Patsy?" she inquired, hanging on to her smile.

Ken nodded. "I have. I had met her before this happened." He ran his hand over the scars on his face. "She cried when she saw me. Patsy is a very caring woman."

"I haven't met her," Mari said. "I'd like to though. Both Jack and Ken talk about Jess and his family quite a bit."

"Jess always invited us for holidays," Ken said. "He has a nice family."

Saber continued to search the room without seeming to do so. There would be others in the crowd. They would want a full team if they planned to reacquire her. She pushed all sentiment away, all regret. Escape wouldn't be easy. She was small and her strength wasn't in hand-to-hand. She was good with weapons, but again, it wasn't her specialty. She could do it — would do it — because she had to. When failure wasn't an option, you found a way to get it done.

"I've only met Patsy, and I really like her."

"She thinks Saber is too young for me,"

Jess said. She was pulling away from him. He could feel her withdrawal as surely as if she were already gone. Something close to panic pressed on his chest until he could barely breathe. He had never panicked in his life. Not once. Not in training, not in combat, not when he'd been captured and tortured. But panic filled him until he could barely think straight.

"Saber." He said her name in a low voice. "Look at me."

She didn't even turn her head his way. She kept that soft, dreamy look on her face, the small half smile, and she looked as if she was very interested in the dancers.

"I'm listening."

Even her voice was perky, damn her, but he knew. He knew with every fiber of his being. *Look at me now!* It was a command, sharp and firm and demanding.

Startled, her eyes met his in shock.

Do you honestly believe that I would betray you? Don't look at anyone else. Look at me. Do you think I brought you here so that bastard Whitney could take you away from me?

He was furious with her — that she could believe such a betrayal. And hurt. God, it hurt like a son of a bitch. He wanted to shake her, so much so that he didn't dare put his hands on her. The table vibrated beneath his palms. Ken shot him a quick inquiry, but Jess ignored him, holding Saber's gaze. *Answer me, damn it, is that what you think of me? That I would hand you over to him after living with you for nearly a year?*

She moistened her lips, her only nervous gesture. She didn't even blink, but stared him right in the eye. Her gaze shifted back to the crowd. His heart slammed hard in his chest, one jolt and his stomach felt as if he'd been sucker punched.

Ken shifted slightly, better to protect Jess if need be. The gesture irritated him. The damn wheelchair again. *I don't need protection and certainly not from Saber.*

The table's shaking. Ken's voice was mild.

She thinks I betrayed her.

That would be a natural reaction. She's spotted the team. She knows Mari and I are part of it. She's not stupid, Jess. If she's running from Whitney, she has to think this is a setup. What would be the chances it's a coincidence?

Get rid of the ego and focus. Jess winced. He heard the echo of that thought and ducked his head, even as he still held Saber's gaze. He let out his breath and tried to see things from her point of view.

"All right, baby. Let's see if I can clear a few things up for you. Ken and Mari are part of a Special Forces team known as the GhostWalkers. Mari escaped from a research facility run by Dr. Whitney. Ken, Mari, and a few of the others came to help because you and I have been under surveillance. I don't know if you're on the run and Whitney's found you, or whether he's watching me, but either way, I figured we needed help."

There was a dead silence as she stared at him, shocked that he'd disclosed as much as he had. Did she dare believe him? She glanced at Mari, but her gaze jumped back to Jess. In spite of herself, her pulse quickened and hope leapt. Was there a chance he was telling the truth? *If you're lying to me, Jesse, I swear I'll kill you before they take me.* She deliberately spoke in his mind to let him know she had power too.

"Fair enough, Saber. But you tell me the truth. I laid my cards out on the table. I expect you to do the same."

"How many of your men are here?"

"Five. And a sleeper hanging back."

She inhaled sharply. He had called in a full team. Each GhostWalker would have a different skill and they would be lethal. "You have a lot of friends." She couldn't hope to take them all. She wasn't that kind of war-rior. Sending up a little prayer that he was telling the truth, she caught at his watch. "Let's go home." *Because if we're going to discuss this, I want it to be between you and me. I don't trust anyone else. And I don't feel safe surrounded by that many enhanced sol-diers.*

He flashed a small, encouraging smile. At least she wasn't making a break for it. *They're supposed to make you feel safe.*

"Well, it's not working." She slid out of the chair, avoiding getting too close to Ken. He was a big man and obviously strong.

"We'll escort you home," Ken said. "And leave you alone once you're settled in and your security is on."

Jess nodded and wordlessly followed Saber out of the club.

Glee filled him. He was ecstatic as he turned on her CD player and stripped off his clothes. He wanted to hear her voice, that sexy, husky whisper that crawled over his skin and into his body, but the music would do and at least he could smell her. He lay in her sheets and rolled around before hop-ping up to drag open the dresser drawers. In the top one he found treasure.

Silky thongs and lacy bras in all colors.

251

He selected several and pulled them out along with two pairs of boy short underwear cut high along the butt. Holding them to his nose, he inhaled and then rubbed them over his body. Every time he saw her now he'd picture her wearing silk and know he had touched them, held them to him, rubbed his shaft until he came again and again with them. He lay back and began, using an almost transparent blue pair wrapped around the length of him, while the music played and his body hummed. He pictured her tied down and helpless, waiting for his attention after the others had beaten Calhoun into a bloody mess. Maybe he'd take her right there by the body. He'd take his time, making her pay for that kiss in the park. Tonight was going to be perfect. His body arched, his hips jerked, and he watched with satisfaction as he sprayed his cum all over her sheets and underwear.

CHAPTER 9

"You haven't said a single word all the way home," Jess said. "I thought we were going to talk."

"Not in the car." Saber knew she sounded clipped, but she couldn't help it. She wanted to believe in him, but betrayal in her business was a way of life. It would be like Whitney to engineer a way to make her fall in love so she could see how futile it would be for someone like her to try to have a life.

Jess glanced at her as he pulled the van into the garage. She held herself stiff — away from him — as though if he touched her she might break. So he didn't, although it was hard to fight his instincts. He turned off the car and sent word. *We're in for the night. Saber isn't going to be going to work. I'll have her call the station and take a sick day. Thanks, everyone.*

They sat in the dark when he switched off the lights. Saber sighed and took the plunge.

253

"I know once Whitney decides he wants you, there's no way to fight him. He has so much power, so much money, and all the newest gadgets available to him. He has research centers set up all over and if one place is discovered, he just moves on to the next. If I don't keep running, I'm vulnerable."

"They took one down just recently. He isn't untouchable, Saber."

"Yes, he is. None of us exist, Jesse. If he wants us dead, we're dead and no one's the wiser. He's building an army and he's got tentacles everywhere. We'll never be safe, either one of us. I know how easy it is to kill someone." She glanced around the large garage uneasily. "I don't want to talk out here."

"Even if he got a bug inside, the frequency would be jammed." It wasn't that she looked scared, more . . . defeated. Whitney had been the one constant adult in her life and he seemed all-powerful to her. "Come on. I'll give you a ride into the house." He knew he shouldn't have offered, she wasn't ready yet to trust him all the way, but she looked vulnerable and fragile and he wanted — no, needed — to comfort her.

Saber opened the passenger door as he hit the lift button, choosing instead to hop out on her side. The moment her feet hit the ground, she knew they were in trouble.

Jesse! She couldn't help the warning, even as it occurred to her he'd sprung a trap. There were no witnesses to see her taken. She'd been stupid. So stupid. She wanted to believe him so much she'd just gone quietly back to the house, and now she was trapped in a small space with no help.

Three men. They were big too. They emerged from the shadows, grinning like apes, standing shoulder to shoulder, menacingly, silently. Just their silence was a threat. The huge, ham-like fists were opening and closing as they slowly spread out. She heard movement behind her and knew she was trapped between the men and the van.

How many, baby?

His voice was calm, reassuring, and it steadied her because he was on her side — there had been no betrayal. She was trained to hear, to feel the rhythm in people, and she knew a lie when she heard one. Jess wasn't lying. He was fighting with her and he was in a wheelchair. She couldn't just escape. She had to win, to defeat. No one could be left standing to get to Jess.

Three in front, one behind me. She had to get to Jess and protect him. They would hear the lift as he lowered it to get himself out of the van. *Take the van out of here, call for help. Your team has to still be close.*

Are you out of your mind? I'm not leaving you. I'm coming out.

He just had to be a hero. It would make it more difficult to fight, trying to protect him while she fought her way free, but she recognized that there was no arguing with him. And the men were moving in on her. *Wait. I'm going under the van and out the back. Don't draw their attention until I'm there.*

Without waiting for an answer, she dove beneath the undercarriage, rolling toward the back of the van. She was small enough to fit without sacrificing an arm or leg as she rolled between the tires and back out into the open. *I'm clear.*

The lift made noise, and it took time. One man burst around the side of the van and she drove her fist into his throat, effectively clotheslining him so that he went down hard, his body hitting with enough of a thud that she knew he was dead. *So much for never killing again.*

She kept running, right at the second man. He was braced for her, so she planted her foot on the side of the van and raced up and over his head, to jump kick the third man right in the temple. She aimed accurately, using her forward momentum to double the force of the blow. She felt rather than heard his skull fracture and he was down even before she landed on the ground.

The second man spun back toward her, one beefy arm reaching for her. She stayed in motion, rolling across the hood of her car to put the vehicle between her and her attacker. *They aren't enhanced.*

Jess burst from the van, thrusting hard on the wheels, accelerating off the lift and whipping the chair around to put himself between Saber and the threat to her. *Get behind me. The other one is coming around.*

Was he kidding? Did he really think he could fight two huge men from his wheelchair? Saber shook her head. The element of surprise was gone with two dead men on the floor. Their friends weren't going to be so gentle with her. She needed to draw them away from Jess.

"What do you want?" she demanded. "We don't have any money."

"Bitch. You killed Charlie."

"He ran into my fist."

"You kicked him in the head," the man protested.

"Sorry, wrong one." She edged her way around her car, keeping him in her sight while she checked on Jess. "It was the other one who ran into my fist."

"I'm supposed to pound the cripple, before we have a little fun with you." He whipped out a camcorder. "He wants a sweet little video made." The smile faded a little. "How old are you?"

"Fourteen. Who wants a video?"

The man swore. "That's bullshit. He wants us to do you, *a kid,* on camera?"

Who is this idiot, Jess? He's willing to kill you and rape a woman, but doesn't want to hurt a minor. Is he kidding?

Criminals have to have some standards, baby. Jess sounded amused.

The attacker standing in front of Jess held a gun and he looked smug. Jess was quiet, coiled. She could feel his energy growing into something powerful and was surprised that the others didn't feel it. The windows in the van, her car, and the garage shimmered. She felt the air expand and contract as if breathing.

"Shoot him, Lloyd," the man near her commanded.

Saber felt the rush of adrenaline as she leapt onto the hood of her car and drove at Lloyd, her legs pumping out hard to smash both feet into his face. Simultaneously, Jess kicked out with one leg from his wheelchair, the ball of his foot hitting the man's wrist with enough force to break the bones. The gun went flying just as Saber's heels crashed into Lloyd's face, driving him backward and away from Jess.

She tried to land on her feet, but she couldn't get away from the body and fell on him. Lloyd went down hard, his arms flailing, and she took a hit to the face that staggered her. She dug her thumbs into his pressure points to keep his hands from her as she scrambled off of him and went for the gun.

The first man tried to beat her to it, but Jess was there, rearing up like an avenging angel, his body between hers and their attacker. He brought the other man down hard, his fingers digging deep into the trachea.

"Don't you move, or I end you now," he hissed. "I'm going to ease up enough to allow you to talk, but it better be what I want to hear. What's your name?"

"Bill. Bill Short."

"Who sent you?"

"A guy paid us. Said his bitch was cheating on him and he wanted the man dead and her taught a lesson. He said he wanted a video of it. He never said nothing about her being fourteen."

Jess clamped down viciously on the man's

throat. "Don't lie to me. You're breaking in here to steal government secrets."

Saber turned away, trying not to smile. Who would ever think government secrets would be lying around Jess's house? When she got herself under control, the man looked as if he might faint. He was sputtering a lot in his denial. "I'm no terrorist. I'm not lying. I'm no spy for a foreign country. And how did she do that?"

There is no way Whitney sent this man after us, Jess informed Saber.

Saber moved around him and kicked the gun a good distance away without picking it up. *How do I call the others back?*

In the house. Use the phone in my office. He gave her the code, his gaze burning into hers. He was trusting her completely and they both knew it. If she was going to betray him, now would be the moment. *Tell whoever picks up "red flag." They'll send my team and a cleanup crew.*

Will you be all right? He was out of his wheelchair and sprawled across the man. She reached down and righted the chair, placing it close to him.

Jess shot her a look of pure annoyance, and she turned and ran. The house was coded, the security some of the best she'd ever seen, but the moment she was inside, she knew it had been penetrated. *Jess, someone's been inside.*

Not this joker, no way could he bypass security. We may still have company.

Saber entered through the kitchen, moving silently in the dark. She had a near perfect photographic memory and if something was moved even a fraction of an inch, the positioning was off enough to trigger an alarm bell in her mind. She could be in a house one time and draw an exact replica on paper, a map to her every target. In her own home, where she'd been living for nearly a year, she knew that someone had moved the coffee mug she always took to work. It was off by no more than an inch on the kitchen counter, but it had been picked up and put back down.

She glided silently across the floor, staying out of the open areas, cautious of triggering any motion alarms. If Whitney was involved in any way, Jesse's office would have been the prime target, and she moved in that direction.

Are you all right? I don't like you in there with no backup. I'm going to knock this one out and join you, so give me a minute.

She didn't want Jess inside, not when she didn't know what she was dealing with. *The place feels empty. I'm tracking to see where*

261

he went, but I'll call your team back first. Stay there, Jess, it's easier for me.

Because you think the wheelchair slows you down.

Was there a touch of bitterness there? That shocked her. Jess had never sounded like that, never complained. Was he upset because she wanted to protect him?

That's silly and you know it. I've always worked alone and it's easier to work the way I've always done it. He would understand that. A team didn't take on a new man in the middle of a planned mission, at least not without taking a terrible risk. She was at the office door.

Yeah, someone had tried to gain entry, but it didn't look as if they'd succeeded. She ran her fingers lightly over the door to check for traps. *They went after your office, Jess. Your boy out there might not have known what he was getting into, but he was a diversion. Someone used him to keep us occupied in case they weren't out of the house before we got home.*

Did they get into the office?

I think security held. The codes are intact. I'm entering now, checking for explosives and bugs.

With what?

Saber didn't answer. She could usually

detect a bug, but not explosives, not one hundred percent of the time. Pulses from transmitters and receivers were easy enough for her, and the office appeared clean. She doubted that the intruder had managed to break in.

Your office seems clean but you'll have to sweep the house. The rest of the rooms are lousy with little listening devices.

You can feel a transmitter? There was excitement in his voice. Respect. *Handy talent to have.*

And heartbeats. She didn't know why she told him. Maybe to warn him. To make him back off. Maybe out of fairness, or self-preservation. But she gave him the truth as she picked up the phone. "Red flag," she said softly into the mouthpiece and then she hung up without further explanation.

Show-off. There was teasing respect in his voice and it warmed her.

His office was a bank of high-tech equipment. The real thing. She knew she was looking at hundreds of thousands of dollars. No way was Jess retired, not with this kind of electronics at his disposal. Most of it wasn't on the market yet. *Nice setup.*

Thanks.

I'm going through the rest of the house. Your team should be here in a couple of minutes.

She really hated leaving him out there alone and was torn. Whoever had been in the house was gone now, she was sure — well, almost certain — but she had to check anyway in case that tiny margin of error just happened to be in effect.

No. Jess kept his voice calm. *I need you out here. Lloyd is coming around. And he's not very happy. I'm not in a great position here. We wouldn't want the two of them to get any ideas.*

He absolutely didn't want her in that house alone — not where he couldn't protect her. He'd already made one mistake in front of her, kicking the gun out of his attacker's hand, and sooner or later she'd remember that. She had an eye — and memory — for details.

He didn't mind playing his wheelchair card if that was what it took to get her back to his side. He had no idea if the house was safe. She was still hesitating. *You'll have to help me back into my chair before the others get here.* Okay that was low, but it worked, he felt her immediate response. Satisfaction and warmth mingled together. She loved him. She might not want to admit it, but she loved him.

"What are you grinning about?" she asked him suspiciously as she entered the garage.

He was sitting on the floor beside his wheelchair, facing Bill, who still eyed him with fear. A few feet away, Lloyd was rolling back and forth and moaning. "You don't look like you need much help to me." But she went to him and caught at the back of his belt when he braced himself on the chair.

He hesitated. He was a big man and he didn't want to take a chance on hurting her, not when he could get into the chair himself. *You're enhanced physically as well as psychically?*

She nodded. *Enough. I don't have the muscle strength a lot of the others were given, but enough to help.*

"Let my arms take my weight." Keeping his eyes on Bill, Jess made certain the brakes were locked before lifting himself into the seat. He could feel her pull, her small body brushing up against him as his weight dragged her forward. "Are you stuck?"

"You're laughing at me." It took a moment to get her fingers from around his belt. She leaned into him, inhaling his scent. "I think you're enjoying this."

"Maybe. It's been a while since I've seen any action."

She studied his face. "Are you telling me the truth?"

"I'm sitting in a wheelchair, baby, and it's

pretty damn real. They aren't going to send me out on a mission unless Ken or one of the others carries me on his back."

She saw him kick the attacker, no question about it, and he was going to have to lie — or explain. Another experiment, another part of him artificial. He was genetically enhanced, physically and psychically. And now he was bionic. There wasn't all that much left of the real Jess Calhoun. Once she knew the truth, fear would creep in, because he was far more dangerous than she had ever suspected. That wheelchair had been his lure, his bait.

"But you work for them." She kept her voice low and she didn't look at him.

"I told you I did. They put a lot of money and time into me and my training, angel face. They aren't just going to let me walk away."

Her head snapped around, her gaze colliding with his. "Or me. That's what you're saying, aren't you, Jesse? You're saying they aren't going to let me go so easily."

"They aren't going to let you go at all, Saber. But there is more than one 'they.' We have the good guys and the bad guys, and you're going to have to pick a side."

"Why? I'm out. Let him come after me."

"He's relentless and sooner or later he'll

find you. He's got a tracking system in every one of you. And I imagine you haven't made him very happy running from him."

"I know about the tracking device. He was putting the chips in our hips, but some of those escaping removed them, so he's using a different system. I'm not worried about it, he can't use it with me." There was no humor in her smile. "Whitney thinks he's superior to everyone, and that's his downfall."

"He isn't going to stop, Saber." He tried to be gentle, but he wanted her to understand the consequences. "You have to join us."

Her eyes flashed. "No, I don't, Jesse. Isn't that the point of what we were all trained to do? Achieving freedom for the people? Well, I may not have had parents and a home, but I'm a person. And I want to be free."

"You're a predator, baby, same as me. We live in the shadows and we come out to hunt." She looked young and fragile standing there while he crushed her dreams. He reached for her, but she stepped back, so that just his fingertips skimmed her wrist. *But you aren't alone, Saber. I'm here and I'll stand with you. We'll all stand with you against him.*

She turned away as the first wave of

GhostWalkers burst into the garage, weapons drawn, faces serious. Logan Maxwell and Neil Campbell came in from either side.

"Two dead," Logan reported after crouching to take a pulse. "Two alive." He looked at Jess. "You both all right?"

"Saber has a bruise coming up on her face, but otherwise, we're good. She checked downstairs, but not the upstairs."

Ken and Mari are on the roof. Logan sent the information to Jess and jerked Bill to his feet. "You'll be taking a little ride with us."

"I want a lawyer," Bill demanded.

"Do I look like a cop to you?" Logan replied. "Don't piss me off any more than you already have."

Neil jerked the man to him. "So you like young girls?"

"No! I didn't know she was fourteen. He didn't tell us that."

"Let's go."

"But, my friends. They killed everyone."

"They didn't kill you or your buddy over there. They saved you for us. So you'd better say everything we want to hear," Neil instructed, shoving the man ahead of him out of the garage.

You're such a tough guy. Logan snickered. *The idiot's going to bawl in another minute.*

Grab this one too. He yanked Lloyd up, uncaring that the man's jaw was dislocated and his nose broken. "Get out of here."

Saber watched the team moving with swift efficiency, taking the house while she stood absolutely still, not wanting to draw attention to herself.

Jess's hand enveloped hers. She tightened her fingers, her heart settling into a steadier rhythm. "Let's go in. They'll have to remove the bodies and clean up in here. I want to double-check my office."

"We haven't cleared the house," Logan warned.

"We'll be in the office. You must have swept that first," Jess said. "And they didn't get in."

"Not the office, but they planted very sophisticated bugs everywhere else." Logan handed him one. "Take a look at this. Not one of ours and not one I've seen Whitney use." He glanced at Saber. "You must be Saber Wynter, Jess's roommate."

She nodded. His eyes reminded her of a hawk, sharp and restless and missing nothing. He made her feel more vulnerable than ever. His gaze dropped to her hand, linked with Jess's. Instinctively she started to pull away, but Jess tightened his grip.

"We'll be in the office, Logan," Jess said.

Send her ahead.

Jess's gaze flicked to Logan's face. "Saber, will you get the door for me?"

"Sure." She moved without hesitation, straight through the garage, turned slightly at the kitchen door with her hand on the doorknob, and glanced into the windshield of her car. There was a handoff of something she couldn't make out, but Logan definitely gave an item to Jess and he slipped it into the bag he always carried on his chair. Her mouth tightened, but she kept walking.

Damn him. So much for being on the team. She was crazy for thinking she could make a place for herself. Essentially she was trading one puppetmaster for another. Because if she worked for whoever Jess worked for, sooner or later they'd be sending her out into the field to do exactly what Whitney wanted her to do, and she couldn't live with that.

She sat on the desktop, swinging her legs, and took a long slow look around. The office was huge, bigger than her sitting room upstairs. There was a framed picture of her with her arms around Jess's neck. His head was tilted so he could look back at her and they were laughing. She remembered him playing around with a digital camera he'd been unable to get to work, but apparently he'd managed to fix it.

She turned her head to watch Jess roll through the door. He didn't have even a smear of dirt on him. "You snake. You said the camera didn't work." She indicated the photograph on his desk.

"It was the only way to get your picture. Here, let me look at your face. You have a bruise coming up."

His hands were gentle as he ran them over the delicate bones in her face. "Are you hurt anywhere else?"

"No. But don't think I didn't notice that cut on your head from earlier. I know your male pride is very fragile, but it looks worse than my bruise."

His eyebrow shot up. "Are we in competition?"

"No." She ducked her head. "You scared me, Jesse. You tackled a killer with a gun." Her heart had been in her throat and she'd been terrified for him, but she knew enough to choose her words carefully. He was a man who believed men should protect women, and worrying because he was in a wheelchair wouldn't sit well with him.

"You kicked him."

"Hey!" Logan's voice drifted down from the upstairs hall. "Jess, we need you up here."

"Be right there," Jess called back and swung his chair around.

Saber swallowed her protest and slid from the desk. "I'll go with you." They must have found her field kit. She'd tucked it away safely but maybe not safe enough. It wasn't the end of the world. He already knew she was a GhostWalker. She'd just have to come up with plausible explanations for some of her equipment.

She went up in the lift, holding his hand, trying to find a way to explain the chemicals in her bag. A small group of men were gathered in her doorway. A faint musky scent warned her it might not be her field bag they'd found. The sudden silence had Jess gliding ahead of her, and between his chair and Logan they blocked the doorway. Jess stiffened and she felt the house vibrate with rage.

Saber avoided Jess's outstretched arm and pushed past Logan to gain entrance to her room. Horrified, she stared around her. Bile rose, but she pushed it down. To have someone invade her room was such a violation, but to do this . . . the room stank as if the occupants had had an orgy. Her clothes were slashed to ribbons and every scrap of underwear was thrown around the room, most containing sickening white blobs. The bed had been neatly made, but one of the cleaners had pulled back the covers to find more underwear coated in semen.

Saber pressed her hand to her mouth, shocked to realize she was trembling. She could feel the sympathy in the room, and was grateful the men didn't look at her. She turned abruptly and stalked out.

"Logan," Jess began.

"We're on it. He left enough DNA here to identify an army. This is a sick bastard, Jess, and she's not safe. If this one is connected in any way to Whitney, he's gone rogue at this point. Whitney would never condone this. He's too . . . scientific. This would be abhorrent to him."

"Funny where people draw their lines. Sometimes I wonder what the world is coming to." He paused and looked around at the cleaning crew. "I want this room stripped of anything he may have touched. Separate her fingerprints so nothing goes out but his. I don't want a flag raised on some remote computer Whitney might be monitoring."

Logan nodded toward the crew and walked down the hall beside Jess. "Whitney knows she's here, Jess. I can smell him. She's in trouble."

"Yeah. I got that."

"And she's gearing up to run. He's too close to her this time, he'll nab her."

"I'm hearing a note in your voice I don't like, so don't beat around the bush, spit it out."

"Unless he planted her."

Jess thrust on the wheels and took himself into the lift. Logan crammed his body in as well. The doors slid shut and Jess rubbed his temples. "He didn't plant her."

"Then how did she manage to find you? You're the one GhostWalker conducting an investigation into our chain of command. Tell me how she ended up on your doorstep. When you couldn't find a background on her I told you she was another Chaleen. They're coming after you because you're a good guy, and that makes you vulnerable. You think the best of people, especially women."

"I didn't think at all around Chaleen, at least not with my brain. They studied me and sent someone programmed to be whatever I wanted. You saw it because you weren't sleeping with her." The doors opened and Jess waited for Logan to step out before he shot out of the small space in a fit of temper. "It was stupid, I'll admit that, but I caught on soon enough."

"She broke your heart."

"She didn't have my heart. She smashed my ego, but my heart was never touched. Saber, on the other hand, definitely could rip the thing right out of my body, so she damned well better not be Whitney's spy."

"Could you kill her?" Logan's voice was low, mild even, but his gaze was cool and steady. "If you had to, to defend yourself, could you kill her?"

Jess remained silent.

"For a moment there, in the club, when she realized she was surrounded by your team, I saw her look at you, Jess. She thought about taking you out right then and there."

Jess swallowed his first response — denial. Hell yeah, she'd thought about it. He wasn't certain how she thought she might get away with it, but she'd thought about it. "I know she did," he admitted. "And she had every right to. Because, if she betrayed me, I'd want to strangle her with my own two hands."

A heartbeat went by. A second one. Logan sighed. "You didn't answer me, Jess. Wanting isn't the same thing. I'm not going to let her kill you. If she makes a wrong move . . ."

Jess shook his head. "I'm not suicidal, Logan. I never have been. I lost my legs, not my mind. I'm better off than most, everything else is in working order. And I'm making some progress with the other thing, enough to think there's hope. But if she turns out to be Whitney's, I don't know if I'd know how to face that, or if I could let you take her out. I just don't know. And it's fucked up to be talking about this like she's not going through enough as it is."

Logan shrugged and walked away, leaving Jess wanting to hit something. In the end, Jess went to find Saber. She wasn't in the kitchen or his bedroom. He knew she wouldn't be out in the open. She didn't feel safe. In his home — in *her* own home — she didn't feel safe. He wanted to yell at someone, hit something. Preferably Logan. Because Logan was right and he was wrong. And damn it all, that sucked.

He knocked on the bathroom door. "Come out of there. I want to take another look at that bruise on your face."

There was a small silence. "I'm fine, Jesse," she finally answered. "I just need a minute alone."

"You've had your minute."

She pushed the door open and glared at him. "I'm the victim here, dragon king, so get over being angry."

"I'm angry because a GhostWalker found

me in my own home, lived here, and I didn't even suspect for months. I usually spot a GhostWalker within seconds of meeting one. Sometimes even before."

"Because of the energy."

"Exactly. There's a feel to it."

"Well. Then I get to be angry too, because I didn't know about you. How'd you figure it out?"

"You slipped up and spoke telepathically."

She put her hands on her hips. "I did not. I don't make mistakes like that." She'd been making mistakes ever since she'd met Jess. She'd never felt such a physical attraction to a man, and then, as time went by, such an emotional attachment. Jess was easy to love. And God help her, she was in love with him.

"You did."

She bit at her lower lip, tapping her foot with her restless energy. "Why didn't you say anything?"

"For the same reason you didn't say anything."

"All right. I can accept that," Saber conceded.

Jess sighed. "You know this can't be coincidence that you're here, Saber."

She closed her eyes briefly. She'd known the conversation was going to circle back to

Whitney. "How many lives do you suppose Whitney has ruined in his quest for the perfect soldier?"

"Too many. So you know this wasn't some mystic coincidence," Jess said. "He must have known you take announcing jobs at small, local radio stations." His throat squeezed tight and his chest hurt as he realized the full implications of where he was going with it. And he had to be right. "He orchestrated that accident. He killed three of my workers to create an opening for you."

"Patsy's fiancé." Saber sank down onto the floor and stared up at him in dismay. "He killed Patsy's fiancé in order to put us in the same place at the same time. How could he know you would take me in?"

"How much do you know about his experiments?"

"In our labs, quite a bit, but other places, not much. I know he trained soldiers, that that was his ultimate goal. He did a tremendous amount of psychic research, and he seemed to be very accurate with his placement."

"We're fairly certain he has some psychic ability. How else would he know which infants to choose, which children? Not by looking. He has to do it by touch. He has a breeding program, Saber. When he does his

experiments, he strengthens the pheromones in his couples to match them."

"You're saying I'm attracted to you because of something Whitney did?" The
thought of that sickened her. For once in
her life she had found something that was
free and clear of Whitney and the endless
tests and observations. Someone good and
decent.

"There's evidence that he does that, yes.
In our case, we can't know for certain, but
it would make sense. He would plan to
throw us together and let his work do the
rest."

She pressed her fingertips to her eyes, calling on every bit of discipline that had been
drilled into her to keep from screaming and
throwing things. Even this. Even her love
for Jess Calhoun hadn't been free will.

She caught movement and lifted her head
as Logan came up behind Jess. "I can't take
all of this in. I think Logan wants to talk to
you." For once she was grateful for the
interruption, because she was not going to
have an emotional breakdown in front of
anyone. "I need to just go somewhere quiet
and think about this."

"Saber . . ." Jess waited until she looked at
him. "Whatever he did doesn't matter. I love
you for who you are, not for how my body

reacts to yours. And he can't make love happen. Remember that, will you, when you're thinking? I'll be in my office."

She couldn't talk with tears flooding her eyes and choking her throat so she turned and went back to the only sanctuary left to her — Jess's bathroom.

Damn. Damn. Damn. He had to follow. Had to run them off the road, keep the two idiots from being interrogated before they gave his description. He wanted to scream and spray all of them with an Uzi. Take them out. Screw them. Screw Whitney. They had no right to interfere in his plans.

CHAPTER 10

Saber stood very still in the middle of the bathroom, her body trembling. The room was large, with cooling tiles and wide, open doorways. Jess could roll his chair into the shower. The Jacuzzi tub was huge and she thought about sitting in it and letting herself cry. Maybe she'd brought this on herself with her voice. She'd deliberately used her voice, tried to summon her watcher from the shadows, and maybe she'd succeeded.

She paced for a while and then tried sitting. Eventually the cleaners left along with most of the GhostWalkers. Only Logan remained, and he went into the office to talk to Jess. They left the door slightly open. She was fairly certain Jess wanted to catch her before she went upstairs, but she had no intention of going up. She couldn't stay in that room. Instead, she crept past the office and into the kitchen.

The room smelled comforting and spicy.

The scent made her feel a little better. She made a cup of tea, but couldn't sit still, shaken and uneasy that someone had managed to get into the house, so close to her — to Jess. The clothes weren't the only thing slashed to ribbons. She'd spotted the picture of Jess she had on her bedside table, glass shattered, frame smashed, and the photograph ripped up.

A prickle of awareness slid beneath her skin, into her mind. She took a breath and let it out. Someone was watching the house. Was it the GhostWalker team? Were they keeping tabs on her? Protecting Jess? She stayed quiet, stilling her mind, trying to feel friend or foe.

The unease that would not quiet gave her the answer: that was no friendly out there that she was picking up. She hurried up the stairs, keeping her steps quiet. If she was lucky Jess would think she'd fallen asleep and he'd work with Logan for a while. The GhostWalkers had more than likely interrogated the prisoners and they'd be feeding information to Jess in the office. That should buy her the time she needed.

In her bathroom, Saber scrubbed her face clean, removing the faint lines along her eyes and around her mouth. Adding color to her skin tone aged her by a couple of years, nothing dramatic, and the eye makeup took away the lost waif look she always had without it. She looked at herself in the mirror and her heart squeezed down hard, her lips trembling as the picture blurred into memories she didn't want to ever think about.

Such a beautiful child, he had said, his hand stroking her cheek while she'd looked up at him. *Such a beautiful child and so lethal, so deadly, one of my greatest achievements. Just sit there and play the game with little Thorn. Wrap your hand around her ankle and feel her pulse. There's a girl. You feel it don't you? Her heart, tapping away, that steady rhythm. Just like the puppy. Keep your touch light. In order to win, they can't know you are there.*

But the puppy died. I didn't mean it. It was an accident. Tears welled up before she could stop them.

At once he frowned, looking severe. *What did I tell you about crying? Do you want to go back into the dark? In the ground where bad girls belong?*

She struggled to hold back the tears, shaking her head, suddenly very afraid. She reached for Thorn's ankle. The little girl was sound asleep, her hair sweeping across the pillow, so white it looked like silk from a corncob. She was only about three, and at eight, Saber felt very motherly toward her. Her own heart beat too fast in anticipation. She had to be careful, keep Thorn from any danger. Stay in control. The doctor wanted her to show control. She moistened her lips and absorbed the rhythm of Thorn's body into her own.

Saber forced her body to relax, to simply take in the sound and feel of that small little heart. She kept her touch light, so light Thorn wouldn't wake up. The thump was so tiny but strong. She knew the exact pathways in Thorn's body, the veins and arteries and neural pathways, every line that fed or was fed by that single organ.

She breathed for both of them, air rushing in and out of their lungs. For a moment she experienced a strange euphoria, as if they were both the same person, one in the same skin, heart and minds totally in tune. And then she introduced the small irregular beat. A thud. Wait. Another thud.

Thorn stirred, pain rippling across her face. Her eyes fluttered open and she looked directly into Saber's eyes. Knowledge was there. Understanding. Thorn had always been so intelligent, far beyond what Whitney ever guessed — or maybe he did — and maybe he was afraid of her.

Saber tore her hand from Thorn's ankle.

"I did it. And I didn't mess up this time." She kept her voice triumphant, with no hint of defiance. But she wasn't touching Thorn again. There would be no second experiment because she was beginning to suspect the doctor would have been happy if she'd killed Thorn. He'd been happy when the puppy had died. She'd seen that in his eyes even when he looked at her sternly.

There was a long silence. She kept her head bowed. Finally he dropped his hand on top of her head. "Good job, Winter. You're a very good girl."

Saber blinked to bring her face in the mirror back in focus. She was now white and ravaged from the memory. Thorn. She hadn't let herself think about Thorn or her sacrifices for years, but if there was one girl, one woman, who could outsmart Whitney, it was Thorn. "Be alive," she said aloud. "Stay alive."

She stared at herself, looking for flaws. Her face was smooth and unlined, beautiful soft skin and very large eyes. She looked so young with her too-slim body and her little girl face. No one would ever suspect her of anything deadly. She straightened her shoulders and firmed her mouth. She had skills and she would use them to protect Jess. Whoever wanted him dead was going to have to contend with her. If it was Whitney, well, she'd always suspected he'd find her someday, and she wasn't about to allow him to hurt or kill Jess. If it was some nutcase fixated on her voice, she was going to remove the threat to Jess once and for all.

Pushing aside the dresser, she crouched low to remove the small grill from the wall. The pipe curved back and she had to reach deep to pull her field kit out. Opening the leather case, she surveyed her options. As she studied the various choices, she sleeked back her hair using a stiff gel and then pulled a skull cap tight over it. She stripped with quick efficiency and dragged on a bodysuit so thin and tight it seemed a second skin. The suit acted as a sealant, keeping cells from being left behind when she took out a target. Her clothes were next, very nondescript, something a teen might wear. She pulled jeans and a T-shirt over the suit.

She took no weapons, but she coated her hands with a solution to fill in all the lines of her palms and fingers, making them perfectly smooth, so she left behind no prints or cells, but could still make skin-to-skin contact. It was a miracle invention, one of Whitney's finest, and yet he hadn't turned it over to the government. The only covert use for it seemed to be his own. Originally she'd stolen several bottles with the idea that she might send it anonymously to a research center, hoping they'd duplicate it, but it was impossible to know which facilities he was associated with.

Saber wasn't an anchor, so death, particularly a brutal one, had debilitating repercussions on her. She couldn't afford to pass out on the job, so she added a small vial of liquid to her armament. If she killed again tonight, she'd just have to take the drug and hope it held until she could be alone somewhere safe.

She had to get through Jess's security to the outside without him becoming aware that she was gone. He was in his office with his friend Logan, looking at something he didn't want her to see. She'd have to spot his GhostWalkers, the ones she was certain were out there, guarding the house and Jess. They couldn't see her leaving or returning.

She pushed open the attic door and leapt, catching the frame and swinging up. She carefully closed the door behind her, making certain it sat perfectly so it appeared undisturbed. She'd tested this route a hundred times, so she could make her way in the dark through the space to the dormer where the ventilation grill was. She followed the heating duct, avoiding a misstep as well as insulation, keeping herself as light as possible as she counted the steps to the small opening.

The louvered air vent was a twelve-inch square. She had already prepared the grill, just in case, loosening all the screws with the exception of one. She had her emergency pack stashed there along with her tools. Quickly she took out the last tight screw and simply waited there in the dark, holding the louvers while she felt the night.

There was someone on the roof. Not the enemy — at least not Jess's enemy. Ken Norton lay up there with a rifle in his hands. Mari had to be close. Again, Saber ignored the oppressive darkness and the way it made her feel until she found Mari's position. There was no sound or movement, neither GhostWalker gave themselves away; instead it was more of a leap in the energy, as if power was alive and lay on the rooftop.

The dormer was difficult to see from the roof itself, and neither GhostWalker had any reason to be looking as long as she moved at a snail's pace and didn't draw their attention. Saber carefully pulled the grill inside, taking care not to scrape it against the frame. Now came the tricky part. She had to slip through the small space to the outside without getting caught.

Movement always drew the eye and GhostWalkers had an unerring sixth sense. With excruciating patience, Saber slipped out of the attic into the open air. When she was dangling just a foot above the steeper roofline, she reached in with one hand and pulled the louvers back in position. Only a very sharp eye would spot that the air vent was slightly crooked. She let go and dropped into a crouch, her small feet making no noise as she landed.

She went still once more and waited, knowing those first few moments were the most crucial. The special clothing from her field pack would reflect her surroundings so that she appeared to fade into them. It was one small trick out of many that helped to make her invisible. She kept her energy as low as possible, changing her biorhythm so that she would give very little away to alert Ken and Mari to another's presence.

She knew the first moment they both became suspicious. Their energy spiked as adrenaline rushed. She continued to stay still, to breathe evenly and keep her heart slow and steady, even as she automatically stretched out her rhythm to include them. She could find a heartbeat in close proximity and work with it, even without touch, but it wasn't as easy or accurate. She couldn't disrupt the rhythm, but she could soothe and calm.

She had previously touched both individuals and already committed their rhythms to memory. Each person's bioelectric activity was unique even in a reversal phase. Saber had a finely honed electrical-magnetic pulse when she wanted to tap into the field her body generated. It was so strong, she had to keep her biorhythm very low indoors and around others to keep from disrupting sensitive equipment, both human and man-made.

The wave was easy enough to disrupt if she was touching her target, but she could still send pulses to coax the rhythm in a direction she wanted it to go. The key was keeping her touch so light it appeared to be natural. She couldn't allow energy to rise around her, giving her presence away to the enhanced psychic soldier.

She waited until both Ken and Mari settled back into their normal rhythms, and then she began to make her way over the roof, threading the needle between the two GhostWalkers. She had trained against enhanced soldiers for years, moving through secured areas where cameras, motion detectors, and just about every technologic advance in security had been used against her. The last line of defense had been dogs and enhanced soldiers under orders to shoot to kill.

She didn't flinch as she eased past Mari, staying downwind, keeping her rhythm low so as not to set off natural alarms. She was so close she could have reached out and touched Mari's leg as she slipped by. She eased over the edge of the roof to the attached garage. If she could have chosen a different way she would have, but it was the only safe way down without risking noise. Even soft sound carried at night and out where Jess's house was located, there was little traffic and no other houses.

She had to get off the roof as soon as possible. Ken prowled the area, quartering every inch repeatedly. He might not sense her, but his radar was extremely sensitive and either he was the most thorough guard in the world, or he was edgier than she'd like. She barely made it over the gutters before he came up on her. Her heart nearly stopped beating.

The surge of adrenaline was almost her undoing. She fought to control her body's reaction as she dangled in the air. The tip of Ken's shoe touched her fingers as he stood, surveying the wooded area across from the

Calhoun estate. She hung directly under him, her body blending in with the shadows of the garage, and she prayed Mari wasn't looking too closely at her husband.

Only when he moved to the other side did she allow herself a small breath of relief as she dropped to the ground. She landed in a crouch, staying low and still, while she "felt" the night around her. Navigating through enemy lines without detection required infinite patience, and over the years, Saber had become good at waiting.

She stretched out onto the open ground and crossed with painstaking slowness, like a snail, crawling with her elbows and toes until she came to the high fence. She crouched at its highest point, counting slowly in her head. This was where she'd be most vulnerable, although because she'd chosen the least likely point of entry, the chances were very low that someone would be focusing attention there at that precise moment. Luck sometimes really was the downfall of a great assassin.

The highest point of the fence was on the most open ground. Few would attempt entry there because they could be seen easily and the fence was difficult to climb. She had no intention of doing so. Behind the low-lying shrubs, she lay in the dirt and painstakingly dug a small depression. Using enhanced strength, she bent the bottom of the fence just a few inches so she could wiggle through. She had to flatten her body as best she could, all the while moving at a snail's pace so as not to draw Ken's or Mari's eye. It would be easy enough to shove the dirt back in place and straighten the few inches of fencing when she returned, and no one would ever suspect she had left the estate.

Once outside the fence, she slipped into the woods and made her way in silence. There was little moonlight, which helped. The area was overgrown with bushes and berries and it would be much more difficult to be spotted.

She let her own rhythm slip away from her mind, concentrating on finding another's. Somewhere out there someone was watching Jess's house and they were emitting energy. In that energy she felt a threat. Her psychic abilities were strong when it came to reading energy and auras. She couldn't read thoughts the way some of the other women had been able to do through touch, but she could feel danger miles away. As she made her way through the woods, the impression of a threat increased significantly.

Saber had to factor in the chance that Ken or Mari would become aware of the intruder and come to investigate, and that meant she needed to be on the alert every moment. She smelled cigarette smoke and slowed her pace, going low to the ground as she advanced on the car hidden in the bushes just off a narrow dirt road.

The vehicle was parked behind several very bushy plants. It was impossible to see from the road, and certainly not from Jess's house, which meant that whoever was watching couldn't be in the car. Saber stayed still, waiting for a sound, anything, to tell her where the watcher was positioned.

The breeze shifted slightly. She wrinkled her nose. Cigarette smoke and perfume — and she recognized the perfume. *Chaleen.*

Saber stayed still, yards from the vehicle, breathing deep to keep her body relaxed and her energy output low. The idea that Jess's former girlfriend was spying on him infuriated her, but she couldn't afford to blow her cover with a surge of adrenaline that would bring both Ken and Mari running.

Chaleen was standing on a large rock beside a tree. She was close enough that at first glance one might mistake her for part of the foliage. She wore a dark navy suit and, incredibly, high heels. Her shoes looked absurd there in the woods. She held a pair of binoculars up to her eyes and was studying Jess's home, a faint frown on her face.

With a little sigh of impatience, she dropped the binoculars, allowing them to hang by the strap around her neck, and stepped off the rock, careful not to ruin her heels. Snapping open her cell phone, she walked toward the more open area of the dirt road in an attempt to pick up a signal. All the while, she continued watching the house.

As she put the phone to her ear, her jacket parted, revealing the shoulder holster and gun beneath her arm. She was wearing slim trousers, and when she took a step, the material pulled just enough to give her hold-out gun away as well. Saber would have bet she had another strapped to the back of her waist, right where the jacket was loose enough to conceal it.

Chaleen began to pace while she talked into the phone, her agitation clear. The energy build-up around her was doubling. Ken and Mari would feel the threat and come looking. It was now or never.

"I'm telling you, we'll never learn anything this way. It's impossible. Do you think Jess is just going to spill his guts to an old girlfriend? One who betrayed him? He's a smart man. You continually underestimate him."

Saber crawled through the brush, stalking the enemy. Chaleen had already betrayed Jess once. She wasn't going to get an opportunity to do it twice. Saber moved her body within striking distance, placing herself in Chaleen's path. She needed Chaleen to take another step and stop. Already Saber began to tune her body's rhythm to her adversary's. The heart, the ebb and flow of blood, the steady pulse — those things became her world. A symphony of sound, the music playing inside of her, etching notes onto her brain where she could clearly see the important pattern and how best to gently interrupt it.

Chaleen sighed and took another step, once more stopping to maintain the weak signal. "Does it matter? He has a girlfriend. Seduction didn't work before and it isn't going to work now. Let me tell you something. Not all men can be seduced into betraying their country. You should have learned that when he was captured and tortured. He wouldn't give up the people he was protecting, not even when he lost his legs. No. Absolutely not. Yes, I believe Jess Calhoun is an operative, absolutely, but he isn't one you can use. Accept it and move on, damn it."

Saber curled her palm around Chaleen's ankle without actually touching it. She could feel the heat now. The life. The blood moving and the electricity as the commands of the brain were carried out. With infinite patience she placed the tips of her fingers over the pulse. Light. So light as to be non-existent.

Saber closed her eyes and absorbed the rhythm, the steady beat and the flow of blood through arteries and veins. She let out her breath at the exact moment that Chaleen did, allowing air to rush through her lungs. For a moment she experienced that strange euphoria that came with blending body rhythms. Sharing the same skin, the same breath, the same heartbeat was unique and incredible, an indescribable feeling. The most difficult moment came with that connection. She couldn't react to the exhilaration. She had to keep that same steady beat so that they were one being.

"I did go see him, but there was no chance to get into his office. I've observed members of his team here, but they're friends of his."

Although her concentration was on Chaleen, Saber's warning system began to shriek at her. There was no sound. Ghost-

Walkers rarely gave themselves away with noise, but the energy coming toward her was very aggressive and it was coming fast. Time was running out. It was now or never.

Saber introduced the smallest blip in the steady rhythm. Chaleen reacted by pressing her hand to her chest.

"Look, I'm telling you this is a waste of time. Jess Calhoun is a patriot and he's given most of his life to his country. I'll be damned if I'm a party to any of this. We're supposed to be on the same side, Karl."

Saber closed her eyes, allowing her breath to escape. Chaleen might be an operative for someone, but she wasn't trying to kill Jess. She wasn't enhanced and there was no way Saber could confirm a connection to Whitney. Slowly, with tremendous care, she lifted her fingers from Chaleen's ankle. The heart wouldn't seize, would remain beating normally, and Chaleen would never know just how close to death she'd been.

"I suggest you put your hands where I can see them," Ken Norton said, his voice low, but carrying a threat that sent a shiver down Saber's spine.

Chaleen snapped the cell phone closed and whirled around to face the Ghost-Walker, nearly stepping on Saber. "Don't point that gun at me. You know who I am and who I work for."

Saber inched her way back into thick brush. If Ken was here, Mari would be covering his back, and that left the way open to get back inside the house.

"I thought the CIA had stopped harassing Jess just about the time he lost his legs. Isn't that when you left him because he wasn't of use to you?"

"He never was of use to me."

"No, I'm betting he wasn't one for pillow talk. Go away, Chaleen."

"Kiss my ass, Norton," Chaleen said.

Saber crawled as quickly as she could through the brush until she was in heavier woods. She ran, staying to the shadows, wishing she could hear more of the conversation but knowing eventually Jess would come looking for her.

It took less than a third of the time to make her way back, as she knew the Ghost-Walkers were occupied with Chaleen. She made certain she stayed small and blended into the night so that she didn't draw Mari's eye. Keeping her energy low, even as she ran, kept the guards' sixth sense from tripping.

Saber leapt onto the garage roof, used it to springboard onto the house roof, and crawled to the dormer. It was a little trickier making the jump and catching the ledge, removing the louvers one-handed, but she had practiced, and she managed to make it into the attic before Ken returned.

Breathing a sigh of relief that she hadn't had to kill Chaleen, Saber made her way back to her sitting room and hastily changed.

"You're looking very pregnant, Lily," Jess greeted, glancing up at the video picture of Dr. Lily Whitney-Miller, daughter of Peter Whitney, the man who had begun the psychic experiments.

Lily sat perched in a chair, her face serious and pale, her eyes wide with concern. "I'm due in a couple of weeks, Jess. And I'm not certain we'll be able to stay here after that, which means we'll lose what little advantage we have. It isn't safe."

"I understand."

And he did. She lived in the house Peter Whitney had built, complete with secret labs and eighty rooms and underground tunnels. The sophisticated equipment inside was his brainchild and he had a back door into it all, so he could review everything his daughter did. Unbeknownst to Peter Whitney, Lily had turned the tables on him and had found a way to tap into his computers, so in effect, they were watching each other.

Lily basically lived in a fishbowl where her father could monitor her at will, but she could feed him whatever data the Ghost-Walkers wanted her to while they tried to track him down. Once her baby was born, she would never feel as if the child was safe unless they moved to another location where Whitney wouldn't be able to kidnap him and use him for his experiments.

"I copied a file on a female child called Winter from my father's computer and made a hard copy for you. In one of his entries a year or so ago, he noted she had changed the spelling of her name from Winter to Wynter, so I have no doubt your Saber is this girl. After reading this file, Jess, I just can't risk it."

Jess swallowed hard as he stared at the photographs spilling across his desk. His throat flooded with tears. "My God. She was a baby. He trained her to assassinate and used her before she was even grown."

Lily's image reflected her own horror. "It's worse than that, Jess. He's got a vision now of a different world, one where he gets rid of birth defects and makes humans into superior beings. He calls it a superior soldier, but he wants an elite force of genius, psychic, and genetically superior humans.

He's a megalomaniac and so fanatical he's lost sight of any reality. I accessed the files of one of the children he used for Winter to experiment on — her name is Thorn and he thought her of no consequence because she didn't show any promise for his ultimate plan. It looks as if he still considers her expendable."

"Now we know what happens to the girls who don't meet his standards. They're on the other end of the experiments."

Lily didn't bother to hide her tears. "I don't know how you're going to stop him, Jess. I really don't. He's a multibillionaire and has research facilities all over the world. He has access to schools and labs and hospitals. He has so many friends in various governments, and the truth is, no matter how they might condemn him publicly, they want him to continue. What he gives them, no one else can."

"That's bullshit, Lily."

"I wish it was. He's my father, but he needs to be destroyed. He's gone past saving doing this." She rubbed her temples, her face lined and worn. There were dark circles under her eyes. "Somewhere he made the descent from greatness to madness. He's completely insane to do this."

"I'm sorry, Lily," Jess said, meaning it.

Lily had suffered enough. He could feel it radiating from her every time she was close to him.

"A child assassin, Jess, trained from the time she was a toddler. She could slip into a room, kill with a touch of her hand, and no one would ever even know it was murder. A heart attack. There is not a single pinprick on the body. She's a perfect killing machine. What government wouldn't give their right arm to have her? Logan gave me the picture you sent. Don't worry, he hand-delivered it, and I've since destroyed it, but she's enhancing her looks to make herself look older."

"I can see that."

"She was trained primarily for covert work. A nice little school where she learned everything needed to slip in and out of any society, any culture, without leaving a trace. She blends. That's one of her greatest strengths. She becomes whatever is needed to get the job done. She's lethal, Jess. One touch. She can kill with a touch."

"I get that, Lily." This wasn't Lily's fault. He had to keep reminding himself he was just pissed off and wanted a target. It couldn't be Lily. She'd given too much of herself to helping the GhostWalkers, but damn it, he didn't want to hear her talking as though Saber wasn't salvageable. They were all killers. Every last one of them.

"He's been tracking her through her radio station jobs. They're watching her, trying to determine if by being out of the compound and away from training she's losing her skills. But more importantly, Jess, they orchestrated her meeting you."

He sighed and raked his hand through his hair. "Then he did arrange the car accident that killed my crew." And his sister's fiancé. How was he ever going to look Patsy in the eye again? And if David's car had been shoved over the cliff, was Patsy's accident an attempt to kill her? If so, why?

"Yes." Lily shook her head. "I'm so sorry, Jess. It's like a game of chess to him. We're all pieces on his board and he moves us around to suit him."

Jess quickly placed a call to the security force to put guards on his sister before spreading the photographs of Saber's childhood across his desk in a surge of shimmering rage. Even the air rippled, the walls breathing as if trying to calm him. "I see his idea of intellectual amusement. Look at the things he did to her. Forced her to kill animals. Tried to make her kill children. Locked her into small dark places folded into a tiny contorted being for hours. Did you see this one, Lily?" He held up a picture

304

of Saber lying on her stomach. She couldn't have been more than thirteen. Several men stood around her with what looked to be glowing hot cigarettes. They had repeatedly touched the hot cigarettes to her skin.

"He didn't want her to move or cry out," Lily read from her copy of the file. "No matter what the discomfort — that's the word he uses in his report — 'no matter the discomfort, the assassin must lie still and wait until that perfect moment to strike.' "

Jess wanted to pound something, preferably Whitney. "She always wears a T-shirt over her swimsuit." He couldn't vent his anger the way he wanted to because he was acutely aware of Lily's tears. She was choking on them, outraged, horrified, and disgusted by the things her father was doing.

"You understand why I can't stay in this house, don't you, Jess?" Lily said. "I can't take the risk that he could get his hands on my baby."

"Of course you and the baby need to be safe, Lily. You've done more than your duty by the GhostWalkers and we're all grateful to you."

"We have to find a way to stop him. I thought it was just the girls in the laboratory where I was. But he has them scattered all over."

305

"That would make sense. If one group was found — or destroyed — he'd have more to work with."

She rubbed her head as if it ached. "I can't find them all. I don't even know how many I'm searching for." She indicated the file on his desk. "Have you read it?"

"I haven't had time yet," Jess said. "Did he use pheromones on us?"

Lily sighed. "Yes. I'm sorry. You'll always be physically attracted to her, Jess, but that doesn't mean you won't ever fall in love with someone else."

"I'm in love with her."

Lily shook her head and leaned forward to stare into the screen. "You're in love with the image she's presenting. Look at her childhood, Jess. She's been regimented, trained, disciplined. She's an assassin. Born and bred for it."

"No, she wasn't born for it, or bred for it," Jess snapped. "She was taken as a child, essentially kidnapped, held prisoner, and subjected to torture. She learned to be what she is in order to survive, Lily. There's a difference. And if you don't know that difference . . ."

A male head leaned into the screen. "That's enough," Captain Ryland Miller interrupted. "She used a wrong turn of

306

phrase, don't read anything into it that wasn't meant."

Jess swallowed his anger. Yeah, Lily misspoke, and Jess's temper was notorious. He had to keep it under control. It was just that the photographs were so heartbreaking. Whitney had documented the journey of a child into an assassin and he'd done it with obvious pride. If ever there was a man who needed killing, Peter Whitney was that man.

As if reading his mind, Lily spoke again. "You understand he could never have an operation of this magnitude — even with all of his money and the contacts and loyalties he's built up — if he didn't have sanction and a lot of help. He isn't doing all this himself. There are too many projects. He may conceive the ideas, but others are taking over the experiments and carrying them out."

Jess pushed back in his chair, this time using both hands to rake through his hair. He needed to see Saber, to touch her, to know that she was all right. He felt bruised and battered after viewing a small part of her childhood. He had been raised in a loving family, with wonderful parents and a sister who adored him. He couldn't imagine what Saber's childhood had been like.

"What else do you have for me, Lily?"

"You aren't going to like it."

"I don't doubt that." He hadn't liked anything so far. Yeah, Whitney had help and whoever he had was trying to send the GhostWalkers on suicide missions. It was Jess's job to find the leak in the chain of command and plug it up.

"He was there. When we operated on your legs, he was there."

Jess felt his heart jump in his chest. The idea of Whitney walking into the hospital and observing his operation with security everywhere was just plain frightening. Lily had been there and Ryland always, always provided her with a guard.

"Are you certain?"

"I was able to hack into your file, and he has all the notes of his observations and conclusions there. He thought Eric and I did a brilliant job. He does say that while you work very hard at physical recovery, you're neglecting the one thing that will make the bionics work and neither Eric nor I have managed to think of it. He wasn't happy with either of us. He thinks we're too focused on other things, me with the baby and Eric trying to play doctor to Ghost-Walkers."

"What should you have told me?" Because the truth was, Peter Whitney was a brilliant man, and if they were missing something with the bionics, he'd know it.

"He mentioned your psychic abilities. You're using physical capabilities to heal, but not mental. He notes that you should be doing exercises and imagery to form the neural pathways to map out the way from your brain to your legs."

"I've been using visualization. You were the one who told me how to work on it. Whitney is full of crap."

For the first time, Lily sent him a faint smile. "He says you're a strong psychic and your brain is very developed, enough that you should be able to form the pathways quickly using visualization through that medium. And I agree with him. You're using the normal part of your brain as well as physical therapy and we're leaving out a vital part of what could springboard you to faster health. Also" — she hesitated and glanced at her husband — "he thought we should have used electrical current to stimulate the cells."

"I'm not certain I like the speculation in your voice, Lily."

Jess reached out and picked up the file on Saber, flipping through the photographs of her life. She looked so young, so innocent and vulnerable. It made no sense that she hadn't touched Whitney's protective streak. How could he look at her and not want to take care of her when she'd been such a beautiful child?

"Jess," Lily said. "He may be a monster, but we should consider his medical opinion on this."

"You want to zap me to see whether or not my nerves respond?"

"Well, electrical stimulation did in fact produce results in lizards who don't normally regenerate a tail."

"Oh, for God's sake, Lily," Jess said.

Several of the photographs slipped out of the folder onto the floor, sliding just out of easy reach. Jess sighed and bent down to pick them up. Saber's hand was there first. It was the photo of her with a small chocolate dog — before and after she'd touched it.

CHAPTER 11

Saber sucked in her breath as she stared down at the photograph in her hands. A strange roaring thundered in her ears. Her heart slammed hard in her chest. There was no stopping the surge of abject humiliation. There she was at eight. Even then there were shadows in her eyes. She could see them. In the series of photographs she was smiling, playing with the dog. By the end she was crying and the dog lay in her lap, lifeless. She still woke up with her heart beating too hard and tears flooding her throat and burning her eyes at the memory of that horrible moment when she realized she had taken that life. She had killed with her touch.

For a moment she couldn't think — or breathe. The roaring in her ears increased until her eardrums ached. *He had exposed the killer in her.* Murderess. Assassin. Evil. She had the touch of death. Jess Calhoun, the only person in her life she had ever truly loved, saw her for what she was.

Jess drew emotions like a magnet and hers were overwhelming. She felt so vulnerable, so ashamed, so disgusting — as if she had no right to be walking on the same earth with him. With anybody. She despised what she could do, what she had done, and for him to see it — to know it — was beyond her ability to cope.

She was vaguely aware of Jess's telepathic touch trying to calm her, to reassure her. She'd been a child. Whitney was the monster, not her. Whitney had forced obedience and he alone was responsible for any deaths.

Saber took two steps back. She wanted to run, but she was frozen. Even her mind seemed frozen. She lifted her gaze to Jess's. She expected loathing. Fear maybe. But not pity. And that made her angry. More than angry. Enraged at the betrayal. "Damn you. You just couldn't leave this alone, could you?"

Jess heard the mixture of rage and shame in her voice. Her gaze flicked to the monitor behind him and he shut it off, keeping whatever had to be said between the two of them.

"Saber, you know I had to investigate you." He struggled to keep emotion — both his and hers — at bay. She looked as if she might shatter into a million pieces.

"I hope you've discovered whatever you felt you needed to know." Her chest was so tight it threatened to implode. Her hand trembled and she tossed the photograph onto the floor in front of his chair. "Everyone's out of the house." She struggled to keep her voice calm and even. "But you've got a couple of your friends watching out for you outside so you'll be just fine if you have an enemy nearby. I'm taking off. I can't stay here." And she couldn't — not with him knowing what she was.

"Saber, stop." He kept his voice low. No challenge, no threat. He shifted his body in his chair, just a slight movement as if easing his position. "This had to come out. You can't hide from it."

She lifted her chin. "I wasn't hiding from it. I lived it." She held up her palm, fingers spread wide. "What did you want me to say, Jesse? I kill with a touch of my hand? That when I was a child, I was forced to kill animals? That he tried to make me kill children?"

He swallowed the bile rising in his throat. "Did he go that far?"

"He forced me to experiment. If I didn't touch them, he would do something awful to them. I learned to be careful fast, and maybe that was the entire point, but I could have just as easily made mistakes, as I did with the dogs. I couldn't always stay in control." She closed her eyes briefly and then glared at him. "I didn't want anyone to know. I had the right to keep it to myself."

"He's never going to give you up."

"You think I don't know that? Do you think I don't know the minute any government gets hold of that file that they'll come after me too? I'm not stupid, Jesse, I'm just not willing to kill anymore." Not for Whitney. Not for the government. She had almost killed his ex-girlfriend. How would he feel about that?

"You can't run for the rest of your life."

A small humorless smile twisted her mouth. "That's exactly what I can do."

"I want you to stay with me."

Her eyes flashed at him. Hurt. Betrayal. Anger. "You've made that impossible. Whoever was on the other end of that connection knows about me. You shared the information. You sent my prints to them and asked questions, raised flags. You knew I was on the run but you did it anyway."

He winced at the stark accusation in her voice. "Saber, you know damned well everything I do is classified. I'd be criminally negligent if I didn't investigate a woman with no past who lived in my home."

"I've lived here nearly a year, Jesse. Why now? Why all of a sudden?"

"I didn't push it before because I thought you were a woman on the run from a husband who hurt you. But you spoke telepathically and I had no choice. Whitney has people everywhere. He's so connected he can place anyone just about anywhere he wants — including the White House. I couldn't take the chance that you might be working against us."

"You know what? It doesn't matter." She had to get out before she began to cry. Once she started, she'd never be able to stop. Jess had represented hope. Home. Love. A chance. It was all gone in one single moment.

She backed out of the room, unable to bear looking at those photographs. Unable to bear that he had allowed someone else to see them. Unable to bear that they even existed in the first place.

"Of course it matters." Jess followed her, tossing the file aside and pushing hard on the wheels of his chair to glide across the floor and keep pace with her. "We protect our own, Saber. No one else is going to have access to that file. There may even be a way to destroy Whitney's data from his computer."

She sent him one smoldering look over her shoulder. "He's backed it up and I can guarantee your friend has as well. They're going to want to *study* me, Jess. They'll want to figure out how I do it and if it can be duplicated. I lived in hell and I'm not going back. Not for you and not for anyone else."

She was moving faster, heading for the back of the house. She wasn't going to take her things. If he let her leave, if he didn't stop her, she would vanish into thin air.

"Saber, don't do this."

"You gave me no choice." She took off running, cutting through the exercise room toward the back veranda.

He had one chance to stop her. She could outrun him in the wheelchair, but not if he used his legs. It was now or never, the most important moment in his life. He forced his body to his feet, his legs shaky, but he was determined. She glanced over her shoulder and her face went white. She skidded to a halt as he took a tentative step, then a second one. He went crashing to the floor, sprawling full length, his body hitting hard.

Jess cursed, fury edging his vision black as he sat up, smashing his fist into his useless legs. Across the room, Saber gasped and hurried back toward him. Then she slowed and stopped again, shaking her head.

"Damn it, Saber."

He saw it on her face. She was going to leave him on the ground. She was really leaving. She spun away from him and started back across the room toward the door.

With every bit of determination in him, Jess pushed himself up, forcing his useless legs to work. He drew the map in his head exactly as his doctors had taught him and sent command after command to the nerves and muscles encasing his bionics. *They would work. Work, damn you. I'm not losing her.* He felt a burst of pinpricks up and down his legs, sparks burning holes through tissue. There was no tentative step this time. He ran after her.

Saber caught at the doorknob to yank open the door. It was torn from her hands and slammed shut, power swelling the room. The window slammed closed. She hadn't known he could do that, move objects without touching them. What did she really know about him? She glanced over her shoulder and saw him coming. And then it registered. Jesse was on his feet.

He was big. Bigger than she'd realized. And strong. She knew his strength. He worked out daily and lifted his body weight over and over with his arms. She never thought she'd see him on his feet, and he was catching up fast, his longer strides eating up the distance between them. His gaze locked on her, fire in his eyes, a fury she'd never seen before, and there was ruthless determination on his face.

The shock of seeing him on his feet stole her breath. She opened her mouth but nothing came out.

You can walk. You miserable son of a bitch, you've been sitting in that chair the entire time making a fool of me and you could walk.

She could barely think with the betrayal. Sheer rage burst through her veins, spread through her like a wildfire. "You rotten bastard. You're a worthless, miserable, *manipulating* liar, no better than Whitney."

Before she could say anything else, Saber's feet were swept out from under her, dropping her ruthlessly to the thick mat. Jess caught her before she landed and rolled so he took the brunt of the landing himself. She found herself on top of him, her body against his, her face inches from his. His arms closed tightly around her, holding her in place.

"Stop struggling, damn it. You're angry and hurt and you feel betrayed. Maybe you even have a right to what you're feeling."

"Maybe?!"

"Yes, maybe, damn it. Put yourself in my shoes. What would you have done differently?"

"Well . . ." She broke off then tried again. "I wouldn't have betrayed you." She pushed at him again. "And you're holding me against my will. Get off and let me out of here."

"Listen to me, Saber. If, after we talk, you still want to leave, then I'll abide by your decision, but not like this, Saber. At least give me a chance to explain."

"Aren't you afraid?" she hissed, furious that she couldn't break his grip.

"Of what? You? You'd never hurt me, Saber, not in a million years."

"Don't be so certain."

"I'm absolutely certain. Do I look afraid?"

"You look like a liar. You pretended to be in that chair when all this time you could walk. And you pretended to care about me when all this time you were betraying me, selling me out to your friends."

"You know better than that." His thigh hooked over both her legs, effectively stilling her struggles. "Stop. You aren't going anywhere until we talk."

"I don't want to talk to you."

He rolled, pinning her beneath his much larger body, and then caught her wrists together so he could use his other hand to force her to look at him. "Well, you have to talk to me, Saber."

For a few moments her gaze warred with his, her body tense.

"Winter," he tried out her real name.

Her head snapped up, eyes smoldering. "What did you call me?"

He took a firmer grip on her. His chair was in the other room and if she got away, she was gone and he'd never see her again, because after that one burst of strength, he had no more feeling — none at all — in his legs. They lay heavy and useless on the floor. "I thought you might like to be called by your given name."

"Don't call me that. I hate that name. He gave it to me and I despise everything it stands for."

"Good. Because I like Saber much better. It suits you." He would always think of her as Saber.

"I'm never going back there, Jesse. *Never.* I'll do whatever it takes to keep out of his hands."

"No way are you going back." He locked his gaze with hers. "I'll protect you, I swear I will, Saber."

"You can't stop him, Jesse, no one can."

"Maybe not as individuals, but as a group, the GhostWalkers are pretty good at defending their own. And you're one of us."

She gave a small snort of utter derision. "Who in the hell is ever going to accept me? You know that's not true."

He went very still as the realization hit him. All the anger, all the fury, as rational as it had been, covered the one thing that she feared most. Saber thought of herself as an unlovable monster. Someone beyond redemption. He wanted to pull her into his arms and hold her tight, but he didn't dare — not yet.

He leaned close to her. "Baby, listen to me. If you don't believe anything else, believe this is the place and I'm the man who can accept you — who wants you."

"Let me up, Jesse," she said, trying to hold on to her anger when she felt it slipping away. She was tired of fighting, tired of running, tired of being scared. Most of all, she was tired of loathing herself. "Although this is a waste of time on so many levels."

The warmth of his body was beginning to creep into the arctic cold of hers, melting the ice around her heart. The caress in his voice, the look of love in his eyes, sent heat curling in the pit of her stomach. She didn't want to think about how much she loved him, or how cute his smile was. Or how hot his body was. She wanted to hate him. No, she didn't want to feel anything at all. "Do you really think anyone is going to accept me into their lives? Your team? Your family? They won't know what I am."

He couldn't help leaning in to inhale the scent of her, to nuzzle briefly the warmth of her neck. "You're the one who can't accept yourself, Saber. I'm used to the different psychic gifts the GhostWalkers have, and make no mistake, you're a GhostWalker."

Tears clung to her lashes and her gaze shifted away from his, even though he held her chin firmly to keep her looking at him. "I'm an aberration. A monster. A child killer. For God's sake, Jesse, you read the file. I made my first human kill when I was nine years old. I'm not like you or the others. I'm a human killing machine. If Whitney could manage to get me an invitation to the White House to a dinner, I could get close enough to the president to kill him right under the nose of the Secret Service and no one would be the wiser. As he was having a heart attack, I could even look as though I were trying to help him, and neither he nor his bodyguards would ever know I was killing him. You tell me how that makes me one of you."

He let go of her wrists and framed her face with both hands. "That makes you exactly like the rest of us — *exactly*. Do you think none of us ever made an accidental kill? We have powers we weren't meant to have and we have to learn how to control them. Every single one of us knows what it feels like to be afraid of what we are and what we can do."

Saber opened her mouth to reply, but then his words really penetrated. She hadn't thought too much about the others and what they could or couldn't do. She didn't know. Jess had just made the door slam shut and he'd been across the room. What else could he do? What could Mari and Ken do? Or Logan? She'd been kept separated from others like her because assassins weren't members of a team. They were loners. They worked in secrecy to carry out their mission. She had never even had a real friend — with the exception of Thorn — and even then, they hadn't seen each other often.

"Let me up, Jesse." She couldn't reason with his body so close to hers and she had to keep her mind on her goal. Survival.

She squirmed, her body rubbing in temptation over his, and he closed his eyes and absorbed the feel and shape of her.

"If I let you up, I lose any advantage I had. In any case, I think you knocked the wind out of me when you threw that elbow. I can't move." His body was as hard as a rock and he made no attempt to hide it from her, moving seductively, pressing her closer into the cradle of his hips.

Color swept along her high cheekbones. "You're moving just fine. Now get up."

"Actually, I can't." His arms tightened possessively, his mouth tasting the scented skin at the hollow of her throat.

His tongue felt like a velvet rasp, moving over her pulse, leaving tiny darts of fire racing over her skin. Her body, of its own volition, melted into his, turning boneless and pliant, catching fire from his, even when her brain screamed at her to not react.

"You betrayed me." The accusation came out desperate because she felt desperate. Jess Calhoun was her enemy because he was the only one who could stop her from leaving.

"Saber, you've been just as well trained as I have. And I know Whitney well enough to know he taught you all about security clearances and need-to-know. You're black ops, covert, and you absolutely know what that means. I work for the government. When it comes to national security, there's no backup in me. I'm sorry if it feels like betrayal to you, but I can't compromise my country because I'm in love with you."

She struggled again. "If you don't let go of me, you're going to end up hurt."

"You want me to let you go, Saber? If you really think I betrayed you, if you really think I'm no better than Whitney, then do it — kill me now."

She held her body stiff, her expression closed to him, but he refused to look away from her. He gave her a little shake. "Do it. I know you can. You hear my heartbeat." He dragged her palm over his chest and held it there. "Either way, you're ripping out my heart, so do it right."

"Stop it. You know I can't." Tears shimmered in her eyes. "I know you aren't like Whitney. Don't push so hard."

"You're afraid, Saber. You're fighting me — us — because you're afraid to be crushed, to give yourself to me when I might betray you. Really betray you. You're afraid to give me your heart because you're afraid I could hurt you worse than anyone ever has. Why would you think that, Saber?" He held her face so that she was forced to look at him when she wanted to turn away from the truth. "I'll tell you why. It's because you love me. You love me so much it scares you.

And you know how I know that? Because I love you, just as much. All of you, every part of you, from that poor little child who was forced to kill, to the beautiful, courageous woman who's trying so hard never to kill again. I love you, Saber. I love you. And, if you leave me, you might as well kill me before you go, because I will be dead without you anyway."

"Stop, Jesse. Stop. You have to stop."

"You can run for the rest of your life, but for what? What kind of life will you have? Alone? Without me? On the run? Stay with me, Saber. I can't promise he won't come after you, but I can promise you that you won't have to fight him alone when he does."

She'd been alone for so long until Jess. Then she'd made a home. A life. She had a best friend who made her laugh. Who could talk intelligently on most any subject. She had a man who made her feel beautiful even when she wasn't. And sexy. She'd never felt that way in her life until he'd opened the door to her and she'd seen the slow burn start in his eyes.

How could she ever bear giving him up and going back to living in the shadows? *Pretending?* His mouth was warm against her neck. His lips felt soft and firm. She wanted this, the hard strength of his arms, the exciting demands of his male body, the pure velvet magic of his seeking mouth. His lips burned a trail of fire from her throat to the side of her trembling mouth. There was no thought of resistance — how could there be?

Saber found herself smoothing her sensitized fingers over the definition of his muscles, feeding her fire, his fire. She was melting, boneless, fierce excitement and moist heat.

Jess shifted his weight, rolled her beneath him, his mouth fastened hungrily to hers, urgently feeding on her sweetness. His hand spanned her throat, feeling for her telltale pulse, the satin heat of her skin. His fingers splayed out, tracing her collarbone, fingertips caressing the soft swell of her breasts. Jess's mouth was merciless, demanding her shyly ardent response.

He slid his hand up the line of her hip, her narrow rib cage, pushing the thin material of her shirt up out of the way as he did so. His palm found her small, nipped waist, rested there possessively, slid around to her back, wanting to explore every inch of her flawless skin. The tips of his fingers touched a rigid raised circle and then found a second one.

Saber stiffened instantly, tore her mouth from his, hands pushing hard against the heavy muscles of his shoulders. His black gaze was riveted to her transparent face, picking up the jumble of confused emotions. A hint of desperation, fear, even revulsion. The smoldering, sultry desire was fading from her haunted eyes, but her lips retained the brand of his mouth.

Jess brought up his arms, locking her to him. "Stop struggling, Saber," he ordered gruffly.

"Let me go. I can't do this. I really can't. I'm sorry, I thought I could, but . . ."

Saber flung herself sideways the instant she felt Jess loosen his hold. She had known he would, he was always so conscious of his strength, careful never to actually hurt her. Jess swore as she tumbled from his arms to the mat, as she scrambled to put a safe distance between them. He caught her ankle, brought her up short.

"Jesse. Let go. I have to get out of here." She sat up, panting for breath, her face white, desperate, the plea in her voice close to terror.

Jesse's heart turned over, every nerve in his body responding to her desperation, but he knew his hold on her was as fragile or as strong as the fingers circling her ankle.

"Settle down, baby," he said softly, gently. "Just sit there, Saber, because I'm not letting you go. Not now, not ever. We belong and you know we do."

"Do you really think this is going to end happily like some fairy tale?" She dashed tears from her face. "I've never even read a fairy tale, Jesse. Back when I first met you and you mentioned them to me while you were teasing me, I lied and said I had my favorites, but I never in my life have read one."

"Well, I believe in fairy-tale endings," he told her. "My parents have been together for years and they're still very much in love. I want a family, Saber — with you."

Her face paled visibly. "Don't say that."

"Don't say what? That I love you? That I want you for my wife and the mother of my children? That I think it's possible for us to have a life together? I have a friend who is married to a GhostWalker. She was raised in an asylum. She starts fires accidentally when the energy builds around her. She didn't think she could have a life either, and believe me, Whitney was after her. She made it out. She can't be around too many people, but she and her husband, Nico, have a wonderful home and a good life. We can too, if we want it bad enough. I want it bad enough. You just have to want it too."

Her eyes clung to his, so blue they were nearly purple, tears increasing the effect. A man could drown in her eyes. Slowly, inch by inch, Jess eased himself into a sitting position. She looked so shocked he wanted to take her into his arms, but he hadn't won — not yet. His hold on her ankle tightened fractionally. "Come here and show me what's on your back that sent you into such a panic."

Saber's eyes widened, startled. She shook her head.

She slid away from him across the mat as he tugged on her leg. Saber lost her balance and sprawled forward, facedown right at his side. He threw his weight over her, pinning her beneath him.

Jess shoved the material of her blouse up ruthlessly, exposing her slender back. Everything in him froze, stopped, his heart, his lungs, his blood, even his brain. Then white hot anger shot into him, consumed him, ate him up. Even seeing the photographs couldn't have prepared him for the sight of her scarred back.

With gentle fingers he traced the line of each round raised scar. "They put out cigarettes on you." His voice was calm, low even, but something murderous and ugly rose up in him, something he hadn't known existed. The walls expanded and contracted. The floor shimmied as he breathed to try to maintain control.

Saber went still beneath his hands, her muted weeping tearing at his heart. Jess bent his head, the warmth of his mouth on her skin, his tongue gently tracing each line, punctuated by a hundred kisses.

She shuddered and he remained still, his lips over one of the scars, while the tension drained out of her and he felt her hips move, an involuntary small shift, but enough to let him know she didn't want him to stop. He pushed her shirt completely out of the way and swept aside her flesh-colored bra.

His hands caressed the sides of her body, beneath her arms, the soft curves of her breasts, rib cage, and waist. His mouth continued to move over her back, a healing, soothing, somehow erotic feather-light touch that stirred her body to life despite every command her brain was trying to give to save her. His hands went lower, to her denim-clad hips, and then slid around to the front of her jeans to the zipper.

Saber caught her breath and closed her eyes against the rush of sensation, her breasts crushed against the mat, nipples suddenly erect and sensitive. His hands hooked in the waistband of her jeans and peeled them from her body. She lay still, face buried in the crook of her arm, tears on her face, her body alive with a sudden growing need.

She wanted him, had always wanted him, from the first moment he'd opened the door. Then it had been purely physical attraction, her body recognizing his in some primal way, but now — now — it was love for him that was so overwhelming, so consuming it had even devoured self-preservation until only he was important. Only Jess. Being with him. Loving him. Forgiving him.

He didn't care that she carried death in her touch. His touch was loving, healing, sexy, everything she'd always wanted and never dared let herself dream about.

Jess tossed aside his clothes. This wasn't the bedroom, it wasn't even the thick carpet in front of the fireplace, but this was where he was going to make thorough, passionate love to Saber Wynter. His hand smoothed over the firm muscle of her buttocks, teeth nipped gently. He pushed against her thigh, allowing her to feel the hot heat of his thick arousal. His mouth sought her bare skin again. He took his time, wanting to explore every inch of her, wanting to know every secret hollow, every shadow. His hands shaped her legs, stroked, and caressed.

Saber moaned softly as he slid his hand along the inside of her thigh and pushed against the rush of damp heat.

Very gently he turned her over and simply stared at her tear-streaked face for one long moment before bending his head to hers. His tongue tasted tears, his lips roamed over her face, her neck, her throat, and settled on her mouth again.

Her arms slipped around his neck, her lips parting to accept him, to draw him into her silky soft mouth. She followed his lead, letting him explore her mouth while she did the same, her touch electric to him, innocent but alluring. He could stay there forever, his soft body against hers, his hands exploring, arousing her, caressing all the while as her mouth moved against his, her tongue stroking his in a small tango of growing need.

Saber lowered her lashes as his lips reluctantly left hers and traveled over her face and neck. Her body raged with fires out of control and needs she couldn't resist. When his mouth closed over her breast, a strong pull sent liquid fire pulsing in welcome.

"Jesse." His name came out in a sigh — a surrender — her hands seeking the defined muscles across his back.

"I know, baby. It's all good. We're good." He murmured the words against her breasts, alternating between suckling, using his teeth with small, gentle scrapes, and swirling his tongue over the nips until she was gasping for breath.

He continued his investigation of every inch of her satin skin, sliding lower over her flat stomach. He found himself smiling at the triangle of silky raven curls at the junction of her legs. Wild. Sweetly scented.

Saber cried out, caught at his hair as he lowered his head and took a long, slow taste. "Jesse." Her hips bucked and her head thrashed as sensations crashed over and into her. She couldn't get out more than his name, and she wasn't certain he could even understand her.

His tongue stroked and caressed, found her most sensitive spot and teased and tortured, stabbed deep, went shallow until she couldn't think or breathe with the building tension. She needed him. Needed something. But soon. Now. In another minute she was going to be begging.

Jess couldn't wait then. Her fire, her damp heat, the feel of her satin skin drove him to depths of craving he had never known. He was always in control, yet he was skimming the edges this time. He wanted to go slow, to be careful, to make certain this moment was earth-shattering for her. With care, he eased aside her knees, poising above her, his dark eyes meeting her blue ones.

"I've never done this before," Saber admitted, her voice shaky.

"I know." But she was trusting him with more than her first time. More than the giving of her body to him, and both of them knew it. He pressed the hot broad head of his shaft against her and began to ease into her, inch by slow inch.

Saber gasped at the feeling of being stretched, invaded. Her body recoiled from his and her hands caught at his wrists.

"Relax, baby, let me do the work, I'll be gentle," he promised.

Her body was a tight velvet tunnel of incredible heat, so small, so fiery. He shuddered with the effort to control himself and waited for her small nod of consent. He gathered her legs over his arms and drew her closer, lifting her as he thrust deeper. Her fingers clawed at the mat for support and her womb clenched.

He could feel the thin barrier protecting her, and he moved again, one strong surge, even as he bent forward, swallowing her soft cry with a kiss. Once again he was still, concentrating on her mouth, on letting her body get used to his. She was so tight, so hot, he desperately needed to move, but he kissed her until she began to relax again and he could see trust in her eyes.

Jess moved then, gentle long strokes designed to keep that beautiful, sultry look in her eyes. Her breathless little cries added to the surging heat. "God, you're beautiful," he said, meaning it.

This was her first time, and despite all the women in his past, he felt as if it were his as well. Not sex. Not lust. Pure magic. Body, soul, mind, hot silk, raging fires, he never wanted this to end. Never. Her body gripped his convulsively, liquid velvet, white hot, and he cried out, all his love, his life, his future in the husky call of her name.

"This is how it's supposed to be, Saber." He could feel his body tighten, heat sweeping up from his legs and pouring through his body. God. He loved her. *Loved* her, with everything in him, everything he was.

He didn't want to stop, wanted to stay in her body, skin to skin, his heart pounding right along with hers. This was love, this agonizing fist of lust that gripped his body and wouldn't let him go. And it was love, the same fist, wrapped around his heart and squeezing with such strength and emotion.

This was what coming together with a woman was meant to be, the frenzy of hunger and tenderness. He had thought it impossible for a man like him to love a woman and have a family, that his need for combat would supersede all feeling for a woman. But he knew now that if Saber asked it of him, he would walk away from the service, give up everything he'd ever worked for in his life, to be with her.

He pulled her closer and bent down to find her lips with his. Long kisses, mouths mating, over and over, losing himself in her velvet heat. He wanted her to feel the way he was feeling, the heat and fire, but more, the overwhelming truth that they were meant for each other — that they belonged. She moved under him, her body tightening around his, the muscles rippling with her orgasm, taking him so that he thought he might be imploding from the inside out.

Saber felt as if she were exploding into fragments, earth-shattering quakes rippling through her body, colors and lights flashing wildly in her head. She clung to Jess, her safe anchor in a raging storm of pure feelings. She had no idea she made a sound, yet her voice mingled with his in the silence of the gym.

Jess eased off of her to lie at her side, one

arm curved possessively around her waist. He could smell the combined scent of their lovemaking, a musky sweetness that seemed to enhance the feeling of joy, of completeness sweeping his body. He felt Saber shiver and realized he couldn't simply jump up and get her a blanket with his legs back to their useless state.

Jess propped himself up on one elbow to study the delicate perfection of her body. She was very small but she had curves and incredible lines to her figure. He bent his head, needing to taste her skin again, his mouth craving the sweetness. "We were meant to be, Saber. Whitney and his pheromones can go to hell. This was us. You and me loving one another."

Saber turned her head, long lashes lifting to study his features carefully. Jess laced his fingers through hers. "I had no idea it would be like that," she whispered softly, slightly awed.

"I'm sorry I hurt you." His fingers splayed across her stomach because he had to touch her, to see his hand on her skin, to feel how soft she was.

"Only for a second," she assured. "Thank you for being so careful." Nothing was ever going to be the same. *She* wasn't ever going to be the same.

"I meant what I said, Saber." His finger-tips brushed the silky V between her legs, touched a tight curl. "I love you. I want you to stay with me."

Just the feel of his fingers on her caused a ripple of intense pleasure, a rush of damp-ness. Beside her, his body was stirring to life and he allowed it, bending his head to a taut, inviting nipple. He would have all the time in the world to make love to her; he was not going to take chances on making her any more sore than she was already go-ing to be. The excitement, the freedom to touch her was incredible.

He lifted his head, feeling her shiver again. "Come on, angel face, let's get you into a hot bath. You're going to catch cold lying here." He leaned into her again to kiss the tip of her nose and then the corner of her mouth. "You'll have to get my chair. It's in the other room." He hated saying that. Needing her to get it for him.

She frowned. "But you ran, Jess. I saw you. And you kicked that man in the garage. How could you do that if you need the wheelchair?"

"It's a long story." He was going to have admit to agreeing to the bionic operation — and that so far, it hadn't worked all that well. This had been the first time he had

had any degree of success. It gave him a measure of hope, but even now, instead of cramps and spasms and pinpricks, he felt no sensation at all.

She sighed. "One you're going to tell me."

"You won't like it."

"Probably not." She caught his face and kissed him before getting to her feet.

Saber gathered up her clothes a little unsteadily, out of long habit putting her shirt on to cover her back. She left it open, liking the stark hunger in Jess's eyes as his gaze dwelt on her creamy breasts and tight, black curls. He made her feel sexy and beautiful.

When she came back with his chair, Jess wasn't the least embarrassed to pull himself, totally naked, into it. Saber was looking at him with such a sensuous, tender look, it made him feel as if he were the greatest lover of all time.

She followed him into the master bathroom with its huge Jacuzzi. Jess could hardly drag his gaze from her body long enough to fill the tub. He got in first because it was easier to maneuver with more room.

Saber stepped into the hot, steamy water. "Just stand still," Jess directed in a slightly husky voice. Very gently, using a soft cloth, he washed the blood and seed from between her legs. His hands were caressing, seductive, producing a rush of warmth, a curl of excitement.

She slid down into the water beside him, gasping a little as the jets swirled bubbles like a thousand tongues licking erotically at her sensitized body.

Jess pulled her to him, settling her between his legs, her small, rounded bottom pressed tightly against his fierce arousal. Her back fit neatly against his chest, his hands came up to caress her breasts floating half submerged, half above the water line. His thumbs feathered gently over her erect nipples, cupped creamy flesh into his palms, his mouth on the vulnerable side of her neck.

"I've wanted you forever," he admitted, his teeth biting her shoulder teasingly. "From the first moment I saw you, I knew you were the one."

"That was Whitney's pheromones."

He nuzzled the top of her head. "I don't think his pheromones could make me feel this way about you, Saber. No, we were meant to be. Destined."

Saber didn't respond. His hands cupping the weight of her breasts, his thumbs sliding in caresses over her taut nipples were driving her crazy. Whatever it was that had brought them together didn't matter anymore. She had committed her heart to him, and that terrified her.

Raging, he punched the wall over and over until his hands were bloody. Failed. It was easy, damn it. *Easy.* Kill the cripple and fuck her over really good. What was so hard about that? But no, they got the crap kicked out of them, and now they were in custody. He'd tried to follow so he could kill them before they could give out his description, but whoever had taken the idiots prisoner had lost him.

Now what was he going to do? What? What? What? He slammed his head hard against the wall, spittle flying from his mouth. He couldn't get near the place, not with all the guards. He had to come up with another place, another location — the radio station. He punched the wall again, furious that his plans had to change.

CHAPTER 12

"Okay, now is the time, while I'm feeling all warm and fuzzy toward you, for you to tell me how you ran after me using your own two legs." Saber tilted her head back to look up at him. She couldn't talk about love. Not without feeling like her heart was going to be ripped out.

"It's classified."

"No kidding? What a shocker. *You* are classified, Jess. *I'm* classified. Of course whatever you've done to yourself this time is classified as well."

"But technically, you aren't in the military because you don't exist."

"You have my file," she pointed out with a small sniff of disdain. "And so does your lady friend."

"Lily. Lily Whitney-Miller."

Saber turned away from him and stared down into the bubbling water. "The doctor's daughter."

"Don't you start on Lily too. Lily gave the file to me, not the other way around. And she's trying to find the other girls — women — that her father experimented on. She saved my life, Saber. I got to know her and I'm telling you, she isn't in league with him."

"How lucky for you that you're so certain."

His eyebrow shot up. "That was sarcasm."

"You bet it was."

"If it's any consolation, she doesn't trust you much either."

Saber burst out laughing. "Actually, that does make me feel better. If she pretended to accept me immediately, I'd be alarmed." She tipped her head back to rub against his shoulder. "What is she doing to you? Dr. Whitney's daughter and the other one. What are they doing?"

"Dr. Eric Lambert," he supplied. "Eric and Lily saved my life."

"And?" she prompted.

He sighed, but really, if Whitney already knew about his legs, what did it matter? "I'm in an experimental program for bionics."

She whirled around, splashing water in all directions. "You're what? I *saw* Whitney's . . ." She trailed off. "Lily Whitney asked you to do this?"

"No, she wasn't involved at all in the beginning. Eric and I were looking at the idea of using the external bionics the army is experimenting with. Eric made a few cracks about a couple of old television shows and how it really was possible to have internal bionics. He said that it had already been tried using a 'smart sleeve' to pick up and register movements of the existing muscles and use that to trigger movement of the appropriate part, but in theory it was possible to regenerate or stimulate existing nerves so the bionics would work completely with my own brain and body. The idea took off from there." He caught her chin when her gaze dropped away from his. "What did you see in Whitney's office? What were you going to tell me?"

She closed her eyes briefly, shaking her head, not wanting him to know, but realizing she had no choice. Not if she was going to keep him safe. She was beginning to realize that loving someone was really difficult. She scooted away from him just in case, because she was going to have to confess to planning a premeditated execution. If Jess condemned her, if he couldn't understand, then there was no hope at all for them. She stared down at the bubbling water.

"Whitney gave me orders to take out a United States senator and his wife. I knew I had to escape. There was no way Whitney would just let me go. Eventually he'd run me down and either kill or reacquire me, so I decided that since I was an assassin and the best way to save my life was to kill Whitney, I would have to do it before I escaped."

She stole a look at his impassive face. Jess waited in silence, giving her no hint of what he was thinking or feeling. She moistened her lips and forced herself to continue. "I knew his schedule at the facility, so I waited for him to come back. He always went into his office late at night to work. The security was unbelievable and he had his own personal guards — enhanced soldiers."

"How many do you think take orders from Whitney personally?"

"Maybe ten enhanced. He has two teams that he keeps with him at all times. They travel with him and answer directly to him for his personal use as well as for his protection. He has others, but they're sent out on assignments for the government. The men who are with him are completely different."

Jess sucked in his breath sharply. "So you're saying aside from Ryland's team and ours, there are others?"

"At least two other teams that I know of

for certain and then Whitney's guards. The men on the teams aren't your enemy, Jess. They're in the same situation you are. They're military and they run covert missions."

He nodded. "Keep going. What did you see when you went into his office?"

"He had a couple of files lying on his desk. One was a file on bionics."

Jess shifted, his eyes sharp and piercing. "What was the other file?"

"The senator and his wife. My targets. He had a picture of them circled with a red marker and the file was very thick."

The only sound was the flow of the jets and the clock ticking on the wall. Jess's gaze met hers. "Could you read the files?"

She nodded her head. "I did. I thought I'd wait for him to come back, so I positioned myself beneath his desk and spent the time reading. He didn't come back. Apparently he had locked the office and left the facility on other business."

"Saber." Jess studied her face, his eyes like that of a hawk, so intent they burned right through her — except that they were cold and distant. "Dr. Whitney's files are encrypted in numerical code."

Saber let her breath out slowly, a chill skittering down her spine, although she was sit-

ting in hot water. "You don't believe me."
She crossed her arms over her breasts, suddenly aware of her naked body. She had tossed the shirt aside, it was somewhere, but . . . She looked around a little helplessly.

"He changes the code all the time, but it's always numerical. *Always.*"

Her chin lifted, and her teeth came together with a small snap, but she forced herself to breathe away her anger. How many times had she believed he was her enemy? Not after making love, but still. "It wasn't code, it was typed neatly in plain English and I lay under that desk for four hours reading both files."

"One of the reasons we have such a difficult time knowing what he's doing is because we have to decode everything on his computer. Lily knows him best, her brain even works in numerical patterns, but it's still time-consuming."

Okay, now her temper was kicking in. She smacked the surface of the water before she could stop herself, sending a plume right at his face.

The water stopped in midair, hung there, and dropped back into the Jacuzzi. There was a small silence while she just stared at him.

"Holy crap, Jesse." There was genuine awe

in her voice. "Why couldn't I get to do something like that? That's just awesome."

"It isn't nearly as useful as you'd think. It takes too much concentration. If anything else had been going on I wouldn't have been able to do it."

"Besides being an anchor, you're a shielder too, aren't you?"

He raised an eyebrow. "We're getting a little off the subject, don't you think?"

She shrugged as casually as she could. "What's the point? I'm obviously not going to convince you, so anything I say is suspect, isn't it? Because, you know, it makes so much sense that Whitney sent an assassin to spy on you. That's not a waste of a serious weapon, is it?"

Jess could see the raw hurt in her eyes and no matter how hard he tried not to let it get to him, his heart was in serious jeopardy. He swore under his breath as he suddenly comprehended the implication of her question. "Saber, *you're* a shielder. That's why in all the months you lived here, I never felt a rise in energy." He hit his forehead with his hand. "How can you shield, but not anchor?"

She cleared her throat. "He said his masterpiece was flawed."

His fists closed and he kept his hands out

of sight. It made more sense to him now, the way she could kill and not suffer immediate and severe repercussions. A shielder was rare. They could keep an entire team from detection. They could shield areas from weapons attacks for a short period of time. Whitney wouldn't want her dead. But if he thought she was flawed . . . "He'd want another one, to work with," Jess murmured aloud.

Saber's fingers curled around the edge of the Jacuzzi, as if she might bolt, but she remained where she was, looking smaller than usual, but her eyes were defiant and her chin looked stubborn and set.

Jess shook his head and raked his fingers through his hair again. "He sent you to me because he wants another one. He arranged for an opening at the radio station and waited for you to take the bait."

Saber shrugged. "You're not telling me anything we haven't already suspected."

"He has a breeding program, Saber. He wants babies. I'm a shielder and an anchor, and although you aren't an anchor, you *are* a shielder too. He knows we'll be physically attracted because when he was busy adding to our genetic code and bumping up our psychic abilities, he made certain of it. He's busy playing God again."

Beneath the bubbling water, Saber pressed a hand to her stomach as if feeling for a child. "I'm not certain what you're trying to say."

"I'm saying you're right, he wouldn't want to get you back, not without you being pregnant."

"He wants me to have a baby?"

"*My* baby. He wants you to have my baby. He has to be convinced that our traits are going to show up in the child, possibly stronger than in us."

She pressed her hand harder. "We didn't use protection, Jesse. I didn't even think about it. How totally irresponsible is that?"

She sounded so close to panic, Jess reached for her and pulled her back to him. "I thought about it, I just didn't care. If you have my baby, I'm fine with it."

Saber shook her head. "This is crazy. Do you see what he's done? He's taking away all our choices. I don't want to get pregnant and worry every second that he's going to take my child away from me."

"He's always going to be hovering around the edges of our lives, Saber. Whitney isn't going to go away because we want him to, no matter whether we're together or whether we choose to have children."

Jess wrapped his arms around her. She

351

was trembling and he needed to comfort her even as he was telling her the truth as he saw it. "He's there, and he'll always be there until he's dead. And even after that there could be others working with him we don't even know about."

She let out a strangled gasp, and he nuzzled the top of her head.

"And that brings me back to the files in his office. Why would he plant something in his office for you to find when he knew he was sending you to me? Because if it wasn't coded, Saber, it was there for you to find and read. Whitney doesn't ever make amateur mistakes. He *wanted* you to read those files."

"On bionics? I could type it all out for you, every single detail in both files, but I have no idea why he would want to give me medical information."

"Unless he knew I was going to be having the operation and needed to get information to me."

"What are you saying, Jesse? That you think he was trying to help? And that would mean he knew months ago that you were going to have the operation. How would he know something like that?"

She sounded frightened and his heart lurched. She was beneath the water, her breasts floating invitingly, her eyes almost violet in her alarm. His hands slipped to her upper arms. "Come here, baby."

He wanted to hold her, comfort her, take the fear from her eyes and replace it with desire. He kissed the side of her neck, bit gently at her shoulder, slid his hand down her arm to try to bring her around in front of him.

Saber's blue eyes darkened. Heated. She moistened her lower lip. "Jess. We have to think about what we're doing here. We're caught in the middle of some giant spiderweb. I'm really afraid."

"Come here." He tugged on her arms to bring her closer.

This time she came to him, a little reluctant, but she moved to stand in front of him. Water pushed between them, the bubbles ferocious, fizzing against his skin, adding to the slow buildup of heat spreading through his body. Keeping her gaze captive, he pushed her legs apart and drew her over him, so she was straddling his lap. She braced herself, using her hands on his shoulders as he cupped her bottom to bring her over his body.

"I know you're afraid of Whitney, angel face, but in the end, only we matter. He's always going to be our bogeyman, but we can't let him stop us from leading our lives. That's our choice. We don't let him rule us or make us afraid to live life."

Her lips trembled and he leaned in to kiss her, capturing her bottom lip between his teeth and playfully nipping and tugging. All the while his hands cupped her bottom, massaging and kneading while the bubbles burst against her bare skin. She rocked her hips, back and forth, a deliberate or compulsive motion that rubbed over the broad head of his cock. Each time she slid over the sensitive head, his body jerked and hardened more.

Jess leaned forward and nibbled on her neck and then teased her earlobe. "I want you to sit on me, Saber, and wrap your legs around my waist." His voice was husky, almost hoarse. The need for her swept over him fast and furious, a vicious fist of lust that only seemed to build as he watched the bubbles fizz and break around her body. He kissed his way down her neck and the slope of her breast. Her body shuddered as he licked the side of her breast and traced the curve with his tongue.

All the while her hips moved in that slow steady rhythm that kept pushing heat through his body. Her breath caught in her lungs and her fingers tightened on his shoulders as her legs threatened to give out.

Jess pulled back to lock eyes with her. He wanted her until he couldn't think straight, couldn't find air enough to breathe. The need had risen sharp and fast when he should have been sated already. Her skin was so soft, all bare, glistening as if the morning had covered her in dewdrops like rose petals. Still keeping her gaze locked with his, he leaned forward and licked at her scented skin, breathing her in even as the pads of his fingers began to explore.

Saber gasped and trembled beneath the stroking caresses. He had to go slow, not simply devour her as he wanted to do. She was all woman, yet this was a new experience and, although she responded eagerly, there was a hesitance that told him she was a little frightened. He had never felt such a fever of absolute need. She tore him up inside with wanting her. For the first time in his life, he actually considered that his control was in jeopardy. His gaze dropped to her nipples, the hard pink tips. He blew out his breath and licked his lips in anticipation.

Saber's body reacted with a convulsive jerk. Her stomach muscles bunched, hands tightened on his shoulders, and once more her hips rocked, sliding the warm, wet entrance over the broad head of his cock. He shuddered, his heart pounding in reaction. That had never happened either, that entire consuming chain reaction of body, mind, and heart dissolving into one single desire so sharp and piercing it became such a physical pain he was desperate for relief. He'd never been so hard, so ready to burst.

Her body was flushed, the creamy mounds of her breasts inviting. He leaned forward until his face brushed against the soft swell, until he could taste with a lap of his tongue. She gasped, a soft moan of pleasure escaping, shredding his control even further. His tongue curled over the nipple in a lapping rasp before his mouth covered her and began to suckle, using his teeth to tug and scrape gently until her fingers bit deep and she threw back her head, arching into him.

His hand slid up her thigh under the churning water. Her gaze, cloudy now with arousal, jumped to his face. He switched his attention to her other breast, interspersing teasing nips with the laving of long, curling strokes. His hand covered her hot, waiting mound and she jumped, her eyes going dark with lust, a soft cry escaping.

"Look at me, baby," he whispered when her lashes swept down to cover her expression. He didn't want that — wouldn't have it. He needed to see her pleasure, needed to see her desire.

He waited, his hand pushed into her heat, his mouth at her breast until she opened her eyes and locked her gaze with his. He slid his finger into her tight depths. She cried out again, eyes glazing over. He curled a second finger inside her, exploring the soft heat, circling her most sensitive spot while her hips pushed hard against his hand. He pushed deeper and her muscles clenched around his fingers, her small, gasping cry sending pulses of fire shooting through his body straight to his groin.

She was in so much trouble. She recognized Jess was binding her body to his. She was in danger of becoming an addict, obsessed with the need for his touch. Pleasure swept through her, and her body grew tight and hungry.

Jess caught her hips and held her directly over his hard shaft. She could feel the broad head lodged in her tight entrance. Fire raced down her thighs and back up into her feminine sheath. Every muscle contracted. He held her still.

"I love how responsive your body is to mine. You love this, don't you?"

How could she not? It didn't seem to matter what he did, where he led, she was going to follow, because she wanted it all — wanted him and the burning pleasure he could give her. She hadn't even known it existed, but now, every time she looked at him, her body was going to flood with heat and need.

Holding her still, he filled her slowly, pushing through the tight, velvet-soft muscles, the fiery channel that gripped him until she had a stranglehold on him. She tried to move, tried to force him to fill her, but he held her firmly and took his time, watching her face and the dazed pleasure flushing her delicate features.

"Do you know how many times, how many ways I've fantasized about having you like this?" he asked, his voice husky, nearly hoarse with desire. "I want to sleep wrapped around your body, my fingers inside of you, my mouth on your breast. When you're in the kitchen in the morning wearing nothing but my shirt, I want to sit you on the counter and devour all that honey simmering hot and spicy just waiting for me."

Her head fell back, a soft groan escaping, his erotic images springing clearly into her mind while he ground himself deep into her, lodging against her womb. Her muscles tightened even more, her womb clenching, her body fighting hard for the freedom to ride him hard and fast. All the while the bubbles fizzed like tiny tongues licking at her sensitive bare skin.

Jess leaned forward and took her nipple into his mouth with a gentle bite, sending waves of heat crashing through her. A small scream escaped, and her nails bit deep. She flooded his cock with liquid fire. Holding her locked in position, he lifted her and then drove her body down while he thrust upward, hard. She gasped as he filled her, his shaft pushing through soft, tight folds, the friction creating a fiery tango of sensation in the sensitive knot of nerves.

She could barely breathe as her body tightened and clenched, every part of her on fire. "I don't know what to do." Because she had to do something or she was going to go crazy.

"Ride me, baby, just like this." His hands urged her into a rhythm. He lifted her hips to let her feel his cock, hard and hot, sliding like so much steel, cutting through velvet folds. His breath came out in a rush and the muscles of his thighs bunched under the onslaught of pure feeling. "Oh, yeah, you're getting it," he encouraged, stopping her just before they were separated. "Does that feel good?"

It was amazing how he stretched her, filling her completely as she moved in a slow downward glide. She moaned softly as she impaled herself on his thick shaft in a long, languorous rocking motion, inducing such pleasure she nearly screamed. His hands came up to tug at her nipples while he drove again and again through her silken heat. Each time was harder and deeper, sending streaks of fire racing through her body.

"You like it hard like this?" His eyes glittered at her, dark with a mixture of lust and unmistakable love. She could see his muscles bunched, his teeth set as he fought for control, fought to keep the pace slow and leisurely while she learned how to pleasure herself with his body.

She could only nod while her hips rose, her muscles gripping and squeezing around him. He was going to shatter her, take her apart before he was done. She lowered herself again while he thrust upward, another slow inch by excruciating inch, killing them both with a riot of sensations pouring into them. She'd never felt so wanton as she arched her body to get a different angle, to feel the thick length of him, as hard as steel, pressed against her throbbing clit.

Her breasts thrust toward him and he leaned in to rake his teeth over the gentle curves. Electricity sizzled, hot and wet from her breasts to her womb to streak like liquid fire through her feminine core.

One hand threaded through her hair and he kissed his way back up her throat to her lips, once again holding her still. She shuddered, her muscles clenching, her body clamping hard around his, the silken walls of her channel milking him even as he kept her hips from rocking. Her head tossed, her eyes dazed and dark with desire.

"You're so beautiful," he whispered. "Like this. Loving me. You're so damned beautiful it hurts to look at you."

Beneath her bottom, his thigh muscles bunched into hard ridges, and then he was changing the pace, taking her over, plunging deep and hard with exquisite purpose, building the heat until it was out of control. Her breath came in ragged gasps as the piercing pleasure built and built until she thought she might not live through it. She felt as if she were burning alive from the inside out, and if he didn't keep filling her, stretching her, if he didn't do something to quench the fire soon, she wouldn't survive.

"Please, Jesse." The soft cry was wrenched from her before she could stop it. There didn't seem to be inhibition or self-respect. She knew she was pleading — begging for release, but the pleasure was too much, it had to end soon or she was going to go insane. Her mind seemed to be shutting down altogether, and her craving for Jess Calhoun knew no bounds.

"It's all right, Saber, love. Go with it. Let yourself fly. Come with me. Just come with me." He gripped her hips and plunged deeper, lodging himself against her womb, swelling thicker and larger than he'd ever been in his life, and his balls grew tight and hard, his thighs shaking.

He moved again, setting a harsh pace, deep long strokes that invaded and receded, each harder and stronger than the last as he pumped into her hot, moist flesh. Around him, her tight, silken channel gripped him hard, milking until the erotic torture nearly strangled him with pleasure. He couldn't stop the bone-wrenching, muscle-tightening explosion as he climaxed, her body melting and rippling around his.

She screamed, the sound vibrating through his groin as he flooded her tight sheath with hot jets of his release, as he surged one last time into her, his hoarse shout joining hers. She collapsed against him, falling onto his chest as he fought to drag air into his bursting lungs. She lay with her head pillowed on his shoulder, exhausted, a limp rag doll, her heart pounding so hard she couldn't bring it under control.

"Are you all right?" he asked gently.

"No. I'm never going to be all right again," she said, meaning it. "Jesse, I was looking for normal. I don't think that's what this is. This is obsession, addiction, something crazy. We could kill each other."

He rubbed his mouth over her neck. "There's so much more. I could spend days, weeks, showing you more."

"I wouldn't survive more," she said, knowing she had to have him again and again. And she wanted — even needed — the more. "What have you done to me?"

"Nothing that you haven't done to me." He stroked caresses over her hair and waited until she stopped trembling, until the little aftershocks lessened to small ripples. "Whatever you're feeling, multiply that by a thousand, angel face, and that's what I'm feeling." He turned off the jets. "The water's getting cold and we're going to turn into prunes."

"Well," she said, wrapping her arms around his neck. "We didn't solve the world's problems, but right at this moment, I'm not caring so much." Because, could he really believe she would betray him if he made love to her so thoroughly? She kissed his throat and nibbled on his chin.

Jess kept his arms around her, holding her to him. "You solved my most immediate problems, baby. I'm thinking we need to get to bed. It's almost morning and we've had a full night."

She lifted her head from where she was tracing the line of his heavy chest muscle with her tongue. "I don't have a bed right now. I'm not sleeping in that room."

"Of course not. I was thinking you'd be sharing my bed."

There was a small silence and she pulled back to look at him. Very slowly she slipped off his lap to move to the side of the Jacuzzi. "I've never done that before. Sleep with someone. Doesn't it make you feel vulnerable?"

"I wouldn't know. I had sex with people, I didn't sleep with them."

"You thought you were going to marry Chaleen, didn't you?"

He shrugged. "We were together, but I don't know that I thought about the future all that much. Maybe at first I thought we'd be together, but after a while, I didn't push it. And no, we didn't sleep in the same bed. I always made some excuse and she was always happy to accept it. That should have told me something."

She raised her eyebrow at him. "You think?"

He slapped water at her. "You can look smug when you want to."

"I know." She really hated the idea of turning her back on him to get out of the Jacuzzi. She didn't mind being naked, but she detested him looking at her back. For some reason, she couldn't overcome the shame, as if somehow she'd allowed the torture. They'd made certain she couldn't touch them, but maybe she could have scared them into believing she would have hunted them down. Now that she was older, that was exactly what she'd do, but back then, she'd been so frightened, and what they wanted from her had been repulsive. She'd loathed herself and her capabilities.

She waited until Jess shifted to first the stair and then the platform before she climbed out and made certain his chair was locked so he could swing into it. She caught up Jess's shirt and pulled it on.

"Chaleen was here tonight."

He straightened up in his chair, frowning at her. "I know that, Ken told me, but how did you know?"

She tried not to look or sound smug, since he'd just accused her of it. "I went out reconning tonight and saw her." She studied her fingernails. "Blew right past both of your enhanced supersoldier GhostWalker guards."

"You got past Ken and Mari? Both of them?"

"It was a walk in the park."

Jess studied her face. It was obvious she was telling the truth. "Ken sent Chaleen packing."

"If the CIA sent her here, Jess, it means they have suspicions that you're more than a SEAL, and if they think that, who knows who else does?"

"You think a foreign government has sent someone to spy on me?" He thrust with his hands, powering the chair through the house toward the bedroom.

Saber followed at a more leisurely pace, holding the edges of his shirt together around her. "Don't you think that's a possibility?"

"I suppose. But I think my radar would have gone off sooner."

Saber put on a burst of speed and caught up to him, catching at his chair to stop him. She waited until he'd turned to look at her. "So, Jess, what if something else is going on here, something not all about Whitney? Yes, I think he orchestrated our being together, but for what purpose? Just to grab me? Why go to all the trouble of the two of us living together for a year? If he provided the opening for the job and knew I'd take it — and who else could have known? — then why not grab me immediately before you called in the other GhostWalkers. Whitney had to have anticipated that move, right?"

"Yes. There isn't a doubt in my mind he wants us to have a child together."

"Well, I don't have a clue why he wanted me to read those files, but this suddenly doesn't feel like Whitney. I don't know why he'd do this when it isn't logical. Whitney may be a megalomaniac, but he has his own logic. He believes himself to be a patriot. He's not going to be giving other countries supersoldiers, so who is leaking the information? Who's looking for confirmation that you're enhanced?"

Jess shook his head, his expression thoughtful. "It isn't Chaleen. Her job is to find out what I'm doing besides working for Rear Admiral Henderson at NCIS. My team has been out on enough assignments to raise a few rumors, especially after the Congo incident. Senator Ed Freeman was involved with that. He's high profile. Maybe it has something to do with the Congo, or the senator."

She nodded. "He was my target. He and

his wife. Whitney wanted them dead. He was in a recent accident and it's rumored he's in a coma."

"He was shot in the head and taken to an undisclosed location. They're keeping his condition very quiet, but you can bet every agency from here to hell and back is looking into it and there are going to be rumors and conjecture about an elite fighting team. Since the CIA was already suspicious, after the senator's disappearance, I'm sure they want answers. What was in his file?"

"Whitney considered him a traitor and wanted both the senator and his wife dead. He actually arranged for me to attend a state dinner and shake hands with the senator. The plan was for me to induce a massive heart attack, and when his wife knelt beside him to do CPR, I would aid her, long enough to release a blood clot into her system. Then I was supposed to disappear before she went down as well."

"You can do that?"

She was so small, yet she held so much power in her slender body. And it was somewhat disconcerting to think she'd been in his home, he'd introduced her to his sister and friends, and he'd never suspected that she could kill with a touch. The innocence in her eyes and the youthful features were all the cover she really needed. No one would ever suspect her. As a shielder, not even Violet, the senator's wife, would have known that Saber was an assassin.

Saber shrugged. "I told you I could."

The significance of what Saber told him sunk in. *She had left the house in full assassination mode.* "You slipped past Mari and Ken in order to kill Chaleen, didn't you?"

She'd hoped he'd missed that. Jess didn't miss very much. "Someone was out there watching you. I was afraid they'd been sent to kill you, so yes, I thought I might do something about it in order to protect you, but I changed my mind."

"Ken came along."

She shook her head. "He would have been too late. If I wanted her dead, she'd be beyond help by the time he arrived. He almost stepped on me."

Jess shook his head, a slow grin of admiration escaping when he knew he shouldn't feel that way. "He's going to hate that."

"Don't tell him. Don't tell any of them." She ducked her head. "I don't want them to know what I do."

"Eventually they'll have to know. You're one of us. We work as a team."

"Assassins don't work with a team, Jesse.

I go out alone. The orders come in and I play whatever part, slip in and out, and no one ever knows it was a sanctioned hit. I'm the weapon everyone's been looking for. I can take out our enemies and no one will ever be able to prove a thing."

"That doesn't negate the fact that you're one of us. We all have different — and lethal — capabilities, Saber. They'll understand."

"Do you really believe they'll walk up to me and shake my hand the way they did earlier? They'll be terrified."

"I'm not terrified of you, Saber," Jess said.

She lifted her lashes. "Well, maybe you should be."

A slow smile softened the hard line of his mouth. Her heart lurched. He looked so sexy. It was no wonder that she'd fallen for him — she would have without Whitney and his pheromones.

"You said that before. I like to live dangerously."

"You're a nut."

"Come on, baby. Let's go to bed." He held out his hand to her. When she put hers in his, he kissed her palm and then placed it on his shoulder so he could maneuver the chair through the wide hallways to the master bedroom.

Saber walked with him. "I've been thinking about this thing with Whitney. We've got him and the sicko who jacked off in my bedroom. Maybe they're connected, maybe not, but I'm leaning more toward the theory that we're missing some vital piece here, Jesse. Something right in front of our noses."

He wasn't going to discount her radar, because he was feeling the same way. Whitney had nothing to gain by snatching Saber before she was pregnant. Not when he'd gone to so much trouble to orchestrate the two of them meeting.

His bedroom was enormous, the four-poster bed dominating the room. It was low, custom built to make it easy for him to lock his chair and slide into the bed without help. The room was always surprisingly neat. Jess tended to toss his clothes over the backs of chairs or onto the nightstand, but everything else was in place.

"I've always been intimidated by that bed," Saber said, stopping just inside the doorway. "It's huge."

"I won't let you get lost. We just have to make certain Patsy doesn't come barging in and find you here or we'll be dragged to the nearest church and married before the day is out."

"Don't even say that. Patsy would be thrilled to catch me in your bedroom. She has visions of you producing like ten kids or something."

He laughed. "My sister would make the best aunt in the world."

"She needs to have children. You'd make a great uncle."

The smile faded from his face. "She was so in love with David. I have no idea how to tell her David died because of me. I never thought my job or the choices I made would ever touch my family."

"Oh, Jesse. Oh God." Saber's hand fluttered to her throat and then shot out to brace herself against the wall. "Patsy."

He stiffened at her tone, pausing in the act of transferring to his bed. "What is it? What's wrong?"

"We have to go to Patsy's house right now."

"Saber, it's four o'clock in the morning. Why?"

She bit at her lip, frowning. "When Patsy was here earlier, I didn't like the way her heart was acting."

Jess straightened up immediately. "What do you mean, you didn't like the way her heart was acting?"

"I don't know. Her rhythm was off."

He looked grim, fierce. "Something is wrong with my sister's heart and you didn't say anything?"

"I tried to get her to see a doctor. I didn't think you knew about me. I was afraid to say anything, but I planned, when I left, to tell you in a letter to get her to the doctor."

"Why did you check out her rhythm?"

His tone sent a chill down her spine. Saber gripped the doorjamb harder. "Someone had dropped a listening device in the pocket of her jacket. It was giving off a small energy field and I picked it up when I was close to her."

"Let's go then," Jess said. "It will take a few minutes for me to get dressed."

Saber hurried to drag on jeans and a T-shirt. Jess hadn't been happy that she allowed Patsy to leave without saying anything, but he hadn't condemned her for it. It seemed that she kept asking him to accept more and more from her. She would have warned Patsy, though. She liked her a great deal and she never would have left without first making certain Patsy knew she had something wrong with her heart.

Guilt didn't ease up as she ran for the van. Jess was already in the garage, rolling his chair onto the lift to take him inside. He caught her outstretched hand as she leapt to join him.

"I'm sorry, Jesse. I honestly don't know if

it's a minor thing that doesn't really matter and will never harm her, but it's just not right."

"I understand." He locked his chair into place and glanced over at her to make certain she was settled. "The thing is, baby, Patsy means the world to me. If anything happened to her . . ." His voice trailed off and the van engine started.

"I know. I'm sorry. I should have told you sooner." She was miserable with shame and guilt weighing her down.

He lost them. *Lost* them. Everything was falling apart. He had to regroup. He could still save this. He went down the stairs to the basement and walked through the wait-ing room. *Her* room. Once he had her where she belonged, her voice would only be for him. She'd speak only when he allowed her, say only things meant for his ears.

Manacles hung from the ceiling and the wall. He had everything laid out for her — ready for her. She would come to love him in time, love the things he could do to her. And she'd know he was her master, the one she was born to please. She'd be what he wanted her to be, live only for him at his whim, at his pleasure. He sucked in his breath. He was so close. No one would ever find this place. Not the cripple, not the supersoldiers, and certainly not that bastard Whitney.

CHAPTER 13

Rain greeted them as they pulled out of the drive and headed for Patsy's estate. Jesse and Patsy's grandparents had left both of them well off, and Patsy lived only a few miles from her brother, the back of her property connecting to the same thick wooded area. A month after Jess's legs had been damaged she had purchased the property next to his and bought into the radio station. It actually took longer to drive to her house than walk through the woods to it, as they had to circle around following the roads.

"What are we going to say to her?" Saber asked.

"I haven't figured that out yet," Jess snapped and then shot her a quick, apologetic look. "I don't know, but I'll think of something."

Saber swallowed hard and stared out the window into the driving rain. The storm was moving in fast. The weatherman had been predicting a major storm for several days and it was finally here, the heavy layer of thick fog blotting out the stars and moon. Lightning veined the underside of the ominous dark clouds swirling overhead, and unease slid down her spine. "I'm sorry, Jess. I should have found a way to tell Patsy without giving away the fact that I'm a trained psychic."

"I'm not upset with you, Saber, just the situation. And I have no idea what to tell Patsy at four in the morning, but I have to go. I feel a sense of urgency, which is silly I suppose, but I just can't take chances with her life."

"She's your family. And I think it's best to tell her immediately and get her to a hospital." She yawned. "I'm actually tired. It's still dark and I'm tired. Amazing."

He reached over and ran his finger along the back of her hand. Her stomach clenched. It was the first gesture of affection or tenderness he'd shown her since she'd revealed she thought there might be something wrong with Patsy's heart, and she instantly felt happy. It was odd caring about another human being. You sort of got sucked in whether you liked it or not, because her affection — and her need to protect — carried to his sister as well.

"I was looking forward to sleeping with you. I love the idea of waking up with you in my bed, wrapped in my arms, your face the first thing I see."

It wasn't fair that he could say things like that to her and make her body go into hyperdrive. But even more unfair was the way he made her heart and soul reach for him. Run to him. Need him. How ironic, considering she'd always been so independent, considering how she'd struggled for freedom. And now Jess was holding her as surely as if she were in a cage.

Lightning flashed across the sky and a few seconds later thunder boomed. The windshield wipers could barely keep up with the pouring rain. Ordinarily she enjoyed storms, but this time her heart pounded and her mouth went dry.

Jess drove down the winding road leading through the thick grove of trees that separated his estate from his sister's. "Don't regret loving me, Saber."

She gave an exaggerated flinch. "Don't be saying 'love,' dragon king. I'm not really used to that yet and I'm letting my mind go there slowly."

"You're crazy about me."

"I'm crazy, that I'll agree with. The rest of

it . . ." She trailed off deliberately and waited for the sound of his laughter.

She loved the sound of his voice, the way it seemed to wash into her body and fill her with warmth and a sense of peace — and she needed peace right now. The storm seemed to be really affecting her, her body wound tighter and tighter, her breath coming in ragged little gasps and her pulse racing.

Jess sent a quick grin, but it didn't ease the fear growing in her. She rolled down her window and inhaled sharply, waiting to feel the night around her. "Slow down."

His smile faded and he did as she asked. "What's wrong, baby?"

"I don't know, but I think you should pull over."

"We're only a few yards before we hit the entrance to Patsy's place," Jess pointed out, but he slowed the van until they were barely moving.

Her heart was racing now and prickles raced across her skin. She tasted fear in her mouth. "Someone is broadcasting tremendous fear. I can hear the heartbeat thundering in my ears and it isn't . . . right."

Jess swore. "Patsy. It's Patsy, isn't it?" He accelerated. "She's having a heart attack."

Saber put her hand on his arm. "No, it

379

isn't that. Pull over and cut your lights. Did Ken and Mari follow us?" She swiveled around in her seat looking for headlights.

Jess did as she asked and rolled down his window as well, trying to feel the flare of energy that signaled something was wrong. Whatever it was, they were a distance away. Saber had to be very sensitive to feel it.

"I'm going in. Pull the van around to the back of Patsy's property and leave the engine running and the doors open. We'll make our way to you."

"That's bullshit, Saber. We don't even know what's going on. We'll wait for Ken and Mari and go in at full strength."

Saber swallowed the lump of fear in her throat. "I don't think that's a good idea. We need them here as soon as possible, but something's not right and I have to try to get to Patsy now." Her hand fluttered against her throat. It was getting harder to breathe. "I have to go now, Jess."

He caught her wrist, his grip hard. "No, Saber."

Her gaze locked with his. "I don't think she's alone."

"We'll wait for Ken and Mari."

"We don't have the time." Her hands trembled. "She's terrified, Jess. You have to trust me, trust in my abilities. I can get into and out of places without detection. I can do this."

"It isn't a matter of trust, Saber. I'm not risking you. I *can't* risk you."

She tilted her chin. "You wouldn't say that to Ken or Mari. You can't get into the house without being seen and you know it. I can. Patsy needs me and I'm going." She tugged at her hand, trying to get free.

"I'm in a fucking wheelchair. What's going to happen if you get caught?"

"The wheelchair has never mattered, Jess. If something happens, you'll get us out. I know you will." Her blue eyes met his. "I trust you completely."

He swore, his gaze angry, furious even, but he nodded his head, jerking her close and catching the back of her head to hold her still while he kissed her. He ground his mouth hard against hers.

She tasted the potent mixture of fear and anger, a fierce need to protect, helplessness, but most of all a predator unleashed. She kissed him back, trying to convey confidence and love all wrapped together.

Jess rested his forehead against hers, his fingers shaping the nape of her neck. "Stay in communication with me. I'm a strong telepath. I'll hear you."

"I will."

"No, Saber. Promise me. No matter what's going on. Don't let your fear or your need to protect me stop you from telling me what's happening. I'll need all the data in order to have a plan of action."

"I promise." And she meant it. Because no matter what, Jess Calhoun was lethal, and if she needed him, he would find a way to get to her.

Jess reached up and flicked the overhead light off. "I'll pull around to the back of the house, but you need to make certain the way is clear. If they have a guard posted, once I turn onto the drive, lights or not, they'll know I'm heading for Patsy's house."

"I'll clear the guard."

He pulled a gun and silencer from a compartment behind the glove box. "Take this and the spare clip."

"What about you?"

"I'm armed. Just be careful." He kissed her again, this time gentle, tender, wanting her to feel loved. "I'll be pissed if anything happens to you."

"Right back at you," Saber said and cracked open the door.

She dropped to the ground and took off running to the deepest part of the woods surrounding Patsy's house without looking back. It had taken precious time to convince

Jess to let her go in alone and she knew what it had cost him in pride. If it were anyone else but Patsy in danger, he would have tried to stop her — and a part of her found that thrilling. No one had ever worried about her before.

Lightning flashed again, this time rippling across the sky in a jagged bolt. Immediately thunder cracked so loud the trees and heavy brush shivered. Saber was drenched within moments of leaving the van, the cold penetrating through her thin clothing. She moved swiftly toward the house. She'd only been to Patsy's house once before.

Saber had been living in Jesse's house about five months and his sister had wanted to make certain Jess was safe with her. Patsy had asked Saber not to discuss their meeting with Jesse, and she hadn't, but trying to hide anything from Jess was next to impossible. He had eyes and ears everywhere and he'd known about Patsy and Saber's meeting even before it was over. Of course Jesse hadn't been happy about his sister trying to protect him, but Saber had instantly liked her for it.

Saber slipped through the trees, approaching the side of the house. The rain poured down through the leaves, the pattern unmistakable, so when the discordant note was

introduced, Saber sank back into the shrub-
bery near the windows and waited. Someone was patrolling around the perimeter of
the house.

She waited, crouched low, breathing away
the stark fear Patsy radiated from within the
house. Even the vicious storm couldn't
tamp down the energy of violence, rather
the wild winds and streaks of jagged lightning seemed to feed it until her stomach
heaved in rebellion. She prayed Jess was far
enough away from the house that he wasn't
picking up Patsy's terror, or there'd be no
holding him in the van.

As the guard approached, Saber dropped
to her hands and knees. The guard was a
short, stocky man with wide shoulders and
an easy swing to his gait. He could handle
himself and that wasn't good. Saber willed
him to stop, hoping she could get a hand
on him, but he kept moving, watching the
drive and all ways to approach the house.
Panic began to creep in, flooding her system
with adrenaline, and she knew Patsy was
close to collapse.

Fighting off the waves of dizziness, she
waited until the guard was almost on top of
her and then rolled out from under the
brush, right at his feet, the gun in her hand
as she squeezed the trigger and hit him dead

center in the forehead. She kept rolling as he toppled to the ground, facedown in the small puddle of water collecting in the flower bed. She landed next to several small ornamental trees, the violent energy crashing over her, piercing her skull like a thousand knives.

She tried to shut it out, pressing her hands to her head, but it was already inside, where she had no filters. There was no way to escape the pain, jackhammers pounding at her skull, the thunder of death, the silent scream of her victim. She rolled in agony, eyes closed, trying to breathe it away. She barely made it to her knees when her stomach rebelled, heaving over and over.

She had to get hold of herself. She was extremely vulnerable and Patsy desperately needed help. Unfortunately, even with a shield, if someone was torturing Patsy — and Saber was beginning to fear it was so — then the violent energy would slide under the shield and debilitate her, as this energy had done. Only an anchor could draw violent energy permanently away. The shield simply kept her energy from alerting others that she was close.

Ordinarily when she killed, she made certain her target was destroyed fast and with as little knowledge or pain as possible.

She introduced a natural means, rather than a brutal blasting away of life. She'd never killed using a weapon, although she was proficient, and she was unprepared for the backlash.

She dragged herself to her feet, stumbling, her head still pounding, every movement jarring her teeth and sending shards of glass through her skull. This wasn't going to be easy. She staggered around the flower bed to the window and unexpectedly the pain eased, and then disappeared altogether. She knew before she turned that she wasn't alone.

Jess! Relief and fear mingled together. She spun around looking for enemies. Jess couldn't outrun anyone or hide sitting in his wheelchair as he was. But without the pain she could think with clarity and interpret what she was feeling much easier.

He pulled her close to him, inspecting for damage. *You can't go in there alone, not after this.* His voice was edgy, angry even, but his hands were gentle as he stroked her hair.

I have to go in there, Jess. Something bad is happening. She didn't want to go in. "Something" wasn't happening. Violence was happening. The moment she stepped foot in the house, the energy would have a target. With Jess close, it would be much easier to deal with, but she would have to get both Patsy and Jess out of danger.

You shouldn't be here. It didn't matter that she wanted him there, it was far too dangerous.

Get it done. I'll be around at the back of the house. Try for the basement, but if you can't make it, go out the attic. You're especially good at that, aren't you? I'll cover you. Just bring her out, Saber.

Saber nodded and turned back to the window. She had almost handed the gun back to him, but hesitated. As awful as the backlash would be, using the gun might be the only way to save Patsy's life. Whoever was in the house with her was playing for keeps, and the guard hadn't been an amateur. What a mess.

She tested the window. Of course it was locked. Patsy had a security system, Saber knew, but considering the intruders in the house, she figured the system was likely off. She didn't have time for finesse, and the room was empty. She waited, elbow poised, for the next boom of thunder. When it came, she hit the glass and reached through to disengage the lock.

It took only seconds to dive through the window and hit the floor, rolling for the cover of the sofa she'd seen during that brief meeting at Patsy's house. The room was carpeted and most of the glass shards had fallen on a long, heavily cushioned window seat, making little noise. She smelled blood the moment she was inside. Fear hit her in waves. Red-black energy washed over and into her with brutal force. She choked and fought back the blackness swirling at the edges of her vision.

Jesse!

I'm here, baby. Breathe your way through it. I'm almost in position.

She could already feel the lessening of the violent energy as Jess got close enough to the house to draw it away from her. And how close was that exactly? Her heart thudded too hard in her chest and she bit down on her lip to steady herself. She couldn't think about Jess and what these men would do to him if they got their hands on him. She had to keep her mind on her shield, build it as strong as possible to mask her presence as she began to search for Patsy.

She concentrated on being small and invisible, fading into the background, moving slow and low to the floor. With the small glimpses she'd had of the interior of Patsy's house committed to her memory, she made her way to the sweeping double staircase that led to the wraparound art gallery. Paintings covered the walls going up the stairs and were displayed in alcoves along with sculptures on intricate pedestals. The curved gallery opened into the upstairs bed- and bathrooms, and already she knew exactly where Patsy was.

Two statues lay smashed on the parquet floor and there was a smear of blood along the wall near what was most likely the master bedroom. She heard men's voices, slightly raised, harsh tones, the sound of flesh hitting flesh and Patsy's cry of pain. Saber made it through the rubble without incident, conscious that she had no time to cover her tracks. If there was a third guard, he would see the marks of her passage, but it couldn't be helped. Terror was coming at her in waves, even with Jess's close proximity. The intent of the intruders was to brutalize, torture, and kill Patsy, and that energy was red-edged and horrific.

Saber ignored her churning stomach by reaching out to Jess, to find his calm, to feel the warmth of his mind.

Tell me.

She couldn't tell him. Nothing would stop him from coming in, and how would she ever protect both of them? *I'm almost there.*

Saber peered into the bedroom. One man stood over Patsy, who was duct taped to a chair, her upper body naked and water dripping from her wet hair and skin. Bruises were already forming on her face, one eye closing, and marks marred her breasts and stomach. She wept continually, shaking her head.

"I don't know what you're talking about. It doesn't matter how much you hurt me, I don't know. My brother was a Navy SEAL but he's in a wheelchair now. Whatever you're thinking he's doing, he's not. He couldn't be."

The man standing in front of her slapped her again and the second leaned in with a long-handled paddle, touching Patsy's breast so that her body convulsed and she screamed as electricity sizzled.

Saber's stomach flipped as she crawled into the room, coming up behind the first man who had slapped Patsy. He was medium height, but strong looking. He laughed and began to unbuckle his belt.

"She likes that, John. She's into pain, you can see she's getting horny. Look at her nipples." He pulled off the belt and swung it at Patsy. "Lie all you want, bitch, but you'll tell us in the end. We want names. His friends. Who he works for. Everything."

The belt left a long welt across Patsy's breasts and stomach. Her body jerked, but she didn't scream this time, she just shook her head helplessly, her eyes wild.

"Tell us or your legs will be smashed just like his, bitch."

Although the men were torturing Patsy, using depraved and brutal methods, Saber wasn't necessarily getting sexual energy from them. Even the laughter wasn't genuine. This was business. They would take Patsy apart — her body, her soul, her mind — until they knew everything she knew, and then they would kill her. It was simply business to them.

"Again, Greg, hit her again." John bent toward Patsy, catching her hair and yanking her head back. "You'll look good in stripes. Of course, we'll stop anytime you want to tell us the truth about your brother."

Patsy's gaze jumped around the room searching desperately for a way out. Saber was now in position, on the floor directly behind the man called John, who still had Patsy by the hair.

Saber placed the pads of her fingers very gently on his ankle even as her gaze met Patsy's. *I'm going to have to kill him right in front of her.* There was anguish in Saber's voice when she confessed to Jess. There was no choice.

Already Patsy's gaze had widened, hope

pushing through pain and terror as her mind grasped the possibility of rescue. Saber blocked out everything but John's heartbeat. Finding it. Melding with it. Disrupting it. She didn't have time for finesse. She had to take him out fast, introducing a massive heart attack.

A solid kick landed in her stomach as Greg attacked, rolling her over, sending her halfway across the room, as John went down, clutching his chest. She kept rolling, aware of Patsy's desperate screams, of the man coming at her, rage on his face, swinging the belt at her body over and over. She felt the blows landing, but she didn't flinch, rolling onto her back, gun in her hand, finger squeezing the trigger over and over, watching as holes blossomed in the body, a small circular pattern in the middle of his throat. If nothing else, she was accurate.

And then everything went black and red as violent energy, anger and pain and brutal death came at her, laying greedy hands on her, grabbing her by the throat and shutting down her airway even as ice picks slammed into her skull from every direction. She tasted blood in her mouth, felt it on her face, wiped it from her eyes. She was dead, but Patsy was safe. As long as there wasn't another enemy close, Jess would come for his sister. The roaring in her head increased and she rolled over, writhing, her body beginning to convulse.

Breathe, Saber. Damn it, you fucking breathe. Jess's voice filled her mind, a clear command from a man clearly used to obedience.

It would have been comical if she weren't struggling for survival. If she could breathe, she'd be doing it. She fought for air, tried coming to her knees, but was driven back to the floor by the pain. She was losing consciousness. Maybe her life.

Jess was there, on the floor beside her, dragging her into his arms, pulling her head back and lifting her stomach. "Take a breath, Saber. One fucking breath, that's all I'm asking for."

The terrible crushing stone on her chest and head eased with Jess's close proximity, but she couldn't hear or see properly. There was real pain now, all through her body, her ribs, her back, even her face. Had the belt struck her a dozen times before she got a shot off? How many times had he kicked her? It felt as if she'd been run over by a truck.

Jess pushed her hair back as he laid her on the floor, careful to keep her body from the blood staining Patsy's ivory carpet. He turned his head quickly to assure himself that Patsy wasn't in any danger. She was fighting the tape, trying to get out of the chair, her horrified gaze on the blood dripping from Saber's eyes and mouth.

"What's wrong with her, Jess?"

"She'll be all right." He sent up a silent prayer that it was true. "Give me a minute and I'll get you loose." He breathed for Saber, trying to find a way to get air into her bursting lungs.

Saber stirred. Groaned. Her lashes fluttered. She gasped and spat blood. Rolling, she came to her knees, clutching her stomach. "Patsy?" She glanced at Jess's sister, her vision blurry. Patsy's color was off, her face pale, sweat beading on her forehead and mingling with the water that had been poured over her.

Jess steadied her. "Can you stand?"

The energy was gone, drawn away from her by Jess's presence, but the aftermath was there, pounding in her head and strangling her lungs. She fought to take a breath, and then a second. More blood seeped from her nose. She wiped away the tracks on her face, spat again to clear her mouth.

"Saber?" Jess's hands went to her hips, holding her as she staggered to her feet.

She had to hang on to his shoulder, cling

to his chair in order to stay standing. "How many, Patsy?"

"Four. I saw at least four, but I thought there were more."

"I only got three of them," Saber said and wiped at her mouth. She'd never been so shaky. Killing with a gun wasn't for her, certainly not this close to the victim and not in an enclosed space.

"Sit down, baby," Jess said, his hands gentle as he pulled her onto his lap. "Just rest for a minute while I get Patsy free."

"She said at least four, Jesse. I only got three." She pushed the gun onto his lap. "I can't use this, not again."

Saber helped Jess cut through the duct tape holding Patsy to the chair. Every movement was painful, but she forced herself to keep going, pulling clothes from a drawer and helping Patsy to put on the soft sweatshirt to cover the terrible marks on her body.

"I can't stop crying," Patsy said, collapsing onto her brother's lap. "I was so scared, Jess. They were going to kill me." She flung her arms around his neck, sobbing, burying her face against his chest.

"I know, honey," he said, trying to comfort her and watch the door at the same time. "We've got to make a run for it." He caught Saber's hand. "Can you do this? I need to know, Saber."

She forced air into her burning lungs, her throat raw, the taste and smell of blood forever etched into her senses. She nodded. "I'm good. Let's get Patsy out of here."

She didn't wait for his piercing gaze to assess her, afraid she'd collapse. Saber inched her way around the bodies, careful not to touch either of them. They were going to make a run for it. A man in a wheelchair, Saber unable to breathe properly, and Patsy tortured and traumatized. "I never realized what an optimist you are," she muttered as she peeked around the corner. "We're clear. Move fast."

The elevator, which Saber hadn't known existed, was to the left of the bedroom. It was small and hidden by the long columns that formed arches to frame the art pieces. With Patsy on his lap, Jess powered the chair with fast bursts of speed across the gallery floor while Saber guarded the stairs.

"No wonder you managed to get in so fast."

"Patsy put in ramps for me at the back entrance because it was easier to maneuver and close to the elevator if I wanted to go up to the second floor." His gaze met Saber's over Patsy's head. He was frowning. Patsy was rocking now, back and forth, making small keening sounds of distress. She looked gray, her skin cold and clammy. *I think she's going into shock.*

Who could blame her? Those men were terrorizing her deliberately for information on you. She wouldn't mind going into shock herself, as battered as she was. She was an assassin, and she'd killed, but not like this, not this brutal, ugly, *messy* death. She did it with style and no fanfare. Quiet and natural as if it were meant to happen. She even tried to lessen pain and fear for her targets.

Saber felt rather than heard movement. *On the stairs, Jesse. Patsy has to be quiet. Get her into the elevator with you and I'll distract them.*

Fuck that. You're coming with us.

She sent him one telling look. The elevator was going to make noise. No matter how modern, it wasn't silent when running. The enemy would know and would be standing at the door, blasting away as it opened.

Damn it, Saber. But he was already using powerful strokes to propel the chair down the hall to the small cage. Saber inserted her body between Jess's and the stairs. She no longer had the gun, but it didn't matter. Her mind would never take another assault and survive. There had to be another way.

Two men leapt onto the gallery floor, rolling away from each other to take cover behind the massive columns. Before Saber could react, the paintings and sculptures began to shake, the floor undulating. She caught at the banister for support, glancing at Jess in alarm.

Take cover, Saber.

She didn't have time for much more than dropping down with her hands over her head for protection as sculptures began to fly through the air. Statues and paintings crashed around and into the columns. Pieces of the frames became weapons, hurtling through the air like missiles.

I think this is considered priceless art, Jesse. Saber peered through her fingers. He was destroying Patsy's art gallery. Glass and plaster whirled in the air so that it created a screen.

Now, Saber. Run. Let's get out of here. We have a better chance outside. Jess cursed himself for shutting down his team earlier. With the capture of the two locals and Chaleen discovered, neither he nor Ken nor Mari had felt any immediate threat. He cursed under his breath as he directed a painting to slam down over the top of the head of one of the gunmen.

Saber moved fast, her small figure a blur as she came rushing toward him. The elevator door slammed shut and they were moving. Jess counted the seconds it took to get to the first floor — an eternity when the two gunmen had only to run down a flight of stairs. He could only hope that both were so shaken by the strange phenomenon of flying art that they remained where they were for a few moments, although they were professionals. They hadn't fired blindly, or panicked, either of them.

The door slid open and he propelled the chair out onto the floor of the small room Patsy used as a den. That was the other advantage Jess figured he had. The elevator shaft was hidden in the walls and all the panels appeared to be smooth. Even if the enemy had a house plan, the location of the elevator doors wasn't included. Patsy had installed the lift within the past year. They wouldn't have any way of knowing which room the elevator opened into.

"You hanging in there, Pats?" Jess asked, worried about his sister.

Her breathing was shallow and her pulse was racing. Her skin was cold and clammy and she wasn't even attempting to hold herself up, slumping against him as if she were too exhausted to move.

"Talk to me, sis," Jess said, powering the chair down the hall to the back of the house, where he'd parked the van beside the ramp. *Saber, something's wrong.*

Saber shook her head. They were in a hell of a mess. She could hear the men running through the house. *They have radios. Someone's outside.*

Fuck. I left the van running. They've got us trapped. Because whoever was outside would be waiting in that van, or at a vantage point where they could pick off anyone running to it. He had two women to protect, and if the enemy got their hands on either of them, they'd have Jess by the balls.

Give me some direction. Saber skidded to a halt.

The basement. Through the kitchen. The door's to the left of the pantry.

Stairs? She was not hiding in a basement while he tried to outrace them in his chair. *Jess, I'm not leaving you.* She didn't care if he used his manly I'm-in-command voice and glared at her, she was sticking to him like glue.

I'll be with you. Just go. Get there fast before they find us.

Saber ran, following Jess's instructions on left and right turns. She yanked open the door. Her heart sank. The stairs were narrow and steep, although there weren't that many of them.

400

Help Patsy.

Saber dragged the taller woman from Jess's lap, getting an arm around her waist. Patsy said nothing, barely opening her eyes, slumping her weight against Saber, nearly knocking her down the stairs.

Hurry, Saber. You'll have to get my chair and then close the door.

Saber didn't look at him, terrified at what he planned. She concentrated on getting Patsy down the stairs. The woman wasn't walking, so Saber had no choice but to half carry, half drag her. She left Patsy slumped on the floor of the basement and rushed back to see Jess swinging his body from his chair and, using only upper body strength, began to descend the stairs.

The muscles in his arms and shoulders bulged with the effort, and she found her breath catching in her throat. There was determination on his face, his mouth firm, eyes glittering with menace. Even on the stairs, pulling the lower half of his body, he managed to look more predator than prey. She swallowed her admiration and jumped over him, landing like a cat beside the chair to yank it out of the way so she could close the door.

The basement instantly went pitch black. For a moment there was silence, then Jess swore beneath his breath and struck a match. "There's a light switch near the door, Saber, can you see it?"

She flicked it and below, back toward the wall, a single bulb lit up. "I take it Patsy doesn't use this much."

"No. Hurry. Get down here. We'll have to turn off the light again and unscrew the bulb so it won't work when they try it."

She was already carrying the chair down to him, taking the stairs two at a time. Placing the chair beside him, she raced to the back of the room and unscrewed the light-bulb, once more plunging the room into darkness.

"They'll be coming, Jesse. They aren't going to be fooled into thinking we're gone."

She crouched down beside Patsy and put a comforting hand on her shoulder, aware of Jess moving toward them in the dark. Only the energy field allowed her to "see" where everyone was. Although she was listening intently for the sound of the enemy, she automatically picked up the rhythm of Patsy's heart — and stiffened.

"Jesse. We've got a problem. Can you get over here now? Feel your way to us? You have a clear path. Right now." She turned Patsy's limp body over so she lay on her back. Pressing her palm over Patsy's heart, Saber looked toward Jesse in dismay.

CHAPTER 14

"Patsy's having a heart attack," Saber said. "If we don't help her now, her heart could be damaged beyond repair by the time we make it to a hospital."

"What the hell are you saying?" For the first time, Jess's composure was truly shaken. "She can't have a heart attack, she's too young."

The wheelchair shot across the basement floor. Jess leaned down to find his sister's pulse, his fingers searching in the darkness. "Are you certain, Saber? I can't tell."

"Yes, I'm certain."

"Do something."

Saber shoved back her hair, sitting back on her heels, one hand pressed to her forehead. Patsy needed help fast. The enemy was searching the house and the grounds and eventually would find them. Jess couldn't run. Neither could Patsy. They were royally screwed unless the Ghost-

Walker team arrived in the next few minutes.

She took a breath, let it out, and laid her palm over Patsy's chest. At once she could feel the heart squeezing, clamping, laboring when it should have beat steadily.

"What are you doing?" Jess demanded, his breath coming in a harsh rasp.

"The only thing I can think of. I'm going to try to trip her heart back into rhythm."

"Using an electrical charge?"

"Do you have a better idea?" Fear made her snap at him and she was instantly ashamed. She couldn't blame him for questioning her. She killed people, she didn't save them. "I'm sorry. You do what you think will help."

Jess swallowed a retort and pushed down the urge to order Saber away from Patsy. "Do you have to sync up your rhythm with hers? Is that how it works?"

"Yes. And we don't have time to discuss this."

"It's too big a risk for you to take." Because he damn well wasn't losing both of them. "Give her to me and we'll make a run for it."

"She doesn't have that kind of time." Saber ignored him, drawing air into her lungs and breathing away her fear of killing

Patsy — her fear of losing Jess. The only thing that really mattered in that moment was saving Patsy's life. And she was Patsy's only chance. For once, she would try to use what gifts she had to help someone.

She felt the jolt as her own heart squeezed hard, shifting off rhythm. Her chest hurt, the pain worse than expected, but she fought it back and concentrated on her own rhythm, steady and true. Patsy moved weakly, bringing up her hand to cover Saber's. Fingers fluttered against the back of her hand, and Patsy's mind moved against hers. Tears burned in the back of Saber's eyes as she felt Patsy's acceptance of their merging. Rather than fight her, Patsy was trying to rise above the pain and fear to help connect.

For a moment it worked, Patsy's heart following direction, settling into a steady beat, but almost at once the jarring pain was back, squeezing down on both of them. Saber moistened her lips, her mouth suddenly dry. She had no choice. If she was going to keep Patsy alive, she was going to have to shock her heart back into a normal pace.

She put her other hand on top of Patsy's, the only warning, and sent the jolt sizzling through her body. The heart stuttered, bumped, picked up the beat, falling into a steady tempo once again. Saber waited, silently counting the seconds, aware of Patsy's heart and the ebb and flow of blood through her veins. She had no idea she was whispering until Jess touched her shoulder and she jumped, shocked that it was her chanting — *please, please, please* — aloud.

"Patsy?" Jess said softly. "Can you sit up?"

"Not yet," Saber said. "Give her a few minutes." The pain was beginning to recede, the tight bands in her chest easing.

We don't have the time, baby. I can hear them coming. I can hold the door against them for a few minutes, but they'll know we're in here. They could burn us out or simply stand at the top of the stairs and spray the basement with bullets. We don't know what kind of firepower they have.

She hated that he was right. She was exhausted, and her body still felt as if she'd been in a train wreck. *Tell me what you want me to do.*

Jess hated the utter weariness in her voice. He had to ask more of her, although he knew the drain of using psychic abilities. She had just risked her life to save his sister and she'd felt whatever pain accompanied a heart attack with the same intensity Patsy had. And Patsy . . . Patsy had been tortured and terrified, driven into having a heart attack — all because of him and his choices in his life. It was a hell of thing for a man to have two of the most important women in his life in jeopardy while he — a man who'd spent his life working to save others — was helpless to save them.

"Can you two make it to the vent leading under the house?"

Saber's swift intake of breath told him she knew what he planned. "We're not leaving you, Jesse. That's not an option."

"Saber, I'm trusting you to get Patsy out of here."

"Not without you. No way. I mean it, Jesse."

He reached out and snagged the nape of her neck, his fingers settling around her to give her a small shake. "Don't fucking argue with me when we're all about to die. Get Patsy and get the hell out of here."

She caught his arm with both hands and rested her head against him. "I can't leave you. I can't."

"Baby, do this for me. I need you and Patsy safe. I can take care of myself, but I can't take care of the two of you. Hurry. We're out of time."

Saber spun away from him and crawled to Patsy. "Can you walk?"

"If I have to," Patsy said, her voice strained.

Saber reached down and took Patsy's arm to help her up. Without looking at Jess she helped Patsy toward the screened vent. It was easier for her because she could "feel" where objects were in the dark. "If you aren't with us in ten minutes, Jess, I'm coming back for you."

"Make it twenty."

"The hell with that." She yanked at the screen until it pulled from the frame. In the dark, no one was going to notice it, not when Jess would be sitting down in the basement in plain sight like a sacrifice. She wanted to scream and throw things in protest, but instead, she pushed Patsy through the opening.

"Where's Jess?" Patsy asked.

Saber took her hand and yanked her forward. They had to go slow, bent over, and find their way. "We have to hurry."

Patsy came with her obediently but she was beginning to be more aware. "Where's my brother?"

Saber kept dragging her along. It was difficult to determine the correct direction, especially since her mind was on Jess rather than on their escape. "Just hurry, Patsy."

Patsy suddenly swung in front of her and

stopped, forcing Saber to do the same. In the dark, she reached out and touched Saber's face, feeling the tracks of tears. "He isn't coming with us."

"No. He could never have made it through here with the chair and he wanted us safe. I'll go back as soon as I know you're out of danger."

Patsy pressed a hand to her chest. "We can't just leave him. Those men . . ." She trailed off and a sob escaped.

"Shh. You have to be quiet. Jesse can take care of himself." Saber sent up a quick prayer that he could, wheelchair and all. He often looked as if he could, and he certainly had psychic gifts, ones that were a little scary when she thought about it. "In any case, it's too late. If we went back now, he'd think we were the enemy. Right now, all he's thinking is that anyone coming at him is out to harm us. That's his advantage — he won't have to think about anything beyond pulling the trigger." While she talked, she kept tugging at Patsy's hand, keeping her moving away from the basement and toward what she hoped was the wooded area at the side of the house.

They were forced to go to hands and knees to continue moving. Saber was used to closed-in places, but Patsy began to shake even more. She pressed her fingers to her mouth, trying to suppress the constant weeping. "I'm so afraid. And I hurt. There's so much pain."

"I know," Saber murmured, shifting her gaze back toward Jess, wishing she could be in two places at one time. "We'll get you to a hospital, but we have to keep moving, Patsy. I'm sorry. I know it hurts, but we don't have a choice."

They were near the screened vent. Saber could see it was much lighter outside. Dawn had crept in, pushing away the night and all cover. She stilled Patsy with a hand to her shoulder, cautioning her to stay quiet and not move. Saber carefully removed the screen and set it aside, all the while listening, trying to pick up any sign of their enemy. When it appeared quiet outside, she signaled Patsy to remain still and she slithered out on her belly, making herself small, cloaking her body as best she could so that she faded somewhat into her surroundings.

Thunder crashed in the distance and the rain fell in a steady downpour, soaking her instantly. She crawled through the flower bed, staying low to the ground as she moved out into the open ground. Once out from the shadow of the house, she spotted a guard near the back porch. He had one foot on the stairs and the other planted on a small shrub as he cradled his gun and peered into the house.

Saber sighed. She could have made it to the woods and safety if she'd been alone, but no way with Patsy. She had no choice but to take him out. Steeling herself for another psychic blast of violent energy, she began to scoot across the ground in plain sight, inch by inch, moving toward her prey.

His radio crackled, jerking him to attention. Suddenly he turned and sprinted right toward her. Saber held her breath and waited. A foot came down inches from her head, another barely missed her hand. Then he was over the top of her and running for the back door. She heard his footsteps pounding up the stairs and the back door slamming.

Jesse. They'd found Jesse. Shaking, she lay there, her face buried in the crook of her arm, her heart thundering right along with the weather. She tasted fear in her mouth. It didn't matter that she'd told herself he was lethal — he was in a wheelchair. What could he possibly do against anyone? He was trapped in the basement. Alone. Vulnerable. And she'd just left him. What had she been thinking?

Saber pushed up off the ground and ran

back to get Patsy. Her vision blurred, but whether it was from the rain or tears, she couldn't be certain.

Jess sat in silence, breathing deep, trying to keep rage from exploding. Patsy — tortured because of him. Saber — suffering because of him. Damn whoever was behind this, because he simply wasn't going to stand for it. Let them come. He prayed for them to come. He was a spiritual man, and if he was condemned to hell for what he was about to do, so be it. He'd go and gladly, because this was unacceptable to him.

"Come on." He whispered the words softly. *Come on.* Whispered the words in his mind, sent them out into the universe to urge his enemies to find him. As if in answer, the door to the basement was flung open.

Come on, you bastard. Walk on in. Let's do it.

He stayed very still, watching as the man crept down the stairs, gun in his hand, his gaze sweeping left to right as he quartered the basement. As he descended, the light from above faded and the man reached for the flashlight at his belt. Jess threw the knife he had strapped to his leg, as accurate as always, so that the man fell hard, gun clattering and head thumping as he slid the rest of the way down the stairs.

Jess pushed the chair close enough to check his pulse. Finding him dead, he snagged the man's arm and began to drag the body away from the bottom of the stairs. It wasn't easy maneuvering his chair while trying to keep hold of the body, but he needed it out of sight fast. The open door, silence, and the smell of blood would lure the others in. As long as they wanted him alive, he had a chance — more than a chance. He'd kill them all, because no matter what else happened, he wasn't going to let them get their hands on the women.

After retrieving the dead man's gun, he parked the wheelchair in the alcove where the heater was located and placed the gun on a shelf facing the stairs. He slipped from his chair and lifted the dead man into it. For the first time in a long while, he was thankful he was physically enhanced. As much as he worked out, he doubted he would have been strong enough to put a fully grown man into his wheelchair from the floor, but with the strength Whitney had given him, he easily lifted the body. He'd already picked out the safest place in the room, the darkest spot with the most cover.

He'd baited the trap, now he had to wait

until they took it. The devil liked to make a man sweat, sending him images of Saber and Patsy in the hands of madmen. They were dead just for what they'd done to Patsy. He'd hunt them down one by one if he had to. And Saber . . . She'd suffered for him. He wasn't going to forget that look in her eyes when she'd known she was going to have to kill again.

The sound of the rain beat down steadily and the seconds crawled by. He heard the first soft footfall and then a second one.

"Henry? You down there?"

Jess remained silent, knowing the men wouldn't fail to smell blood. The open door was an invitation. He remained still, patient. He heard a whispered consultation. He simply lay there waiting. They would come because they had to. They had gone to the trouble of torturing Patsy for information. They would surely want him.

A figure appeared in the doorway, stepped hastily to the side in a crouch, sweeping the basement with a flashlight. Jess concentrated on the gun he'd left on the shelf. It rose in the air, levitating just about the height of a man's chest before firing. The flash was bright in the room, and the flashlight clattered to the ground. The man holding it clutched his stinging hand and swore as the

415

room once again was plunged into darkness.

"Calhoun. We know you're in there. Come out into the open and drop your weapon." The voice came from outside the room.

Jess glanced at his watch. Saber and Patsy should be clear of the house. If he made a mistake, both should still be fine. He tested his control, felt the concrete under him shift slightly. The walls shimmered uneasily for just a moment. The stairs creaked.

"Calhoun, don't make this hard on yourself. Ben just came in and we've got your sister."

Your sister. Not both women. Saber would never allow them to take Patsy from her. If they had captured Patsy, they'd have taken Saber as well. They were lying. Even with logic telling him both women were safe, his heart still stuttered. He felt the floor quiver, always a problem when he was upset. Control was of vital importance when you could shake apart a house.

"Calhoun. Let's just talk."

The first man, already inside, began to make a cautious move to find cover. The gun hovering over the shelf fired a second warning shot, and the man brought up his gun and sprayed the basement with bullets.

"Stop! What the fuck is wrong with you, Stan? We need him alive."

The gun fell silent, although Jess could hear harsh breathing. The man giving orders stepped to the door's edge and flashed a light over the basement. He caught the splash of blood and the shadowy figure of the man in the wheelchair. Swearing, he tried for a better angle.

"I think you killed him, Stan."

"He was shooting at me. What the hell was I supposed to do, Bob?" Stan felt around for his flashlight. "The damn thing's dead. He put a bullet in it."

The two men remained where they were, observing what they could see of the body, taking care not to expose themselves to further gunfire. Jess had positioned the chair so only a part of it could be seen from the door, the rest hidden by the alcove. He remained silent. There was a third man still alive, and Jess willed him to enter the basement. He couldn't attack until the man was inside, but he remained stubbornly cautious.

"Get your ass moving, Specialist," the one near the doorway urged. "And you'd better hope you didn't kill the bastard. I'll cover you."

Jess felt the beginnings of a smile. Yeah, dark hair in the doorway had it right. He was a bastard. He lived for this.

417

"Hooah, Sergeant." Stan started down the stairs and the second man moved onto the landing. His gun was steady on the body slumped in the wheelchair. Jess remained still, silently urging the third man to join the party. For a moment it looked as if it wouldn't happen.

"Keep the talk down until we have the bastard," another voice snapped.

Bob moved completely to one side, giving the other man, who was obviously in charge, the better position. Immediately he stepped inside the room as well, shifting to the left of his partner.

The door to the basement slammed closed behind them, plunging the room into darkness. The two men closest tried to open it, pounding and rattling the doorknob, swearing and kicking at it, but the door held fast.

The stairs and landing began to shake, gathering momentum until nails and screws began to pop out of the frame and drop to the floor. There were shouts. Stan fired his gun, the sound deafening in the small space. The flash blinded everyone even more.

"It's an earthquake," Bob yelled. "You're going to shoot one of us, Stan. Just hang on until it's over."

The shaking grew worse until the boards on the landing and stairs began to break apart. Stan yelled hoarsely as he fell and the two other men followed, one grabbing at the rail and swinging by his arm before dropping to the floor below.

"Son of bitch. Son of a bitch." Stan scuttled across the cement toward the wheelchair, his gun aimed at the dead man's head.

"It's a fucking earthquake, Stan," Bob shouted again.

"This is no earthquake," the one in charge snarled.

"It's him, Bob, you moron. It's *him*. I told you it was true. I'm killing the son of a bitch." Stan pulled the trigger several times, the bullets tearing into the body in the wheelchair. The body jerked with the force of the impact and the dead man slumped over, sliding down in spite of the belt holding him to the chair.

Stan crawled closer, moving around the protruding wall housing the hot water heater. Jess rolled swiftly into position, each move already mapped out in his head. His arm slipped around Stan's throat and clamped down hard in a half nelson. Stan thrashed wildly. He was a big man and his feet drummed on the concrete as he tried desperately to break the stranglehold Jess had on him.

"Stan! What the hell? Get a light, Ben. We need a light," Bob shouted.

There was an audible crack and Stan's feet went still. Silence settled into the room. There was only the sound of heavy breathing as the two intruders fought for air, adrenaline rushing through their veins.

"Stan?" Bob said again, this time his voice low, a conspirator's whisper. "Answer me."

"Get over there and check it out," Ben said in an undertone.

"Screw that. We need a light."

"Yeah, you find one. I dropped mine when your little earthquake took out the staircase." Ben's voice dripped sarcasm.

There was another silence. Bob sank down onto the floor, his back to the wall. His eyes were beginning to adjust again to the dark as dawn crept over the horizon. He could just make out the shadow of Stan's body lying on the floor beside the wheelchair and another body slumped in the chair. "I think they're both dead."

"Check."

"You want me to check?"

"Damn straight. Check so we can figure out how to get the hell out of here."

Bob lifted his gun and fired a round into the head of the man in the wheelchair. "I'm not taking any chances. If he was faking,

he's dead now. Cover me, Ben, just in case."
Bob began to crawl toward Stan, keeping a careful eye on the motionless man in the wheelchair.

Jess concentrated on the lightbulb Saber had unscrewed. The moment Bob was beside Stan, where he could have reached out and touched Jess, the bulb spun back into place, flooding the room with blinding light. Jess kept his eyes closed until the bulb reversed direction and the light went out after one flash. He was on Bob instantly, catching his head in his hands and twisting violently. Again there was a satisfying crack and Jess was back in the shadows.

Silence reigned. Ben sighed and pushed with his heels, sliding his body into the rubble left from the staircase. He crouched underneath what was left of the landing.

"So it's true. You are one of them." He shoved his gun into a shoulder harness and reached for a pack of cigarettes. "Don't kill me until I have a last smoke." He lifted his hands into the air, showing the pack and lighter.

"Go ahead." Jess's disembodied voice bounced off the walls coming from every direction.

"You're pissed about your sister."

"Yeah, you could say that."

The lighter flared and Ben bent his head toward the flame. "I can't blame you. It's a job, you know, nothing personal." The lighter snapped off and the end of the cigarette glowed red.

"You tell yourself that."

"You gonna kill me?"

"What do you think? You tortured her. You were going to rape and kill her. You're a dead man."

"I figured as much."

Jess watched Ben take a strong pull of the cigarette. He wasn't going down easy. He was trying to buy himself time to think his way out of the mess he was in. If he could locate Jess's actual position, the man thought he'd have a chance. "Are you going to tell me who sent you after me?" He'd help the man buy time while he bought information.

"I don't think so." Ben took another drag of the cigarette, pulled it from his mouth and stared at the red tip. "Sooner or later they're going to get you, and there's some satisfaction in that." He toed open the door to the gas water heater and flicked his cigarette toward it.

Jess had been waiting for a move and he stopped the cigarette in midair, let it drop, tip down, and mash itself on the concrete.

"That was no earthquake."

"No, it wasn't."

"You're the real fucking thing."

Ben's gun swept up and he sprayed the basement with bullets in an up-and-down pattern going across the room. His finger remained steady on the trigger even when the gun began to shake in his hand, began to put pressure on his wrist, turning slowly, inevitably, inch by slow inch toward his own body. He broke out in a sweat, his heart thundering in his ears, fighting with every bit of strength he had, but he couldn't stop the turn or remove his finger from the trigger. He heard himself scream as the bullets tore into his body, one after the other, ripping through him.

"Yeah. I'm the fucking real thing and that's for what you did to my sister, you son of a bitch. It might not have been personal to you, but it was very personal to me."

The words were low, whispered in Ben's left ear as he fell back. He turned his head and stared into cold, merciless eyes. Jess lay stretched out on the floor beside him, only inches away, his face set in implacable lines. Everything blurred. He heard the gun clatter against the cement, and his hand flopped onto his chest. He couldn't feel it and his vision grew dark. He coughed. Gurgled.

Spat. Ben tried to lift his hand, but he couldn't tell where it was. He died, staring at Jess's uncompromising and very unsympathetic gaze.

Jess shifted into a sitting position. "You didn't suffer nearly enough for what you did to Patsy," he told the dead man. "And I'm going to find out who sent you and rip his heart out. But meanwhile . . ."

He trailed off and looked around him. He was going to have a hell of time getting out of the basement now. Cursing, he made his way to the wheelchair, using his hands to walk. Dumping the body, he wiped the blood from the seat and back as best he could. Flicking a quick glance toward the light fixture, he waited until the bulb screwed itself back in, and light flooded the basement once again.

It looked like a war zone, with bodies strewn everywhere and blood splashed from one end of the room to the other. He folded the chair and locked it in a closed position. This was going to be tricky. Using the bionics always was. They could fail at any time and leave him in a vulnerable heap on the floor. He hit his leg in frustration. He'd suffered pain and the threat of bleeding out, countless hours of physical therapy, and he still couldn't use them.

He looked up at the door, allowing it to swing open. His strength was becoming a problem. Like all GhostWalkers, even those who trained as he did, mental psychic challenges drained his strength faster than anything else. Slow tremors invaded his body. He had no intention of letting the other GhostWalkers — or worse, Saber — find him lying on the floor in what amounted to a slaughterhouse. Nor was anyone carrying him out. No one.

He forced himself to stand, using his mind to command his legs. Pain sliced through his head, and his body shuddered with the effort. He broke out into a sweat. He could move objects with semi-ease now. The more he practiced, the better he got at it, but moving his legs, making them respond, was both painful and difficult. And now he was fatigued, not a good thing when he was trying to make the bionics work. He should have let them try an external power pack, but he'd been stubborn, wanting his legs to be part of his body, not some externally powered robotic limbs.

He dragged the chair to him and placed it under his arm. He had to jump into the doorway, taking the wheelchair with him. And he had to land on his feet or he'd fall backward onto the basement floor — and

Ben's dead body.

Stiffening his back, he blocked out everything around him. Sight. Smell. Danger. He visualized his legs with veins and arteries and flashing nerves firing like sparkplugs in a car. He sent the signal from his brain to the nerves as he crouched low and leapt. He felt the power rush through him, the coiled readiness of the genetic enhancements springing into action. Though he hated what Whitney had turned the Ghostwalker program into, Jesse loved the rush using his physical enhancements always gave him. Loved it. Before he'd lost his legs, he'd lived for it.

He landed in the doorway and took a step forward, then a second. Exhilaration swept through him. He was doing it! He was walking again. He'd almost forgotten what it was like to stand, to feel his legs under him, to walk upright, his body once more his own and under his command. He felt tall. He hadn't been tall in a year. It was amazing to walk, to feel free. He'd learned appreciation for things most people took for granted, and he swore to himself he'd never take them for granted again.

His legs began to shake, warning him he was overdoing. He set the wheelchair on the floor near the back door and took another step to walk around it. He didn't want to stop, wishing he could just walk out into the rain and keep going until he found Saber.

Jess reached for the back of the chair, and his legs gave out, dropping him to the floor with no warning. One moment he was standing, the next he had crashed onto the tiles, the force of the fall splitting open his knees. He tried to go with it — he knew how to fall — but it happened too fast and he slammed his head against the wall.

Cursing, dizzy, he dragged himself into a sitting position and hit the wall with his fist in a fit of frustration. So much for the new and improved legs. With a little sigh he reached for the chair again. The back door swung open and he rolled, bringing up his gun, his hands steady when the muscles in his legs spasmed and cramped. He lay on his belly, his body stretched out, legs jumping, with his gun aimed.

A low, one-two whistle eased the tension in him. He rested his forehead on his arm for a moment, frowned when he lifted his head and saw his arm was smeared with blood. Wiping at his face, he rolled over, sat up, and sent the exact same one-two whistle back, but he didn't lower his weapon until Logan stepped into the room.

"You look like shit. Who beat you up?" Logan crouched beside him but kept his weapon clear and ready as he examined Jess's face.

"You ought to see the other guys." Jess pulled his face away from Logan with a small glare. "There's nothing wrong with me."

"You've got a hell of a cut on your face."

"My sister was tortured and someone kicked the crap out of my woman. I don't think a little cut is anything to worry about."

"Really? Well, you're bleeding like a stuck pig. I thought maybe one of them got you with a knife."

If Logan was looking for an explanation, he wasn't going to get one. Jess reached for his chair. "Where's Patsy?"

"Saber's got her safe in the van. She wanted us to take Patsy to the hospital so she could come look after you herself."

Jess winced. "Go to hell, Logan."

Logan frowned. He'd always teased Jess about being in a wheelchair. Jess had never reacted with anger. "You all right?"

Jess dragged his chair close with one hand and locked the wheels. "Yeah. I'm just pissed that I brought this on my sister."

Logan stepped to the door of the basement and peered down. "Holy crap, Jess.

428

You *were* pissed off."

"The bastards got off easy."

"Couldn't you have left one alive so we could interrogate him? The two we got earlier aren't part of this. They were amateurs hired by some bozo as sacrificial lambs, maybe to set you up to see what you could do. But this was professional."

"No, I couldn't leave one of them alive. They *tortured* my sister. What would you have done?"

Logan swung his head around, his gaze meeting Jess's. The easygoing mask slipped to reveal the predator underneath. "If I'd gotten to them first, they would have died hard and mean. They were lucky."

There was a moment of silence. Logan turned away as Jess heaved himself back into his chair. Jess wiped at the blood on his face, his hand lingering to hide his expression. Having walked made sitting in the chair all the more difficult, as if it was the first time all over again. His lungs burned for air and he fought down rising panic. He didn't dare look at Logan. He needed out of there. He needed Saber.

The back door was still open and he thrust at the wheels hard, propelling his chair out onto the porch. It was light outside, and raining hard. The wind felt good on his face, but the tightness in his chest didn't go away. He heard the door of the van slam and looked up.

She came to him out of the rain, water plastering her hair around her face, slicking back the springy curls. Her eyes were enormous, almost purple, her mouth inviting. The sight of her shook him, warmed him, eased the terrible weight in his chest. She had bruises coming up on her face, her cheek was a little swollen, and she walked with a limp, although she was trying to hide it. She was the most beautiful thing he'd ever laid eyes on. Her gaze locked with his and his heart somersaulted at the relief there. The shimmer of tears — for him.

"You made it." Her voice was husky, as if she might be choking.

"Was there any doubt?"

She stopped in front of him, swallowed hard and shook her head. "No, of course not. But it's good to see you." She pressed her palm to the cut on his head. "Since we're taking Patsy to the hospital, you can get this looked at."

He didn't tell her he was using an experimental drug for an experimental program and he needed his own doctor, he simply caught her hand and pulled her to him so

430

he could taste her wild, exotic flavor and lose himself in the dark excitement of her soft mouth.

CHAPTER 15

Saber really didn't like Dr. Eric Lambert. He and Lily Whitney-Miller had arrived at the house with Captain Ryland Miller in the evening after things had settled down in order to take care of the cut on Jess. She expected to dislike Lily, knowing the woman knew all about her past, yet it was Lambert who set off her initial alarms.

Unlike Lily, Eric Lambert wasn't a Ghost-Walker. He might work with them, but he had no firsthand knowledge of what they suffered, what their lives were like. He studied them, and he patched them up when they went down, but the bottom line was, he experimented on them — just as Peter Whitney did.

The GhostWalkers were government assets. Resources. Weapons. They thought of Lambert as their friend, but he thought of them as a top secret arsenal. It was next to impossible to watch him interact with Jess and Lily as if they were his friends and colleagues while listening to his elevated heart rate and smelling his fear every time she got near to him. And it was tempting to get near him. To offer her hand when she knew he was so afraid. And damn Jess for telling Lambert about her abilities.

She stared out the window in Jess's bedroom into the rain, wishing everyone was gone so she could go yell at him. Pick a fight. Make it easy to leave. *Lily and Lambert knew.* And if they knew, eventually the government would come knocking on the door and expect her to do a little job for them. She'd told Jess it would be like that, but he'd given her up anyway. He was too trusting, thinking everyone was his friend. A big happy family.

Moron. Idiot. Naive. She pushed the heel of her hand hard against her forehead. *What is wrong with you?*

Saber? Jesse's voice sounded in her mind.

Whoops. She was really distracted to make such an amateur mistake. It was exactly how she'd given herself away in the first place. She was so connected to him, she barely noticed when she reached for him anymore.

Well, you're an ass. You told that slimy little doctor Lambert about me. I told you what would happen once everyone knew. He's a government man. In a couple of weeks we'll be getting a knock on the door and an engraved invitation to some social event where I'll get to use my special talents for the good of mankind.

That's not true, baby. First of all, Eric's not like that and he's not "everyone." Second, I didn't tell him. He doesn't know.

He knows.

There was a small silence while he digested that. *Are you certain? You're tired and maybe a bit cranky.*

Saber sucked in her breath. Cranky? He thought she was cranky? Her blood pressure was shooting through the roof, she wanted to scream at him, but she forced a calming breath to stay under control. *He knows and I'm not cranky, I'm angry. I can fight one enemy, but not several, not all at once. He's government all the way and he'll trade all of us in in a heartbeat if he's given the order.*

Frowning, Jess cast a brief look at Eric Lambert. The doctor looked the same as he always did, laughing with Lily, teasing her about how she looked as if she'd swallowed a basketball. Saber didn't know him and she was so worried about anyone finding out about her past. There was no real way Eric could have known. Saber was seeing

434

things where they didn't exist. *You're para-noid. And exhausted. Why don't you go to my room and lie down. Eric's sewing up the cut and they'll leave. We'll get some sleep and you'll feel much better.*

First I'm cranky and now I'm paranoid? Saber's voice went low. Cold.

Jess winced at the ice in her voice. "Lily, come on. Enough already."

Lily studied the cut on his head, frowning as the blood continued to seep in spite of the hours that had passed since he'd first been injured. "I told you to be careful. We're using Zenith on you and that drug is dangerous."

Eric held up his hands. "I'm going to wash up."

"You know where the bathroom is." Jess waited until he was out of the room. "You assured me that you were going to destroy the file on Saber."

"I did." Lily straightened up, stretching her back out.

"But you told Lambert about her?"

"No, of course not."

"Why of course not?" Jess took the pill she handed him. His head was throbbing. They'd spent most of the morning at the hospital, staying with Patsy while the doctors ran tests and treated her wounds. Once they knew she was in good hands — and he'd put a guard on her door — Jess and Saber had returned home and waited all afternoon for news from the cleanup crew at Patsy's house. Saber still hadn't been to bed and she still intended to go to work. She wasn't — he was going to make certain of that — but she needed sleep desperately and so did he. He just wanted everyone gone so they could be alone and he could hold her.

But Saber was wrong about Eric Lambert knowing the truth about her. Jesse hadn't told him and neither had Lily. He breathed a sigh of relief.

"He isn't one of us." Lily ducked her head. "That sounds terrible, Jess, and I don't mean it that way, but he could never understand our lives. If Saber stays, she's going to have to be protected. Her skills will have everyone after her, even the good guys — especially the good guys. And what Whitney did to her as a child . . . He forced her to kill animals, animals a little girl would love and want to have for pets. He put her in the position of having to have perfect control or kill a friend — another child — toddlers even. How can a child get over that kind of trauma?"

Jesse was glad to hear Lily refer to her

adopted father as "Whitney." She was finally coming to terms with the fact that he was a monster beyond redemption, and she was beginning to distance herself from him emotionally. Jess was certain that was a good thing. "I didn't think about that."

"You wouldn't, Jess — you came from a loving home. Saber wouldn't have known what a mother and father was, not for years. She grew up training. Her life was all about rigid rules and constant learning. What do you think those first few years were like?"

He was ashamed to admit he hadn't given it much thought — at least until he saw the pictures of her childhood.

"It's amazing that she's still here with you, that she could learn to trust anyone as much as she does you. You're probably the first person she's ever confided in, or shared any of the real Saber with."

She was making him feel worse by the moment. He hadn't wanted to think about Saber's trauma, or even acknowledge there was a threat if she stayed with him, because he didn't want to lose her. "She's probably being paranoid, but she thinks Eric knows about her."

Lily went very still. "Jess. Why would you doubt her? She was raised in a world even you can't comprehend. She has to be very sensitive. We haven't even begun to discover what she can do with her abilities. When a GhostWalker 'thinks' something, it's most likely true. Look at you. Until you were in that chair, you hadn't developed your ability to move objects and yet now you're incredibly strong. You 'thought' you might be able to do it and played around a little bit, but because you didn't have time, you didn't bother with it. There're so many others with hidden talents they haven't begun to tap. If Saber says Eric is treating her different, I wouldn't ever think she's paranoid, I'd believe her."

He didn't want to believe her because he didn't want to accept the consequences. Logan knew. For sure, Logan knew. Was it possible that he had told Eric? Jess rubbed his head again. He was too tired to think. "I need to go to bed, Lily."

"I know." Lily packed up her equipment. "How are the bionics coming?"

"It's frustrating. I'm beginning to think we should have gone with a power pack even though that would be limiting. I can't keep function and I sure can't trust it." His frustration and anger were in his voice, but he couldn't help it.

Eric returned, leaning into the doorframe. "Are you visualizing? Using your psychic abilities to rebuild the pathways?"

Jess sent him one smoldering, dangerous look. He wasn't in the mood to be lectured. He'd done enough visualizing to get fifty pair of legs working, and he was still sitting in a chair, taking falls that put stitches in his head, humiliating him in front of his friends and Saber. He wasn't going to take bullshit from anyone, not even a friend.

Eric held up his hand. "Don't take my head off, I was only trying to help."

"Well, don't." Jess glared at him. "Just who told you about Saber?"

Lily's hands stilled on the medical bag. She turned and looked at Eric. The doctor stood there, looking uncomfortable, toeing the doorframe. He shrugged. Jess remained silent, waiting, *insisting* on an answer. Because whoever ratted her out was going to get the beating of his life.

Eric scowled at him. "How the hell would I remember? I'm around all of you all the time. Does it matter?"

"It matters if you make her feel uncomfortable in her own home."

Irritation crossed Lambert's face. "This is your home, Jess. I've been in it hundreds of times over the last year. She's not like the rest of you and you should know that. And frankly, if anyone should be feeling uncomfortable in it right now, it's you. Because as long as she lives here, you're putting your life and the lives of everyone that comes here at risk."

"What the hell does that mean?" Jess spun his chair all the way around to glare at his doctor.

Eric straightened, glaring right back, refusing to be intimidated. "What do you think I mean? She kills with one touch. What happens if she gets a little tired of her man? Or she's angry and out of control? She could kill you in your sleep. Just holding your hand. Leaning in to kiss you good night. The rest of you, you're trained. Disciplined. She's a wild card, Jess, and one none of the GhostWalkers can afford."

"You don't know what the hell you're talking about."

"That's the problem and you know it. I *do* know. She's a killing machine. Lily thinks so too, but she's too polite to say it. I'm your friend and I don't want you dead."

"We're all killing machines, Eric."

The doctor shook his head. "Not like her. She's deadly, Jess, and she's got you wrapped around her little finger until you not only can't think it, you can't entertain the idea of it. What do you think is going to happen here? You know about her. You're a liability to her. The moment she decides to pick up and leave, you're a dead man. She can't be controlled."

"And the rest of us can?" Lily snapped.

"To some extent, yes. You all have loyalty and discipline. You serve your country. You have ideals and goals. You're a team and those men and women are your family and the ones you trust. What is she loyal to? Who does she trust? Not you. Not any of you. And she sure doesn't want to serve her country."

"How the hell do you know what she wants or doesn't want?" Jess growled.

"She's out for herself. She ran from Whitney but she sure as hell didn't try to come in, did she? She didn't go to the nearest fort and say she had to speak to a commander. And I also know she's something that should never have been created."

Jess heard no sound, but instinctively he knew Saber was there. He looked up, met her violet-blue gaze, dark and stricken. She blinked and her face was a mask.

"I'm going for a walk, Jess. I'll be back when your friends are gone — *all* your friends." She spun on her heel and walked away.

It's pouring, Saber. Go to bed. I'll be there soon.

441

I don't want to be in the same house with them. As long as they're here, I'm gone.

We need them.

You need them.

Her voice choked and his heart sank. He swore and glanced at Lily. She had tears shimmering in her eyes.

She held out her hand to him. "We'll go. I know what it's like to feel like a freak. To have to live differently than everyone else. All of us do. It doesn't matter what gifts we have, people are going to look at us in the same way Eric does."

"That's not true," Eric denied, obviously upset. "I've never looked at you in any way other than as a friend and colleague."

But there was Dahlia, one of the women Jess had been a handler for, a woman who started fires when the energy buildup was too severe. She couldn't safely go out in public without an anchor. No doubt Eric would consider her a monstrous freak as well. Jess pressed two fingers to the spots throbbing above his eyes. Why hadn't he realized Eric might think of them that way, and if Eric, a doctor who helped them, did, what would most of the rest of the population think?

The walls breathed in and out and the ground rippled again. "Damn you, Eric.

What the hell was that? You don't come into my home and insult my woman . . ."

"*Your* woman?"

"Yeah, *my* woman, and then think I'm going to be all right with it. I want to tear out your fucking heart right now." Jess actually moved his chair closer to the doctor but stopped at the look on Lily's face. "You know what? It doesn't matter what you think. You don't know Saber." He held up his hand to forestall any reply. "Look, Eric, thanks for all you've done, but maybe it would be better if you didn't come back."

"For God's sake, Jess, we've been friends for years."

Jess rubbed his eyes. "Saber is in my life to stay, Eric. She isn't going away, and knowing how you feel about her . . . well, enough said." Because he still wanted to smash his fist in Eric's face for making Saber look so lost.

"Talk to you soon," Lily said. "Get some rest."

"Yeah, I'm tired. I need to sleep for a while," Jess agreed. "Thanks for sewing me up."

Lily picked up her bag. "Be more careful, Jess. Until you can get the bionics working properly, you shouldn't risk practicing without someone with you."

He waved his hand in acknowledgment, but didn't reply. He needed them gone. And he sent word to the others that the house was secure and they could leave. Ken protested, along with Logan, but he made it clear he wanted them gone. Because he needed Saber to be all right more than he needed anything else right then. He wanted her to feel safe and secure and that her home was a haven, a sanctuary for her.

It didn't matter that Eric made a kind of weird sense. He didn't care. Maybe someday she would get tired of him and want out, but he couldn't imagine, not for one moment, Saber killing anyone for killing's sake. She detested it. She feared making mistakes. She wasn't the killer Eric believed her to be.

Saber waited until the last GhostWalker left. They had gone reluctantly and she could only assume Jess had sent them away. Still, she waited until dark before she went back into the house, and even then she crept in, not wanting to see him. He was the only person in the world she'd ever called friend, the only person she'd ever loved, but how could he hear those things about her and not have doubts? Even she had doubts.

For a moment she stopped, covering her

face with her hands, listening to Jesse's breath, his heartbeat. She couldn't face him. She might not have the courage to ever face him again.

The minute she set foot on the landing, Saber began stripping. She hadn't been able to stop crying, and between her tears and the rain, she was soaked. She used the second bathroom, avoiding her room altogether. She couldn't face the idea that someone had been in there touching her things, even after the cleaners had removed all the evidence.

She stepped into the shower, allowed the steamy water to cascade down on her, warming her cold skin, doing nothing for the ice deep inside her. She was upset with Jess, with his friends, but most of all with herself. What had she expected? That they'd all just embrace her into their lives? That they'd want her to be a part of them? That she could fit in somewhere?

She hadn't even been certain she'd wanted it. Okay, that wasn't true. She'd been *afraid* to want it. Afraid it wasn't real. She shouldn't have hoped. Hope was for fools. Hope was for people, not monsters.

A shudder ran through her body and her chest hurt, crushed beneath some heavy, tearing emotion. The raw burning in her throat refused to go away no matter how many times she worked at swallowing the lump. She leaned against the tiles, her knees weak, legs shaking so much she was afraid they would give out on her.

An hour later Saber lay on the sofa on the upstairs landing, staring up at the ceiling. Her small lamp dispelled the darkness but gave her little comfort. Sighing, Saber slipped from the bed, wrapped her arms around her waist, pulling Jesse's shirt close around her body. On bare feet she padded down the hall to sit on the top stair, needing to be close to Jess but not wanting a confrontation. After all, it was a no-win situation.

Below her, something moved out of the shadows. Jess. Saber could make out the outline of part of his chair and one powerful shoulder and arm. His face was still hidden in the darkness. Of course he would be down at the foot of the stairs, needing the same feeling of closeness. Saber drew her knees up to her chest, rested her chin on them. It gave her a measure of comfort to know he was there.

"Why don't you come down here?" he suggested softly.

"I can't, Jess," Saber replied, her voice muffled, throat raw and torn from the

446

earlier heart-wrenching sobs. "I just can't."

There was a small silence. A red glow and the aroma of pipe tobacco drifting up the stairs indicated his state of mind. "It won't get cleared up if we don't talk about it."

Saber rubbed her forehead. The headache wasn't going away anytime soon. "What's to say?"

"He was wrong about you."

Her eyes began to burn all over again. She pressed her fingers deep to try to stop the tears. Crying was a weakness, one she'd never been able to overcome. "Maybe. If I don't know, how could you?"

"Because I know who you are. I see inside of you. You know yourself that using telepathy gives you glimpses into a person's mind. I feel what you feel. I can see what you're thinking. You aren't a killer, Saber. You kill reluctantly." He sighed. "The truth is, between the two of us, I have much more of a killer mentality. I don't feel remorse. Dead people don't haunt me at night. When I thought I was stuck in this chair, I missed the action, the adrenaline, the danger. I like the life. You don't."

"I made mistakes, Jess. I could make more."

Jess was silent, very aware of her fragile state of mind, the battle raging in her. She

447

sounded so lost. So forlorn. He was walking a tightrope, needing to find a way of reaching her. Eric had reconfirmed all her own doubts about herself. If only he could touch her, hold her, he might have a chance. They were separated by a flight of stairs; it might as well have been the Grand Canyon.

"Listen to me, angel face," he tried again. His voice was sheer black magic, a dark sorcerer's powerful weapon, the only one he had at the moment, and he used it shamelessly. "We need to talk this out. Come on down, honey. I'll make hot chocolate, we can curl up on the futon with the fire going and settle it all, just the two of us."

His voice touched her like fingers, soothing, caressing. Half mesmerized, needing him, Saber stood up slowly. Part of her wanted to run down the stairs, fling herself into his arms and be comforted. The other half of her, the sane half, recognized the danger, the shaky line separating standing on the fence and making a commitment. She actually walked down the stairs thinking she was going to do it, just sit on his lap, lay her head on his shoulder, and everything would be all right.

Self-preservation took over. She'd hoped once. Believed once. Hoped and believed in him, yet with her own eyes she'd seen her file, pictures of her as a child killing a puppy. That had been one of the worst moments of her life and he'd witnessed it. Not only Jess, but his friends. Saber eluded Jess's outstretched hand, hurried into the middle of the living room.

"I can't let this happen. Don't you see? I *want* to be with you, to stay here, to believe it's all going to come out right, so the moment I let you hold me, I'll let you convince me even though I know it's impossible." Tears glittered on lashes. "And it is, Jess. It's impossible."

Jess found himself holding his breath. Saber couldn't possibly know what she looked like. Wild, beautiful, large violet-blue eyes luminous with unshed tears, blue-black curls spilling like a halo around her delicate face. She was clad only in his shirt, the tails dipping nearly to her knees, the sides riding higher, revealing an enticing glimpse of bare thigh. Her small bare feet only seemed to increase the feeling of intimacy between them. Beneath his terry cloth robe, his naked body stirred hungrily.

"You have to be willing to listen," he said gently. "I believe this can be resolved."

"Do you?" Her chin lifted, eyes flashing. "Do you really? Or are you just lying to yourself?"

Something dark and dangerous flickered in the depths of his eyes. His mouth hardened perceptibly. "I don't lie to myself."

"Really? What about your 'friend' Eric? Or the fact that you allowed them to talk you into the bionics program, or that they're using Zenith on you? Did you think I wouldn't recognize the signs of that drug? That was in Whitney's file, the one in plain English, not math code. It was his suggestion Zenith be used in small dosages, did you know that? You sold me out to them, whether you intended to do it or not."

"Bullshit, Saber. You're picking a fucking fight with me so you can leave." He knocked the ashes from his pipe into the ashtray beside him and tossed the pipe aside. "I would never sell you out, not for any reason. I had you investigated, like I was supposed to. It would have been criminal of me not to, and you can't condemn me for that. I have no idea how Eric found out about you, but it wasn't through me and it wasn't through Lily."

"How would you know? Because she told you that? Of course she told you and you believed her. But you didn't believe me when I told you he knew." She backed away when he glided closer.

"Damn it, Saber, we have no chance of

straightening anything out between us if you're going to insist on behaving unreasonably."

"Unreasonably?" Saber echoed it, her voice swinging out of control. "You think I'm unreasonable because I don't like it that my past is known by all your little friends? That your friends think I'm a freak and a monster? God! What the hell do you want from me?" Tears sparkled on her lashes. "You want unreasonable? I'm out of here, Jesse!"

Saber whirled around and ran through the house, heedless of the dark, of the furniture. Ignoring Jess's hoarse yell, she swung the kitchen door open and rushed outside onto the grounds. She had no idea what she was doing but she had to get out of the house. Her lungs burned for air and she felt like the walls were closing in on her. Outside, the grass was squishy and wet beneath her bare feet. She ran into the middle of the backyard and paused to look wildly around her, not really comprehending what she was doing, where she thought she was going. The world around her was crashing down and everything she dreamt of was lost.

The night was as turbulent as she felt. Trees swayed in the wind. She turned up her face to the dark ominous clouds, allowing the rain to mingle with the tears on her face. The shirt molded itself to her soft curves and became nearly transparent.

Jess followed her into the tumultuous night, something wild and savage rising up in him to match the elements. "Saber!" His voice carried across the distance separating them, harsh, hoarse, commanding.

She spun around to face him, frightened, untamed, beautiful in the unrelenting storm. "I can't stand it, Jesse." It was a cry torn from her heart, her soul. She was so lost and there was no way out, no way back.

Above her, the sky ripped open, a jagged white streak cracking across the dark rolling clouds, for a moment throwing the grounds into sharp relief. Jess caught a glimpse of her, the shirt nearly nonexistent, plastered to her body and emphasizing her breasts, the darkened, erect nipples, the narrow rib cage and flat line of her stomach and the dark V at the junction of her legs. She looked like a pagan sacrifice, her slender arms outstretched to him, her pale face strained and vulnerable.

His body hardened. Not a subtle, enjoyable change but a savage, painful jolt, the need so intense, so ferocious, it was like nothing he'd ever experienced. "Come here." His voice was rough with lust.

Saber looked across the yard at him, at the raw hunger etched deep into the lines of his face. Desire glittered in his eyes, dark and rough. His body was starkly aroused, the bulge thick and impressive, tenting his robe. The breath stilled in her chest and every stomach muscle tightened and bunched. Spasms went off in her womb, little bursts like sparkling rockets. He was a dark obsession that drew her beyond control.

She came to him, he to her, meeting on the edge of the lawn. He caught the back of her legs in his hands, slid his palms up her unexpectedly hot skin to her firm buttocks. His grip was strong, possessive, as he kneaded flesh.

Saber moaned as his exploring hands urged her closer. Not bothering to remove the thin, transparent material covering her flesh, Jess bent his dark head to her nipple. His mouth was hot on her aching breast, the shirt abrasive. It was wildly erotic, sending waves of such urgency through her body she could barely stand. Cradling his head to her breast, she lifted her face to the wild sky, allowing the rain to wash away the tears.

His hand skimmed up her inner thigh, moved higher to caress hot, moist velvet. Saber moaned again, needing, wanting, a sudden frenzy of hunger she couldn't control. Jess lifted his head, dark eyes burning black. He caught the front of her shirt and as another bolt of lightning ripped across the sky, he jerked brutally, parting the material so that the light exposed her creamy rain-wet skin. The shirt fell unnoticed, a rag in a pool of water at her feet.

Jess caught the nape of her neck, dragged her to him, fusing their mouths together, dominating, barbaric, taking, demanding her compliance, her submission. His body was burning, a painful unrelenting arousal. Saber's soft little throaty cries, her wandering hands, and the sweet taste of her did nothing to appease the pain — it only fueled the fire already burning out of control in him.

She tore her mouth from his, her hands pushing aside his robe, exposing the magnificence of his hard, masculine body. She knelt, wrapping her arms around his waist, her lips on his skin, tasting rain, moving sensuously over every defined muscle, exploring, taunting, deliberately feeding the desperate urgency she could sense in him.

Jess cried out hoarsely, caught two fistfuls of her silky hair, bunching the mass in his large hands, his body trembling, fighting for control. He jerked her head back. In the bright streak of lightning they stared into each other's souls.

"I'll never let you go," he warned softly, implacably. "Be certain, Saber, if you come to me like this, you're mine. If you do this, you're mine." Because she was going to destroy him. Utterly destroy him with her mouth and body. She was already taking him to a place he couldn't come back from.

"I have to have you, Jesse." The admission was stark and raw, and she dropped to her knees in the wet grass as he scooted his hips forward, bringing some relief to his aching body.

Her entire body was going wild with need, her control nearly gone. She wanted it gone. She wanted this — Jess — his body needing hers, burning for hers. She craved the dark possessive lust building in his eyes and the way his body responded with such heat, growing thick and long and hard with his need. She didn't care about his friends, or what they thought, only Jess and the way he looked at her.

She was hungry for the taste of him. She needed to feel the hard length of him filling her mouth, watch his eyes go opaque and glaze over, hear his breath go ragged and see his chest rise and fall, hear his voice turn hoarse with pleasure. She cupped his tight sac in her hands, ran her fingers in a caress over his hard shaft. Watching his face, she leaned forward and ran her tongue over the mushroom head, tasting sex and lust and love mingled together.

His cock jerked. "Damn it, Saber. We could both be in trouble."

She wanted to be in trouble. She wanted him wild and rough. Still keeping her gaze locked with his, she leaned into him with a long slow lick, curling her tongue under the base of the flared head.

His eyes went hot and his fingers bunched in her hair, forcing her mouth toward him. A muscle ticked in his jaw as she blew warm air over him. She opened her mouth to accept the demands of his body, her tongue moistening her lips in anticipation. He made a sound somewhere between a growl and a groan and dragged her head to him.

Saber took him in, inch by slow inch, deliberately prolonging his agony, her gaze locked with his as she drew his thick shaft into the silken heat of her mouth. He tasted of sizzling passion, rich and male, and she needed more. She watched him as he drew in harsh breaths, as he jerked at the robe, shoving it down until it bunched behind him. All the while his hips thrust in an almost helpless rhythm.

She could feel him pulsing against her tongue, filling her mouth, stretching her lips. The power was incredible — that she could do this to him, this sexy, virile man, that he could trust her and want her so that he couldn't take his eyes from the sight of her, so that groans rumbled in his chest and his body shuddered with pleasure.

She licked at the underside of the broad head, and then sucked hard. His thrusts became more urgent, deeper, the hands in her hair controlling. She drove out his control, so that his hands were rough in her hair, tugging at her scalp, sending delicious little currents of electricity down her breasts to her groin. Her womb clenched every time he thrust deeper, each time a groan escaped. She learned to keep rubbing her tongue on the sensitive spot on the underside at the head of his shaft. The more she did, the more she swallowed him and sucked, the more the reward. His breath hitched in his lungs and his cock jerked and throbbed in anticipation.

"You've got to stop, baby." He used her own hair to pull her away from him. "If you don't, we're going to have a major problem."

She took one last satisfying swipe with her tongue. She loved the look on his face, the raw pleasure, the stark desire. He tugged her to her feet, his hands gripping her hips, urging her to climb on him.

All around them the storm raged out of control. The rain beat down. Thunder crashed and occasional flashes of lightning lit up the sky. The series of storms was just getting started, bringing in winter with a vengeance, but it did nothing to cool the raging heat between them.

Her body slid enticingly over his, soft skin against the hard muscles of his thighs as she wedged her knees on either side of his hips. Deliberately, her gaze locked with his, she lifted her body above his. "I really do love you, Jesse. So much I don't know what to do with it," she whispered.

He loved her with everything in him. Everything that he was. "Don't cry, baby, you're still crying."

He cupped her bottom, thumbs caressing, his body straining, aching, demanding. She was a white-hot, tight sheath urging his possession. He urged her over him, driving up through her feminine channel, wanting to shout as pleasure burst around and through him. Jess forgot everything he had ever learned about control. He matched the fury of the storm, unrestrained, turbulent, fiercely wild. The cool rain, her hot body, the lightning flashes, the crack of thunder, it all became mixed with their union. The storm merged with the wild pounding rhythm of their bodies.

He didn't ever want to see that look on her face again. So torn. So sad. So afraid. "I'm going to love you forever, Saber." He gripped her harder, gave her a little shake even as he surged deep inside her, locking them together. She was fiery hot, gripping him tightly, the slick silken walls rippling, clamping down and milking him. He leaned forward, pressed his mouth against her ear even as his body coiled tightly. "If you never trust anything else, trust in how I love you."

He exploded, the hot release jetting deep inside her while her muscles convulsed around his. She cried out, threw her head back, and wept with the night. He called her name, but his voice was lost in the whipping wind.

When the tremors had subsided, Saber lay against his chest, exhausted, spent, unable to stand, unable to move long enough to separate their bodies. In spite of the cold, the heat rising between them caused little beads of perspiration to mingle with the drops of rain on his skin. Jess's heart pounded with alarming force, and he had to fight to control his breathing.

Still locked deep in Saber's body, Jess

spun around and glided out of the storm with sure powerful thrusts on the wheels of his chair. The kitchen door was standing open, evidence of their fast departure. He closed it gently, sliding the bolt in place, the sound very final. Saber hadn't moved, clinging to him, her eyes closed.

As he glided through the house toward the master bath he could feel his body rippling with the aftershocks of her pleasure. He smiled, rubbed his chin on the top of her head, and just held her, thankful to have her. They might have all kinds of things to settle, but she'd committed to him and he couldn't ask for more than that.

Jess rolled the chair right into the wide, specially built shower stall, adjusted the water, and turned on the spray. The warm water felt wonderful, dispelling the cold of the night rain.

Saber slowly, reluctantly untangled her body from his. Jess's hand cupped the side of her face, pushed wet strands of raven hair from her cheek. She couldn't look at him, couldn't believe she had behaved so wantonly, couldn't understand how her body could have felt so much pleasure in such a savage act. She stared down at her bare toes. She was totally nude, no robe, no clothes, in the shower with Jess. His wheelchair was dripping wet, a faint smear of mud being washed away from where her feet had touched the back. His terry cloth robe was soaked and scrunched around his bare thighs and back.

Saber blushed, not quite believing the evidence of their wild, abandoned behavior. Jess caught her chin firmly, his smile infinitely gentle.

"Loving," he whispered, his thumbs caressing her fragile jaw, openly reading her thoughts. He kissed her forehead, skimmed his mouth over hers. "I was loving you."

CHAPTER 16

Jess stared down at Saber's face. She lay curled up, sound asleep, exhausted, one hand flung out toward his pillow — and him, he hoped. The small lamp beside the bed spilled light across her face. Her skin was soft and luminous, her lashes long, lying like fans against her skin. He held her close, his body around hers, his hand under her breast, his cock pressed tight against her buttocks. And God help him, he was as hard as a rock.

He laughed softly, the tightness in his chest finally easing. Patsy was in a hospital being taken care of and Saber was in his bed where she belonged. He bent his head to brush a kiss in her hair before shifting to slide from the bed to his wheelchair. Saber needed the sleep and he needed to get busy and finish the investigation.

He and Logan had tried to recover the data on the recorder and hadn't been successful, but Neil should have been able to do something with it. There were a few GhostWalkers who were very good with sound and Neil should have managed the recovery. Hopefully there was a message waiting from him.

More importantly, for the first time, he had a positive direction in which to take his investigation. The men who had come after him were definitely army. Ryland Miller and his team would want to know. They were conducting the investigation into their handler, General Rainer. Once they all had the same direction, Jess was positive, they'd make progress.

And he had to do something about the bionics. If he couldn't get his legs moving, he would have to consider the idea of wearing the external pack. Even if he could walk part of the time, he couldn't ever rely on his legs, so they were useless to him in their current state.

"Jesse." Saber turned over, her lashes lifting, her gaze meeting his.

"I'm here, baby. Go back to sleep, I'm going to work for a little while. You're exhausted." And the bruise on her face stood out starkly against her pale skin. He had discovered a few others on her body as well, one particularly bad one on her hip from where she'd been kicked. Every time he thought about the jeopardy he'd inadvertently placed his sister and Saber in, he felt sick inside.

She pulled the sheet closer around her shoulders and smiled at him. "I love the way you look, Jesse."

Her voice was so drowsy and sexy, he felt it vibrate through his body, heating his blood, stirring his senses.

"Go to sleep. I'll come wake you in a few hours."

"You'd better. I have to go to work tonight." She yawned and then smiled at him, her lashes already drifting down. "Or my boss might fire me."

Her boss was already thinking about firing her. He was altogether certain he could not survive her going to work, not after what had been done to Patsy. "A couple of the guys will be over, so don't come walking out in my shirt and nothing else."

"Good tip." Amusement tinged her voice, a slight smile curved her mouth, but she didn't open her eyes.

Jess left her to sleep, showering and dressing, using his racing chair rather than the heavier electric one to take him into the office. It took twenty minutes for Logan and Neil to show up, and he could tell by their faces Neil had managed to extract something from the recorder.

"You're going to hate this," Neil greeted.

Logan glanced around. "Where is she?"

"She?" Jess frowned at him. "You mean Saber? Do you really want to piss me off, Max? Because I just spent a couple of hours looking at the bruises on her face and body. I saw her lying in the fetal position on the ground, from the psychic backlash after firing a gun and killing a man — for me, for Patsy. I wasn't close enough to draw the energy away and you and I both know without an anchor, even a shield won't help. She knew it too, but she still did it."

Logan poured himself a cup of coffee from the pot on the desk. "I'm going to look out for you whether you like it or not."

"Then let's get this over. Tell me how she's different. Eric Lambert has the same objection to her, but he isn't a GhostWalker. You can kill. I can. All of us do kill. Does it really make a difference how we do it? You have no problems with Mari or Briony."

Logan sighed. "Mari is a soldier and Briony doesn't have a mean bone in her body."

Neil cleared his throat. "What about the other women? Flame and Dahlia?"

Logan swept a hand through his hair. "I know Dahlia. That's different. To be honest,

I didn't trust her at first. And Flame — she can kill with sound. So yeah, she makes me a little nervous too."

"*I* can kill with sound," Neil pointed out.

"It isn't the same thing."

"Why?"

"Because women don't belong in combat. They shouldn't be running around killing people. They're supposed to be the gentle sex. *We* take care of *them.* They should be having babies and cooking dinner not killing people. What the hell is going on in the world when we think it's okay for women to have guns?"

"Flame, Dahlia, and Saber don't need nor want guns, bro," Neil pointed out.

"Well that's just a fucking great relief to me," Logan snapped.

There was a stunned silence and then both Neil and Jess burst out laughing.

"I suppose they shouldn't be allowed to vote either," Neil said.

"Would you like her better if I told you she can cook?" Jess asked.

Logan glared at them. "Go ahead and laugh. It isn't right."

"Good God, Max. You're a fuckin' male chauvinist," Jess said.

"So what if I am? What about you? Don't pretend it doesn't freak you out just a little that that woman can kill with one touch. What if she's on her period? You ever see a woman with full-blown PMS? My mom used to lose her mind. I'd go to a friend's house for a week until she'd call and say it was safe to come home."

"Okay, I've gotta go with Max on that one," Neil agreed. "Think about it, Jess. The ability to kill with a touch and a woman with PMS. You gotta have some big balls to live with a threat like that."

Jess let out his breath. "I have to admit, I never thought about it."

"It could be ugly," Logan said. "Really ugly."

"I'll just have to keep her pregnant."

"Yeah. That'll work," Logan rolled his eyes. "Don't you watch movies? Ever see a woman in labor? Or having a baby? One hard contraction, my man, and you are toast. The husband's life is already at risk without the woman knowing how to kill. Seriously, Jess, you've got to think about this long and hard, and think with your brain, not with other portions of your anatomy."

"You're just trying to scare me," Jess said, glaring at them.

Logan and Neil burst out laughing.

"Go to hell, both of you." Jess poured a

cup of coffee. "You're a couple of bone-heads. Are we working here or what?"

"I brought this for you." Neil pulled a disk from his pocket, the smile fading from his face. "I'm going to let you listen. It took a while to clean it up and get the conversation. There's still some background noise, but I think you'll recognize a couple of voices." He pushed the disk into the computer. "I'm saving the original and you'll see why."

There was a moment of silence and then the sound of footsteps. "We can't afford to let any of them live, Senator, not one. I don't care if they're out of it or not. You've got to shut that program down. The biggest danger to us right now is that megalomaniac, Whitney, and the abominations he creates." The voice was muffled, and a little distorted, but Neil had managed to amplify the sound enough to catch the words.

"I'm trying."

"Try harder. Whitney knows about us. He's going to find a way to bring us down and you'll go down with the rest of us, Senator. We'll all be charged with treason and my guess is, some of us will be taken out and shot before we ever go to trial. Do you think the president is going to want anyone to know that we've been selling secrets to terrorists and funding them for years on his watch? No one is going to want that information made public. They'll kill us all, and Whitney's supersoldiers will be the ones pulling the triggers. The man's mad as a hatter but they won't terminate him. We've got a few people in key places who feed us information, but it isn't enough. You have to find a way to take him down."

"I'm doing my best." The voice was clearer, as if perhaps he was the one with the voice-activated recorder nearest him.

Jess leaned in to pause the recording. "That's Senator Ed Freeman. This had to be made before he was shot. Who's the other man?"

Neil shook his head. "I have no idea. I've been trying to match the voice with voice prints I have, but so far, no luck."

"The senator sounds almost as if he's afraid."

"Listen to the rest of it," Neil suggested and once more activated the sound.

"Whitney's going to keep going until he's killed. There's no other way to stop him. You've got to kill all the women in his breeding program — *all* of them. We can't have them adding to this mess."

"He doesn't trust me. I think he's trying to have me killed."

"He must know you were instrumental in sending out a couple of his GhostWalkers to the Congo. Get it done. And when I say all the women have to die, I mean *all* of them."

"Violet is helping us," the senator hissed.

"She's the one who told him about Higgens. If she hadn't tipped him off we would have gotten the bastard then. Instead, Higgens is dead and Whitney is in the wind."

"She didn't . . ."

There was the sound of a knock on a door, hinges creaking, and then more footsteps. Both men went silent instantly. Chairs scraped.

"No, no, keep your seats."

The recorder went off abruptly. Jess and Logan looked at each other. The tension in the office rose.

"Was that who I thought it was?" Logan asked.

"That was the vice president," Jess said. "He has a very distinctive voice. He just walked into that room. You don't think whoever was talking to the senator is in the White House, do you?"

"Could the rot really go that high up?" Logan took a deep breath. "They're talking about selling out our country from the White House."

"We're dead men," Neil said, "if we don't find these people."

"They're traitors," Jess snapped. "Fucking traitors and we're going to find them. Isn't Higgens the man Ryland had to kill?"

"He must have been part of a much larger ring and we thought we got it, but we didn't even get the tip of the iceberg. When you're talking senators and someone working in the White House . . ."

"Or the Pentagon. The recording could have been made there as well."

"We know the conversation takes place somewhere the vice president would visit. Neil, can you isolate any background noises?"

"I tried. The recording was damaged. I don't know who could have put the recorder into Louise's private safe."

"The senator's wife? She's a GhostWalker. But she also had made some kind of deal with Whitney to save her husband's life. Whitney put out a hit on him. When she made the deal, she sold out the girls in the breeding program."

"It was one of Whitney's soldiers who put a bullet in his head," Jess confirmed, "although any of us would have been happy to. The senator is responsible for Jack and Ken's capture and torture. He handed them

471

over to Ekabela in the Congo. Prior to that, Whitney had targeted the senator for assassination using Saber. She escaped instead of carrying out the order."

Jess took another drink of coffee, his frown deepening as he tried to puzzle it out. "So we've got two factions. We have Whitney who is a madman, making weapons for his country and thinking he's as patriotic as all get out."

Logan nodded. "And we've got some group, small or large — I'm guessing large — selling our secrets to the highest bidder. They're in top government positions and we know they're also in the military — at least some of them."

"The bastards who went after my sister were army," Jess confirmed. "We need to talk to Ryland Miller as soon as possible and get this information to his team."

"Whoever was talking to the senator is the one giving orders to the admiral and the general, sending our teams out on suicide runs. It has to be him. We've got his voice now. We should be able to nail the bastard," Neil said. "I'll keep working to clean it up and see if I can enhance it even more."

"And try again to get something on the background noises, see if we can maybe figure out exactly where the conversation is taking place, which building," Logan added.

Neil nodded. "I doubt I'll get too much more. It wasn't easy cleaning it and pulling up what I did get."

"Was there any more of the conversation?"

"Not that wasn't damaged beyond my abilities to recover. I can ask Flame, she's a genius with this kind of thing, but I wouldn't count on getting much more. I think the man must have been standing a distance from the recorder."

"He couldn't have known the conversation was being recorded," Logan said.

Jess snapped his fingers. "But the senator might have. Listen to the things he said. Short answers. Nothing too incriminating. He might have been the one recording it. Violet would be likely to urge him to get some insurance. I don't know how the senator got involved with them, but I'll bet he wanted out."

"Then he tries to bargain with Whitney, an exchange of information — especially if the senator's wife is targeted to be killed," Logan filled in. "Whitney didn't sell out those women, nor was the senator going to rescue them, he was trying to show Whitney what he knew, that he'd keep quiet in exchange."

"Then why did Whitney have him killed?"

Neil asked.

"We don't know if he's dead."

"It was a confirmed head shot. I doubt if he survived, and if he did, he's a vegetable."

"Then Violet is going to want revenge. She can't go home to Whitney and she can't come to us. She's out there alone with everyone wanting her dead," Jess said. "So what's she going to do? She plants the recorder in Louise's office, because she's heard the rumor that I'm conducting some kind of investigation."

"We're making a big jump here," Neil said.

"Maybe," Jess agreed, "but it fits."

"Talk about a pissed-off woman," Logan said. "See, I have a point. She's a loose cannon and no one knows whose side she's going to come down on. In the meantime, everyone had better watch their backs. Now you see what I'm talking about with these women. Gun or no, she's dangerous as hell."

"At least she's got good cause, and you ought to be happy, Logan, she was protecting her man," Jess said.

"Too bad she had the wrong man. What a waste."

Jess burst out laughing. "You're such a hypocrite, Logan. You say the women shouldn't be enhanced, but if they are, you don't want to share them with anyone."

Logan shrugged. "I'm a complicated man."

"You're a nutcase."

The smile faded from Jess's face. "You're a smart nutcase, Max. Before Saber escaped, she was in Whitney's office and she found two files out. One was on the senator. She didn't talk much about it, but when I ask her tonight, I'm going to bet she'll tell me it documented treasonous acts."

"That would at least confirm our speculations."

"And there was a file on bionics. Both files were in English, typed out and left right on the desk for her to find. Whitney always, *always,* uses mathematical code. I asked Lily and every single time she's accessed a file on the computer it's in code."

"Which means he wanted her to see those files," Logan said.

"Exactly, but why?"

Logan studied his face. "I think you already know."

Jess was silent for a moment. "You're wrong about her."

Logan looked startled. "That was an abrupt change in subject."

"She saved Patsy's life. There was something wrong with Patsy's heart and Saber knew it. Patsy had a heart attack, Logan. She would have died without Saber. She might be able to kill with a touch, but she can give life as well. You might want to think about that. It could be your life she has to save one day."

Logan held up his hand in surrender. "I don't know why or how we circled back to this, but I'm more than willing to be wrong. I don't like risking you, but if she was mine, I'll admit, I'd risk everything for her."

"We're good then?"

"We're good." Logan shoved out of the chair and set his coffee cup aside. "I'm taking off. It's getting late and she's going to be up soon. She won't want us here."

"She doesn't like you knowing about her past," Jess conceded. "But she'll get over that."

Neil placed his mug beside the coffeepot. "I'm heading out as well. I'll get the recorder to Flame and see what she can do with it. You know we're close if you need us. Martin's taking the watch tonight. And I'd like to point out, and you can tell her, that I don't know, nor do I care, anything about her past. She's one of us."

"Thanks, Neil. I'll make her aware of that." He grinned up at Logan. "It's only Max she has to avoid. And great work, Neil.

I couldn't get anything off that piece of junk."

Neil laughed. "Our strange little skills come in handy."

"Yeah, they do." Jess thought of his sister as the men went out. If Saber hadn't zapped her heart to get it going, she'd most likely be dead, or her heart irreparably damaged. Saber could do things with her talent — good things. And he had an idea that that was the reason Whitney had left that file in plain sight for Saber to read. He had a feeling convincing Saber of what needed to be done, though, was not going to be easy.

He sat for a long while observing her sleep. She was curled up like a kitten, her springy curls blue-black against the pillow, matching the color of her feathery lashes. He enjoyed seeing her in his bed. She looked a little lost without his body beside hers, but he liked that as well.

As he sat watching her sleep, his body hardened, began to make demands. He took his time divesting himself of his clothes, never taking his gaze from her slender body. She looked so right in his bed. He dropped his shirt and then struggled out of his trousers, wincing a little as his body tightened and thickened in anticipation. She looked a beautiful invitation with her hair tousled and her lips slightly parted, lying in the too-large bed.

"Stop staring at me." She didn't open her eyes.

"I want to swim."

"Go swim and leave me alone."

"I'm not supposed to swim by myself. My doctor said so."

She made a rude noise, but still kept her eyes stubbornly shut. "You swim by yourself all the time. Since when do you listen to your doctor?"

"Think how bad you'd feel if I drowned."

Her lashes fluttered. "I'm thinking I might help you drown. If you go away, I can sleep for . . ." She lifted her lashes a bare centimeter and peered at the clock before settling against the pillow again. "A couple more hours."

He rested his chin on his palm, elbow on the side of the bed, leaning in to put his face inches from hers. "Did you know that you're grumpy when you first wake up?"

"Just because your friends left doesn't mean you get to bother me."

He should have known she would be aware of others in the house. The knowledge just made him proud of her. He tugged on the sheet. "Swimming. Exercise. We can skinny-dip."

"You really aren't going to go away, are you?" She opened her eyes and glared, then her gaze widened and she flushed when she saw he was naked and more than alert.

He laughed at her. "Nope."

"You aren't exactly the dream man I thought you were. You're relentless when you want something."

"I'm your dream man." He dragged the covers off of her and slid his hand over her stomach, up to her breast. "I want something now." He bent his head to the invitation, enjoying the way her stomach muscles bunched and her breath caught in her throat when his mouth settled around the offering.

Saber closed her eyes, circling his head with her arms, holding him to her breast while his mouth pulled strongly, sending flashes of fire arcing through her bloodstream. She was all too aware of his other hand drifting down her body, sliding over smooth skin, moving lower and lower. Her hips jerked in anticipation of his touch. He moved his palm to her leg, gliding up and around to her inner thigh.

Her pulse pounded in her blood. Waiting. Needing. Wanting. He had to touch her. In that moment, with his mouth pulling strongly at her breast, his tongue sending waves of heat crashing through her body and his hand moving over her skin, she saw her future, time stretched out before her clearly. She would never be free of her need of him. She would crave his touch with this same intensity — for all time.

Saber ran her fingers through his hair, keeping her eyes closed to better absorb the sensations. Heat and fire. A coiling. It was amazing how he could bring her body to such life. "This is such a perfect way to wake up," she murmured, still drowsy, arching her back like a cat.

"I agree." He kissed his way down her ribs to her intriguing little belly button. "Do you know how soft your skin is?" His voice was low and rough, that husky tone that excited her, that told her he was focused wholly on her.

She lifted her lashes to see the raw desire etched deeply into his face, the stark need in his eyes — for her. His hands were hard on her hips, turning her body so she lay across the bed, dragging her closer to him, his gaze greedy, centered between her thighs. Her breath caught in her lungs as he opened her legs. His hands stroked caresses along her inner thighs, moving slowly toward her heated center. She ached for him, her body pulsing with awareness and need.

His lips feathered down her abdomen, tongue teasing nerve endings into tiny explosive sparks. He said something low and rough, his voice sensual, eyes darkening, adding to the need building inside of her. The warm, drowsy feeling had been replaced by sheer need. She was shocked how fast desire built inside of her, reaching a fever pitch, and he was only kissing her skin, touching her. There was something sinfully sexy about the harsh stamp of lust on his sensual features as he tugged on her legs, widening her thighs apart, using the width of his shoulders to keep her body open for him.

He lowered his head again and his breath was warm. Her body jerked in reaction but he held her firmly. His tongue stroked a long deep caress and she cried out in a broken tone. His mouth settled over her, his tongue flicking as he suckled at her. He suddenly speared his tongue deep. She moaned and nearly came off the bed. He was strong, stronger than she'd remembered, and he held her hips, pinning her in place while he feasted.

His tongue thrust deep and hard, over and over, circled her clit, and he suckled again, sending fireworks exploding all around her. Her fingers bunched the comforter as she whipped her head back and forth, writhing beneath the sensations ripping through her body as his flicking tongue threw her into orgasm.

"Jesse." Her breath came in ragged gasps. "Slow down. You have to slow down." Because the pleasure was skittering too close to pain, the buildup too fast, the orgasm too furious. She felt out of control and unable to catch her breath or think straight. Already another orgasm was building rapidly, winding her tighter and tighter, taking her higher and higher.

He growled low in his throat, the vibration sending a spasm through her womb as her muscles clenched in need. He shifted again, his tongue sliding over her one last time, tasting her heat. He pulled his body onto the bed and rose above her on his knees, catching her hips in his hands and lifting her.

Their gazes locked. He looked wild, his eyes almost black with desire, his face glistening. The head of his heavy erection pressed tight against her entrance. She swore her heart stuttered. The air caught in her lungs. And then he plunged into her, driving deep through soft folds and tight muscles, lodging so deep she felt him against her womb. He stretched her, invading, forcing her body to accommodate the intrusion of his thick shaft. Pleasure washed over her at the intensity of the friction, through her, rocking her until she wanted to scream.

Jess began a fast tempo that had her rising to meet him, desperate for release. The powerful strokes took her higher, forcing her body into a tighter and tighter coil. The temperature rose, until she felt as if she was burning, melting around him, until the tension in her just kept building beyond anything she could ever have imagined.

"Stay with me, baby," he ordered. "Hold on, Saber. Let me have you. God. Baby. Give yourself over to me."

She hadn't realized until that moment that she was thrashing beneath him, her head tossing, her nails digging into him, hips bucking. She was fighting herself, not him. The gathering storm inside of her was too much, too big, too frightening. It was more than her body, it was all of her, and if she gave herself up, sacrificed everything, trusted him that much . . .

He held her thighs apart, surging into her, forcing her to keep climbing with him. She could feel her body pulsing, tightening around his, gripping hard, clenching and rippling. There was no stopping even if she wanted to — and she didn't want to. Her vision blurred, her breath came in sobbing gasps as the explosion rippled through her, building like a wave — a series of waves. High. Hot. Continuous.

Her body was tight, fiery tight, her channel squeezing and clamping down, her flesh melting around his driving cock. He felt the first rush of her orgasm, the slick, heated cream, the fierce grip of her sheath around him, and his own release was there, erupting fast and hard. He held her tight while the waves burst over them, and the explosions finally began to subside.

He collapsed over her, his breathing harsh as he fought for air. Sex had never been that good with anyone else, and he was damn sure he wasn't going to take a chance on losing what he had. He rolled over and lay beside her, his fingers tangling with hers. Beside him, Saber gave off heat, her muscles still bunching in the aftermath.

She turned her head and smiled at him. His heart actually jumped in his chest. The sight of her, sprawled out naked beside him, his scent mingling with hers, expression just a little dazed, made him a little light-headed.

"Marry me."

Beside him, she gasped. Stiffened.

Jess sat up. "Marry me, Saber. I want you in my life forever."

"You can't ask me to marry you, Jesse. Good grief, what are you thinking?" She was genuinely horrified and it showed on her face.

"I just did."

"Well, no. Of course no." She sat up too, pulling the sheet around her.

"Why?" He should have been hurt and maybe that would come later, but she was so distressed and shocked he felt the need to comfort her.

"Why?" she repeated. She pushed the heel of her hand against her eyes and shook her head before looking at him, her expression saying he was a moron. "A million reasons, but first and foremost, Jesse, you have parents."

There was a small silence while he struggled not to laugh. "I don't understand your logic here, baby."

"You understand my logic very well, Jesse. I can barely manage when Patsy comes to the house. She's wonderful, but she's like the real thing."

Now his mouth did twitch. He covered it with his hand and shook his head, more confused than ever. "Do you really think you're making sense? Because I have no idea

485

what you're talking about."

"Patsy. Your parents. Family, Jesse." She thumped the pillow hard. "Are you crazy? I'm really upset that you would even consider marriage with me."

"Why? Do you think you're going to get into an argument with my father about politics or something and decide to give him a heart attack at the dinner table? I can't see that happening, Saber. They can drive me crazy, but I've never wanted to kill them, not even Patsy when she's interfering."

Saber covered her face with her hands. "You have to stop. You're pushing me too fast. We just . . . you just . . . I can barely keep up with what's happening between us and you want more from me." She clutched at the sheet again and peered at him, distress on her face.

"Marriage is supposed to be a good thing, Saber."

"It's not. It's absurd."

Jess leaned close to her. "You aren't really upset over this, are you?" Silence met his question. He pulled her into his arms. "Is it such a bad thing that I'm in love with you? Don't you want to be with me?"

She rocked back and forth, shaking her head.

"Is it scary to think of spending your life

with me? Is it because I'm in a wheelchair?"

She glared at him, sliding off the bed, still holding the sheet around her in a show of modesty. "No. Not at all. I am insulted you would even think that —"

"Because I think I've figured out the problem with the bionics. We can fix them. *You* could fix them."

She stopped, her jaw dropping, mouth open in shocked disbelief. "What? Why would you think for one minute that I could fix the bionics?" She felt absolutely vulnerable — naked, unable to talk when she didn't have her clothes. On the edge of desperation, she looked around her. "I may have read the file Whitney left out, but I'm not a doctor and I don't understand half of what was in it." She looked exasperated. "I can't find my clothes."

"Saber, look at me."

"I have to go to work."

"In the report Whitney mentioned something about electricity being used for regeneration, did he?"

She spun around, her face going white. "I know you're not talking about that ridiculous article he cited. Biologists manipulating the electrical fields in tissues to regenerate amputated tails of tadpoles at a stage when they can't regenerate? Not that.

Because there's a huge difference between a tadpole and a human being."

"What else did the article say?"

She swirled the sheet around her, holding it close. "It doesn't matter. I know where this is leading and I'm not going to do it."

The discussion wasn't going well, Jess decided. She was tense, her fingers twisting together, knuckles turning white as she gripped the sheet. She had a stubborn look on her face. Her mouth was set firm and her chin high.

"Just tell me what else it said."

"There was something about electrical fields helping to, and I'm quoting here, 'control cell identity, cell number, position and movement, which is relevant to everything from embryonic development to regeneration to cancer and almost any biomedical phenomenon you could imagine.' I don't want to know what that means in terms of your bionics, Jess. You can't just introduce electricity into the body. It can kill you. I ought to know."

"Or it can be used to save someone, the way it did Patsy."

She shook her head. "I'm not having this discussion with you. I'm not. I don't care if you get angry with me, I'm not risking your life. I won't do it. And you'd better keep those two friends of yours away, because neither one of them is doing it either." She sent him a smoldering look, controlled fury in her eyes. "I'm going to work. Never, and I mean *never,* bring this up to me again."

She turned to walk out of the bedroom. The door slammed closed, trapping her inside the room.

Chapter 17

Saber turned around slowly, trying to tamp down the anger suddenly churning in her stomach. "Open it."

Jess reached down to the floor to scoop up his trousers and shirt. "We need to talk about this, and since I can't chase after you . . ."

"Don't you *dare* play your wheelchair card on me," Saber hissed. "I don't deserve it. I'm going to take a shower and find clean clothes. I'll talk to you when I've calmed down. Open the door, Jesse."

Jess realized getting her to say she would talk after a shower was the best he was going to get. If he made her any angrier, she wasn't going to listen to anything he had to say. "After your shower we can meet in the kitchen."

She stood waiting, tapping her foot in silence.

"It's easier to close doors than open

them," he admitted. "I'll meet you in fifteen minutes."

Saber yanked the door open and stalked through to the hallway. She ran up the stairs, furious with Jess, angry that he would risk his life. He had a good life. Most people would have given anything to have what he had. A family. Parents who loved him. A sister like Patsy.

"Damn you, Jesse," she yelled and slammed the bathroom door.

It didn't improve her mood to find the stack of brand-new clothes neatly folded, tags still on, waiting for her. She wouldn't have minded had Patsy bought them, or even Mari, but she suspected Mari wouldn't have thought of it and Patsy was in the hospital. No, this was from Lily. All the sizes were correct and there was just about everything she would need.

She took a deep calming breath and stepped under the water, turning her face up to let the hot stream run over her. She couldn't blame Jess for asking her to try to help him walk, as much as she wanted to. He would never have been a SEAL or joined the GhostWalkers if he didn't have a strong need for action and risk. He had to be intensely patriotic and he desperately needed the use of his legs to get back into action.

As she shampooed her hair she thought about patriotism. She detested everything about Whitney and tended to want to believe the monster had no good qualities, but he was a brilliant researcher and his training methods did bring results. She was afraid of the dark, yet she could move through a house unerringly to find her target in complete darkness. Her natural personality was to be emotional, yet she could be tortured and not cry out. She wasn't good at pain, but she'd learned to accept it. And why did Whitney fool himself into believing that the end results justified the means? Patriotism.

Whitney was a patriot. She washed the soap from her hair and added conditioner. The GhostWalkers were all patriots. "I'm not." She said it aloud. Said it defiantly. She wasn't killing because some bastard high up in the government decided someone else needed to die. What was wrong with everyone? How could they trust an order that came down from someone they didn't even know? Someone who could care less about them. Someone who maybe even had their own agenda, or was as loony as Whitney. It made no sense to her.

She dried off, repeating to herself that she was *not* going to let Jess persuade her. It

492

was the height of stupidity. But with a sinking heart she knew if Jesse said just the right
thing, looked at her a certain way, she'd give
in — because she loved him. And love
seemed to make her do really stupid things.

She dressed carefully, hoping to provide
herself with a little armor, and went back
down to join him. Jess always took her
breath away with how handsome he was.
She'd seen him once standing and he'd
been an imposing sight. She felt safer with
him in a wheelchair. Was that the reason
she wanted to say no? Was it more than her
fear of harming him? She hoped not. She
hoped she wasn't that petty, but for the first
time in her life she'd been happy. Jess standing, walking, working as a GhostWalker
would change everything.

She crossed the room to avoid getting too
close to him. She perched on the countertop and folded her arms, waiting for him to
speak first.

"You have to be open-minded, Saber."

He even smelled good. Her heart ached
looking at him, drinking him in. It would all
change. Didn't he realize that? She
shrugged. "I'm trying to be, but you have to
be open-minded too, Jesse. There are a million reasons not to try this. One misstep
and instead of regenerating a nerve, I could

give you cancer."

"Before we get into all the reasons we shouldn't try it, angel face, just tell me what you remember of the report."

Saber's blue eyes glittered at him. "I think you're crazy to even consider doing anything Whitney advises."

"Whitney may be insane, but he's still a genius. If he thinks he has a solution to making the bionics work without a power pack, I'd like to hear it." He kept his voice calm and even.

"He has a solution for a lot of things, Jesse, and none of them are acceptable in a civilized world."

He refrained from arguing. She'd stall as long as he let her. "Just give me the information."

"Fine."

She shrugged, but he noticed she twisted her fingers together and held them tightly against her middle as if her stomach was churning in protest. He wanted to put his arms around her and comfort her, but he stayed still, knowing she had to come to terms with the idea of using her talent on him by herself.

"Apparently it's been known for some time that using electrical currents on wounds can regenerate lost limbs and even repair severed spinal cords in a variety of *fish and mammals. Fish,* Jesse. *Mammals.* Not humans. No one has tried what you're suggesting."

"Humans are mammals," he pointed out.

"Don't even try to be funny." She jumped off the counter and began to pace with quick, restless steps. "This isn't funny, Jesse. What you're asking me to do . . ."

"I know it isn't funny," he replied. "But there has to be something to this."

"Maybe." She pushed at her hair, making it more tousled than ever. "Whitney concluded that the neural pathways need electrical stimulation for regeneration, and that without it, any attempt will eventually fail. There are drugs that stimulate growth, but he concludes that they will never push the neural pathways to form correctly. The downside appears to be that if you overstimulate, it can cause excessive cell growth and cause tumors. *Cancer,* Jesse. That's what he's talking about."

"But without the electrical current, there's really no hope."

She whirled around to face him. "I knew you'd jump on that. I knew it. Whitney doesn't know everything. He doesn't, Jesse, and he's capable of terrible things. I've seen it. I've been a part of his experiments and believe me, he doesn't revere life. We're inferior to him. He wants the *perfect* soldier, and we're not quite up to his standards, so if he needs to find out how far electrical current can be used before it causes cells to become cancerous, he has no compunction about doing so."

"I'm aware of that." Jess kept his tone low, careful not to let the energy swirling in the room near her. He was worried enough without hearing what he already knew. "But you can manipulate the electrical current and read my rhythm at the same time, can't you? Isn't that what you do?"

"Nothing is that simple. I'll admit that the report supports findings that bioelectricity plays an important role in cell regeneration and that electrical induction of *tissue* regeneration may have some application . . ."

"Not *some* application, Saber. *Significant* application."

"Maybe. But you want neural pathways reestablished from your brain to your legs. The nerves are damaged. You have no feeling."

"I have some feeling now. Since they operated and put in the bionics. You saw me walk. Something is happening to allow that. Before the operation, I couldn't move my feet. Now I can. I have to concentrate, but I can do it."

"There you go, then. Give yourself more time."

"I would be walking by now if it was going to work."

"You don't know that, Jesse, and you're risking cancer." She knelt in front of him, looking up. "Please, for just a minute, put yourself in my place. How could I live with myself if I ever harmed you? How could I go on? Do you have any idea what you're asking of me?"

He framed her face with both hands. "Yes. I know I'm going to do this. If you don't help me, I'll ask Lily and Eric, and neither of them can monitor me the way you can. I'm asking you to do this because I believe you're my best chance."

His thumbs brushed against her soft skin as he stared down into her eyes. It was difficult to ignore the fear he saw there, but he was going to try the experiment. He'd had too many operations and had worked too hard to give up.

"Do you have any idea what this will do to us?" she asked. "The changes it will bring?" She had to bring it up. He had to go into this with his eyes open.

"Having me on my feet can only make things better."

"Is that what you really think, Jesse? Because I love you enough to try this madness with you, but you'll go back to active duty. You will. It's what you live for. You and your team will be all over the place and where will that leave me?"

He shook his head. "You're part of us, Saber."

"How? How am I part of your team? How could that ever be? I assassinate people and I do it alone."

"You can heal people, Saber. You could be the ultimate safety net for all of us."

She opened her mouth to retort, but closed it abruptly. Could that be true? Was it possible she could really use her talent for something other than death? She'd helped Patsy, but that had been a fluke. She ducked her head, not wanting him to see her expression, knowing that he'd stirred hope and it was there in her heart, in her mind. She'd always thought of herself as a kind of terrible plague people should avoid.

"Saber? Honey, look at me. You're amazing. The things you can do are amazing. And if you can do this for me, imagine what you could do with someone wounded. I've thought a lot about this."

"I could screw up big time, Jesse. My childhood was a training ground to kill, not save lives. I need to practice and I don't want it to be on you." She was listening to him, wanting it, wanting to be someone different, wanting the prize he was holding out to her, but there was a cost. She wasn't willing to gain her new life at the expense of his.

"You can already read my biorhythm, right? You monitor my pulse, even my blood pressure. Start slow. See what you can do. We don't have to do the regeneration all in one day, in one session. Neither of us knows how it will work."

"It's an experiment, Jesse, and a darned dangerous one. If Lily did this, she could have the equipment ready in case anything happened to you."

"She could have equipment ready after the fact, but *you* can prevent disaster from happening in the first place. You'll know if my heart starts to go crazy, or anything else goes wrong."

"Maybe — but you're betting your life on a very big maybe."

"And the other thing, Lily has no way of monitoring the cells themselves. She would have no way of knowing the cells were becoming overstimulated, so she would be guessing at the electrical pulses used. You'll be far more accurate."

"Jesse," Saber shook her head, holding her shaking hand out in front of her. "You don't have a clue of the process any more than I would have for moving objects. You're guessing because you want it to be true."

"Am I?"

Saber closed her eyes and let her breath out. Eric and Lily couldn't know the amount of electrical current to introduce. How could they? Their guesses would be less precise than hers.

"Okay. But you tell Lily."

"She'll want to be here, and I want to start now."

"I don't care. We can start, but you tell her what we're doing. If she has advice or objections, I want to hear them."

"I thought you didn't trust her," he grumbled, pushing his chair down the hall to his office, with Saber walking behind him.

"I've changed my mind."

He unlocked the door and waved her inside. Saber took the most comfortable chair and waited until he brought Lily up on the monitor. As Jesse explained what he wanted to do, the dawning excitement on Lily Whitney's face made Saber's hands clench the armrests of her chair. "Jess! I should have thought of that. It was there in his file about cell regeneration, but I didn't think about Saber. Can you really do that? Is it possible, Saber? Can you monitor him internally and know when to stop?"

Saber shook her head. "I have no idea."

"I studied your file. You're unique. I've never run across anyone else like you, with your talent, so this would be such a gift to the GhostWalkers if you could actually use electrical currents. There's so much I could teach on manipulating cells for wounds. This could be historic . . ." She broke off. "I'm sorry. I get carried away sometimes. You must be really frightened thinking about trying it on Jess."

"It terrifies me," Saber admitted. She still found it hard to trust Lily — to trust *anyone.* "No one has any idea if it will work or even how to do it."

The thought of Jess without his wheelchair was scary. She hadn't realized how much she relied on that chair to keep her safe. She'd seen glimpses of the real Jess Calhoun, confident and skilled, a warrior, a SEAL, a GhostWalker. He would demand she give everything and he'd give just as much. What if it worked? What if it didn't? She could barely breathe she was so close to panic, and that was simply — unacceptable.

"If you want to try with me here, I'll be

glad to help monitor him," Lily offered. "I'm not sure how much help I'll be, but we can talk about it as we go."

Saber twisted her fingers together and tried to look calm. "That sounds best. Then, if he goes down, you can get us help fast." Her eyes met Jess's. "You'll have to have your legs stretched out."

"That small couch is a futon. I rest in here sometimes," Jess said.

"Is that what you do when I think you're hard at work?" Saber said, trying to inject a light note into the situation. *She* was liable to have a heart attack before they were through she was so scared.

As Saber pulled off the cushion to unfold the frame, she heard Lily rattle papers. "While she's fixing up the room, Jess, I may as well let you know we got the identities of three of the four men who attacked your sister. The fourth man is a ghost. He's dead. I mean he was listed as dead before he ever arrived in Sheridan. The other three were all army, just as you suspected. And the ghost was a Ranger. Special Forces. He took the psychic exam, but didn't pass it. Didn't score any psychic ability. He was supposedly killed in Afghanistan."

"I'll bet that was the one they called Ben."

"Ben Fromeyer. Supposedly deceased a

couple of years ago," Lily said. "But here's the really interesting thing, at least to Ryland. Two of your dead men served under Colonel Higgens before he was killed. Higgens is the man who tried to have Ryland and his GhostWalker team destroyed. We thought he murdered Whitney."

Jess noted that once again, Lily distanced herself from her father. "Higgens was selling secrets to other countries. Conspiracy, treason, espionage, murder — the man was a real piece of work."

Lily nodded. "Ryland thought he stopped him."

"But maybe Higgens was just a cog in the wheel," Jess mused. "And it's been moving right along ever since."

"That's what Ryland thinks. He wants to discuss this with General Rainer."

"He can't until Rainer is cleared. You know that, Lily."

"He won't. But in spite of the circumstantial evidence, Ryland doesn't believe the general is involved."

"Rainer's army, and he was a good friend of Whitney's."

"I know. I know that. But Peter Whitney never sold out his country. Higgens wanted him dead because he found out about the espionage ring. That part was very real.

Whitney faked his death and went underground so he could continue with his experiments, but you can bet he's still got every single government contact he had before."

"Does that include General Rainer?"

Lily shook her head. "Absolutely not. The general has been very good to the Ghost-Walkers. Without him, Ryland's team would be on the run." She looked past Jess to Saber. "Saber is ready, Jess, if you really want to try this."

Jess didn't make the mistake of hesitating. One look at Saber's face told him she was ready to run. He pushed his chair close to the futon and locked the brakes so he could shift onto the open bed. Saber handed him the two pillows that he kept on the shelf in the frame, and he stretched out, positioning his legs so Saber could touch them easily.

She sank down beside him and tangled her fingers with his. "Are you certain? Very certain you want to try this?"

He could feel her trembling and raised her knuckles to his mouth. "I need to do this, Saber. If there's a way I can walk again, then I have to try."

She took a breath and let it out, glanced at Lily, who nodded encouragement, and moved down to the end of the futon where she could circle Jess's ankle with her fingers. His skin was warm, so the circulation was working. She had to calm her mind, put away any possibility of mistakes, and listen, find his rhythm and hear what was happening in his body.

In actuality, it was more than hearing — Saber *felt* the movement of blood. Felt the way everything worked, as if it were her own body, as if they shared one skin, much like it felt when Jess made love to her. That same breath. The euphoria. He was so strong, inside and out.

She moved one hand up his leg to his calf, trying to feel the electrical pulse, that field of energy always present. She had to map the electrical properties of the damaged cells. She could identify them and keep the map in her mind, one of her greatest gifts. Lily and Eric had believed that with the DNA Whitney had given Jess during the genetic enhancement, and with the new drug accelerating cell repair, they would be able to stimulate the damaged nerves to work, but clearly the damage was far too severe.

"Tell me what you're doing."

She moistened her lower lip with her tongue, the only sign of nerves. "Obviously, Jesse, I'm in uncharted territory. If the damaged cells had been usable, physical therapy would have been enough along with the other things Lily and Eric have tried, but the therapy failed. Before I can stimulate new nerves to grow, I'll have to get rid of the damaged ones."

Jess linked his fingers behind his head. "That makes sense."

She flashed him a brief, tentative smile. "I'm glad you think so. And I sure hope you're right about Dr. Whitney, because I'm using everything he said in that file. According to him, many areas of the body have their own built-in programs for regrowing themselves if they're damaged. To heal myself, or someone else, in theory, all I really have to do is trigger one of those programs and the body will do the rest."

"Let's do it then."

Saber sighed. She'd said "in theory." He had chosen to ignore that part. To trigger the program she needed to send a steady stream of electrical signal to the right place at the right time. The body's own biological regrowth program for that particular area would take over and do the rest. It sure beat trying to micromanage the regrowth process herself — that is, if Whitney was correct in his findings. She could just watch it kick in after she jump-started it.

"Come on, Saber, let's do this."

She scowled at him. "You know this isn't quite as easy as you want it to be. For one thing, aside from having never done it, I have to learn all kinds of little details. I have to be careful when healing wounds to apply the electrical current in the right direction. If I blow it, the wound would open up instead of close. This is going to take a little time until I figure out what I'm doing."

He rubbed his hand up and down her arm. "I'm sorry. I know it's going to work, Saber. If you do this, I'll be able to walk again."

"Well, don't talk to me anymore. Let me visualize this." Because she was scared now. She'd killed over and over again with the touch of her hand. Now she was going to do something good for a change — if she didn't blow it and do further damage. And she was going to have to follow Dr. Whitney's instructions verbatim. He had written that report for her to read, knowing she would read it and retain every word. He had described in great detail what needed to be done and how to do it. First she had to shrivel up the damaged nerve segment, using a targeted burst of electrical current. Then she needed to grow a new nerve segment to replace it.

Growth of new nerves — neurogenesis — took a special application of her skill. Like an artist, she would "direct" the electrical field from one point to another — across the gap where the damaged nerve segment used to be — "painting" where she wanted the new nerve pathway to appear. This would set up an electrical field across the space she was visualizing, and nerve cells would start growing in the direction she had "commanded."

She started tentatively, and found that for growing neural pathways, a pulsed electrical current worked much better than a steady one. With persistence, she could generate an entire nerve segment. It was an amazing feeling. The nerve cells felt like plants sprouting in her mind; she visualized them that way. Some would push out tentative tendrils that would grow around neighboring cells. Others would retract if they touched other cells.

Once she grew some new nerve cells, she "fired" them repeatedly — just as if Jess were using those nerve cells over and over again, to break them in and to trigger growth of even newer neurons hanging off of them. If she generated more current, it resulted in faster growth of new nerve cells . . . but she also had to be careful to not overdo it and "fry" the new nerve segment she was creating.

It was an exhausting business, but she grew more confident as she realized the useless tissue and cells were being replaced by healthy muscle and nerves. She concentrated on the most damaged areas, around the bionics where the electrical signals had been severed, and stimulated the growth in those precise muscles and nerves needed to drive the bionics.

Growth of new muscle tissue required a little something, she discovered; it was actually easier than regenerating nerves, but required great precision for long periods of time. If she applied just the right amount of electrical current at just the right place on the edge of the healthy muscle tissue, she would trigger a biological program already built into the body, a program for regrowing new muscle tissue to replace old damaged tissue. She just had to keep the level of current steady to keep the body's program running and sit back and "feel" it do the rest of the work. It sure beat having to micromanage all the zillions of muscle cells. She was so exhausted, she wouldn't have been able to continue.

She pulled her hand away from Jess's legs, aware of the time passage only because she was swaying with weariness. The room had been so silent while she worked, and when she glanced at the monitor, Ryland was watching with his wife.

Jess lay very still for a long while, so long that Saber's heart began to accelerate. She touched his shoulder. "Are you all right?"

He glanced at her and then at the monitor. "Yes. I feel fine. Just not any different. While you were working my legs were warm, and I actually felt a couple of zaps, but now I'm not feeling much of anything." He sat up slowly.

Lily smiled at him. "If you don't see any improvement within twenty-four hours, you should try again. This is amazing, Saber."

"Only if it worked," Saber said.

"I'd like to stay and talk, this is really exciting, but I think I'm going to be having a baby here pretty soon."

"You mean in a few weeks," Jess corrected.

"I mean in a few hours. If you need anything else, call Eric. I'll be out of touch for a while."

Ryland stuck his head around Lily, a grin splitting his face from ear to ear. "We're having a baby, Jess!"

Jess laughed. "I can see that. Good luck to both of you. Let us know everyone's all right the minute it comes into the world."

"I will," Ryland promised.

Lily blew a kiss to Jess. "Be happy, you two."

The monitor went dark and Saber flicked it off. She turned to Jess. "I can't believe she sat there in labor the entire time. I would have been freaking out."

"I don't think you freak out much, Saber," Jess said, catching her hand and tugging until she was back beside him.

"What is it?" She pushed back his hair.

Jess lay back against the pillows, trying to hide his frustration, rubbing his hand over his shadowed jaw to hide his expression when he really wanted to pound his legs with his fist.

"What?" Saber flashed a slow smile as she shook her head. "Did you think anything we did was going to meet with instant success and you'd miraculously stand up and walk? It even took a tadpole twenty-four hours to grow a new tail, and you, my impatient friend, are a lot larger than a tadpole."

He scowled at her. "You could be a little more sympathetic."

"Over what? You being a little kid who wants instant gratification?" She leaned over and kissed his nose. "There. It was all out

511

of joint, but I've made it better."

"It's not better." He pointed to the left corner of his mouth.

She rolled her eyes, but leaned closer, her lips feathering across his until she found the corner and pressed briefly. "You're such a baby."

He pointed to the other side.

Saber caught his head in her hands and kissed the right corner of his mouth and then settled her lips over his. Teasing. Nibbling. Sliding her tongue along the seam of his lips. She felt her stomach tighten, her womb clench with need. It didn't take more than looking at Jess to want him. Kissing him was incredible. She loved his mouth, hot and sensual and a little ruthless.

His hand moved to the nape of her neck, holding her still, while his mouth took control of hers. His other hand urged her down on top of him. She straddled him and slid her arms around his neck, pressing close to his chest.

He kissed her over and over, deepening each kiss, demanding more and more until she felt as if she was melting in his arms. "If I didn't say it before, thank you. And if it doesn't work, thank you for trying. I know you were afraid."

"If I forget to tell you," she whispered

against his mouth, "I'm very much in love with you."

"Then marry me."

She sat up abruptly. "Not that again. Honestly, Jess, you're relentless when you want something."

He tugged on a curl. "I can keep you safe from Whitney."

"Maybe. And maybe you'll get me pregnant and we'll have to go underground like Lily. She's leaving her home in order to keep her child safe."

He shrugged. "We can go up into the mountains near Jack and Ken. They have a fortress up there. It's all good, Saber, as long as we're together."

She moved from his lap. "Come on, dragon king, let's go eat. I haven't had food yet and I've got to go to work." She needed something after expending all that energy.

He slid his body from the futon to his chair. His right calf jerked. He caught his leg and positioned it. "I'll cook tonight. You can explain why you don't think moving to the mountains would be a good idea."

"Your parents, for one thing, Jesse. And Patsy. After you moved here, Patsy followed you and then your parents bought a house as well. You told me that yourself. You just can't leave them."

He laughed at her. "You're really grasping at straws, aren't you?"

"Why marriage?"

"Because I believe in it. My parents have been married for over thirty-four years. They're still very much in love. I don't think the real thing comes along all that often, so I'm grabbing it and hanging on."

"How can you be so sure that it's not pheromones?"

He caught her hand again, tugging until she was beside him. "Sex with you is fantastic, no doubt about it, better than anything I ever imagined." His grin turned wicked. "And I can imagine a lot. But the truth is . . ." His smile faded and he brought her onto his lap, his arms enfolding her close, sheltering her against his heart. "I'm so in love with you I can't think straight. One has little to do with the other. I wouldn't feel like this if it was all pheromones."

She bit her lip. "You thought you loved Chaleen enough to ask her to marry you."

"She was pretending to be someone she wasn't. I thought she liked all the same things I did, and I didn't know what real love was. I mistook a sexual attraction for the real thing. I think I knew all along, but I didn't want to know because a home and family meant so much to me. You're the real thing."

"What if you're wrong?" she persisted, turning her face up to his. "You could be wrong."

He slid his hand around the nape of her neck, the pad of his thumb caressing her face. "I'm not, Saber."

She shook her head. She was tired already and she had a show to do. "I've got work tonight. Do you think we could talk about this later? I'm starving."

"Fortunately for you, I called and had dinner delivered earlier. I just have to heat it up."

"You cheat," she accused, sinking into a chair. Her hand was shaky as she pushed it through her hair. "That was more difficult than I imagined." She had to hide the effects of the psychic drain from him or he'd insist she stay home, and she needed a little time to put everything in perspective. But she was exhausted.

"It makes sense, you're using energy to direct an electrical current. And you worked for over an hour and a half."

"I didn't notice the time passing," she admitted. "Whitney's file was actually more helpful than I would like to admit. Everything he speculated and how to do it was dead on." She hadn't deviated at all from the instructions, too afraid of doing harm.

He put a plate in front of her and turned back to get his own. "You said you read the second file, on your target. Senator Ed Freeman was your target, right?" He looked back at her when she didn't answer.

Saber's gaze slid away from his. "I don't like talking about what went on before I came here. I'm trying to be someone else and forget all of that happened. Maybe, just maybe if I could help you, I wouldn't feel like the villainess of the world all the time. And maybe your friends wouldn't look at me like they expected me to fry them with my gaze."

Jess put his plate on the table and rolled his chair beneath it. His legs were twitching, both of them, tiny sparks of pain zapping him. He didn't dare mention it, not when she was so certain she could harm him. "You're too sensitive. No one looks at you like that except you. What happened to you made you who you are, the woman I'm in love with, Saber. And we need to figure out who is trying to kill the GhostWalkers."

"Whitney is a good start."

"Maybe. Possibly. But then maybe it's someone else and Senator Freeman was involved in espionage." The pins and needles were painful and his muscles cramped and spasmed.

She shrugged. "Whitney thought so. Freeman's father was friends with Whitney but apparently they had a falling out over Whitney documenting the senator's involvement with a General McEntire, who was part of an espionage ring. I saw the evidence and it was pretty damning. The senator looked a legitimate target to me, but then evidence can be falsified fairly easily."

"I don't think Whitney made anything up, Saber. Freeman set up two GhostWalkers for capture and torture in the Congo. He's part of a ring trying to destroy us, although it doesn't make sense because he's married to one of us."

"Violet. I read about her," Saber said. "Whitney wants her dead too."

"He would if they were selling secrets to foreign countries, especially now with all the terrorist attacks. And I can't blame him. Freeman was about to be named as a vice presidential candidate. Can you imagine what he'd have access to?"

Jess's legs were jumping. Beneath the table he pressed his hands down hard on his knees in an attempt to control the involuntary spasms. Pins and needles were like hot pokers stabbing into his flesh. He broke out in a sweat. He had meant to have her stay home from work, but he didn't want her to see him like this.

Deliberately he glanced at his watch. "Have I made you late?"

She grabbed his arm and turned his wrist over. "Oh no. I've got to go. Brian's going to be pulling out his hair. I'm sorry about the dishes. You heated up the food, I should clean up. Just leave them for when I get home."

She rushed around the table, dropped a quick kiss on his head, and catching up her purse, paused at the door. "If you need me tonight, you call me, Jess."

"I'll be all right." She had to leave fast or she was going to notice he was in trouble.

"Your friends will be hanging out tonight, right? Watching over you?"

The anxiety in her voice turned his heart over. "Yes. Now go, Saber. I'll be listening."

She smiled at him and hurried out the kitchen door to the garage.

Jess put his head down on the table and prepared himself for a long night.

CHAPTER 18

"Hey!" Brian frowned as he strode across the floor, reached for Saber's chin, and lifted it so he could inspect her face before she could jerk free. "What happened to your face? Who hit you?"

Saber touched her cheek. "I forgot about that. It looks worse than it is, Brian. Some . . . people attacked Patsy, and Jess and I happened along and there was a bit of a fight."

Brian's eyebrow shot up. "You got in a fight? And the boss? Is he all right? Who would fight someone in a wheelchair? And who would attack Patsy? She's the sweetest woman in the world. Is she all right?"

Saber laughed and sank into a chair. "Do you have any more questions?"

"A dozen or so." Brian gave her a reluctant answering smile. "But tell me if Patsy's all right."

"Yes. She's in the hospital. She had a

heart attack."

Brian's color paled. "A heart attack? But, she's too young."

"I think she had a heart problem and with the assault on her, her heart couldn't take it and reacted. She's in the hospital and she's better."

His boyish good looks suddenly hardened, and for one brief second he looked scary. "Who attacked her?"

Saber shrugged, trying to appear casual. "I have no idea who they were." Usually she liked the radio station at night, sitting in the booth, talking to unseen listeners, but she was so tired and so many things had gone so wrong, that maybe it wasn't such a good idea to come in to work. Now she was looking at Brian as if he were a suspect. "Do you know Patsy very well? I didn't think she came to the station that much."

"Actually Jess interviewed me for the job at his home, not here at the station, and Patsy was there. I was new in town and she had coffee with me a couple of times. Not like a date or anything, she was just being nice to me. But I like her."

Saber grinned at him.

Brian raked a hand through his hair. "Not like that. Don't start. And at least tell me if Calhoun is all right. He must have been really upset over his sister being attacked."

Saber settled into her familiar chair. "Yeah, you could say he was upset. He's pretty amazing for being in a wheelchair. I was impressed." She tapped the mike, a habit she couldn't break, her restless fingers moving everything around within reach. "It feels good to be back."

"That nutcase that keeps calling you," Brian said, "I've been listening to the tapes over and over and he's distorting his voice, not a lot, but enough that I'm beginning to think that it's someone you know. And some of the calls were prerecorded."

Saber's head snapped up. "What do you mean, prerecorded?"

"I don't think he's there. I think . . ." He broke off abruptly and shook his head.

"Oh no, you don't. You can't just stop there. This whack job records his distorted voice on tape and then calls the station and uses the recording?" That made no sense at all.

"I think he arranges for the phone to call in automatically, like the telemarketers, and when the phone on our end answers, the recording kicks on."

"Why would he do that?"

"You tell me."

Frustrated, Saber glared at him. "You're

driving me crazy. Men are crazy. Whoever said they were the logical sex? You've obviously been thinking about this and you must have a theory."

"I'm not stupid enough to tell it to you, because it's so far-fetched. Figure it out yourself and tell me what you come up with." He glanced at the clock. "You're on in five."

Brian had jinxed her for the entire night. She just couldn't get into her normal rhythm. It wasn't a bad show, but she didn't shine, that was for sure. Why would someone use a device to make a call demanding to talk to her? What if she'd agreed to talk to him? What if he'd gotten past Brian? So the object of the phone call hadn't really been to talk to her at all.

Whoever had broken into her house likely would be the same nut. Surely, there couldn't be two separate people fixating on her. So why would he call and not be on the other end of the phone to talk to her if she took his call?

Her gaze strayed to Brian several times over the course of the next few hours, her body slowly growing tense. She studied his face. He had a boyish face, laugh lines around his eyes, his mouth always ready to smile. But when she really examined him, it occurred to her that those boyish good looks could be hiding something much more sinister beneath. Goose bumps raised along her skin.

She did another short broadcast, talking about nothing she could remember, her mind suddenly consumed with the reality that Brian moved with grace and carried himself like a man who could handle himself. And what did she really know about him? He'd arrived in town right before she had. *And he saw Patsy occasionally.* Her pulse thundered in her ears and her mouth went dry.

Had he said that to subtly warn her that he could hurt Patsy anytime he wanted? When had she let her guard down enough to stop being suspicious of everyone around her? She snuck another look at him — the set of his shoulders, the smooth way he moved. He was good at his work, easy to work with, he fit in.

What was she thinking? Where was she going with this and why was she suddenly tense and apprehensive? She bit down hard on her lip, distracted enough that she nearly missed her cue. At Brian's frantic signals, she sent her soft, whispery siren's voice out over the airwaves, gave a little commentary, and introduced the next run of songs. All the while her mind was turning over the puzzle, trying to piece together an answer.

Feeling Brian's gaze on her, she turned and glared at him through the glass. She signaled him to come into the booth. Brian sauntered in, looking cockier than ever.

"I want to hear your theory."

"What's yours?" he countered.

"If I know him, obviously he'd have to disguise his voice."

Brian nodded. "My feelings exactly." He leaned one hip lazily against the console and regarded her from his lofty height.

Saber leaned close to him, moving her hand until it rested close to his arm right above his wrist. She drummed her fingers beside his arm, using her nervous habit to cover her movement. "And if he used a recorder, is it possible that he wants to be in two places at the same time?"

She tuned her heartbeat to his, listening to the rhythm, allowing her body to sync with his. If he was nervous, it didn't show in his body rhythm. His heartbeat and pulse were steady. Her fingertips very lightly slid against his skin. "Like if it was you, Brian, you could call and still be here to take the call." She made certain as she made the suggestion that even as she sounded casual, she checked to see if there was even a slight abnormality in his pulse.

He grinned at her. "Me? I like you, honey, but not that much. It's a lot of trouble to go to, and I'm kinda on the lazy side."

Absolutely no change in his rhythm. If Brian was lying, he would be able to beat a lie detector with no trouble at all. She didn't believe he was that good. She slipped her fingers back to the surface of the console and resumed the "nervous" drumming. "It was a wild idea, but actually not a bad one. If the person is someone I know, wouldn't it be a great way to keep suspicion from them? They could be with me when a call came in."

"If you're thinking Jess, I just can't go there. I'm sure the man's a perv, but if he wanted to get all freaky with your things, he'd have done it long before now."

Everything in her stilled, but she hung on to her smile and the cool mask that was her face. Young. Innocent. So sweet and vulnerable. *How had he known that the intruder had gotten into her things?* No matter what he said to cover his tracks, Brian knew about the intruder, and no one should have that information. It hadn't gone outside the GhostWalker circle at all.

"Not Jess, you dope." She injected the right touch of humor.

She caught a glimpse of her face reflected in the glass surrounding her, and it was her heart that jumped. She was wearing her death mask. The innocent teenage one. Guileless. Little white teeth gleaming in a smile, eyes shining and friendly. She despised that mask, but there it was, an automatic reaction. She glanced down and found the pads of her fingers against his pulse, her body already syncing their rhythms. Even knowing from the easy relaxed rate of his pulse that he wasn't the stalker, she instinctively had prepared to kill him to eliminate a threat, if she'd been wrong.

She jumped up so fast she knocked over her chair. Suddenly she wanted Jess's arms around her, protecting her — or Brian. What was she thinking? That she could settle down with Jess in a fairy-tale world and have the happily-ever-after?

"What's wrong, Saber?" Brian leaned down and picked up the chair, giving her a puzzled frown. "You really aren't considering that it's Jess — or me — are you? If you're afraid, I'll call Brady in. Hell." He righted the chair and held up both hands palm out. "I was only trying to help. I didn't want to scare you."

"No, no, Brian." She forced another baby-faced smile. "I've got an irrational fear of bugs, and I saw that spider." She pointed to the little arachnid crawling innocently on the edge of the console. "I just reacted without thinking."

Brian grinned at her and used his thumb to squash the spider. "I never expected such a girlie reaction from you."

Saber rolled her eyes and forced an answering grin. "Well, don't tell anyone." She moved around him back to her chair, keeping her heart rate under control. She waved him out of the booth and turned back to the mike, talking nonsense and flirting a bit before she set up the next round of music.

Her first thought had been to eliminate the threat to her. She had been trained as a child to kill and she thought if she just refused, if she just walked away, she would be like everyone else. She'd stop and it would be over. But everywhere she went she had to take herself with her and she was an assassin — a trained killer. Her every instinct had been to destroy the threat.

She glanced through the glass at Brian. He was joking with Fred, the janitor. The kind older man cleaned the station every night, and Brian always, *always,* talked to him. Treated him with respect. Brought him food even, some little thing he'd found and thought Fred should try. Brian even got along with Les, the man who took his job during the day.

No one got along with Les. He kept to himself, was rude and insulting to and about women, and resented working for and having to take orders from a man in a wheelchair. He was good at his job, but basically he was just plain creepy . . .

Her breath came in a little rush. *Les?* Could the whack job be Les? But if it was Les, then how had Brian known about the intruder ruining her clothes? Patsy didn't know. Only the GhostWalkers and . . . She picked up the phone. Jess answered on the third ring.

"Hey, quick question." She glanced around to make certain no one could overhear. Brian was busy with Fred, not paying any attention. "Who knew about the whack job in my room?"

"The team of course."

"Would they say anything?"

"No, of course not. Why?" Jess's voice was filled with suspicion.

"No reason. I'm just trying to figure things out. Anyone else know? Patsy, for instance?"

"How the hell would Patsy know? Lily and Eric knew. I briefed them when we talked about . . ." He broke off, hesitated, and then supplied, "Things."

"You meant me. You discussed me."

"Among other things. You're too sensitive, Saber."

"Well, how many people know about you, Jesse? Not your SEAL background, but the GhostWalkers? Does Patsy? Your parents? Who knows? Who goes around discussing you?"

"What is wrong with you tonight?"

"I can't talk right now, I have a show to do."

She hung up, furious all over again. Damn him for sharing her life with those others. She didn't know them. She didn't trust them. They weren't part of her world.

Brian knocked on the window and held his palms up in inquiry. Swearing under her breath, she leaned in to the mike and began another commentary, all the while her mind churning with myriad possibilities — or none at all. How had Brian found out? He had to be the intruder, but seriously — she studied him again through the glass — it just didn't add up. No one that creepy could keep up that kind of pretense for long — could they?

She was grateful when three o'clock came around. She was going to have to discuss this with Jess. Just the possibility of being in such close proximity to a man who had broken into her home and violated her privacy in such an obscene way had her twisted up inside.

Brady the security guard was waiting to walk her to her car. Brian stopped to say good night to Fred, and Saber breathed a sigh of relief. She didn't want another prolonged chat with him before she had a chance to talk to Jess.

"It was a good show," Brady greeted. "I listened while I did my rounds."

She sent him a sharp glance. Now she was paranoid. Brady was a friend of Jess's from his navy days. He'd been a SEAL and had started a security service. Why shouldn't he listen to her show while he made his rounds? The job had to be boring most of the time.

She forced a tired smile. "Thanks. I wasn't into it like usual, so I'm glad the show didn't sound too bad."

Brady was a big man and light on his feet. He had the restless eyes of a lot of the SEALs, scanning their surroundings as they moved across the parking lot to her car. She stayed close, her hand brushing his arm occasionally, the touch so light he barely felt it, but it was enough to allow her to feel the steady rhythm of his heart.

Saber drew in air, let it out, concentrating on the steps to the car, all the while watching Brady, aware of every body movement. Tension built and she couldn't stop it. Everything felt wrong. A step out of place, but she wasn't certain why. Time slowed down, tunneled, while her heart beat the same rhythm as his. Brady was her guard. He'd been walking her to her car for nearly a year, yet all of a sudden, she no longer felt safe with him.

"What is it, Saber?"

His voice was quiet. She felt the concern in him and forced herself to smile again. "I don't know. I'm a little skittish."

Brady put his hand on her arm and swept her behind him as they approached her car. "You should have said something. When you think something is wrong, it usually is." He pulled his gun from his shoulder harness and stepped toward her car.

"Brady, let's go back inside," Saber said. "I feel exposed out here."

There was little cover in the parking lot. A few trees and shrubs spread out, but most of it was asphalt. She glanced around uneasily.

Brady immediately stepped back toward her. The bullet caught him low on his thigh and spun him around. He went down hard, his large body sprawling out, but his gun was still rock steady in his hand. Saber dropped down and crawled to where he lay.

"Get to cover."

"How bad?" She put both hands over his heart to feel the extent of the damage.

Brady shoved at her. "He'll be coming to finish me off. Get the hell out of here, Saber. There's no cover."

She caught his arm. "Push with your feet. Hurry."

"Leave me. You've got to get out of here." But he pushed with his heels as she dragged him between the cars.

"Shoot out the lights."

Brady didn't ask questions, he fired several shots. Glass shattered, raining down from all four corners of the lot.

"Well, at least you're a good shot." She renewed her grip on his arm. "Keep moving."

"I hope you have a plan."

"I always have a plan." Saber kept dragging him, staying low to the ground. Let their attacker think they were sheltering between the cars. "I can see in the dark, like a cat, Brady. Keep moving, we only have to make it to the edge there."

"There's a dropoff."

"Yeah, I know." She'd studied the area

thoroughly over the past year, committing the landscape to memory just in case she had to escape fast. She figured this qualified.

"Saaaaber." The voice sounded eerie coming out of the dark. "Saaaaber."

"Great. It's the whack job sperm donor. Sheesh."

Brady muffled his snort.

Saber pulled at his arm harder, silently cursing that she didn't have the kind of strength needed for carrying big men. Whitney had physically enhanced her, but more with the ability to jump, to turn herself into a pretzel, get in small places. Her strength was more than adequate for lifting herself and dangling for long periods of time by her fingertips, but Brady was nearly dead weight. She was beginning to sweat, fearing they might not make it.

"When this is over, lose a little weight, Brady," she hissed in his ear.

"It's all muscle, ma'am."

There was little moon, so he couldn't appreciate the eye rolling. She could see the stain spreading now, inky black in the dark. "What is it about Navy SEALs? Do you all have to be so macho?"

She was talking more to distract herself from the task of pulling Brady's large body and the fear of a bullet striking them. She kept close to the cars as long as she could before dragging him into the open. They had to go slow, not draw the eye. Hopefully their attacker would be concentrating on watching between the cars. It would make sense for them to try to stay concealed and the cars were the only real cover available.

"Saaaaber." The call came again. Distorted. Taunting. Disturbed.

They stayed silent as they made their way with painstaking slowness across the ten feet separating the asphalt from the rough terrain. The wild grass was kept low around the edges of the parking lot to minimize the risk of fire.

"Be ready with your gun, Brady," she whispered. "We're going to be very exposed right here. Hopefully I can get you onto the grass without drawing his eye. It's going to hurt like hell. Are you ready?"

Brady gripped his gun and nodded.

Saber backed onto the curb, staying as low as possible. She hooked Brady under his arms and heaved, dragging him over the bump. His breath left his body in a rush, but he remained silent as they fell backward onto the grass. They lay gasping for breath, Saber under the upper half of Brady's body.

She put her mouth against his ear.

"There's a ledge, a large one, just behind us. I'm going to try to get you there. Let's just rest for a minute." She could feel Brady's heart racing. His pulse was thready. He was heading toward shock. His skin had gone clammy. "Can you hang on a little longer, Brady? I'll get you help as soon as I can."

Brady managed a brief grin. "My backside's a little raw, ma'am."

In spite of the gravity of their situation, she found herself smiling back. "Come on, tough guy, let's move."

All the while she was listening for a sound, anything that would tell her where their attacker was. She watched the parking lot as she dragged Brady backward. Now that they'd been in the dark awhile, eyes were adjusting, which wasn't a good thing. She felt the need to move faster, but forced herself to keep their pace slow.

She saw a figure move, running from the side of the building to the shelter of one of the trees. Her heart jumped. She took a breath and allowed adrenaline to give her the rush she was going to need.

"He's over by the smaller of the trees closest to the station. Keep your eye on him. If he goes for the car, can you hit him? Are you good with that gun? Because, seriously, if you're not, I am. The thing is, though, it will make me sick — really, really sick — to kill."

He was silent for a moment, his grin widening. "Just how good are you with a gun?"

"I've had a lot of weapons training and I qualify as an expert marksman."

"You're just full of surprises. And mean as a snake. You want that son of a bitch dead, don't you?"

"I want him gone. And I don't want to have to worry that he's going to come after me again." She didn't know any other way to shoot than to shoot to kill.

They were right at the ledge now. She didn't want Brady to drop to the other side until he fired the shot or gave her the gun. They'd only have one shot at it. Once he'd given away their position, she'd have to stash him and draw the attacker away from him. Her only hope was that the madman didn't want to kill her right away. Whatever this was — whoever it was — it had nothing to do with the army and the investigation Jess was conducting. The man was a stalker — her stalker.

They lay in the thin grass, willing the man to go toward the cars. He called out Saber's name again, the sound so strange she realized he had to be using a device to distort the tone enough to disguise it. *She knew him.* She always identified people by their particular biorhythm, the way their body was unique. She had to tune out everything else and just hear him if she was going to recognize him. And that meant she couldn't do it until she could get far enough away from Brady so his heartbeat wouldn't interfere.

Everything to her was an electrical current — a kind of code — and she knew if she could get close enough, her body would pick her stalker's rhythm up.

"He's moving," Brady said.

She blinked to bring the shadowy figure into focus. He took a couple of tentative steps. Brady brought the gun up.

"I might be able to hit him," he said. "The company van is blocking him, but I might tag him if he comes out into the open."

"Go for it if you think you can."

He flicked her one quick glance and then shifted to get into a better position. His hand was shaking. Sweat dripped into his eyes.

Their attacker crouched low, looked left and right, and then ran toward the cars. The sound of his boots hitting the asphalt seemed overly loud in the silence.

Saber took the gun from Brady's hand, aimed, and squeezed the trigger. The bullet caught the man low, slamming him backward. The sound of the gunshot reverberated across the parking lot. He yelled and fired off several rounds as he went down, shooting wildly. The barrage of bullets hit cars and trees and went into the dirt, but didn't come close to them.

Saber pushed to her feet. She had very little time. Already the violent energy was rushing to overtake her. Brady tried to catch her with an outstretched hand, but she brushed past him and ran toward the downed man, the gun rock steady on him. She had to finish him before the energy hit her and she went down. There was no one else to protect Brady, and his wound was serious.

"Don't!" Brady called sharply.

She was aware of him struggling to get to his feet, but she couldn't stay and help. The wounded man thrashed on the ground, cursing aloud, and she gripped the gun harder, her stomach churning. She willed him to turn the gun on her. She didn't want to kill him in cold blood — like an assassin. She wanted it to at least be self-defense.

She made noise as she ran, deliberately making her footsteps loud, hoping he'd bring up the gun, but he kept screaming and rolling on the asphalt. Saber skidded to a halt, brought up the gun, and stared down into the face of the man who had violated her sanctuary — her home.

"Les." She let out her breath, a little shocked that the day soundman could have been stalking her for the last few weeks. He barely spoke to her, in fact the rare times they worked together, he was surly and mean.

He spat curses at her, the gun still in his hand, but he didn't lift it, only drummed his heels against the asphalt and raged as if demented. She could see he'd been wounded in the stomach. The pain had to be excruciating.

"Saber!"

If she was going to kill him, she had to do it now, squeeze the trigger and be done with him, but she couldn't. She stood there shaking, the energy swirling around her in blacks and reds, swallowing her up so that her vision darkened and she went to her knees.

Brian ran up behind her and the terrible churning in her stomach, the pounding in her head, lessened significantly. When he dropped his hand on her shoulder, it disappeared altogether.

"Are you all right?"

"Brady's been shot. We need to call an ambulance."

He reached down and helped her up, removing the gun and tucking it into his belt. "Did he hurt you?"

"No. But he's been the one calling and he broke into my house and did disgusting things in my bedroom. I don't understand this."

"No? Les was sent by Dr. Whitney to watch you and report back to him."

Brian drew a gun from beneath his shoulder and kicked at Les with the toe of his boot while Saber stood there, mouth open in shock.

"How would you know that? Who are you?"

"The theory was neither you nor Jess would pay much attention to someone not genetically enhanced. And you didn't. It was a test of sorts, one you both failed. You even disliked him, but you didn't bother to find out why. That's a weakness, Saber."

He brought up the gun, aimed it, and fired. A hole blossomed in the center of Les's forehead. Saber jumped and stepped back, horrified.

"You should have killed him. You never would have been safe as long as he was around. He's been deteriorating for months.

He obsessed over you."

"Brian." Saber inhaled sharply, trying to keep panic down. He wasn't close enough to touch. And he didn't take his eyes off of her. "Do you work for Whitney?"

"You already know the answer to that and it should have occurred to you why you were so comfortable at work." There was a definite reprimand in his voice.

"You're an anchor." *He* was the reason she wasn't writhing on the ground with jackhammers pounding at her head from the aftermath of violence.

"And a shielder." He flashed a quick grin. "One of the rare ones — like you."

She raised her chin and took another step back. "You'll have to kill me, Brian, because I'm not going back."

His eyebrow shot up. "If I'd wanted to take you back, I would have knocked you out at work and gotten the job done."

"I liked you, Brian. You're very good at what you do."

"You don't have to stop liking me. I'm no different from you. I do a job. My job was to look out for you and I've done it. The next time you have a maggot on the ground, Saber, kill it. You've been taught right. Just because you don't want to work as an assassin anymore doesn't mean all of your training should be thrown out. You should be able to keep yourself alive."

Brian glanced over at Brady. "I've got to go. There are a couple of people I want to see before I take off."

She took a step toward him. "Not Jess."

"Of course not Jess. Back off, Saber. I wouldn't want to have to knock you out. I don't like seeing bruises on you. I'm going to see Patsy, just to make certain she's all right. I'm not going after Jess."

"She has guards on her," Saber felt compelled to point out. She *liked* Brian. She thought of him as a friend. And she was stunned that she had worked with him night after night and never once caught on to the fact that he was a GhostWalker working for Whitney.

"He's evil, Brian. You have to know that."

"I'm a soldier, Saber. Just like you. I take orders."

"You're not in his breeding program?"

"That's a rumor, nothing more."

She shook her head. "You're lying to yourself because you don't want it to be true. Why do you think he let me go? He wants Jess and me to have a baby."

In the distance they heard the wail of sirens. Brian didn't look away from her. In his eyes, on his face, she saw respect — the respect of a fellow soldier — admiration for what she could do.

"I do my job, Saber. Go where they tell me and carry out orders. I'm going to see Patsy and then I'll be gone. You stay out of trouble."

"Brian, get another assignment. Anyone but Whitney. Ask for a transfer to one of the other GhostWalker teams. Someone is out to kill all of us and we have no idea who. Not Whitney, but someone high enough up that they can mess with assignments. Some of the GhostWalkers have been sent out on suicide missions. You need to know that and all the men on your team need to be aware of it as well." She talked fast, keeping her voice low, aware of the janitor and two other security guards hesitantly coming toward them.

He smiled at her. "You take care of yourself. I have to get out before the cops arrive. Be safe, Saber. And don't let your guard down."

She was going to miss him. She watched him walk over to Brady and held her breath as he crouched down, took a pressure bandage out of his jacket, and handed it and Brady's gun back to the ex-SEAL. Brian went over the side of the mountain, using the exact escape route Saber had scoped out months earlier. He would have a car and a pack stashed close by.

She ran over to Brady and knelt down beside him. He tore open the packaging with his teeth. She ripped at the material of his trousers. His thigh was soaked with blood.

"Here, give it to me. The paramedics will be here any minute."

"Brian's military," Brady said. "Man, I didn't catch that. He blended so perfectly."

That was what a GhostWalker like Brian did. A chameleon, becoming who and what everyone expected. She shook her head. She'd heard of them, of course, but Brian was the first one she'd encountered. They could become anyone.

"Yeah, he's military."

"He executed that man."

She didn't reply, but sat back, rubbing her hand over her face, exhausted. Without Brian to pull the energy from her, she felt the aftereffects, although most of it was already dispersed. She held out her hand. "You have a cell phone." Because all she wanted to do was talk to Jess — hear the comfort of his voice.

Brady lay back in the grass beside her. "My pocket."

She glanced at him sharply. He was gray,

with beads of sweat on his face. "Hey! You'd better not be thinking of dying on me."

Alarmed, she bent over him and pressed her fingers to his pulse. At once she felt the rhythm of his body. She could read it easily now, after working with Patsy and Jess. He was losing too much blood too fast. Swearing, she knelt beside him.

"Close your eyes and try to relax. You're going to feel warm, maybe even hot."

A faint grin told her he wanted to give her a snappy comeback, but he didn't have the energy to deliver it.

She sent out a tentative current, reading the feedback until she found the tiny nick in the artery. She closed herself off to all sights and sounds and sent a small pulse of heat to repair the tear. The electrical current stimulated cells to step up the repair process as well as closing off the artery.

Brady caught her wrist as she sank back on her heels. "What are you?"

She grinned at him. "I'm top secret, my friend." And she could save lives as well as take them.

She found his cell phone and flipped it open to call the one man she needed to share that piece of news with.

CHAPTER 19

"Logan and Neil checked out Les's home and most of it was stripped clean. All but the little homemade dungeon he apparently had waiting for you," Jess said.

Saber shuddered. "There are just some things in life it's best not to hear about and Les's dungeon is one of them. What do you mean the house was stripped clean? Weren't there any prints?" She felt awful. So tired she could barely stand, and twice now she'd had nosebleeds. She'd covered it up at the police station when she was giving her report, but all she wanted to do was crawl in a hole somewhere.

Jess leaned forward in his chair to reach the cup of coffee she put on the table in front of him. It had been a long day with the police, checking on Brady at the hospital, visiting Patsy, and then talking with Logan and Neil. Saber hadn't even gone to bed. They lost both soundmen at the radio station and he sure as hell didn't want Saber to go in to work. He didn't want her away from him.

"There were prints, but they didn't tell us too much that we didn't already know. I ran his prints when I hired him, and nothing popped out at me. It seems he failed to mention on his resume that he spent a couple of years working at the Whitney Research Center in California."

"Brian said Les was reporting to Whitney, but he was a very sick man. Do you think Whitney knew he was sick and that's why he sent Brian as well?" Saber asked. She yawned and pressed two fingers to her throbbing temples, trying to stop the incessant pounding. "It's all too complicated for me to figure out."

"They found recordings of Les's ramblings. Most of the recordings were missing, so I'm assuming the ones referring to Whitney were taken, but there were enough left to show his descent into madness. It seemed to happen over time."

There was something in his tone that had Saber going on alert. She reached across the table and caught his hand, waited until his eyes met hers. "It had something to do specifically with me? Did Whitney set him up?"

"We don't know, baby, but it's a possibility."

She jumped up and turned away from him to pace across the floor. Even her legs felt rubbery, her body trembling with weakness.

"Whitney had another man like this working for him, a very sick doctor. Logan thinks it's part of a larger research project Whitney's conducting." As Saber went by him, Jess caught her arm to stop her. "We all believe that Whitney has psychic ability. That he reads people. How else would he find infants with psychic ability? He isn't the kind of man to have a couple of deviants working for him unless he wanted to study them."

She frowned and pulled her arm away, not wanting him to notice she couldn't control the trembling. "Whitney sent him on purpose? How could he know that he'd come after me like that?"

"He didn't. He wanted to see. At least that's what we think."

"And he sent Brian along just in case."

"He probably didn't want to take a chance that anything would happen to you before you had a baby. If Brian is a shielder, then at this time, I know of only four of us. Kadan, you, Brian, and me. He needs more children to be born because it's so rare and

548

obviously he thinks we're his best bet."

"Great. I can never have a baby."

"We'll have babies," he said softly, reaching for her again and drawing her close to him. "I've already talked to Ken and Jack about purchasing land close to them. We can build a fortress up in the mountains. A few of the others may join us and we can protect the children."

"What about Patsy? It bothered me that Brian was so insistent about seeing her."

Jess was silent for a moment, turning things over in his mind. Brian risked being caught to see his sister. Granted, the guards weren't GhostWalkers, but they were well-trained men from Brady's security force. When he'd spoken with Patsy she had admitted Brian had come to say good-bye.

"Patsy's never met Whitney, has she?" Saber asked.

Everything inside of Jess went still. His thoughts were already heading in the direction of Saber's and it scared him. If Whitney had managed to observe his operation at a major hospital with GhostWalkers around, he certainly could waltz into the hospital where Patsy was.

"Oh God. Hand me the phone. I want her protected at all times. We've got to get her out of that hospital and into some place we can better guard her."

Saber shoved the phone into his hand. "Maybe I should get over there." She didn't want to. She wanted someone else to handle all the problems so she could just crawl in bed.

Ken, you and Mari get over to the hospital fast and guard Patsy. I'm afraid Whitney may make a try for her.

Then you wouldn't have any protection. Neil is meeting with Kadan today and the others were called to work.

Jess glared at Saber, frustrated that Ken would argue with him. "You're not going without me. I'm sending Ken and Mari there as well." *Get to Patsy. We'll be right behind you.*

You're vulnerable here, Jess.

Damn it. Don't you think I know that? Go!

"We've got to get over there, Saber. If Brian was interested in Patsy, Whitney must have somehow paired them using his pheromone enhancers. He won't let her go."

Saber had reached for the van keys, but she dropped them back on the table and stopped, turning to look at him. "What does that mean, Jesse? You don't think Brian could have genuine feelings for Patsy?"

"What difference does it make?" he snapped impatiently, reaching past her for

550

the keys. "Let's go."

"You go."

Jess whipped his chair around. "Don't do this, Saber, not now. Patsy could be in danger."

"Brian isn't going to hurt Patsy. And in any case, he's long gone. She said he left, remember? And Ken and Mari won't let anything happen to her. I think you should go and see for yourself, but I'm tired. I've been up nearly twenty-four hours, been in a shoot-out, and used up all my energy trying to heal your legs. I'm going to bed."

"Damn it, Saber. This isn't the time to get pissed off. I wasn't talking about us."

"Yes, you were. You think I'm going to just let that go, Jesse? Brian is after Patsy for no other reason than because Whitney paired them? Patsy is beautiful, far more so than I am. She's sophisticated and educated and most men would kill to have her. She isn't anything at all like me. If you don't think Brian could be attracted to her for herself, then no way in hell did you fall in love with me on your own."

He raked a hand through his hair, wanting to shake her. She was exhausted. He could see it on her face. And hurt. He could see that in her eyes. But the truth was, she was looking for a way out because she was afraid — of him, of Whitney, of being involved in a family, of being part of the community of GhostWalkers.

"You've always got one foot out the door, Saber. No matter how much I tell you I love you or that I want you, no matter how many times I tell you that you're my world and I'd give up everything for you, it isn't going to matter if you don't feel it too. I can't make you want to stay. And I'm not holding you against your will, as much as I'd like to."

He threw the keys back on the table. "Do you think I'm proud of the fact that we didn't use birth control? Do you think a man like me ever — *ever* — forgets something that important? I wanted you pregnant. I wanted you to have my child growing inside of you because you wouldn't leave me. You'd need me to take care of you and the baby. I hate that I did that. That I even thought that. That's as much of a trap as Whitney had you in. If you stay with me, it has to be because you love me and want to be with me."

"It's so easy for you, Jess. You have it all. The parents. Patsy. Your friends. Everyone respects you. I come from nothing. I don't even have a name or a birthday. I can do all the things Patsy can do because I was educated for the purpose of fitting into any society to kill. That was my main goal for everything I ever learned."

He spread out his hands. "But that isn't who you are. You've lived here going on a year, Saber, and I can tell you, I have more of a killer instinct than you. Brian knew that or he wouldn't have blown his cover. He'd still be here watching us, informing Whitney and seeing my sister. But you wouldn't kill Les."

"I would have killed Chaleen. When I thought she was a threat to you . . ."

"But you didn't. And that's the point. It isn't in your nature. I see you. Who you are. Who you can be. For once in your life stop running from yourself and have the courage to take what you want. I'm right here. In front of you."

Saber sank into a chair and rested her head in the crook of her arm on the table. "I'm so tired, Jesse, I can't think anymore. Go see Patsy and make sure she's fine and I'll sleep for a while, and when you come back we can talk."

His breath caught in his throat. Something was very wrong. Saber didn't get tired — not like this. He should have noticed the moment they were alone together. He rolled his chair closer to her and put his hand on her forehead. She wasn't running a fever and that could only mean she was feeling repercussions from trying to heal the damaged nerves and muscle in his legs. It wouldn't be unusual for a GhostWalker to have problems after using psychic ability. Many had brain bleeds and other major physical problems. He should have considered that.

"Come on, baby, let's get you to bed. I'll call Eric to come over and check you out, just in case."

"No, I don't want that man near me, and I'm just exhausted. I can hardly function, let alone think. Please just go see Patsy, you won't worry so much if you do. I'll be fine here." She let him pull her out of the chair and onto his lap. She nuzzled his neck. "Tell me about your legs. So much has been going on I haven't had a chance to ask you if you think I helped."

"I think you saved my legs for me, baby. I spent the evening while you were working swimming and relearning how to use my legs. It's interesting. I know how to walk, but I actually have to remember, think each step through. But I only fell a few times." There was excitement in his voice.

He pushed the wheelchair through the house toward his bedroom. "I'm resting my legs right now. Eric said not to be stupid and overdo, even though I really want to go running." He kissed the top of her head. "Go running. Did you hear that, Saber? It's possible that I'll be running in a few days and *you* did that. *You.* You're a fucking miracle, babe. My own personal angel."

She sighed softly and murmured something he couldn't catch, her small body relaxing into his.

Jess slowed his pace. She had fallen asleep in his lap. Even with his astonishing news, she had crashed — big time. His mouth went dry. He wasn't a man to feel panic, but he wanted to call Lily and ask her if it was normal for Saber to have this reaction. Unfortunately Lily wasn't available to him. Ryland and she had gone underground with the baby being born. A boy, Daniel Ryland Miller. Jess was certain he would see them up in the mountains when they bought land in the same vicinity.

A thin red streak flashed across the room right in front of him and Jess slammed the chair to a halt and dove for the floor, taking Saber with him. They landed hard, Saber beneath him as half a dozen tiny red beams hit the wall.

"Shit. Shit. We're under attack. Are you hurt? Did I hurt you?" He stayed low, trying to get a look at her and move them at the same time.

"I'm fine." Her voice was utterly calm. "But I'm really getting sick of this. Let's take them out for good this time, Jesse. This is our home."

"Crawl forward, toward the exercise room. I've got things stashed in there we'll need."

She didn't ask questions, but scooted, more on her belly than hands and knees, going fast as the first canister of gas blew through the window and exploded. She closed her eyes and held her breath. She knew her way around the house without sight and she went unerringly, Jess right behind her. She could feel his body skimming over the top of hers as they moved, Jess crawling with her, his body shielding hers.

Her arms and legs felt like lead, but now she was beginning to lose her temper. *Is your office secure?*

They can eventually get it open, but when they try to blow it, and they will, they'll get a few nasty surprises. It will also trigger a meltdown in the hard drive. Everything will be wiped clean.

They don't know you can use your legs. You can use them, can't you? That was her biggest anxiety. If Jess needed a wheelchair, they were in for trouble.

I might not be fast, but I can use them. Keep going, baby, it's getting bad in here.

He all but pushed her through the door to the exercise room and slammed it shut. They stayed low to the floor, taking in deep breaths of clean air. Saber crawled over to the cabinet holding the towels, grabbed a couple, and shoved them into the crack.

"What am I looking for?"

"Move the cabinet out," Jess instructed. "There'll be a keypad. Code in 'red flag.' Count ten seconds and code in 997342. That will get the door open."

Saber punched in the codes as quickly as she could. Tracers were zinging through the kitchen and living room, and the thunk of the canisters of gas could be clearly heard as they hit the floors or walls.

"I need the laptop. Hurry. I can lock this room down. They're going to try to kill us, Saber. Have you ever been in a combat situation?"

"I trained with weapons, but without an anchor I have a bad reaction. I'm an expert marksman, though, and I'm very good with a knife."

"You can't hesitate, Saber. You're going to have to shoot to kill. And stay right by me so we can do this."

She had the steel door built into the wall behind the towel cabinet open. There was an arsenal there as well as gas masks and the latest in body armor. She pushed the laptop into his hands and turned back to the weapons.

Jess flipped the top open and powered up the laptop.

"This room was built specifically for this purpose."

She sent him a quick glare over her shoulder. "Nice that you told me. What other secrets do you have?"

"Okay, I've got it up and running. Am locking it down."

Coverings slid into place over the windows, thick steel to prevent the gas canisters and attackers from entering.

"Bullets aren't going to penetrate the walls and doors. The coverings won't stop them, but it will slow them down until our team shows up."

"What else does that thing do?" She began pulling weapons and ammunition out and tossing them to him.

Saber shoved guns and knives into her waistband, taped one to her ankle and another to her wrist. She threw him a vest and donned one herself and then added the gas masks to their growing pile.

"I need the small suitcase. Hurry, Saber."

She dragged it off the shelf and gave it to him. "I hate to ask."

He flashed a quick grin. "I've tapped into the security monitors and you can see them. I count six. They're coming in."

"We're overloaded." She traveled light and all the weapons were a bit much. Still, she strapped them on and went back to him.

He began pulling materials from the suitcase.

Saber stared at the contents and then at him. "A bomb? You're going to make a bomb?"

"It's mostly already made. I just have to arm it." He positioned the claymore mine in the middle of the door and ran a thin trip wire to the door handle and signaled her to the other side of the room. "They'll be coming into the house in another minute. They know we're inside and they've got us surrounded. They'll try to blow the door, and the claymore will take out anyone on the other side."

"You're crazy, you know that?" But she was beginning to feel safe with him. He was a soldier and very methodical. And he had planned for just such an attack. He was perfectly calm and very confident.

He flicked her a wicked smile. "You got it

right, baby. I'm a GhostWalker and we were born crazy."

Saber had the sudden urge to laugh. He really was crazy. "You like this, don't you? They're tearing up your house, and you're stoked about it."

"We're moving anyway." He indicated the wall around the swimming pool. "Get behind that. There's a grate in the cement."

Saber had looked at that grate hundreds of times, assuming it drained any water that splashed from the pool. "You have an escape route."

His eyebrow shot up. "Doesn't everybody?"

"I must be slipping. I didn't suspect." But she should have. Jess was no lamb. No Navy SEAL was. Add in the GhostWalker program and she should have been searching his house for his arsenal. "Is the house wired?"

"You're making me proud, angel face. Hell yes, it's wired. Pull the grate." He indicated the monitor.

She could see shadowy figures moving through the smoke surrounding the house. Two tossed hooks over the upstairs balcony while others surrounded the house. They rushed, blowing open the doors and windows. Glass and wood sprayed into the air and shot across the interior of the rooms to slam into walls. The house shook ominously.

Saber ducked her head and Jess swept her behind him with one arm. "Stay close. The energy is going to be racing toward us and it's going to get ugly."

She planned on staying very close to him. His solid frame was comforting and his complete confidence inspired the same in her. The first rush of adrenaline was wearing off, leaving her more exhausted than ever, the psychic drain taking its toll. She rested her head against his broad back, and he reached over his shoulder to curl his arm around her neck, holding her to him while they both stared at the monitor. Saber held her breath.

Two men entered through the front door in standard two-man formation.

"They're military," Saber said. "Look at the way they're moving."

"I believe the late Colonel Higgens had a lot more to answer for than we gave him credit for. I think he was part of an espionage ring that reaches all the way to the White House."

The two men separated, rifles at the ready, and began a cautious exploration of the living room. With the gas masks on, they looked like monsters as their shadowy figures moved through the swirling vapor.

"If they think you've uncovered evidence of that, they'll want to kill you for certain, Jesse. They aren't going to be taking prisoners."

"I have that feeling."

Jess watched as the two climbing the ropes made it onto the balcony. One pulled out a very large-looking knife while the other had a gun. They tried the door, and when it didn't open, the one with the gun fired several shots. The two in the living room were too disciplined to react to the gunfire. They swept the room efficiently, quartering the area, checking thoroughly.

Jess kept his eyes fixed on them, so much so that Saber stopped watching the split screens showing every entry point and watched the living room. She felt the jump in Jess's pulse, the slight tension in his body as the man sweeping to the left of the room approached the doorway to the kitchen. The soldier took a step, then a second one. She saw a light flash red on the strip along the bottom of the screen. The soldier stopped abruptly, staring down at his foot, and the very line of his body screamed horror. He said something to his partner, who backed up, looking wildly around him at the floor.

"Pressure switch. Now they know who

they're dealing with. Fucking amateurs want to play with me in my own house."

Jess leaned his head back and kissed her. His mouth was hard and hot and commanding. She could feel the heat radiating from his skin and feel the rush of excitement flowing through his body.

A thousand butterfly wings brushed at her stomach and in spite of the situation they were in, her body reacted to his heat. "And all this time I thought you were so sweet."

He laughed softly. "The wheelchair was my friend. If you had met me before I was in that chair, you would have run." His eyes were locked on hers. Dark with the excitement of combat. Smoky with raw hunger. Sharp and piercing, revealing the true predator that lived in his skin.

She pressed a kiss to the back of his shoulder. "I would have run like a rabbit."

Her gaze shifted back to the monitor, her heart picking up the acceleration of the soldier in the other room. She could taste his fear. She wasn't made for this kind of combat. If she could have, she would have closed her eyes, but it was impossible to look away. The soldier shook, his rifle visibly trembling while his partner turned and ran from the living room to the stairs.

The soldier in the living room yelled

loudly, but it didn't slow his partner down. The running man's sole hit the third stair, and the explosion rocked the house. Saber's body jerked and she turned away from the screen, unable to watch as the body lifted into the air along with half the railing and several stairs, slamming into the ceiling and raining down wood, plaster, and body parts. The second explosion followed closely on the heels of the first as the soldier in the kitchen jerked his foot in automatic reaction.

Jess whirled around and pulled Saber into his arms, sheltering her as violent energy rushed through the house, walls serving as no barrier, the red- and black-edged waves seeking a target. He wrapped her up, putting his head over hers, holding her to him while the energy washed over them like a tidal wave. She felt stabs of pain, but they passed quickly as Jess absorbed the violence.

Because her rhythm automatically synced with his, she felt the racing current. Instead of pain, Jess's body attracted the energy, soaked it up and processed it — and that startled her. She'd never actually thought much about how an anchor worked with that much energy, but it was as if he'd gobbled it up, absorbing it into his system to be used for other purposes. She could understand how he might be an adrenaline junkie. The violent energy infused him with strength, and the need for action.

"Are you all right?" Jess kissed the top of her head, stroked one hand down her hair, even as his eyes stayed glued to the screen.

She nodded. The two soldiers entering through the upstairs heard the explosions downstairs and they were sweeping the rooms in a hurried, but much more cautious manner. Two more were entering through the kitchen, and that made her heart jump — they were closest to the exercise room.

"Doesn't it upset you that so many people want you dead?" she whispered.

"No, it just pisses me off. These men work for whoever is betraying our country — and whoever that is ordered them to torture my sister. I'm taking them all to hell, but before they go, they're going to know they fucked with the wrong family."

She felt the resolve in him, the absolute conviction that he was taking his enemies down. The confidence that was beginning to bloom in her increased, spreading and growing. The other GhostWalkers had the same mentality as Jess. They would stand together and fight back. There would be no running, no lying down to allow someone to destroy them no matter what the odds. She wanted that. She wanted to feel that same confidence. Be part of that tight-knit group willing to band together against all odds and believe absolutely that they could win. More than that — she wanted to belong to this man with his fierce pride and courage.

"Okay."

The soldiers upstairs were at the top of the landing looking down into the destruction of the living room. One shifted position slightly to get a better look, hands on the railing as he bent over. Instantly a red light blinked on the bottom of the laptop screen.

"Okay what?" Jess asked.

She looked up at him, at the strength in his face, at those piercing ice-cold eyes alive with the cunning of a true predator.

"I'll marry you."

His gaze slid over her upturned face, and a slow smile softened the hard line of his mouth. He caught her chin. "And you'll have my children."

"You don't want very much, do you?"

He took her mouth with his, the flare of heat instant, the taste of joy evident. Even in combat he could melt her.

His arms were around her, his tongue dancing with hers when the next explosion rocked the house. The soldier holding the railing had shifted position and the pressure switch had blown.

Jess held Saber tight, kissing her, his lips moving against hers. She felt the vibration rush through him as he drew the energy to him like a magnet. Electricity zinged through her — through him, a physical wave nearly sexual, almost euphoric.

She let out her breath and caught at him for support. "Jesse. That's so dangerous."

"And addicting. Every psychic gift comes with a high price tag. It would be easy to become addicted and need that kind of rush." He flicked a glance at the screen and swore. "The bastard on the landing has an M203 attached to the bottom of his M16."

Saber's breath hitched in her throat. She knew that was a grenade launcher and she wanted no part of that.

"He's going for my office," Jess informed her.

Saber imagined hearing the distinctive click and then the thump as the grenade was sent streaking through the hall into the door of the office. The house shook as the office door blasted inward.

Once again Jess drew Saber close to him as the wave of energy rushed over them. Jess studied the soldier on the landing. "He's directing everything. See, he's staying to cover just in case either of the two coming from the kitchen steps on a switch. He's lost three men, and he knows the house is wired, but he's as cool as a cucumber. He's going to sit up there with his little grenade launcher, safe while everyone else takes the risks."

"Are we going to get out of here anytime soon?" Saber asked.

"I have a couple of things to take care of, baby."

"Like staying alive?"

It looked like a war zone on the screen. She didn't want to wait around until the intruders blew open the door to the exercise room.

"I have to make sure the office is destroyed with everything in it and I've got to kill every one of these bastards. The cops will be showing up any minute and I don't want any of them to die because I ran."

She couldn't argue with that, but she wasn't certain she believed him. The calm, easygoing man she'd been living with for the past year was riled, and he wasn't going to cut and run until he'd taken out the men who had threatened his family. In a strange way it made her feel safe knowing he was that kind of man. But she also felt as if she should grab him and drag him into their bolt hole. She didn't trust his legs. He hadn't walked one single step, and the wheelchair was on the other side of the door.

"One man is approaching the office. The door's gone. Let's see if my failsafe works. All data on the computers should be corrupted beyond repair even if they managed to get a hard drive intact, but just in case . . ." He murmured aloud, talking more to himself than to her.

Saber leaned closer to peer at the monitor. Smoke and dust swirled thickly. A soldier wearing a gas mask emerged out of the rubble and stood at the entrance to the office, staring inside. He turned and looked up at the man on the landing, holding his thumb up to indicate they'd found the computers. She felt Jess go still, and then his adrenaline spiked. His arms tightened around her, pulling her into his chest, his head going over hers.

The initial explosion shook the house, the ground, but didn't stop there. More followed, each blast louder than the last. The energy came at them in a series of waves. Saber was left feeling sick, her head pounding. Even with Jess's presence absorbing all of it, the initial rush was a shock to her body.

Jess raised his head to take a quick glimpse

at the monitor and swore. He caught at her, for the first time standing, pulling her up with him, dragging her down toward the grate. "Get down the steps, take the gear. Move fast, Saber."

She couldn't see what had alarmed him, and she didn't wait around to find out. She caught up as many weapons as she could, tossing the gas masks down into the tunnel before she dropped into the hole. The stairs were narrow and steep, leading down to a very small tunnel. She could walk upright, but she knew Jess would never be able to.

"Jess, we don't have your wheelchair."

"I can walk. I won't be winning any races, but I really can get my legs to work." He was already swinging his body through the gap and reaching for the stairs with his legs, pulling the grate after him. "Go, he's blowing the door."

She watched him come down the stairs, bending to keep from hitting his head as he neared the bottom. She wasn't running down that corridor until she knew he was safe.

"Go, damn it."

"Are you sure you can do this?"

He gave her a little push, indicating she should run ahead of him. Saber whirled around and sprinted down the length of the tunnel. She was very small and could move fast, but from the little she'd just observed, Jess was still unsteady on his legs. He was also tall, with broad shoulders. He had to stoop and turn his body at an awkward angle to get through the winding passageway.

The blast was loud, reverberating through the tunnel. Smoke and dust poured in. A thin trail of red light led the way as they followed the corridor deeper into the earth. The sides were shored up with thick timber and wire over the dirt walls.

"They're in," hissed Jess. "The one trying to get data from the office is toast, and the first one into the exercise room won't have a chance, but we'll still have the one with the grenade launcher, and we can't be caught inside this tunnel."

"Are you certain they won't get your files? What about the one you had on me?"

"I destroyed it. Run, Saber, stop worrying about me. In another minute we're going to have someone shooting at us with a grenade launcher."

Saber could feel him right behind her, so she accelerated her speed. She wasn't particularly strong, but she was fast. Gene therapy had seen to that. "Your beautiful house is being destroyed." She'd tried not to think about it too much, but the loss of the first place she'd ever thought of as home was devastating.

"It doesn't matter."

"It does. It's the first home I ever had. I loved it." Her vision blurred and she wiped at her eyes, the gas mask clunking against her arm.

The tunnel curved and began going up again. She could see that just ahead the thin red line abruptly stopped. "Where? Tell me where to go." She slowed, seeing nothing but a dead end blocking their way. They appeared trapped.

He put his hand on her shoulder and reached up to feel above them with one hand. Immediately the tunnel was plunged into complete darkness. There was no light coming in from anywhere to help with the unrelenting blackness.

Her breath caught in her lungs. Jess seemed larger than ever, more solid. He gathered her close and put his mouth next to her ear. "None of it matters, you know. *We're* all that matters. You and me. Wherever we are together, Saber, that's our home. You'll love the new house I'm going to build for you."

He reached above her again and found the latch that hid the door in the ceiling overhead. A head leaned in from above and Ken grinned at them.

"You've been having fun without us," he accused.

Jess caught Saber around the waist and lifted her out of the tunnel. She blinked as the light filtering through the forest struck her in the eye. The house was on fire a short distance away. Ken caught her in firm hands and pulled her all the way up, setting her to one side in order to reach down for the equipment Jess had.

Saber could see they were surrounded by grim-faced men, all holding rifles as if they knew how to use them. GhostWalkers. Jess's GhostWalkers. She turned to watch the house burn, her heart heavy. Mari stepped up beside her and took her arm.

"I'm sorry about your home."

The sympathy was unexpected, but for the first time, she felt as if she might really be able to be a part of these people. She didn't feel anything but sympathy and a determination to keep her and Jess safe. Maybe, just maybe, she was already home.

CHAPTER 20

"Jess, you're back." Ken Norton glanced at his watch. "Four in the morning and you're getting married tomorrow. You cut it close, bro." He was crouched low on top of the boulder guarding the entrance to the Norton land.

Jess and Saber were temporarily staying in a cabin the Norton twins had up in the mountains of Montana.

Jess paused on his way in through the twisting trail. The night was moonless and the clouds obscured most of the stars — just the way they liked it. "I didn't have a lot of choice. The meeting with Rear Admiral Henderson and General Rainer went as well as I could expect, I guess, but neither of them were very happy that we'd been investigating them."

Ken shrugged, cradling his rifle in his arms, his eyes making a sweep of the tree line below. "I doubt if you or Ryland offered much in the way of an apology."

"Hell no. We gave them our findings and a copy of the tape. The original is here and we're keeping it that way."

"You'll be happy to know the escrow went through. You officially own eighty-six acres up here. Ryland and Lily are purchasing land as well. In fact they're buying up everything they can in the hopes that more of the GhostWalkers will settle here later. I've been messing around a little with ideas for buildings we can more easily defend." Ken shrugged his shoulders. "Was hoping you'd take a look later."

Jess nodded. "Definitely. I want to start building as soon as we can. Patsy is willing to build her home near mine so I'll know she's safe as well. That means we've got to put up two homes next spring."

"I'm glad she finally agreed to come. She and Saber still talking about owning another radio station?" Ken's inquiry sounded mild enough.

Jess's smile was faint. He knew exactly what Ken was thinking. "Don't go worrying. If it comes to that, we'll do it up here. I know it would be a nightmare to protect them in town."

"Where do we stand with it all?"

"About the same. The espionage ring is

still in place, and unfortunately several army personnel are involved along with a major player in the White House, which pretty much means we're fucked. Violet is on the loose with her own personal agenda and Whitney is busy manipulating everyone."

Ken grinned at him. "Yeah, well, we like life interesting."

"I've got to get back and catch a little sleep before the big event." Jess tried to sound casual when he was anything but. He couldn't wait to see Saber — to hold her in his arms.

Ken snorted. "She's a little pissed at you, my friend. Don't expect a warm reception when you crawl into her bed to — er — sleep."

Jess smirked at him and walked up the path toward the cabin, waving at one of the guards crouched high in the cliffs overlooking the property. He had spotted several of the GhostWalkers patrolling and knew they had arrived for the wedding. His wedding. He grinned like an idiot, just thinking about it.

He'd been gone seven days while he was meeting with the admiral to give him the findings of the investigation. But now he was home and determined to see Saber.

He had hated leaving her behind, and

she'd been less than happy about it, but he felt she was safer under the protection of the GhostWalker team.

He slipped through the open window and just stood there a moment, drinking in the sight of her. She was so beautiful she made his heart ache. Stripping quickly, Jess climbed into bed, pulling her feminine form into his arms.

She cuddled into him, curled like a little kitten, as his larger body wrapped around hers protectively. Her blue-black curls felt like silk against his face and her soft skin invited his touch. He inhaled her, pulling her scent deep into his lungs. His body was already hungry, his mouth craving the taste of her.

He stretched, moving his legs, reveling in the miracle of being able to do so, then leaned into her and kissed the nape of her neck, his hands sliding up her rib cage to cup her breasts. He was a big man and she seemed so fragile, yet he knew there was power in her — steel in her. She would stand beside him no matter what happened.

It was a luxury to be able to touch her, to wake up to her soft curvy body. *His.* He smiled again and pushed the sheet from her, sliding his body over and down hers.

"What are you doing here?" Saber didn't

open her eyes.

Her drowsy voice was mesmerizing, sliding through his system like a drug. "Go back to sleep. I want to indulge myself a little bit."

"You left me and I'm mad at you, so go away."

He slid his hands over her soft skin from her breasts to her belly. She didn't open her eyes but she frowned at him.

"You don't deserve me. Go. Away."

"It's our wedding day."

"It was. I was abandoned. Left behind. Deserted. I'm dreaming of retaliation right now and you're disturbing me."

He brushed the tip of her breast with his lips, feather light. "What kind of retaliation?" He felt her stomach muscles bunch in answer.

"I'm finding one of the very hot Special Forces marines to take your place. He will adore me and never leave me."

"He will get his throat slit and you will be punished severely. Go back to sleep and dream about a proper retaliation such as killing me or something. That's much more appropriate. And no jarhead could ever take the place of a SEAL, baby." He bent to bite gently, his tongue bathing away the small sting.

"Ow!" She pushed at his head. "Go away."

His mouth closed over her breast, suckling strongly, tongue dancing over her nipple, flicking and teasing until she was arching into him and the hands that had been pushing him away were pulling him closer.

"Fine," she muttered. "I guess I'll keep you."

He laughed and kissed his way down her belly, caressing her thighs and pushing them apart. He lay over her, his hands on her abdomen, his arms locking her hips in place while he bent to taste her. Beneath him, she jumped, her hips jerking, but he held her still and took several long, satisfying licks. The honeyed taste of her was sexy as hell, and he decided waking up should be all about indulgence. He could have his way every morning and be a happy man all day.

"You're so beautiful."

Her body was flushed, her thighs tight. Muscles bunched in her stomach and dew glistened on the tiny corkscrew curls guarding the treasure he was after. He held her open to him, and bent his head and drank, tongue stabbing deep, circling her clit and drawing out nectar.

Her body thrashed, but he held her firmly, giving her a small smack on her bottom. The little flair of heat sent more honey his way. He lapped it up in appreciation. "Stay still. This is my time, you can do whatever you want later — after all, I have to show you navy men are up to the task."

Saber moaned, clutching at the pillow to keep from lifting off the bed. His tongue was like fire, stroking little flames around her clit. He suckled, the sound sexy, sinfully wicked. A sob of pleasure escaped and she clawed the sheets, trying to stay still for him. His eyes went hot and dark with lust as he felt the first tremors in her body.

"Oh, yeah, baby, come apart for me." His finger swept over her slick heat, pushing deep, and she felt the rush of an orgasm overtaking her. Instantly he bent his head again and used his sinful mouth to increase the strength of the quakes, his tongue probing deep, until she went wild, thrashing under him and crying out his name.

Jess grinned as he pulled back. She was so beautiful with her eyes nearly opaque and the signs of his mouth all over her. He kissed her thighs and laced her fingers between his own, stretching her arms over her head and pinning her hands to the mattress as he bent forward to find her mouth with his. He could kiss her forever. He planned on kissing her forever.

He took his time kissing her over and over,

deepening each until he could feel the same urgency in her as he felt. He shifted, sliding from the mattress, wanting to be on his feet, dragging her body to the edge of his bed.

"What are you doing?"

"Anything." He lifted her hips and bent to drink again. She cried out brokenly, her breath coming in ragged gasps. "Everything." He licked another offering of warm honey and then straightened over her. "Open your mouth."

He looked huge standing over her like some avenging god, but she couldn't resist the driving hunger in him. She wanted to taste him, wanted to see how far she could drive him before he lost control.

"This is supposed to happen after the wedding," she pointed out as he pushed his hips closer, nudging her lips with the broad flared head of his heavy erection.

"You're my wife," he said. "In every sense of the word, you're my wife."

She let him wait a heartbeat before she licked the small pearly drop from the head. His hips jerked and he caught her hair in his hands like reins. She laughed as he pushed into her mouth eagerly. The sound traveled up his shaft like a vibration and she felt him shudder, saw him throw back his head and close his eyes.

She took him deep, her tongue teasing along the underside of the broad head, finding the most sensitive spot, while her hand circled the base, fingers caressing. She loved him with her mouth, suckling hard and flattening her tongue only to shift back to a slower pace. She matched her rhythm with his, the heartbeat, the quickening breath so she could follow more easily what pleased him best. Everything seemed to please him. His hips began an urgent thrusting, and she felt him thicken more, harden into silken steel.

It was Jess who pulled away, his breath coming in harsh gasps. "Not so fast, woman of mine. You're going to kill me."

"You deserve to be killed for leaving me."

He caught her easily and flipped her over onto her stomach, yanking her back so that her hips hung over the bed. One arm banded around her waist while his other hand immediately went between her legs, finding the moisture that told him she was more than ready for him. He pushed his finger into her and her muscles clamped down greedily.

"You're so damned hot, Saber." He pressed one hand to the nape of her neck, holding her against the bed while he continued to probe with his other hand, plunging his fingers deep and then withdrawing until she was moaning and pushing back against his hand.

Jess immediately removed the temptation of his fingers and replaced it with his heavy erection. She tried to lunge back, to impale herself on him, but he made her wait, holding her helpless while he pushed inside of that fiery, tight channel, inch by slow inch. She was almost too tight, her silken sheath gripping him until he wanted to roar with pleasure. He withdrew and entered again with that same excruciatingly slow push, absorbing the way her body tightened around his, clamping down with heat and fire, living silk moving and contracting around him.

Her breath exploded in a little sob and she tried again to push back harder, to force the pace she wanted. His fingers tightened on the nape of her neck. "Not yet, baby, take it slow and easy."

He didn't want slow and easy any more than she did, but he wanted her desperate for him. He wanted her to crave him the same way he did her, to feel that hunger clawing and ripping at her until she would do anything to have him give her release. He rubbed the soft, firm skin of her buttocks, massaging as he slowly withdrew and then watching as he disappeared into that secret feminine channel.

When she thrashed again, he plunged hard and fast. She sobbed, her muscles clenching around his, her hips rocking as he drove in harder, holding her pinned to the bed, driving so deep her bottom nestled against his stomach. His cock throbbed almost painfully, swelling more, stretching her feminine sheath.

Saber couldn't move, couldn't do anything at all but lay there facedown, keening, as he pistoned harder and harder into her. The hot friction sent sensations rocketing to every part of her body until it seemed that every part of her ached for release. It was all the more erotic hanging over the bed, unable to move while he took his pleasure and gave it back tenfold. Each hard thrust of his cock sliding through her velvet folds felt like flames dragging over her.

He began to pump hard and fast so that she couldn't possibly control the pleasure bursting through her body, the tightening of every muscle, the building and building until the mind-numbing explosion sent quakes and shudders through her body. Her muscles convulsed around the heavy shaft, squeezing harshly, until, with a hoarse cry, he climaxed with her.

Jess lay over the top of her, his breath coming in gasps, his heart pounding. He slipped his hands beneath her body and cupped her breasts, kissing the nape of her neck while they lay locked together. He could feel her body rippling around his cock and he responded with small jerks of gratified bliss. She'd drained him, left him sated and happy, but somewhere deep inside, that dark craving was already beginning all over again, his mind alive with his fantasies and all the things he could do to pleasure her.

"I love you, baby." He stood with reluctance, not wanting to separate them, but knowing he was heavy. He let his cock slide from the heat of her body.

"You're going to be in such trouble when Patsy finds out you're here," Saber whispered, turning to him, circling his neck with her slender arms.

"Yeah well, I'd brave just about anything to be with you." He lifted her, kissing her, wanting her to feel how she shook him up inside. "Are you good with this? With living here? With being a part of all this?"

"And if I wasn't?"

"You're my world, Saber. If you aren't happy, then I'm not happy." He kissed her again and set her on the bed, coming down to her, his smile cocky. "Then I keep working at convincing you until you know this is where you belong."

Jess bent his head to nuzzle her belly. Someday his child would grow there. *Their* child. He would carve out a life for them any way he could, and God help anyone who tried to take it away, because he wouldn't have mercy if they came at his family again.

"I know where I belong," she said, her fingers twisting in his hair. "I know exactly where I belong."

Jess Calhoun was her man, her other half, and wherever he was, that was her home. Whoever he was with, that was her family. And if anyone tried to take it all away from her — well, there was a whole side of her that she was suppressing, but it was there, waiting and ready to protect her own.

Saber Wynter, soon to be Saber Calhoun, had finally stopped running — both from Whitney and from herself. At long last she knew who she was and where she belonged. She'd made a home for herself here, a life, with Jesse. So, maybe it wasn't the normal life she'd always dreamed of — and maybe it never would be.

But then again, who needed normal?

This was so much better.

ABOUT THE AUTHOR

Christine Feehan lives in the beautiful mountains of Lake County, California. I have always loved hiking, camping, rafting, and being outdoors. I am happily married to a romantic man who often inspires me with his thoughtfulness. We have a yours, mine, and ours family, claiming eleven children as our own. I have always written books, forcing my ten sisters to read every word, and now my daughters read and help me edit my manuscripts. Please visit my Web site at www.christinefeehan.com.

HQ
MID-YORK LIBRARY SYSTEM
1600 Lincoln Ave.
Utica, NY 13502
(315) 735-8328

A cooperative library system serving Oneida, Madison
and Herkimer Counties through libraries

www.midyork.org